DAVID G BAILEY was born in Lincolnshire
of Ely, also studying in the Fens and the Bla
USA, Caribbean and South America as well as
Midlands, he travels to write reports on insuran

After his debut as a published author in 2021 with an adventure fantasy story aimed at and beyond young adults, *Them Roper Girls* returned in 2022 to a world more recognisably our own. With humour and compassion, it traces in their own voices the lives of four sisters over more than sixty years from their 1950s childhood, as each tries to make her own way in the world against many challenges – as often from within the family as outside it!

A husband of one of the Roper sisters takes centre stage in David's latest novel, *Them Feltwell Boys*. With the same gritty realism and sometimes dark humour found in the earlier novel, Ray Roden's crude attempts at teenage love are seen in counterpoint to his cynical womanising as an adult. Even if he is prepared to change, will it be in time to save his marriage and career?

To read more of and about David's work, including a quarterly newsletter and new content daily comprising extracts from diaries and other writing over more than fifty years, visit his website www.davidgbailey.com.

Other novels by David G Bailey

Seventeen: or the Blood City Tommy O'Reilly Benefit Tour (fantasy adventure)
Them Roper Girls (contemporary fiction)

Them Feltwell Boys

David G Bailey

SilverWood

Published in 2023 by SilverWood Books

SilverWood Books Ltd
14 Small Street, Bristol, BS1 1DE, United Kingdom
www.silverwoodbooks.co.uk

ISBN 978-1-80042-255-1 (paperback)
ISBN 978-1-80042-256-8 (hardback)

British Library Cataloguing in Publication Data
A CIP catalogue record for this book is
available from the British Library

Page design and typesetting by SilverWood Books

'I don't think he'd ever given up hope of being two wildly different people at once: the favoured scholar, the bully.
In fact, of course, the two persons he wanted to be shared the same roots. He wanted to do well at school for the same reason that he must continually be fighting, taking offence. There was a desperate anxiety in him to be on top, always, everywhere.'

Edward Blishen (from *This Right Soft Lot*)

'Objects in the Rear View Mirror May Appear Closer Than They Are.'

Jim Steinman / Meatloaf

In conscious and unconscious loving memory of
Joyce Elizabeth Bailey (1927 – 2023)
Mary Agnes Harper (1935 – 2004)

Chapter 1

I first met her at the TB clinic. That was what I used to say. I thought it sounded kind of romantic. Actually, it was just a room at the Whitefriars hospital. I can't remember what the tests were. X-rays I assume, with the nurse saying the radiation is nothing to worry about, then making sure she's in another room altogether when it hits your chest. Maybe they took blood, tested your lungs by having you blow into a machine, one that will take every last bit of puff from you and still be unimpressed.

I thought tuberculosis had died out a million years ago. Apparently not, since Uncle Jack and Aunt Margaret both caught it. My cousin Janet tested clear. I was never told whether it was hereditary, contagious, infectious or what. Although they only lived ten miles away, that was a different county, different schools, so I only saw Jan odd times at holidays, christenings or weddings. We had not yet discovered funerals.

The distance between the women of the family, the in-laws, was much more than ten miles. The brothers Peter and Jack would enjoy a pint together at those same family occasions. They obviously didn't care enough to make it a more regular thing, not enough to break the custom of our family where women ruled the social side. Still, we all had to be tested, despite not having been near the sufferers on any regular basis. We did not see them during their convalescence either, which as far as I know was local. Mountain sanatoria were evidently not, or no longer, an indispensable part of the recovery process, since our part of East Anglia was at or below sea level, nowhere for so much as a hill start in a driving test.

We were all clear, Mum, Dad and me. My aunt and uncle did make a full recovery. I never found out what Tina was doing in the clinic that day; perhaps having treatment for anaemia or anorexia, if her extreme pallor and skinniness were anything to go by. I probably wouldn't have remembered her at all except for the long blonde hair, almost white. If I'm honest I didn't remember her enough to make the connection. She was the one, at our second meeting, to remind me of the first when, in our grammar and high school uniforms, we sat briefly together in a waiting room without exchanging a word.

Although I liked Uncle Jack and other male relatives well enough, my hero was Mum's brother Dan. His sisters always said he was spoilt as a child, hinting or sometimes saying outright that even now, in his early thirties, he had not left that childhood behind. Through his twenties he had a variety of jobs, and women, some of whom even I had to jib at calling Auntie. He had only married the once. I loved Aunt Jackie dearly, but that was not enough to keep her with us. 'She said after me she could never love another man,' I heard Dan say once with a kind of rueful bravado. It was only as I grew a little older I saw the double edge to this remark; later still when I could put it into the context – Jake it was who told me – of her living quietly with another woman who worked at the Metal Box.

By the summer I was approaching my third year at Washtown Grammar School, Dan – working as a lorry driver – had moved into a small flat on the Feltwell side of town. His relationship with his dad had taken a blow with every new job, woman, tattoo and drunken night out, basically with every adult year he failed to adopt the same settled pattern of life as Grandad Will.

Over Sunday dinner a week earlier, on the strict condition of no drinking with me in his car, Dan had pocketed Mum's permission to take me to Hunstanton. 'No problem, we'll wait till we see the sea before we crack the first can,' he had promised.

The Blacksmith's Arms did not have a sea view, nor did Dan's pint of lager come from a can. He put a top of lemonade on it, making sure I had noticed as we retreated to the garden. We were the first customers of the day.

'If your mum asks, mind, that dash takes all the strength out of the beer, makes it like a shandy.'

'Why couldn't I have a shandy then?'

'Steady Eddie, you can have a shandy later if you like, to impress your girlfriend.'

'What girlfriend?'

'Shame I didn't get a sandwich, could of toasted it off your face.' He leaned across the table to frame my cheeks with his hands, leaving the cigarette in his mouth. 'I don't know her name. Forgotten it tell you the truth, but you'll find out soon enough. We're off on a double date, mate. See I'm a poet and don't know it.'

If Uncle Dan did have a girlfriend lined up for me, she would be my first. I was past the stage of seeing no useful purpose at all to females of my own age, without yet having found a role for them in my life. It didn't help that the Grammar was boys only. Washtown High for girls was across the river. Our only sight of its pupils was on the buses to and from the different establishments. The convent school was over the road from our main gate, and there was a brief window of opportunity to mix there as classes ended each day. Like the back seats on the bus, this was open only to older and bolder boys than us. Even our Catholic James 'Jambo' Haslett was no use. He had been at the Convent in its primary section, to be turfed out with all the other boys at the very age you begin to see the benefits of mixed education. He had no contacts, or none he was admitting. I envied Jake – my best mate since our own primary in Feltwell – his mixed secondary modern. He was not yet in the front line. Still, he could get a view from the edges at breaks when sometimes a girl was separated from the herd to be mauled by a pack of boys.

Grandad Will kept a caravan on site at Hunstanton all year round, letting it to relative strangers (there was no advertising, so all came recommended by someone he knew) as well as relatives. He was shocked the first year Dad said we would be going somewhere different for our summer holiday, somewhere we had to pay for accommodation. This turned out to be another van – there were strict limits to Dad's sense of adventure – further down the Norfolk coast. We were now on our third year at Caister-on-Sea, smaller and quieter than 'Sunny Hunny', which suited Mum. Dad and I liked its proximity to Yarmouth; he for the variety shows with people he watched on telly all year, I for the much greater volume of arcades, amusements and fairground attractions it offered.

As we pulled into Searle's, I thought at first Dan must have some errand for his father. We went straight to the four-berther, in the back row before vegetation began sloping untidily upwards away from the sea. He knocked on the door rather than use one of our keys.

My first impression of the woman who answered was a fine pair of legs, visible to mid-thigh under some kind of beach-wrap thing as she stood two steps above us. She came down one of these to bring her face level with Dan's. She kissed him on the lips, I noted, but not at length. Easing him to one side she joined us at ground level, barefoot on the rubberised mat with its blurred 'Welcome'.

'Hello there, you must be Ray. Glad you could come with your uncle today, he said you might. I'm Julie.'

I shook the proffered hand, a ring on its third finger but none to match on the left. She was hardly taller than me, a pretty face without much make-up as far as I could tell, the shape of her head clearly defined by blonde hair cut shorter than mine (or Dan's – he was joking about getting a ponytail 'to finish off your grandad').

'Cat got your tongue?' Dan used a favourite phrase of Mum's. 'He's not normally shy, must be nervous about his date, like me.' Allowing her to re-enter the van first, he used one hand to give her backside a boost.

'No need to be, you haven't got a date yet, neither one of you. Tea or coffee? Or would you rather have a cold drink, Ray?'

Why was there nowadays so little space in caravans compared to when I was a kid? This one was roomy compared to the tourer Grandad also had, kept at home. Dad had been obscurely annoyed when he bought that, although it served well for our Caister holidays after that first independent one. There was more opportunity for Dan to grab Julie's waist as she ushered us by her at the small gas stove, into the slightly broader living area. 'This is Christine, my daughter. You've already met Dan, sweetheart. This young man is his nephew, Ray.'

I was instantly reassured that Dan had been joking with me. No way the child sitting in the window, a pile of newspapers spread all over the table in front of her, was girlfriend material. More likely I had been brought along to babysit her.

'Hello, Dan. Mum, how can I expect anyone else to call me Tina if you won't make the effort? There's so many Christines at school, I only wish you'd named me Christina at least in the first place if Tina was too much bother. Have you got a nickname, Ray?'

'No, there's not a lot you can do with mine.' I was not going into David Carlton who'd tried to make Roland Rat out of Roden, Ray in my early days at Grammar. I had smacked him in the face, his lip trembling as it fattened.

'Tina here' – the old smoothy hadn't remembered any variant of her name half an hour ago – 'is a lot cleverer than you, mate. This one does all right in his schoolwork.' High praise indeed from Dan, before putting me back in my place. 'Can't play football though. Tina's top of the class in high school.'

'I was in my first year, not this last one though.'

So she was in the same year as me! She had the grace to look embarrassed, sitting there in a green bikini top which had nothing whatsoever to fill it out.

'She's not always as clever as she likes to think.' Julie was standing between me and the table. 'Still needs her mum's help with the *Telegraph* cryptic crosswords, don't you? Perhaps Ray would like to give you a hand with it while I make the drinks.'

I would rather have read the football pages, but Dan had already snapped up the *News of the World* (had Julie bought it specially for him? If so, it revealed an unexpected depth to their relationship). Whatever he said, I had no fear of any girl being brighter than me. I sat down at an angle from her, making her turn the puzzle so I could see it.

I had no idea what I was doing. The clues made no sense to me. Half a dozen were already filled in. Soon realising my silence was due to ignorance of the conventions, not sulkiness or an attempt at superiority, she tried to help, and wasn't too cocky about it.

'"A pen's rote badly – that's common language!" "Badly" probably means it's an anagram, for them I like to write the letters in a kind of circle then see what order fits. We've got an "E" already from "SMEE" – Mum did help me with that one, "Pirate's ungrammatical introduction". I was annoyed because I've read *Peter Pan* and seen the film and pantomime and everything like a thousand times. Are you listening, Mum? Any idea? Or Dan?'

My uncle grinned at me over the top of his paper. He was quick with figures, not so hot on words. 'I told you, boy. She's a terror. You wouldn't be top of the class if she was in it.'

'I'm not top anyway,' I snapped. I didn't mind doing well at school, it kept Mum and Dad happy. Still, I didn't want to come across as a total swot, here or anywhere else.

I was not left to stew too long in the alphabet soup Tina was stirring with every appearance of enjoyment – *she* must be a real swot. I didn't expect Dan to hang around drinking tea for long. Sure enough, he soon offered to take us all for lunch somewhere along the front. I kept quiet about Mum's carefully packed sandwiches.

I stood outside with Dan while he smoked a cigarette, leaving Julie and Tina the caravan to get themselves ready. They emerged looking no different to my unpractised eye, except that they now wore hats: Julie's one of those broad-brimmed straw things against the sun, Tina in a baseball cap worn back to front. It was a Yankees one, which was a point in her favour.

'Do you like United as well, you know they're linked with the Yankees, merchandising and all that? Apart from being the best, that is.'

'Excuse me? Oh, you mean the hat. No, I only wear it because I like the logo. My Dad took us to Yankee Stadium and bought it for me. Which United do you mean?'

'There's only one.' Even if she could do poncy crosswords, there were still important life lessons I could teach her. I didn't want to tread nearer on the matter of her dad. My uncle's arm around Julie as they shuffled along behind us suggested he was off the scene. Divorced was fine. Dead I didn't want to risk bringing into the conversation.

'I suppose you mean Manchester United.' She followed my nod at the ball I was dribbling along the prom, playing it off the wall now and again. The name and crest were right there on it. 'I don't think Dad likes them. He doesn't see football much now anyway because he lives in the States.'

'What is he, a Yank?'

'No, he's English. We were living in America but Mum had to come home to have me, something about being born in Yorkshire, God's own country he always calls it.'

'You might have a chance of playing for the county the way they're going.' I had already consigned Mr Whatsisface to the Elland Road terraces, where he was welcome to stay.

'I doubt it, I'm not very sporty.'

'Not a problem.' I picked up my ball, looking back at Dan for confirmation that we would be going up the stone steps to the Saracen's Head, next to the Kit Kat club. I could not think of Tina as anything but much younger than me, which meant I could talk to her normally. I was not beyond a bit of showing off all the same, wanting to impress her by my familiarity with Hunstanton. I somehow assumed it wasn't her normal sort of holiday place.

I got my shandy at the Saracen's, even if Dan did cut my order back from pint to half. I was grateful he put it in a glass, since I saw the barman give him one of those cans, pop tasting like it, not the proper thing with real beer. Julie had half a lager and lime, Tina a coke she drank from the bottle, through a straw.

I had no expectations of getting Dan down to the beach for a kick about. He picked up on my intentions the third time I tried to pass the ball through his chair legs.

'Julie, is it all right if Raymondinho here takes Tina down to the beach for a paddle? I think he's worried about missing the Punch and Judy show if we keep him here any longer.'

18

Looking at her daughter, she saw no objection if no bursting enthusiasm either. 'Come here and let me put some sunblock on first, you know how you burn,' she said.

'There you go, boy. Have this for a donkey ride or ice cream or something – and not just for yourself. No skinny-dipping. Look, me and Julie may not stay here all afternoon' – she remained expressionless at his enquiring glance – 'I'll tell you what, how about we meet right here again about half five? Is that OK?' I knew he wasn't asking me. 'If you like I can give him Dad's key to the van, so they can go back if it starts to rain or anything and we've gone for a walk.'

'Walking in the rain, you romantic devil? I'm going to have to bolt the caravan door every night if you're wandering around with a spare key. Does that work for you Chris – Tina? We can perhaps get some fish and chips for tea?'

It was walking down one of the stone ramps to the beach that she reminded me of our first meeting. If I was flattered at first that she remembered me from the TB clinic, I had to set her right when she said I'd looked proper nervous as they called my name.

By unspoken agreement we walked a hundred yards away from the Saracen frontage, where Dan was bringing another couple of drinks out to the balcony bar. It was my turn to be rebuked when we put our clothes together, removal of her denim shorts revealing the bottom half of the green bikini. I only asked where her bucket and spade was.

'I didn't bring them. Your uncle told me you'd sulk and start crying if I didn't play with your stupid football. Let's go in the sea before one of the big boys takes it off you.'

She was game enough, I'll say that. At first we pat-a-caked the ball to each other, standing waist-high in the water. I started heading it, and she had a proper go at that, not closing her eyes and letting it bounce off randomly, like her nut was a fifty-pee piece. Her hair was still very long, pulled back tight from her forehead and ears, gathered up somehow behind so it wasn't in the way.

I soon saw, as she dived to pursue the ball when I slammed it past her, that she was a much better swimmer than me. Had to be, since I couldn't swim at all. There were a good few people in the water. I was keeping half an eye out for anyone I might know from school, so I could put on an air if necessary of having less fun than I was.

Luckily Tina did not suggest a swim into deeper water. Perhaps she really wasn't sporty. As I had expected, she tired of the ball game sooner than I, suggesting we walk further along the front. Despite the heat of the day, she shivered briefly when we left the sea.

'Want to borrow my T-shirt?' I awkwardly thrust out the red singlet, Dennis the Menace standing proud on it in some material between plastic and Velcro, not altogether pleasant to the touch.

'No thanks. I like it though.'

'All you have to do is join the fan club in *The Beano*, then you can send away for one. You still have to pay for it, mind.'

We agreed not to bother with ice creams, to save our money for the amusement arcade. Again, she was a good sport. She stood her share of games, didn't ask me to do that stupid one where you put your feet on coloured pads and jig about to music, wasn't quite as hopeless at air hockey as I'd expected. I didn't beat her by that many.

Outside the big, free-standing entertainment complex, couples and families were picnicking on the green leading up from beach to town, many of them probably waiting for their homeward excursion buses. Cannily I kept us to the lower end as we passed, with the girl to my left so I could appear to be talking to her while scouting for flashes of flesh, always more exciting than the matter-of-fact display of bikinis on the beach.

'Do you think we've left them enough time for sex?'

I thought she was referring satirically to a couple of teenagers eating face ten yards away. When I realised she meant Dan and Julie, to my horror I blushed. 'You shouldn't talk about your mum like that,' I then made matters much worse by saying.

'Why not? She always says we should be able to talk about everything to each other. Not that I always want to, not about my stuff.'

Having no wish to hear about her 'stuff', whatever it might be, I felt some need to defend Uncle Dan against the imputation that he would rush Julie back to the van for sex as soon as we were out of sight; not so much to cast him in a better light, more to save us being billed as stock comedy nuisance kids. 'I wouldn't be surprised if they're still at the Saracen's, been there all afternoon. Else he might have taken her to the Con Club. I went there with him once, they've got a full-sized snooker table.'

She did not seem persuaded. 'I don't mind, you know. Your Uncle Dan's all right. Have you got a girlfriend?'

'Whatever Elizabeth says I bet Ken takes more responsibility than you ever do for our kids. I sometimes wonder if Denis is getting into drinking at his friends', you know the Puerto Ricans treat beer as a soft drink.'

'It is Medalla *Light*. You've got to expect it, he's nearly seventeen now. It's Kim you need to keep your eye on. You see the way these little girls go out, dressed in next to nothing.'

'Denis isn't sixteen yet. If you can't set a good example at least don't encourage him.'

'Ken said he wanted to talk to me about Barbados tomorrow. How would you fancy a posting there?'

'Barbados? Could be worse places I suppose. Like Hong Kong.'

These were choppy waters. While grateful for Ken's intervention in the Far East, she blamed him both for allowing the situation to develop and then not punishing her husband severely enough. Ray decided to fight another day, but could not resist a parting shot before taking Sanjo out for his late-night walk. 'Yeah, like Hong Kong, where our daughter was born, none of it's been any good really, has it?'

'You behaving yourself then, Ray?'

Ken's abrupt way of beginning his review meetings was nothing new, though Ray was more used nowadays to the leisurely Caribbean pace of things, along with elaborate Spanish courtesies. You were often on the coffee and liqueurs before you learned what lunch was all about. 'Well, I had a detention last week for not handing in the reinsurance returns on time, and Janet is always threatening to ground me, otherwise not too bad.'

'Never mind ground you, I'm surprised she hasn't decked you before now. Is she happy enough here?'

'Yes, she doesn't work for Sovereign, does she?' The edge to his tone was to indicate that work was work and his private life his own. Ray was admittedly at a disadvantage there, in that he had left the boss no option but to intervene when he managed to tangle up the two in Hong Kong. Ken had gone above and beyond then, helped out as a person. It was no less than the truth when he added, 'She would cook you a dinner though, says you're always welcome during your visits if you want a change from eating well.'

'Tell her thanks, I don't have my old appetite. Since they gave me the Eastern Front to watch as well as this side of the pond I'm always on a plane, always with a gut-ache.'

'You sure that's not one too many G and Ts?' For a moment Ray thought he had gone too far. The monobrow arrowed briefly chinwards before Ken laughed, showing a set of teeth to make American dentistry proud (a legacy of his own time in Puerto Rico). 'Pot and kettle, my lad. I don't want to know how much vodka you get through over here. Might be good training for a new posting, if you've been giving any thought to that.'

'You know me, Ken. Go with the flow, take what's offered as long as Jan will follow with the kids. I don't believe in long-term planning. Have you been doing some thinking for me?'

'Jesus Christ, a year ahead is hardly long term. You need to show a bit of initiative, can't rely on Staffing to sort you out a new job every time – look how they left you there in Hong Kong, too long probably. Don't want to make the same mistake here. It's all opening up for us in eastern Europe. I want people I can count on there, but I might make an exception for you. Could be a move to make your career.'

'Or scotch it.' Ray did not remark that no sparrow fell on Ken's patch without him taking the keenest interest. Perhaps he rather than Staffing was the one who had made Ray do extra time in Hong Kong. 'Sending someone to Siberia isn't normally a sign of special favour. Especially when I was waiting for you to offer me Barbados.'

'Barbados? Oh yes, I mentioned it last night, didn't I? I'm afraid you're not going to be as lucky as I was, we haven't had an expat in Bridgetown for years.' He paused a moment, as if in fond remembrance of his own posting there. 'You might have a bit of spare capacity as we're going to switch the US Virgin Islands over from you to Jaime. It makes more sense with Puerto Rico, both US jurisdictions.'

'I thought you were the one who made the switch the other way when they were setting my unit up? You know it represents nearly half my premium income?'

'More like a third, don't exaggerate. I was persuaded into the change, let's leave it at that. You always bitch to me about Dumpy and Hairpiece anyway.'

Had Ray really shared his nicknames for their USVI agents Frank Bridges and Joe Makepiece (B & M Insurances) with Ken, knowing he never forgot anything. 'I don't say I enjoy working with them, but they're my biggest

'There you go then, that's fine. Jan couldn't give up work soon enough once she'd tricked and trapped me.'

'What did she do?'

'The usual, she got preg... oh, you mean what did she do for work. She worked in Sovereign, believe it or not. Could do a good job here like she did in the UK, except she's never had the visas to work on our postings. Does a bit of volunteer stuff here, a library and the Commonwealth Association. We'll have to get you signed up for that too, piss-ups round each other's houses every month or so mainly.'

Ray was joking about the pregnancy, in the sense that she had only told him about it once he had already booked her plane ticket (whatever his mother might persist in believing). He didn't mind at all. His longer-term life projection of being divorced with two kids by age thirty was still very doable at that point, the more so if you counted the son she already had. He liked to brag of his adventurous move within twelve months from being a bachelor living in South London to a married man with two children in Southeast Asia.

Jan not only took the wheel on their way home from Cerromar but refused to stop at Pepito's to play pool, or allow Ray to accept Eddie's invitation (admittedly half-hearted) for a final drink at his Howard Johnson hotel – during the next week he would be moving into a beachfront flat in Isla Verde. Pointedly Ray poured himself an NBA hand of vodka as soon as they got home, taking it with a tint of diet coke on his evening walk with Sanjo.

Tonight he was inclined to be talkative, over the phone outside and back home with his second sextuple. 'What did you think of Uncle Eddie then, kids? Never mind that rubbish on telly, answer your Uncle Dad.'

'He's cool,' Denis allowed.

'He's cute,' Kim granted.

'Hold up, darling, I don't want to hear you calling anyone cute unless it's a baby or a puppy. They say he looks a bit like me. Did you think so?'

'No Daddy, you're old.'

'Jan, I wish you'd have a word with that Kimberley Maria. She gets cheekier every day. Don't think I don't know where she gets it from as well.'

'If you want to help with the washing-up, get yourself a tea towel.' Jan ungently repelled his advance.

'Christ, I'm only trying to make conversation, you moan enough when I don't.'

'That's right, because you only want to "make conversation" when you're bored or got a few drinks down you.'

Ray sulked for a while, until the children were in bed. 'Get off,' Jan warned, opening her eyes briefly as he sat down by her outstretched feet on the sofa. She was still wearing the light summer dress from the club, legs bare.

She tolerated his hand massaging her ankles. When he began to inch up her calf, she said 'Ray' in no welcoming tone. He was ready for the lunge of her right foot at him when he moved a bit higher. 'Leave me alone, you're drunk.'

It was hardly worth arguing about her increasingly liberal definition of 'drunk' to include evenings he could remember the next day. 'It's me and thee then, lad.' He tried her further by inviting Sanjo up to bed. The dog evidently decided she was not deeply enough asleep for him to risk a smacked arse, looking up only briefly from that arse and the leathery balls at which his head was often to be found.

Feeling sorry for himself and – why not admit it now? – a little affected by the vodka on top of beer, Ray did not have the energy even for porn. The days when he would use Sunday evenings to map out his coming week at work were as remote as those of Alfie and Annie Rose, him reading their adventures to the kids as they lay either side of him in bed. Weekly advance planning might have served him yet, but nothing too strategic as at the end of the month it was announced that the Sovereign Group had been taken over by SRG.

Chapter 2

'Ray? Ray, are you a virgin?'

Luckily, I'd heard the question running the length of the bench desks behind me. It was in the same vein as 'Are you a heterosexual?' except it would snare not those boys with a limited vocabulary but the ones too inclined to boast. It was understood that we were all virgins in 3A. To say otherwise would invite open laughter or forensic questioning.

Slaphead Selby's deafness allowed us to talk freely enough in his maths class. My questioners, Stevie Thomas and Milky Underwood, would only ever raise their hands in Slaphead's lessons. Never with a maths answer or question; in asking to be excused, or for a window to be opened, their delight was to address him as 'Greaser'. If he ever heard it as anything other than the formulaic 'Please sir', he chose not to make an issue of it.

No doubt it was an eye to career progression rather than any sudden awareness of the world of mockery in which he lived that led to Slaphead's departure in the middle of our third year. The first inkling of a merger between grammar and high schools came from our dour geography master, Arthur 'Bolton' Blackburn: 'It's going to be bad enough having to teach girls, without you behaving like one already, Tanner.' Bolton, obviously confident of his place in the larger school, would indeed survive the river crossing with us that summer, as various of his colleagues would not.

Of my immediate schoolfriends, the one I would have bet on to get a girlfriend first when we reached that promised land was Mick Turner. He had already given up playing for the school football team on Saturday mornings, to help his mother on their fruit and veg stall in the town market. He would wear woollen gloves in winter, with their fingers chopped off at the top joint to allow him to handle change. We might have laughed to see those on another boy.

Hoss Jenkins had needed all his sixteen stone to drag Mick off Tom Wilkins, a boy in the year above us who fancied himself enough to call our mate a 'little pikey bastard'. Hoss had to shoulder his way through the ring of boys chanting 'FIGHT! FIGHT! FIGHT!' in the same way as he had come to Anthony Holding's rescue when that boy fainted dissecting a frog in his general science class the year before. Wilkins had the more severe head injuries, though.

After playing football for the school myself on Saturdays and eating fish and chips in town, I would take my kit bag round to Omie Newnham's house. He had brought his nickname from primary school without being able to source it. A more valuable legacy was his friendship with Mick, perhaps the only person at school to call him Stephen. That friendship gave him a certain immunity; his popularity he earned on his own.

Omie's house, a semi with one main room downstairs and a bay window onto the street, was our Washtown centre of operations. He lived there with a younger brother, generally ignored by us all, and his mother. Mrs Newnham was welcoming without being all over us. None of us ever talked about our parents, but I assumed she had a job including weekends, since she was never much in evidence.

Jambo Haslett and I both lived in Feltwell, six miles out of town, far enough to disqualify our houses as gathering points. As he had been commuting to town since his convent beginnings, we had no shared history of Well Creek County Primary.

'Are you Ray Roden?' Jambo asked.

'You know fucking well I am, Haslett. You've heard me say so at the start of every class for a week.'

'I know, I meant… we both live in Feltwell.'

'Yeah, I live in the village, not in some poncy house halfway to Norwich. What about it?'

'My mum used to know your mum. They were at school together, so she said I should say hello to you.'

'Why? Haven't you got any mates? Afraid of the big boys from town? Omie here's from town, I bet he could do you.'

'He probably could.' In the embarrassed smile they exchanged was the beginnings of a friendship that developed beyond me. It was not until long after our playground introduction as first-term first-years that I started to get jealous of it. By the time we entered 3A, Jambo and I would usually sit together on the bus home from school, even though he was not a footballer.

There were at least two keepers ahead of Omie for the school team, so when I fetched up in Victoria Street, no doubt smelling of sweat, salt and vinegar, he and Jambo were often already there. While Mick joined us less frequently nowadays, we would always stop at his stall in the market, and he could sometimes bunk off with us for half an hour.

I suppose we all had pocket money of some kind, though it was as bad form to talk about this, or show off spending power in any way, as it would have been to ask how much Mick earned for his Saturday shift. Records were the only thing I remember any of us buying, other than food or drink for which the Methodists' Tea Shop was a regular haunt. Nobody chucked you out of there however long you sat before, after or without consuming.

Our taste in music was far from uniform, still formed in part by or in active rebellion against that of our parents. Dad liked brass bands, which was fine, music so far from ever being heard by any of us that it could cause no embarrassment. The same was true of Mrs Newnham's radiogrammed collection of Country and Western, with an honourable exception made for Johnny Cash. Jambo asked me if I thought 'Boy Named Sue' reminded Omie of his absent dad.

'Fucked if I know. He never says. If it was his old man's record he wouldn't've left it behind if he was a dad like Sue's, would he? Omie hasn't got a guitar either.'

'No, but there might be an empty bottle of booze in that cupboard his ma keeps locked up. Someone told Omie that bit in the song where he says he's the beep who named you Sue, was to block out "son of a gun". Hardly sounds worth bothering, does it?'

'I asked Dan and he said it was "son of a bitch". Still hardly seems worth bothering.'

I was growing out of calling Dan 'Uncle' unless he forced the word from me when we were wrestling, which we hardly ever did any more. He treated me more as an adult in his use of language now, without stopping from taking the piss out of me whenever he could. I would still sometimes stay overnight at Grandad Will's for him to pick me up in the small hours to ride in his lorry.

'Why doesn't Grandad like you?'

'Who says he don't?' Dan shot back from the driver's side of the cab.

'Well, you don't seem very good friends with him.'

'Are you good friends with your dad?' He had the irritating habit of machine-gunning questions at you, distracting you from what you were trying to talk about. It was worse when the questions found you short of a confident reply. This one was ridiculous, but I didn't want to fall into a trap, so took my time before answering.

My dad Peter's lifestyle was far nearer to Grandad's than Dan's, though he was not noticeably close to his father-in-law. All my life he had worked as a dragline driver on the Wash, taking whatever overtime was available. At home he would mainly watch television and smoke, leaving the ceiling above his armchair with a big yellow stain, like it was the underside of a mattress somebody upstairs had wet. He had watched me play football when I was at primary school, was keen on me doing well in class at grammar, never told me off much, but a friend…?

'That's different, you can't…' Despite my deliberations I almost stepped right in it, saying you can't be friends with your dad, which would obviously let Dan wriggle off the hook completely. 'You can't say it's the same, you're both grown-ups, you could go up the pub and stuff.'

'Have you ever known your grandad go up the pub?' This time it was rhetorical. 'When I was a boy I used to think that's exactly what we'd do when I grew up, but he'd already stopped drinking by then, half a shandy at Christmas is about his limit now. That's what being married with kids does to you, boy, every single time.'

'Dad still goes up the pub,' I said stoutly, not wanting to think I might have sold him short, even if only in my own mind.

'Six pints on a Friday night and four of a Sunday dinnertime with me, all in the Swan, that's not your dad any more, not like he was before he got so damn p-w'ed by my sister.'

'What's p-w'ed mean?'

'If I wanted you to know, I wouldn't have used the initials, would I? If you catch your old man in a good mood you can ask him, but don't *ever* ask your mum, she'd have my guts for garters.' Perhaps realising this would not be a solid enough gobstopper, he added, 'And she won't let you come in the wagon again.' He reached across to ruffle my curly hair, knowing I hated that even worse than when he used to play Desperate Dan, scraping his unshaven chin all over my face. 'Don't look so serious, mate. If I'm still around when you grow up, I promise I'll keep right on drinking and we can go up the pub together as much as you like.'

Dan had unconsciously provided us with many hours of activity indoors at Omie's, from the card games he had taught me. Jambo had picked up some of these at Grandad's when Dan was still in residence, happy enough to stop

36

playing Subbuteo, at which I always beat him. I usually beat him at cards too. Newmarket, Chase the Lady (rechristened Hunt the Cunt by Mick one half-term), variants of whist or rummy all featured, with our favourite for three players – unusual in being only playable by that number – Sergeant-Major. This was a version of whist Dan had played in the army, when he and his mates were too broke for brag (we were always too broke for brag, which doesn't work with matches).

Despite disagreements over the cards, many of them, it never got physical between the four of us, Mick acting as a silent regulator. Every boy had a good idea where he stood in the unwritten table of hardness. Keeping in one's place helped keep the peace. Mick was at the top, able even to give the boys in higher forms an upset (as Wilkins had discovered). I was in the pack behind the leaders, challenging for Europe if not the league title. Omie and Jambo were mid-table, unthreatening yet unlikely to go down. So at least I thought. Maybe I thought too much about the table.

We were happy enough, I would say, in our boys' world with our boys' games. We were not frightened by the prospect of the merger, as some older lads undoubtedly were, too long institutionalised after the natural co-education of infant school. Still it would be a change, for the boys a change of location as well as classmates.

There was no grass at the Grammar. We played football every break as well as before and after school, on the paved playground. There would be at least a dozen games going, with regulation balls you could buy from what was optimistically called the tuck shop: a window in a wall halfway up the slope to the headmaster's garden. There was a measly selection of chocolate bars and sweets, with the hard-plastic-panelled, perforated balls found to offer least threat of smashing a window. Slightly bigger than a tennis ball, they would only become dangerous to property when on their last legs. Stuffed with paper and taped together so much as almost to obliterate the plastic from view, on a wet day they could become as painfully unpredictable as a cricket ball.

Although our playground matches were the best thing we could do with our time (only Omie as yet was into cigarettes, nicking them singly from his mum), it was a luxury to have our games lessons on the school's football pitches. It meant a trek of over half a mile, across the river and into the trees on the edge of town, but it was always the last double period of the day, so we didn't have to worry about closing bell. The girls' school was hardly a hundred yards from

Willow Road, which would be an improvement; better yet, it was rumoured to have ample fields in its own grounds.

There was no question of any joint activities during the year leading up to the merger, unless it was at a level far above our third-form heads. We all knew where the high school was, expected to turn up there in September after the summer holidays. That would have been our first sight of the hallowed turf, if not for Monkie's habitual idleness.

Mr George Redmonk was our history teacher. Even his eyes were lazy. They would appear fully closed as he read from a hardback on the least interesting, most conspicuously irrelevant topics of English and European history during its most eventless periods. Perhaps they *were* fully closed at times, his featureless delivery of the material surely from memory rather than an engaged reading of the *Corn Laws*, the doings of the Elder or Younger Pitt – who cared which, they had both been dead a thousand years? – or the epochally poxy *Treaty of Utrecht*.

Our own heads were bowed over our 'rough books', scribbling as much as we could catch of his monologue. Homework would be to transcribe it fair into our orange history exercise books; revision to learn it by heart; exam to regurgitate it. If we'd had a book each, Monkie could have dozed in earnest while we studied quietly.

He could, unfortunately, no more be trusted to doze than we could to work quietly. There would usually be at least one incident to evoke our teacher's other nickname. Maybe a head would be not only bowed, not even only resting on the desk, but vibrating against it from a snoring none of the rest of us would have disturbed for the world. Maybe someone would ask Monkie to spell 'Hohenzollern' once too often, forcing him to his feet to blazon the word across his pristine blackboard. Maybe he was just in a filthy mood. Then Redmist would appear.

He was a cracking shot with the blackboard duster, though he was reduced to hurling stubs of chalk after that split Mark Edwards' head open one day. Edwards never dared say, but the word was he got a personal apology and a new pair of glasses in compensation for the stitches. He had been doubly unlucky, sitting near the back of the class so the missile had gathered momentum, and being caught by the wooden not the wiping side of it. Redmist learned to be a little more subtle, levitating and walking boys with the minimum of exertion on his own part – a firm grip on the hair immediately above their ears, which was profuse on almost all of us at that point in history.

As we came to the end of summer term, exams done and form placings set, whipping both carrot and stick from our teachers' hands, Monkie at last came up with a new lesson format. Not for him a fun quiz, or any of the other devices employed to avoid total anarchy or total apathy – Morry Davies was best in music, letting us bring in our own stuff (until Parkins and Powell, squabbling over playing order, snapped the arm off the old record player). Monkie announced a field trip. His debut grin should have warned us.

There were textbooks after all. A whole cupboardful. It looked as if all the other years were also being forced to learn their history exclusively through the medium of Monkie. Perhaps he would have argued that was right and proper, the very definition of a teacher's role. In other classes, we would hand in our books at year end. There must have been some arrangement for transferring them from South to North Brink. Monkie evidently hadn't read the memo. He proposed we carry the books across to the girls' school.

They weren't heavy. Only two boys were excused lifting duties, Morton who had a withered arm, and Yarley who was excused everything. We had never seen him in gym kit. Omie, Jambo, Mick and I hit the streets together.

The novelty soon wore off. The cardboard boxes had to be gripped from underneath with both hands, an uncomfortable posture which soon had us revising our opinion about the weight of their contents. By the time we reached Clarkson Bridge, Mick was fed up, not so much at the load as at having to listen to Jambo's moans about it. Omie had already stopped for a breather twice, on the excuse of a fag carefully shielded from any passers-by. I was glad he had taken the initiative to pull up.

The stone balustrade on either side of the bridge, separating its pavements from a straight drop into the Nene thirty feet below, was no more than four feet high. 'Fuck this for a game of soldiers,' Mick muttered, hoisting his box onto a shoulder then pitching it over into the water. It sank like a brick, one copy of *The Age of George III* escaping, struggling momentarily to stay afloat before the monarch's bewigged head on the cover became sodden and disappeared to the bottom of the filthy river.

'What you all fucking gawping at?' Mick asked.

'What about Redmist?' Jambo spoke for all of us.

'What about him? You dumb fucker Cranham, jogging my arm like that you've made me drop the books into the pissing river. Don't blame me if I have to grass you up to Old Monkie.'

Sweat was pouring down the face of Chubby Cranham as he toiled up the bridge's slight gradient, chin on his box of books as if afraid it might otherwise blow out of his hands. Whether because he was too involved in his misery to hear Mick properly, or as part of a general policy in dealing with him – a sane one, on the whole – he kept his head down and struggled past us.

'You all saw it, didn't you lads?'

'Yeah course we did, Mick, but do you think Monkie will swallow it?'

'I don't give a rat's arsehole. It's last period. I'm off home now. If he remembers it while September good luck to him.'

Monkie had told us to ask for Miss Barton on arrival. She didn't seem enough of a looker to justify his close attention to her when we found them there together, so perhaps she was going to be his boss. He must have driven round from our school, the bastard, without a single box of books in his rotten car.

If Miss Barton was going to boss Monkie, she had her girls to direct us. The one who led Omie, Jambo and me to a storeroom (downstairs rather than up, thankfully) was as tall as any of us. Alison's moustache was also a worthy competitor to any of ours, her hair a severe square cut, a perfectly straight line across the back of her neck we noticed as we followed her. There were perhaps six inches of leg between the top of her navy socks and the pleated blue skirt. None of us bothered to measure too closely, even as we followed her back up the stairs.

'Well done, boys,' the teacher said briskly as we came back into her view. 'I'm sure Alison's been tremendously impressed by your muscles.' (If so, she gave no sign of it.) 'We probably shouldn't, but I think we can let you cut across our lawns to get away home a little more quickly.'

Monkie grinned, obviously pleased that this shortcut had not been allowed or known to us when we were still humping his books.

So they weren't pitches or fields here, but lawns. Certainly, something like lawn tennis was going on, courts stretching away from the school buildings parallel with the river. It differed from the games I liked to watch on telly (for the shots of the women serving) in that there were no rallies going on. It was an achievement if one girl managed to dish it up over the net and the other to get it back. They looked to be about our age, their white skirts shorter than Alison's uniform.

There was a mixture of smiles, blanks and whispered confabs at the net as we sauntered along, desperate to seem independent of Alison striding ahead of us. We couldn't even be trusted to find a five-barred gate in a flat field, it seemed.

We were alert to any hint of mockery, not responding to the odd disguised wave, fingers waggling at us without any extravagant arm gestures. Still, I could not decently ignore it when someone called my name.

'Who's this then, mate?' Jambo whispered from behind me as she came running towards us, dragging her opponent with her, arms still linked as she spoke first to our guide.

'We can take these visitors off your hands now if you like, Ali.'

'What about Miss Harmister?'

'Oh, she's in the copse' – a backward nod of the head, like a horse spooking away from a treatless hand – 'with the real tennis players. She won't be out till the bell.'

Alison was not convinced. 'I've been given the job, so I'll do it. Up to you if you want to tag along. I didn't ask you to if she does turn up.'

Now that we had swelled to an awkward sixsome, the newcomer suddenly lost a bit of her assurance. No way were Jambo or Omie going to break the silence, and I kept quiet too.

'Aren't you even going to say hello, Ray?' She was almost hiding behind the other girl, a dumpy little thing with dark freckles all over her face and a thick braided pigtail hanging down either side of it.

I pretended to look behind me for someone called Ray. She was nibbling at a hank of white hair, her face turning red. 'Yeah, how are you?' I relented. 'Don't think much to your backhand.'

'I'm better at football. This is Angie, my best friend, we both really hate tennis, don't we Ange?'

'I'm Stephen...'

'Leave off. This is Omie, and this is Jambo, they're my bestest friends in the whole wide world.'

Perhaps he had learned it at Convent, that smooth bastard Jambo, shaking the girls' hands and giving them what looked a shy grin they wouldn't know was to hide the braces on his teeth. Omie followed suit, unworried by any nicotine stains on his own gnashers.

'I'm Tina,' she proclaimed, challenging me with her eyes to reveal the secret of her name. She hadn't changed that much, taller no doubt, still no tits, tanned legs worth a look though, about twice as long as her friend's and with less skirt to cover them. 'How's your uncle, Ray, Uncle Dan?'

The enquiry seemed neutral enough. I had never seen Dan with Tina's mum again after the day at the seaside, knew that whatever they had going on it had not lasted long. 'He's all right. How's Julie?'

'She's great, she's married now. Ray and I were once almost cousins, weren't we?'

I wasn't going to join her blethering. I was sweating that she would say something to make me look ridiculous in front of my mates, already planning the conversation once we were safely out of the school grounds.

'Dan? What's he got to do with these young ladies?' Jambo stuck his snout in again.

'Nothing.' I lifted my head briefly to point with my chin at Tina, without looking her in the eye. 'He used to shag her mum, that's all.'

Chapter Two

Leaving the house the day Martin was expected, Ray heard Kim ask, 'Mum, what's the Alamo?' Before Jan could answer, Den was in there. 'It's a place where a load of Americans died like rats in a trap. Every one of them died.'

'Don't mind him darling, your dad will tell you when he gets home. He's seen the bloody film enough times.'

Ken Thompson seemed to have little appetite for the conference call following the merger announcement. He gave Jaime and Ray the most cursory of greetings before reading out, word for word, the press release they had already seen. He concluded with obvious relief: 'That's the information duly "cascaded". Any comments or questions?'

'I suppose congratulations are in order for keeping the secret so well.' Jaime's usual courtesy was in his voice, though the comment was barbed.

There was a pause before their boss replied. 'These things are kept within a very small working group on both sides. There are all sorts of legal and stock market implications that make secrecy as you call it – confidentiality is the English word – essential.'

The Big Man was hitting back. There was nothing wrong with Jaime's English.

'So in practice what do we have to do next?'

'You have to sell the deal, Ray. And I mean that, whatever your private feelings may be about it. The comms people will be sending out all sorts of specimen letters to brokers, customers, staff, but never mind all that bumf, the way you carry yourselves will be crucial.'

'You know what the staff's concern will be, Ken. Job losses.' Ray made the point, though Jaime had over a hundred people to worry about to his half dozen.

'All I can say there is, you're luckier than a lot of our friends around the world. It will be far more complicated where both companies operate in the same market. In the Caribbean SRG tend to focus on the Dutch islands, is my understanding.'

'I know they pulled out of Puerto Rico years back, because I used to work for them here.' Jaime had been sitting back letting Ray lead the conversation from their end, but now he leant forward over the speakerphone. 'I was wondering if that attitude will carry through into the new group, shutting down our operation.'

'Too early to say, and the same for Ray's islands. I'm sure you'll both have a chance to show your mettle. There will be regional merger groups set up, teams from both sides of the house. My initial thought is to nominate the three of you for the Caribbean.'

'The three of us?' Ray knew perfectly well who they would be.

'Yes, I think Eddie can do a lot of the legwork, obviously keeping in regular touch with me and my counterpart in Amsterdam. Mr Van Houden will also be naming a team, probably out of Curaçao. You'll have to get together with them as soon as possible. Meanwhile get out into the market, you around the islands Ray. I'm counting on you to be ambassadors for Sovereign. Why has it suddenly gone quiet?'

'Nothing.' Ray spoke when it became clear Jaime would not. 'As it happens I've already got flights booked to see Jonno in Tortola tomorrow. How much longer will we be Sovereign? What's the new name going to be?'

'No idea on that. On the merger they want regional blueprints within three months. There's plenty to do, so unless there's anything else for now…?'

'Sounds like we'd better get into the market.' Ray raised his glass of water in an ironic gesture of cheers, which put a smile on Jaime's face for the first time that day.

The owner of El Rancho de Che had reached an accommodation with Ray, after an initial wariness on both sides, once they had agreed the islands were a piece of shit not worth one Argentinian or English life. As usual, he brought the first beers personally, shaking hands with Ray and Jaime after depositing the frosted mugs and bottles on the table between them. With his unfailing instinct for when it was appropriate to pull up a chair himself, he decided this was not the moment. The eight or nine other diners were enough to half-fill the place, without threatening their regular corner table.

'Jesus, we'll be reporting to that little shit before long if Ken has his way. Don't tell me he wasn't sent out here deliberately.'

Ray knew it was going to be a long lunch – they never had a short one at Che's – and he did not fancy spending it in defence of his new assistant manager. 'I get the feeling he's already wishing he wasn't here. Probably worried there won't be anything for him to go back to in London when he's shown he can't hack it overseas. Can't hack two years shagging his way round the Caribbean.' Ray hardened his heart.

'There may come a time when we'd all be glad of two years.'

They were on their third round when Nelson Cano arrived from the gym. Jaime's sales and marketing VP seemed to think that helped with his cholesterol, blood pressure, triglycerides or something else on which Ray preferred not to know his own numbers. Plates of cheese and meat empanadas, and chorizo in a heavy garlic sauce, beat Nelson to their table, as he glad-handed people at three others before taking his seat.

Friends since their teenage years courting two sisters from Caguas, Jaime and Nelson became brothers-in-law then *compadres* with the birth of their first children. Jaime was still married to the younger sister, Gloria, while the other was the first of Nelson's three wives to date. Whatever his family loyalties, his fidelity to Jaime in a work context was absolute. Unless his boss told him to worry about the merger, all he needed on it was a quip or a soundbite good enough to stop it interfering with his production of new business.

By the time they had finished their main courses, they were ready to face the market. It came to them. For form's sake they took a coffee into the larger back room, marking the end of the eating and the start of their serious drinking. They shifted tables together in the inclusive Puerto Rican way, brokers, agents and major clients passing through as afternoon became evening: Paco, Rafa, Tito, Juancho, Victor, Edwin, Pepe, Emilio, Tony, Chago, Eduardo, Diego, Gustavo, Luis Ramon, Ramon Luis, Pablo, Joey, Johnny, Chito, Hector, Manolo, Peyo, Georgie, Kike, Oscar, Rafi, Moncho, Alex, Tato, Nello.

They drank Medalla, Coors, Bud, Palmolive (the local name for Heineken, smoothing away life's harder edges), Finlandia, Absolut, Jose Cuervo, Beefeater, Tanqueray, Franjelico, Red Label, Black Label, Buchanan's, Don Q Cristal, Palo Viejo, Cointreau for Nelson after his fifth stiff vodka, feeling he shouldn't overdo it and the orange flavour must be from good vitamins.

Drunken repetition was not a problem, since it was the same message for all. The biggest news in Sovereign's centuries of existence was a good thing. If there was any cause for concern, didn't they think the Puerto Rican bosses would have been shifted at least marginally from their normal habits on the day of its announcement?

Ray was never in any later than the office's nominal opening time of 8.30, though it was increasingly rare for him to be at his desk much earlier. He was always there after its closing at 4.30 too. During the period in between, a diligent time-and-motion study might have detected some absences longer than the statutory thirty-minute lunch break.

He never aspired to be the last to leave. There were always affairs going on. With the open-plan office laid out like a deck of cards, it was quite a trick to remember which were the pairs, amongst those dotted around at desks where the computers had long been logged off anything related to insurance. He did not suspect Eddie of any such liaison – not yet anyway – and was surprised to find him when he returned from Che's towards seven.

'Fall asleep at your desk, mate? You mustn't stay too late you know, cramps the style of the ones without a home they want to go to.'

'That would be me as well. I'm not complaining but I haven't made any friends in the block yet. I'd like to invite you and Janet round for a curry one night, with the kids would be fine.'

'Yeah, ta, sounds good. Probably easier for you to come to us, but we'll have plenty to do around here for the foreseeable anyway, with the merger and all.'

Irritatingly, the boy had followed him to the door of his office. 'I had plenty to do this afternoon. Ken came through, said he was looking to talk to you and Jaime, he forgot to stress earlier that we should prepare op plan figures on the basis of transferring the US Virgin Islands out of Caribbean Coordination and into Sovereign Puerto Rico.'

'I got that message loud and clear, no need to remind me, leaves us with the British Caribbean mainly, also known as the square root of fuck all. Our expense base will never stand that cut in premiums, especially now you're on board. I suppose the Big Man told you you're on our merger steering committee or whatever they call it?'

'He did. Another thing I should probably have mentioned first, I don't know if Jan got through to you in the end, she tried here more than once. Several calls from the islands too, good job you'd already sent the agents the email about me, mostly they wanted to hear any gossip behind the main story.'

'I was busy this afternoon. I haven't got any gossip myself, but if you're not in a hurry to go we can carry on chatting downstairs.' Flicking through the tear-off message slips on his otherwise clear desk, he found a new name: Eric Horsevole, followed by three of Marta's unapologetic question marks. Why did it never occur to the secretary he shared with Jaime to ask the person at the other end of the line for a spelling, rather than expect him somehow to enlighten her? Seeing the company name of their new Dutch partners, he guessed it was his Caribbean counterpart at SRG. Tomorrow would be soon enough to get back to him, or the day after. He must not appear to be at the guy's beck and call, put himself at any disadvantage.

However unappealing his empty apartment, it was evidently more attractive to Eddie than joining Ray at Frankie's joint, on the ground floor of the Hato Rey office block where Sovereign occupied the seventh. Ray checked in almost daily for lunch at the bar or evening wind-down drinks, often both. Frankie swore the only reason he didn't offer breakfast was that he already grew sick of the sight of Ray and Larry.

The bar area was enclosed to the left, down a couple of steps which had unfortunately inspired someone to a sign over its doorless entrance arch: Frankie's Valley. Larry was at his normal place, to the left of the bar counter as you went in, where the short stroke of its L met the back wall. In the body of the restaurant only two tables were occupied, one by four women, the other by a couple of not-so-young lovers.

'You been poisoning our new mate?' Ray accused their Martinican host François Nguyen. 'Said he'd had a lunch here but no way could I get him down this evening.'

'That'll be the company, not the restaurant. Anyway, last thing I need is another English asshole who's only going to drink beer. I already hardly have space for proper drinks with so many crates of Medalla out the back.'

Ray had never bothered to get Larry's history or citizenship clear. It was enough that he still spoke like an Englishman, despite many years stateside, including a spell in the US army. He was an engineer of some kind, working at construction projects on the island when he worked at all. His shaven head was baked leathery brown by the sun.

'I was heading off, dead in here tonight, but I'll stand another one. Lusa?' He held thumb and forefinger three inches apart for the prettier of the two barmaids Luz Angela, indicating the measure of Chivas he expected in his personal green glass and designating it 'a half, honey'. He appeared in Frankie's at least once every day it was open – all bar Sundays – often staying for several hours more than Ray, who did after all have a wife and kids at home.

It was perhaps a little late for the kids when he thought of leaving Frankie's, Lusa already let off and the main room in darkness, but he did include Denis and Kim in his offer of any kind of carry-out meal as a water-tester to Jan over the phone.

It was scalding. 'That's the best you can do? Where the fuck have you been? I've been trying to reach you for hours.'

'Calm down, what you shouting for? It was a busy day, you know the takeover, I was in meetings. And you haven't called lately cos I've been sitting at Frankie's for a little while unwinding a bit.'

'So glad you can "unwind a bit" after your stressful day. How many times do I have to call before you answer me? How far down do I rank behind your work and your friends and your other women? It's not as if I was calling to ask you to pick up a pint of milk on your way home or something, how often do I call you at all? I know better than to disturb you when you're so busy in your "meetings", you never answer after midday once you've left the office to get pissed. I speak to Marta more than I do you. I thought, just thought you might be *slightly* interested to know Denis has been expelled from school. Drugs.'

Chapter 3

The girls' school premises were bigger than the boys', certainly, but not twice as big. Forms one and two had therefore been jettisoned, so that children would now enter WGHS at thirteen rather than eleven. It was galling to have reached the fourth form – only in July had we tossed our caps into the Nene, as they ceased to be a compulsory part of uniform – and find the ladder chopped off beneath us. We had a single year's worth of kids to lord it over.

There were now four classes in each form rather than the two (A and Alpha) at Grammar. With the war already lost there was no point in fighting any battle for separation by gender, so each of 4W, 4G, 4H and 4S contained a mix of boys and girls. Having been together since 1A, Mick was the only one we lost to 4H as Jambo, Omie and I fetched up in 4S. It had a form master rather than mistress, and one already known to us: Hoss.

It would have been delicious to see the bachelor Hoss finally have to cover sex in a mixed class. In 1A, when we had one weekly lesson of general science, he had been forced to bluster his way through the schoolboy error of asking us a question to which he did not know the answer. Given an apparently free choice of which of the seven characteristics of living things we would like to study, the class spoke as one for reproduction. We never got to it and now I never would, having chosen physics over biology.

Signposted to our forms and form rooms by paired prefects (both male and female looking horrendously uncomfortable in most cases), in that first period together the interaction between the genders in 4S was stilted. Left to choose their own desks, the pupils were standing around in single-sex knots of three or four, the boys in their navy blazers and grey trousers gravitating like a murky sediment to the back of the room. Omie was there before Jambo and me. I was pleased that with satchel, sports bag and his arse he had secured the three rear left corner seats, less pleased that his arse was parked in the prime corner one.

We had seen little of Omie during the long summer break, which had been important in the sentimental education of Jambo and me. We spent a lot of time together in Feltwell, even though he remained inept as ever at football. He never bothered to join in our games at the playing field, nor to court my Well Creek mates who remained suspicious of him. 'See you, Ray,' Kev Brown, the best player in the school year below mine, remarked one day as Jambo appeared, knowing I would lose interest in the game and wander off to mess about on the swings.

Our summer football was always prone to interruption anyway, by teens from the travelling community that worked the villages over fruiting. Jealous of their own womenfolk – there was one exceptional beauty, Morwenna, I lusted after but dared not pursue, despite some encouraging smiles from her – they were always on the lookout for village girls. They treated them with no more respect than the village boys did, but had more money.

I don't know how far it went between Tom and Gloria. He ruled three or four younger brothers, and was usually a genial enough mediator between the travellers and ourselves. If she was not his sister, he also kept a protective eye on Morwenna. He was the only one who troubled to learn any of our names, though to be fair we made little effort in the other direction.

Gloria Carney was not from Feltwell but was hanging around our playing-field that summer. At fifteen or sixteen a year or two older than us, she had perhaps left Lockwell Secondary Modern. Dark-haired like Tom and Morwenna, it was maybe through the girl she became close to him. Despite the mutual suspicion, it was a reality that many of us spent long hours with what Nana Joan still called 'diddicoys'. There were only so many employers of casual fruit pickers. Jambo worked in the strawberry fields with me at Grandad Will's that summer.

Most of Tom and Gloria's relationship was in the open, but occasionally they would disappear into the caretaker's tool shed, the caretaker long since disemployed with his tools, the padlock and its hasp long since sprung. Despite the council's original high hopes for the playing field, it was already ours.

Jambo was as attracted to Morwenna as I, and equally fearful of doing anything about it. Gloria was also untouchable, first because of her age and secondly because of Tom. All we did was moon around the swings and the panelled roundabout, pretending to be engrossed in our own conversation while always keeping a prurient, covert eye on the girls.

Tom and Morwenna had already gone, hop-picking in Kent or wherever the next stop on their migrations was, when we were treated to more than a knicker-flash, courtesy Sam Hopkins. He was another sporadic visitor to our field, not welcome for a long spell after he broke the wooden crossbar on one of the under-sized goals the council had provided us by swinging on it. They removed the debris, but never replaced it.

I had the impression Gloria wouldn't stick around the playing field much longer. She was so bored she was even talking to Jambo, who had a bit more politeness or nerve than me.

Sam probably knew Gloria from Lockwell. Again a bit older than us, he might have been a more logical successor to Tom, yet preferred to egg on Jambo while boasting of his own successes with girls.

'Go on mate, you want to get in there, you can tell she's gagging for it now that did's taken his big dick away. You should at least be getting a bit of finger pie by now.'

All Jambo did was give that grin of his.

One evening Sam decided to take the lead. There was a football game going on as he made a playful grab at Gloria. She shook him off easily but did not leave. He came back over to us. Totally without reason he put me in the same man-of-the-world bracket as himself, the two of us taking the piss out of Jambo for his lack of initiative. 'Be ready, Jambo, cos in a few minutes you're going to see your first hairy twat – unless you count Mick Jagger.'

It was like when a fight was brewing. Everyone knew something was going to happen. Sam set off after her again. She ran like the girl she was, ineffectively, looking back over her shoulder. The footballers temporarily left their game: Jake was there, Kev, Buzzy, Ade, Willie, and no one to look out for her.

It was all over very quickly. Sam caught hold of her and pinned her to the ground, hands beside her head. He was close enough to have kissed her if he wanted, straddling her waist.

She didn't struggle much. I don't know if Sam would have used more force if she had. Once he felt her relax, he slid down her body, flipped up her skirt and pulled her white knickers down around her ankles.

She lay quite still, a dozen boys gaping at her bush. I might not have known exactly what to look for underneath it. There was nothing to see from my angle to one side other than the thick rug of black hair. Nobody said

51

anything. Sam sportingly stood back so as not to block the view. Gloria looked up at the sky.

Nobody moved to stop her when she got up after thirty seconds or so. Nobody had touched her. She did not seem fazed by the assault. There were no recriminations, not a hint of tears. I suppose she went home. It was only as she mounted her bike, unhurriedly, that I fully realised what we had seen. It was only then I got a hard-on, not my first but one I still remember.

Somehow the stripping consolidated Jambo as her boyfriend. I don't remember what was said the next day. He would sit on the roundabout with her, arm awkwardly round her shoulders. Once he put his hand up between her legs, under her skirt, yet without going on to touch her. They snogged a bit.

I don't know where all the other girls in the village were that summer. For a while Gloria held us all spellbound or, to put it more accurately, cuntstruck. If we had had telephones we would surely have called Mick and Omie down. Boys who had missed out on the show, ones we never normally saw, started hanging out down the field.

Jambo was not jealous or overly possessive. He did not demur when Sam suggested it was only fair we all had a chance to snog Gloria. Strangely enough, neither did she.

This time there was a modicum of privacy. Jambo was first into the shed where she waited, then Sam. There were three or four more of us, jostling around and bullshitting each other outside. When Sam came out, ostentatiously swiping his fingers under his nose, it was my turn.

Gloria was fully clothed, standing in a corner. There was one plastic window to the shed, so filthy it prevented spying and did not bring in much light. I was nervous as hell, yet there was no way I could back down with all my mates outside.

I walked the few steps across to her. I put my hands at her waist. She was slightly taller than me. I moved in for the kiss, to feel her hands gently pushing at my chest.

'Hop it.'

It never occurred to me to disobey Gloria. A small part of me was relieved to be dismissed. Nobody was in the shed very long with her, and none of us spoke about it afterwards, so perhaps I was not the only one she baulked at. She had not spoken loudly, eventually came out as self-possessed as ever to sit with Jambo on the roundabout. As rejections go, it could have been much worse.

I went off to Caister with Mum and Dad. The only women there were the dancing girls in the end-of-pier variety shows and the improbably proportioned ones on the comic postcard stands. Jambo, on the other hand, was launched. The thing with Gloria had fizzled out, he told me on my return. He was now seeing another girl, one Vicky Cooper. He had the crucial attribute of not being discouraged by refusals or even outright insults. Perhaps conscious of her own overbite, Vicky had mocked his dental work cruelly and long before eventually letting him into her house.

'Did you screw her then?'

'No.' Jambo was relatively discreet about his relationships with girls, which might have been another reason they liked him. While I was pleased he hadn't got all the way, he let me assume he had enjoyed other freedoms. There was little expectation at that stage of girls doing anything in return. It was all a question of how much they would allow you.

Jambo would bike to see Vicky somewhere in another village he would not even name, let alone share her address. At some point they realised they would be schoolmates come autumn, if not classmates. Apparently she made it clear they would not still be going out at that point. Going out was maybe stretching it, since he never mentioned going anywhere but to her house, which she closed to him well before the holidays ended.

'Is she here then, mate? Omie, Jambo had a bird over the holidays.'

Jambo put his hand over his mouth to avoid being overheard by the class (though it was a characteristic gesture anyway). 'Yeah, that's her over there.'

I was disappointed. She was sexy, with a real figure. 'He's had his head between them tits, Omie. And more. Aren't you going to say hello to her?'

He wasn't. During that whole school year, we would never see the slightest exchange between him and Vicky Cooper. Which did nothing to make us doubt his story of their summer afternoons.

Valerie Anderson, one of two girls who had passed the eleven-plus from Well Creek Primary with me, was also in 4S. We had not spoken through three years of standing at the same bus stop, so there was no reason to start now. The only other girls I knew at all were huddled as close as they had been by the tennis courts at the end of summer term. Only when register was called would I remember the other one's name as Angela – Angela Graham, it turned out – and learn that Tina's surname was Gibson. I wondered if alphabetical-order seating at the high school had hothoused their friendship, then thought perhaps Tina had changed her surname when her mother remarried. I didn't know how these things worked.

I was no more inclined to approach Tina that first morning than Jambo was Vicky, despite some prompting from Omie and him (less malicious than mine had been). I didn't regret the flood of tears from her that my mention of Dan's relationship with her mum on the day of the textbooks had provoked. If she wanted to be a little girl that was her problem. I was, though, a bit miffed that she blanked me as comprehensively as Vicky Cooper did Jambo. It wasn't supposed to work that way.

Tears were something new, or returned, to our lives. Only the most pathetic first-former at grammar school would have cried at anything. These high school girls, *fourth* years, fourteen or fifteen years of age, were at it all the time. In class, in the corridors, in the playground, presumably even more in their toilets; alone, with one friend, in a group, in front of teachers; we set up a roaring league, headed after a month or so by Angie Graham with sixteen sightings.

The class of around thirty was split more or less evenly between boys and girls. Daily repetition of the attendance register meant we soon knew everyone else's name. While a Monkie would undoubtedly have delegated the telling of this to some lick, male or female, Hoss boomed out the names himself. At Grammar it had been surnames only, here first were given as well. The girls were not expected to be addressed as brusquely as we had been. It was comical to see how some of the teachers, Monkie amongst them, suffered more than having to learn them by having to utter the chummier Ray, James, Stephen and Michael rather than Roden, Haslett, Newnham and Turner. Some boys also struggled initially to respond to names nobody but their grandmother had called them in years.

Looks had been as unimportant as academic prowess in determining your ranking at grammar school. Hardness and footballing ability were what mattered most. In our ranking of the girls, looks were the only factor.

It would have been unreasonable to expect from a population of fifteen more than two or three stunners, with about the same number of grotesques. Amongst the latter, along with six-foot-three Barbara Beckford (4H had a midget, Mick countered) and Roarer Graham (not from anything physical but her propensity to tears, which made her easy prey to our bullying instincts), was our supervisor from the history books portage. Alison Bright was not even registered for the roaring league. None of us were quite sure where to put her, so it had to be with the untouchables.

Valerie Anderson, not at all the podgy swot I remembered from our childhood, was respectably mid-table, the pretty face now sculpted into focus offering the prospect of further advancement. We noticed the girls often hung about in pairs, one good one bad by our binary reckoning of sexual attractiveness. Val's bad friend was a bus girl from another village, Sandra Martin. It was not until weeks had gone by that we would assign any notice, much less the ultimate badge of a nickname, to any other constituent of 4S's amorphous mid-range female body.

Nobody would have denied a place at top table to Vicky Cooper. Although, if Jambo was to be credited, she had a very firm moral compass, from which she would not deviate in any circumstances, she just didn't look that way. There was sexual promise in her least provocative of gestures, or so it seemed to us. Maybe it was her breasts.

If Vicky Cooper was perfectly happy in her own company, friendly enough to all (except Jambo) but without any favoured companion, Cathy Strain was rarely seen outside a group, like a prize quarterback for whom team-mates are expected to make the blocking sacrifices, with Beanpole Beckford browsing at altitude to warn of any approaching danger. Cathy always had a messenger, a delegate from those who jostled to walk the school at her side, if she should need to make contact with a boy. Her skirts were always the shortest in class. As if granted some special dispensation – and Hoss was certainly not going to enquire if it were so – she wore tights while all the other girls were still in knee-length navy socks. Yet it was understood these were no signs of invitation, at least not to the oiks of 4S. While she might deign to answer a fifth-former, even offer a smile to an upper-sixth prefect, we knew we had to await her summons.

I was slow to realise that Tina was in the same category as Vicky and Cathy. So was she. The shortness of *her* skirts seemed more due to a sudden growth spurt than any sexual calculation. If she wore a bra, it was redundant. She was open and friendly to all, crossing the male–female divide as easily as she did the much bigger one between those who were attractive to the opposite sex and those who were not. When she wore her hair in pigtails she looked ten years old, whereas the same style gave Cathy Strain the appearance of a young woman offering her husband a birthday treat. For all that, Tina was right up there in the sex league, which had nothing to do with either popularity or personality.

One would hope that if the teachers had such a league they kept it to fifth and sixth-form girls, and even with them very much on a theoretical level. The other side of the coin, with teachers as potential objects of attraction, was new to us all (except maybe Richard Watkins, who had fetched up in 4G). Our gym teacher Alex Calderwood was a good bloke for a jock. Woodie seemed genuinely embarrassed to find girls constantly mooning around after him. He was more used to preventing his male charges on school trips mooning out the bus window.

Within the female faculty, led by deputy head Old Ma Granger, the only one worth a second glance was Mrs Jackie King. The fact of her Christian name being known signalled her place in the staff pecking order, as head of domestic science. Her succulent body was unfortunately off limits to my mates and me by virtue of her subject. It was an optional one, perm two of three with the others being art and woodwork. Only Jambo had the slightest interest in art. I hated woodwork. Still there was no way to sign up for cooking. So we thought, not knowing the sweets it would bring those who did.

While we boys shied away from home economics, the girls showed up in force for 'Dai Hard' Lewis's Latin. His nickname owed nothing to any of his wartime exploits. He had been somewhere in Africa. His stories of those times never had anything to do with fighting. At Grammar I had come to imagine his service as another version of his later career, sitting in a hot room with thirty or so young men, most of them bored out of their brains. My only addition to the picture of our Nissen hut classroom – left behind at the merger – was a lazy ceiling fan.

Dai's nostalgic digressions, though lengthy and in themselves tedious, were nevertheless universally welcomed as a break from our own labours. I suppose he must have taken us through the cases, the declensions, the conjugations, in fact I have a trace memory of reciting them in the same way we had our times tables at primary school. Once beyond these, however, when not in Sierra Leone circa 1945 we were back in 50 BC rehashing the no-more-interesting Gallic Wars of Julius Caesar.

Homework was unvarying, a number of lines to work through, enough to fill the next class as we construed them sentence by painful sentence. Dai would usually begin with the next boy in line from the previous class, but was too canny to do so every time, keeping us all up to the mark.

While we were striking camp in the fields of France, or grappling with ablative absolutes, our female counterparts across the river were cutting pictures of togas from magazines to stick in their exercise books. Their teacher possibly had no knowledge of the language the skirt and sandal-wearers spoke, but her classes were such fun that a disproportionate number of girls signed up for Latin O level.

There was a surfeit of activity in the roaring league the day we – eight boys, bravest of the brave in Caesar's legions, and over twenty girls innocent of battle – got our first test results. Poor Vanda Docherty leapt five places with her strongest showing since she realised all the boys referred to her only by her initials. Dai was sympathetic yet unwilling to soften his marking standards. In November he was still doling out nought out of twenties, albeit with the occasional 'but improving' to the most easily discouraged. At the end of Christmas term, the boys occupied the top eight positions in the class. By the beginning of Spring term in January at least fifteen girls had been reassigned to other O level options.

Tina Gibson was one of those who persevered. Old Dai took a bit of a shine to her. He was the only teacher she did not ask to change to her preferred version when he addressed her as Christine. Naturally she knew no more than the other girls at the start of the year; unlike some, she was a quick learner.

She was precocious in other ways too. Before the end of September, while most of us were still not talking to girls on an individual basis, Brian Retchless was squiring her at breaks, walking the playing fields hand in hand and sometimes seeking out the areas where a limited degree of privacy could be had.

I had no idea what she saw in Pukemore, as I began to tag him, gaining some currency for the nickname at least amongst my own mates. He had never done anything to distinguish himself at the Grammar, yet was now revealed as a ladies' man, no more interested in the roaring than he was in the football or hardness leagues. Tina's presence on his arm made it impossible even to make the easy cracks about his selection of cookery as a subject – perhaps it was in those classes they had somehow got together.

It was hard to bear that someone like Pukemore had come up on the blind side, especially after the summer successes of Jambo. He did not waste any more time on Vicky Cooper, but adopted a kind of scatter-gun approach to a group who called themselves the hockey horde (quickly, inevitably, translated by us to hockey whores). Alison Bright was the centre-half and captain, with half a dozen others the nucleus of the team, their effectiveness on the field not always in inverse proportion to their degree of femininity. Of Maureen Wheatley, Lesley Carrick (the other girl from Feltwell), Janes Gault and Harewood, Nicky Stannett, Pat Wilson and Susan Tierney, only the last two were in 4S. Whenever they would accept his company Jambo hung around them, as well as joining the larger group during breaks. He seemed to be targeting centre-forward Tierney, but with Jambo you could never be sure.

Mick had not hung around in 4H, bagging its league leader. Caroline Peacock, who lived on the same bus route as us, was either shy or disdainful of talking much on the occasions Mick walked her to the Cattle Market and happened to fall in with Jambo and me. She was one of those girls with extra-long hair, jet black in her case. Omie and I took to calling her, carefully out of their earshot, Mick's squaw.

Although both of us cloaked it with disparaging comments about her and everything she was letting Pukemore do to her, we were both equally smitten with Tina Gibson. While I could clearly see Omie's infatuation, at the time I did not acknowledge or even recognise my own. She had been a little more relaxed in my presence since hooking up with Pukemore, smiling if he and I exchanged a greeting. She was friendly enough with Omie too, but openly flirtatious to some of the other boys in class. Her choices seemed as eccentric as that of Pukemore; Steven Barnes was called 'FA' because his huge lugs made him look like the Cup; Richard 'Wah Wah' Worsfold was more confident now than in our first year, when he had been forced to wait through most of registration every day before having to stutter his name.

While girls loved nothing better than to talk, they were generally more respectful of teachers than were boys in keeping quiet in class. Tina was a leading exponent of a trick they had presumably brought from high school: the note. Under the pretence of recording whatever Sir or Miss cast before us, she would scribble something on a piece of paper, fold it various times then pass it to a friend. This might be done in a casual half turn, ostensibly to stretch, dropping it on Roarer Graham's desk behind her; by a more daring dig in the ribs to warn Valerie Anderson in the desk ahead of incoming; or by a flick across an aisle, Pukemore often having to scrabble to retrieve it from the floor.

I rarely had anything to say to my mates that could not wait until break. Mum always put something in my blazer pocket, which I had to eat before the bell to avoid cutting into my own time or having to share. This was not so difficult with a bar of chocolate, more of a test with a packet of Golden Wonder cheese and onion. I did not welcome the possible attention drawn to me when Tina pinged a tightly folded square off her thumb almost into my lap. She wasn't getting a crisp, I knew that much.

Licking the crumbs off my fingers, shy as much of any attention from my mates as discovery by Dai – Pukemore didn't take Latin, Omie did – I read my first note in her childish handwriting. 'I suppose you know half the girls in class fancy you. Not surprising!!!!'

Chapter Three

There was much less traffic on the way to work than normal. That was always the case when schools were out, as they were today to prepare for the storm, but Ray suspected there would also be a good deal of absenteeism amongst the workforce, authorised in advance or not.

The WOSO radio station was of course full of Martin, from the news bulletins to the banter of the DJs – a notch or two more hyper than usual – to opportunistic advertisers who would probably have already sold out of their flashlights, first aid kits, anything that might help in a hurricane, by the time today's listeners could reach them.

He knew the sell-by date to reduce his insurance exposures on the British Virgin Islands had passed. He could almost have wished the whole portfolio had been transferred to Sovereign Puerto Rico along with the USVI rather than stayed with him a year earlier. The visit to Sovereign's agent in the BVI's capital of Road Town on Tortola – scheduled originally to assure the local insurance commissioner of Sovereign's continued commitment to providing coverage in his islands, then coinciding with news of the merger with SRG – seemed a long time ago.

'That went down like a lead balloon.' Ray was sitting with Eddie Jemson and David Johnson out of the bright midday sun in the open-air shade of the Captain's Table, off Road Town's main drag.

'It's the way you tell 'em, Ray.'

Ray never looked forward to meetings where he had to present, even informally and on something as cut and dried as the merger, even to an audience as undemanding as Patrick Wright and his smattering of subordinates at the Financial Services Commission. He had missed a fortifying Bloody Mary before catching their early-morning Starburst flight from San Juan and was aware that he had not sparkled. He should have known better than to expect any reassurance from their agent. 'Fuck off, Jonno. Nothing much *to* tell, what did you expect, a full dog and pony show?'

'I'm only messing with you,' Jonno replied. 'We've done our duty, let's hope you're not back in three months telling them you're pulling out.'

'If anyone's back in three months it'll be young Jemmie, our jewel in the crown. He won't tell you, but he's been sent to switch out the lights on all the tin-pot agencies around the Caribbean.' He turned to the supposed switcher-offer, sitting very upright in his chair. 'Never mind dog and pony, it's a real one-man-and-a-dog show here, Eddie. I'm surprised Jonno didn't bring Shanks to the FSC this morning.'

'It's not quite like that, David...'

'Jonno's fine, lad. And don't worry, I don't take anything seriously from this plastic Manc.'

It was a relief to be out of the suit jackets Ray had felt it appropriate to wear for the visit to the regulator, where Commissioner Wright had listened politely to what he already knew about the Sovereign and SRG deal. 'Thank you for troubling to visit us on this matter. We had in fact already been informed of the deal by B & M, as representatives of SRG. I understand for the moment you will be maintaining the two separate licences.'

Between the FSC meeting and the Captain's Table, Ray had berated Eddie for not having discovered and briefed him that Sovereign's agency in the US Virgin Islands, B & M after its principals Frank Bridges and Joe Makepiece, was also present in the British Virgins, representing SRG. He now took this matter up with Jonno. 'I knew Joe Hairpiece has always been sweet on you but not that he already had a foothold here. Has him or fat Frank said anything to you about the deal?'

'As a matter of fact I was at this very table' – he gestured at its checked cloth and the placid harbour waters beyond, crowded with craft of all sizes – 'only last week with Joe and Erik Horstwald.'

Ray shook his head as if deeply disappointed. 'Good of you to mention it. They already looking for a merger here?'

'You know Joe's been prepared to buy me out for yonks.' Jonno was not at all abashed. 'He's mellowed over the years, even prepared to let me keep my own name on the door. I think he thought I was joking when I said the dog would still be coming in.'

'You're seriously considering it then?'

'I am. I don't see me ever going back to live full-time on the Wirral, especially without Sally.' Ray looked at his shoes, even though it had been two years since the death of Jonno's wife and his eyes no longer filmed up every time he mentioned her name. 'I want to start slowing down a bit, even if retiring full-time here isn't an option either. They freeze your UK pension if you do that, you know.'

'Yeah, I remember you saying so.' Ray did not want to hear that whole story again. 'So you're looking for a lump sum, nest egg or whatever you want to call it? Not that I'm blaming you, mate. It must be hellish living here.' It was his turn to gesture at their surroundings, taking the opportunity to call over more beers. Always with half an eye on the waiter when in drinking mode, he rose to his feet when he saw the man greeting an attractive woman who was pointing over at their table.

Ray had forewarned Jonno if not Eddie that they would be joined for lunch – none of them had yet thought of eating – by Emilia Rosso, an account executive with multinational correspondent brokers Martinez y Asociados in San Juan. 'Emilia specialises in large accounts, around the islands as well as in PR. In fact you do some work with B & M in the USVI, isn't that right, Emi? Did you know they had a presence here too?'

The new arrival was modestly enough dressed in a trouser suit, yet the waiter was more than attentive in helping her to get out of her jacket. She did not seem fazed at being plunged straight into business discussions.

'As far as I know B & M's work here is mainly limited to countersigning on the odd multinational account, but I know they're hungry for business. I haven't come across SRG at all.'

'They don't mention any registration here on their website.' Eddie had been stewing quietly over the rollocking from Ray for not having picked up on their new colleagues' licence in the BVI.

'So what did old Whore's Hole, or Erik as I'm sure you already call him, have to offer you, Jonno?'

'Erik' – he gave Ray a covert V-sign while addressing them all – 'was very polite, very correct, but I don't think he'll be offering me their pen. As you know better than me, SRG have always avoided most of the islands in the main hurricane path. If that policy applies to the new merged company, my best bet might be to do a deal while I still have some leverage, not with SRG but with Joe. He's got various other carriers anyway, while of course I've always been entirely faithful to my dear friend Ken, and now this scally.' He brought the V above the table to indicate Ray.

'Jan's faithful to me as well, but she can still be a pain in the arse. I tell you one thing old Wrighty said this morning that could be good for us. If he can get the government interested in insuring their whole Road Town complex – hospital, social security and all the other government departments housed around it – there'd be a nice chunk of premium and commission. I don't say Sovereign would be able to swallow the whole amount, but that's where Emilia and her colleagues might come in. I'll let her talk a bit more about Martinez y Asociados if she likes, but they're the correspondents in PR for Fawkes Fordham. Where do they rank now, Emi?' Ray glanced at her. 'Top five anyway, of worldwide brokers. If you get the local inside track, I'm sure they could help us with the international reinsurance market for whatever my friends in London don't want for Sovereign. What do you think, mate?'

Eddie was scribbling in a notepad pulled from the jacket behind him. Emilia seemed ready to speak, but Jonno answered first. 'Joe was talking about it as a fronted risk, but I guess if Sovereign were to retain a proper share that would mean normal commission levels on it, not a reduced fee?'

'Now you are upsetting me. At least give me first option to put a deal together. You do your bit in terms of gathering the information here, I'm sure Eddie will help out if you need him, and this is definitely one of Emilia's areas of expertise. I'll put my shoulder to the wheel with London.'

'You putting your shoulder to the wheel, that alone would be worth the price of admission.'

Ray's alcohol intake in Road Town was relatively restrained. He had always followed the precept of an older, wiser insurance soul from his early days with Sovereign at Northampton branch: don't ruin your weekend, the worst hangovers are best handled on company time so at least you're getting paid as you suffer. Today was Friday, and in the back of his mind he knew he might still have tough meetings to face.

Jonno had shared a bottle of wine with Emilia over their catch of the day, while Ray stuck with stubby Red Stripes. Eddie had switched to soda water after the first couple of rounds. Before the broker left to catch her earlier flight, Ray was pleased to see that Jonno had been growing quite confidential with her; there must be life in the old dog yet.

'Best place on this shithole island, Eddie,' Ray enthused as they pulled up at a Riteway supermarket on their way to the Beef Island airport. He loaded his until then unused sports bag with Fray Bentos meat pies, Heinz baked beans, Bisto gravy powder and other delicacies of English cuisine not so readily available in Puerto Rico. 'So I don't starve when Jan refuses to cook for me, mate.' He winked at Eddie as he threw in a bargain pack of Kit Kats for the kids and a chess set of Ferrero Rocher for the wife. It may not have been much as a peace offering, but flowers would have made her either laugh or more insanely suspicious than she already was.

Ray was trying hard not to think of what awaited him back in San Juan. His departure for the airport from the spare room to which Jan had banished him the night before had not beaten her exit to drive the kids to school, but he had done his best to phone her from Jonno's office before they adjourned to lunch. He knew she had a meeting with the school principal but not the time of it. He struggled to remember details of her rant the night before, when Jan had refused to let him wake Denis – as if he would be sleeping, he had argued in vain – to talk about his behaviour. He had apparently been caught smoking dope with two other boys, the status of whose fathers – both known to Ray – had given him some comfort. Mark Prestwick's dad Henry moved in the highest levels of San Juan society. Mauricio Sanchez was a take-no-prisoners local lawyer, who Ray could not see letting his boy Pancho be expelled for anything short of a triple murder. Unable to raise Ray the day before, Mauricio had spoken to Jan, who was bitter that she would be forced to face Principal Medeiros while the other kids had fathers turning out to support them. Ray thought to get the scoop on the meeting by a phone call to Mauro once back in San Juan, before going home to face his family.

Jonno was a generous host and would invariably see off visitors with a farewell beer and shot at the relaxed airport. As Ray hit his friend up for a Jose Cuervo, the sight of a Blue Curaçao gave him an idea.

'Jonno, didn't you tell me once you used to go over to the Dutch islands for the diving?'

'That's right. A while back now though.'

'Listen, I'll be there next week to meet your new buddy Erik, why not come along?'

'What for?'

'You're our star producer now, mate. The idea is we'll talk about our businesses with each other. I wouldn't expect you to sit through all the merger bullshit but you could maybe give us five minutes on the soundness of your account. Do some diving if you've still got the puff, have some beers with us in the evening. I'll even let you put the flights and hotel on your agency expenses account with us.'

'Where's the catch?'

'No catch. It won't hurt for the Dutchman to see you're with us and not B & M. If we mention the government business as part of our plans it will put down a marker to keep them – and him – away from it. No catch, just common sense and a bit of fun for us both.'

Eager as he had been to confront Denis the previous evening, Ray was reluctant to do so tonight. There were no missed calls from Jan on his phone and he had only been able to leave a voicemail with Mauro, so he changed his plans to drive straight home from the office (where Eddie had dropped him from the airport to pick up his car) in favour of one for the road in Frankie's. He had no fear of an extended session with Larry, who usually left early on Fridays to see his live-in, referring to it as 'date night' purposely to nauseate Ray. He had not left yet, though, so Ray decided to seek some of the parenting advice he remembered Jan sarcastically suggesting he urgently needed the night before.

'Do you ever see your kids, Larry?'

'Not in fifteen years. Maybe twenty.' He immediately dispelled any notion he had been counting the days.

'Did you have problems when they were teenagers, like drink or drugs?'

'Listen buddy, I've never had a problem with drink or... oh, you mean a problem with *them*. You shitting me? That was half the reason me and the old lady broke up. She said the old Mary Jane was harmless, I should keep more of an eye on Laurence's drinking – she always called him Laurence, talk about getting a boy off to the wrong start.'

'A lot of people think drink's worse, don't they?' Ray offered tentatively.

'Sure, a lot of dopeheads and hippies and wasters do that exact thing. Look, I don't know doodly dick about drugs and I don't want to, but the army taught me plenty about discipline. When she thought she should take that over for the kids I said fine, but I was outta there if I couldn't be master in my own home. I thought I told you all that before, don't say you got problems with one of your sprogs. I bet I can guess which one.'

Larry got on well enough with Den, but it was Janet and Kim who brought out all his chivalrous and protective instincts. Whatever his problems may have been with his own wife and kids, he had charmed Ray's, despite his drinking partnership with her husband stacking the odds heavily against him with Jan.

'They do say it's the boys that are the most bother. I might have to enlist you to give him a military dressing-down, a proper telling off.'

'Telling off? That's what women do. Don't treat him like a sissy mate, that's the best advice I can give you.'

Luckily their *marquesina* or carport was wide enough to demand no great skill in avoiding Jan's black Plymouth. It was later than usual for him to arrive on a non-poker night, though he did have the excuse of having travelled abroad during the day. He half expected the door to be locked against him. Not so, and at least Sanjo was happy to see him.

She hardly turned from her patio seat facing the unlit pool when he came through the living room to her. He could see she had been crying, which was even worse than her anger. It happened very rarely. He hated it. 'Come on, baby, I'm sorry I couldn't be with you today. I didn't hear from you but I finally managed to get through to Mauro. It's not so bad, is it?'

'Not so bad for you, no. If you mean Mauricio Sanchez, he took the lead, talking to Principal Medeiros about the need for due process. I said I'd sue their arses if they tried to exclude our son, and might anyway for letting him smoke dope on their premises when he's never done it at home.'

She was talking to him. That had to be a good sign. 'And what did he say to that?' he prompted.

'He said the teacher who caught them might have been a bit what was it, "over–zealous". He felt obliged to give us all the guff about Eugenio Hostos Academy's zero-tolerance policy, and how if a child is expelled for drug-related offences any siblings are out as well, but I could tell we'd knocked the wind out of his sails.'

'You what? So Kim would be dragged into it, totally innocent?'

'Now I've got your attention, have I? Either sit down and listen, or make me a drink while you're up. I see you've had your fill as usual, important business trip my arse.'

Ray knew it was no use trying to justify himself, but he could at least pour himself a rum and coke far stiffer than the generous one he fixed her. 'Did the mighty Henry Prestwick show up?' he asked on his return to the table, taking a seat this time beside his wife.

'Yes he did show up, unlike some, so don't take the mickey out of him. He seemed a bit of a stuffed shirt to me, but you could tell old Medeiros was impressed. He's got a couple of other kids in the school, so they'd be having to expel about half a dozen if they pushed it, quite the little scandal not to mention the loss of fees. It was lucky whichever of the boys had it managed to ditch the evidence into the bushes or whatever, so unless one of them admits to it they can't get any of them with possession or trafficking.'

'Come on Jan, trafficking? We're hardly talking the Cali Cartel here.'

'I know, and they'll get away with a warning about their behaviour this time, but that doesn't make it all right. Other than charging into his room and throwing your drunken weight about – which you won't be doing tonight any more than last, by the way – what do you propose doing about it? What do you think Denis needs?'

'A girlfriend probably. Look, I'm not taking the rap for this. I've never smoked in front of him.'

'No? Last Christmas giggling in the kitchen with his Uncle Alex, Little Jan and her boyfriend, don't you think he may have wondered what that was about? God, Kim could probably have told him if they didn't hear it direct from one of their other cousins. Playing dominoes was never that hilarious!'

Maybe he had gone a bit *too* generous with the rum. The intention had been to relax rather than refuel her anger. 'Come off it, love. Don't pretend you didn't do your share of weed in your long-hair beads and sandals days. We used to be able to laugh about that.'

'It was over twenty years ago, you prick, not on our last trip home.'

He suddenly felt very tired as well as drunk; nevertheless, he tried to respond calmly. 'I think it's more a matter of discipline. "Don't do as I do, do as I say." That was all we were told.'

'And how did that work out for you, Ray? That's why I won't have you trying to lay down the law when you're sozzled. Don't you see what's wrong with that?'

'I never hit the kids, never would, you know that. Have it your own way if you don't trust me to talk to Den, like you always do.'

'Have it my own way? That's rich coming from you.' She drained her glass and stood up, a little unsteadily. It occurred to Ray the drink he had served may not have been her first of the day. 'You can go ahead and sulk some more in your new digs. Don't even think about trying my door.' (So he was now a mere lodger in the spare, the matrimonial bedroom somehow hers alone.) 'And you *will* be talking to Denis, just as soon as you can spare a sober half hour in your busy bar and island-hopping schedule.'

'*Calle Matadero*, Slaughterhouse Street, and here you come like an ox with no idea what's about to hit you.'

Bowling was not something Ray had ever done in his boyhood or youth. If there was a tenpin alley anywhere nearer his village than Peterborough he didn't know of it, while the more sedate indoor or outdoor versions featuring jacks and shuffling old codgers were as remote to him in those days as the possibility of golf. Prejudiced against it also as an inherently American pastime, he had to concede he was now living in a US commonwealth. Sovereign had held a staff party at the Matadero alley, so huge it might even once have been the slaughterhouse itself. Kenneth had winked at Jaime's choice, which was not necessarily what the human resources team had in mind as a team-building activity.

Despite forcefully put objections by Jan that he was effectively rewarding bad behaviour, Ray had opted to bring Denis this Saturday morning. Jan and Kim would usually come too, but he had suggested they might like to reward their own spotless selves by a trip to Plaza Las Americas, largest mall in the Western world (or so his Puerto Rican friends bragged to Ray, without making that any reason for him to visit it).

Den was in subdued mood, perhaps unable to gauge that of Ray as they had not spoken at any length since Jan's visit to the school. Ray hoped their conversation wouldn't be as heavy going as the one with her the night before.

As they put their bowling names up in lights – an austere 'M' for him, 'The King' for the boy – and rental shoes on their feet (a visit to the alley or a game of golf were the only things that would induce Ray to wear socks of a weekend), he continued trying to keep things light. 'Lesson number one: M is for maestro, which is me, and *muerto*, which is you, deader than any of the poor beasties that ever stumbled through these doors.'

'The King is *not* dead. I always like to give you the first leg so we get to play the full three. I know you stomp off if I beat you two nil.'

Ray was glad to see Denis relax a bit during that first game, after a couple of early gutter balls. He had chosen a lane with nobody on either side but, halfway through, an industry colleague – Max Kozlinsky with his own loss adjusting firm in Old San Juan – appeared to their right with three kids all under ten.

'Too high for golf, too low for bowling.' The twenty-stone Max waddled over, indicating Ray's score of 107 by raising a few of his chins.

'Yeah well, you know, have to take it a bit easy on the kid else he'll go home crying to his mummy. Den, this is Mr Kozlinsky.' He put a hand on the slab of his friend's upper arm. 'What did *you* do wrong?'

'Excuse me?'

'Out with three kids, it must be some kind of punishment from the missus. Can I get you a beer?'

'Sure. I don't mind a bit, I've always loved bowling.'

'I can see you've put a few hours in.' Ray had indeed noticed with some envy the smoothness and consistency of Max's action. 'Got any tips for a duffer like me?'

'You're beyond help, Ray. It's all about being relaxed. Get the right dosage of these' – he emptied the small can of Medalla in one easy pull – 'and make sure when you let the ball go your thumb's pointing at the ceiling.'

'OK, cheers mate.' He gave him a thumbs up.

It was only fair to test the advice before passing it on to the lad, it might put him off his game. It didn't help Ray's much, but that was probably because he hadn't yet achieved the first part of calibrating his blood alcohol level. He was not going to have more than a couple of cans, despite the fact he felt it was a six-pack chat coming up. Telling himself it was Denis who should be nervous didn't seem to help.

It was a point of honour with Ray never to throw a game of any kind with any kid over five years old unless he was trying to get into its mother's pants, so when Denis took the second leg it was fair and square, 132 against a feeble 97. He was only trying to be a good parent in passing on Max's vertical thumb tip before the decider. He had genuinely noticed that his better shots all seemed to have that characteristic. Of course, it did initially make you a little bit self-conscious, you had perhaps to get worse before you got better, no pain no gain.

'Muh muh muh muh muh muh muh muh, the M strikes again, the Matador *mata*, the Monster monsters, two and one after a fiercely contested third leg. All right, you don't have to gimme five, but you do have to shake hands. At least we both got into three figures on that last one. Keep following Uncle Max's tip and you might be in my league one day.'

'Your non-league you mean. How about double or quits in the arcade, you can choose the game?'

'No fear. Take a tip, son, always end on a win. Here's a couple of dollars, go on the machines yourself then we'll have something to eat.'

The days when Ray could keep up with Denis on electronic games, whether handheld or as here banked in an annexe to the main bowling alley, were long gone. He must be getting plenty of free plays, he thought grumpily as he sat alone eking out a can of Medalla, watching Max take his kids' humble adoration for yet another strike. At last though, they were settled facing each other, over a polystyrene plate of fried chicken and fries each to occupy their eyes while they followed Jan's orders.

'You know we've got to have a talk, don't you?'

'I guess.'

'You don't guess, you know. I understand you want to fit in with the Americans and Puerto Ricans, but it can go too far, the language you use is important.'

'My teacher said she's pleased with my Spanish.'

'I am too.' He tried to recall if he had ever heard the boy speak it. 'I know you're a clever lad, Den, and I know that doesn't necessarily stop anyone doing stupid things. How long have you been smoking dope then?'

'I like the way you automatically assume I was. Just like Mum.'

'Well I kind of gathered… you mean you weren't?'

'No, I was. But it's the way you assume things, all of you.'

'Your mum's concerned, Den. We both are.' It was hard not to show the vexation that his briefly raised hopes had been immediately reset to naught. 'Why did you do it?'

'Why do you drink?'

Expecting at least some attempt at a response or considered argument, Ray had taken a big bite of chicken and crammed a gravied chip in after it. He took his time swallowing them before replying. 'You know what my favourite advert is? It is now, anyway. It's the one where you see a clean-cut all-American dad agonising over this sort of discussion – except his son's got a nose piercing

70

to make it clear he's a bit off the rails but basically a good kid. And the strapline, the message, is "Don't Be Ashamed of Being a Hypocrite." I won't be. I'm not setting myself up as any kind of example, mate. I'm telling you. It may not sound fair, but that's life. Tough titty sometimes. I'm not accountable to you, but you are to me.'

'Are you accountable to Mum?'

'Den, don't think I don't see what you're doing. This is not about me. We can have a talk about why I drink if you like.' ('When you're drinking with me, aged twenty-one or over,' he didn't add.) 'But that's not for today. Today it's you on parade. Is it a habit, or was it a one-off?'

'Depends what you mean. Mark says his dad says it's not habit-forming, weed.'

'Oh, and Mr Prestwick's happy with all this, is he? I don't think so, and know for a fact Mauricio Sanchez isn't. Don't expect me to get into a debate about it. Bottom line, you're lucky not to be expelled already, and in that case your sister would be too.'

'What? But Kim hasn't...'

'I know. At least I hope I know. It's one of the school's BS rules. If a pupil is ejected, out go their siblings too.'

'But that's not fair.'

'Refer back to earlier in our conversation. Can I count on you to stop doing this. Not for me, for your mum and Kim?'

'Why not for you, don't you care?'

'Christ, yes I care, of course I do. I don't want you to feel under pressure to perform for me is all, any more than I want you to be like me.'

'Why, because I'm not your son?'

Again Ray restrained himself. 'Don't try playing that card, please. I'm not going into the whole nature versus nurture thing, the biological parent claptrap, you can't dodge me that way. You're my son in my heart and like Forrest that's all I have to say about that. I don't want you to be like me because I want you to be better. That shouldn't be so hard. Son.'

'And what if Pancho and Mark carry on?'

'Ah, the famous peer pressure. I'm glad I flicked through all your mum's parenting books last night, haven't slept better in weeks. Pancho and Mark. I imagine their dads are having a chat with them too, probably going a lot better than this one. Can I tell your mum you understand what you've done was wrong and it won't happen again?'

The boy stirred his last chip into the still sizeable puddle of ketchup. 'Well, I'm sorry to have caused all this fuss and upset everyone, I guess that was wrong, and on the second bit all I can say is I'll give it my best shot.'

Ray didn't know whether to knock chip, container and cutlery off the table or burst into tears. He couldn't help feeling the conversation might have gone better. Still, when they got out of the car back home after a silent journey, he could not bear being on the outs with the boy. They had a long series of shared catchphrases from movies otherwise forgotten.

'Good talk, son.'

Den almost seemed to have been waiting for Ray to stop being so grown-up from the speed with which he answered him. 'Good talk, Dad.'

Ray hoped he could convince Jan it had been. He needed to find a way back from the outer darkness of the spare room.

Chapter 4

'Good afternoon to you all. My name is Anjelica Crossan, but the girls will know I don't have the voice, or actually the temperament, of an angel.' Some of those girls tittered dutifully. We boys stayed on silent alert. 'I also have to say there is no truth to the rumours that I am going into business with the former grammar school French teacher Mr Blackwell.'

Only a couple of the girls giggled this time. Old Ma Crossan was beginning to falter, seeking safety behind her piano. Music was still compulsory at the mixed school, in a stocking-filler kind of way of one lesson a week.

'I'm so excited at the prospect of a mixed choir. I've introduced myself, now I would like each of you to do the same. I'm hopeless with names, but I guarantee I will remember each and every individual voice.' She clapped her hands, as if applauding her fabulous gift. 'All stand up please, give those lungs room to function properly. Right, who wants to go first? We had some great fun with "Lilliburlero" last year, didn't we girls, but I can probably manage to keep up with whatever you like. "Jerusalem"?'

She plonked a few notes on the piano without looking at the keys, smiling fiercely. None of us had a clue what she was on about.

'Come on boys, don't be shy. Isn't any brave soul prepared to sing a few words for us?'

So that was it. If she expected volunteers, she was sadly unaware of our collective squaddie mentality. Anyone who cared or dared to open their mouth to give song would not only break the ice but plunge instantly through it to a lonely watery grave. She asked us individually, with no success. When we sang as a class she may have detected some voices almost as deep as Alison Bright's. Relinquishing the keyboard to an evident pet, Geraldine Smart, the thin woman in woolly tights wandered the rows of desks, black hair swept theatrically clear of those magic ears, unable to absorb basic factual information like a pupil's name yet capable of distinguishing each and every one of us individually from a fragment of song.

If she couldn't name us, she couldn't shame us. I had no illusions about my own voice and kept my trap firmly shut throughout. Others would participate with brio, as long as her back was turned to them. I could hear Omie improvising alternative scatological lyrics, like he did every year to the hymns at our Thanks and Commemoration ('Wanks and Menstruation') service in St Peter's.

My inhibitions at singing in public in no way extended to our back room downstairs, where I would listen to the radio and tape music from it. Thursday nights I would invade the living room to shush my parents and tape also from *Top of the Pops*, which they could tolerate as it clashed with no soap. Old Ma Crossan would surely have been proud of my voice projection if not its quality, since it occasionally drew Mum in to ask me to turn down the volume a tad. She would sometimes insist on lighting a fire for me in there, or pop her head round the door to see if I wanted anything mid-evening before bringing in later a crisp-sandwich supper. She didn't knock, and didn't need to. My only vice, other than the singing, was to read and reread Tina's notes.

Considering I hadn't expected that first one, saying half the birds in form four fancied me, I'd managed to get a reply off sharply enough. Something to the uninspired effect that *all* the boys fancied her. Lacking her expertise, I landed it on the floor beside her rather than on her desk. She left hurriedly at the end of class, without speaking or even looking at me.

There was a lot of that – not speaking, not looking. We moved during the day between classrooms, were not always taking the same subjects, and only in a few were within pitching distance of each other. Even so I would sometimes come home with a pocketful, particularly as she could manage three to my one. Ever the dutiful student, I would not allow myself to unpick them till my homework was done; once I'd finished, they would be slipped into the few album sleeves I had, the most flattering fragments including that first one reserved for one of my *Motown Chartbusters*.

I was never forced to colour as violently as FA did when Dai Hard enquired if he would 'either stop reading billets-doux in class or share them with us all'. Tina was not the only girl to keep up such a correspondence but undoubtedly the most prolific, and to my mind promiscuous. It would have been worse than singing for Old Ma Crossan to share any of my treasures with anyone, yet there was nothing shameful, startling or remotely sexual in them. I would learn that I counted Roarer Graham among my most fervent admirers, and Pat Wilson the crop-haired hockey full back, but little directly about Tina's own feelings. That didn't stop me from imagining the tone of her missives to FA or Wah Wah might be quite other, or that she might be mocking me in the ones she sent to her female friends.

Couples in our year strolling the grounds together at breaks, as she had once with Pukemore, were very much the exception. Perhaps she had grown bored with the isolation or with him, though unbelievably they still seemed to be on what could only be called friendly terms. Mark ('Jason') King, a redhead who lived up the road from school, could be forgiven a bit of hand-holding as the price of having lucked out with Vicky Cooper. Jambo seemed unperturbed by this, himself now an accepted groupie of the hockey horde without putting down a firm marker upon whichever one his heart was set.

Omie and I continued to play football at dinnertime, when we could get in close to an hour by wolfing our food down – a long-established Grammar custom. In the shorter morning and afternoon breaks we would hang about in a crowd of six or seven: Jambo and Mick sometimes still; Carl Walters from a village the other side of Washtown from me, with whom I'd got into the habit of walking to the Cattle Market for our different buses after school; FA sometimes; Jason less so once engaged with Vicky; John 'Pint' Smith; and Philip Brown.

We would talk football, of course, telly still, girls increasingly. Our girl talk was generally scurrilous or scornful. The ones who openly disdained us, the Cathy Strains, the Sarah Wallinghams – her boyfriend was in the upper sixth, for fuck's sake – or those we feared might be out of our league (Tina was in this category, as was Vicky Cooper still despite her dodgy picks from amongst our mates), those girls came in for the most speculation about how far they would go. Hard evidence was lacking, but someone had always heard something from someone else.

A different defence mechanism came into play with the less attractive girls, or 'dogs', as their sexy sisters were often 'bitches'. There was none quite as criminally obese as our Tubbo Wyatt, but deviations from the physical norm were usually punishable, as with Beanpole Beckford. There was an uneasy feeling about how far to take mockery with the three-foot-nine Fiona Price from 4H, not so much from pity or a sense of fair play but because she was rumoured to have punched fifth-former Nev Cousins right in the bollocks when he greeted her as 'Bridget the Midget'. We would rarely accuse each other of fancying ugly sisters, but it was equally important to ensure they didn't fancy you, by being as unkind and obnoxious to them as possible.

They had their own defences, naturally. One going back probably as far as Romulus and Remus' first double date – before the Sabine women, whose rape Dai Hard stoutly maintained meant nothing more than 'a carrying off' in Latin – was that of beauty and the beast. The beauties might occasionally parade together, but were more characteristically competitive and even spiteful. How we laughed at hearing the queen of 4W Sarah Wallingham's dismissal of Tina as 'pretty, but let's face it she's got tits like golf balls'. Sarah was never seen in a group of girls – it didn't occur to us that perhaps they all hated the bitch – but Tina was rarely without Roarer Graham at her side.

The girls' other defence was their greater interest in the game. While we hardly troubled to differentiate them except by looks – pop songs weren't the only things for which we compiled top tens – they would find out whatever they could about us. At one point they even made it into a silly game, four or five of them swarming up to a boy at break with ten or twenty questions, in the breathless format of a teen magazine. And it worked. However much you prepared a terse 'no comment', once Pukemore had suavely responded, then Jambo to a twittering of hockettes, you were only waiting for your turn to show off, preparing your answers and fretting you might not be amongst the earliest nominees.

'So, Mr Roden, could you spare our readers a few minutes of your valuable time?' Tina waved her familiar's glasses case at me as a microphone. Notepad at the ready, Roarer was at her one elbow, Pat Wilson the other, with Susan Tierney, VD and Val Anderson also in attendance. Val and I did nod and occasionally exchange a few words with each other nowadays at the Feltwell bus stop on the rare occasions I wasn't running to board. Her presence would keep me honest on our shared primary school days if they should figure in the celebrity profile.

'Right then Ray, if I may call you Ray' – seeing I hadn't shoved them aside to join my mates – 'we'll start off with a few easy ones. Birthday?'

'Yes, once a year. All right, November eleventh, Armistice Day. But I wasn't born at eleven o'clock.'

'A Scorpio, like me,' Tina squealed, Roarer looking a little crestfallen. 'Middle name or names?'

'Monk's pleasure.'

'Sorry?'

'None. My father said they couldn't afford a middle name when I was born.'

'Brothers and sisters.'

'Lend me your ears. Same as middle name. I'm an only child, or you can put spoilt bastard.'

'I'm an only child too,' Tina told her friends.

'You and Ray must be made for each other,' VD said with perhaps a hint of sarcasm.

'Any pets.'

'Nick, a black lab.'

'Oh they're lovely, I've got a golden retriever,' Sue Tierney piped up, as Tina – did she not have a dog? – hurried on to the next question.

'Favourite sport? I think we can guess that's football. Favourite team?'

'United. And don't anyone embarrass yourselves by asking which.'

Despite her gameness in the shallows at Hunstanton on a day that was already becoming part of our private mythology, Tina was not a great one for football or any other sport. 'Best friend?'

'Best mate, Jake. You don't know him. But here at school probably Mick Turner' – it was hard to give up on the illusion that hardness was the thing girls most prized – 'or Omie.'

'Best female friend?' Tina rushed on.

I was ready for that one, after nearly spewing myself when I heard Pukemore say it was his mum, always. 'I don't believe in friendship between men and women,' I said airily. 'There's only one sort of relationship they can have, and I think we all know what that is.'

'I think we all disagree with you,' Susan Tierney said coolly, to an approving nod from Val and a sudden hush from the rest. 'Any proper relationship, even a sexual relationship as I assume you mean, has to be based on friendship or it's not worthwhile.'

This wasn't in the script. My smooth man-of-the-world demeanour, as I had seen it in the mirror, morphed instantly to spiteful schoolboy. 'You've been listening to Jambo too much. I can tell you what sort of relationship he's after with you if you like.'

'Never mind, what about first love?' Tina took charge again.

'United.' Didn't sound quite as witty as I'd hoped.

She let that one pass. 'First kiss?'

'That would be Nick.' A moment of horror as I thought they might already have forgotten my dog and think instead of say useful midfielder Nick Holton in 4G – their hockey pal Nicky Stannett would have been almost as embarrassing. Val came unexpectedly to the plate before anyone else could speak.

'I know that's a lie. Wait till I tell Debbie Finch you've already forgotten her.'

Fair cop. There was a brief spell, up to age nine perhaps, when it was the done thing to have a girlfriend at Well Creek Primary. Debbie might honestly have qualified as a first love. We had certainly kissed, and not without an element of sexuality to it, albeit wholly instinctive and obviously pre-pubertal. And then – had it been across one summer holiday? – it had suddenly been babyish to hang around with girls, football became more important to me and my mates. Or was it some withdrawal on the part of the girls themselves, a tactical feint in the wider strategy of returning to the field better armed in a year or two?

I answered the next few questions absently with Debbie on my mind: pet likes, Nick; pet dislikes, cold gravy on hot meat; favourite teacher, Phwoar Jackie; career ambition, anything that gets me out of this shithole with enough money not to have to come back. The bell for the end of break was going as they put the final one.

'Personal ambition? To be divorced with two kids before I'm thirty.'

Although the girls had no way of knowing it, not even Tina, this was a nod to Uncle Dan. He'd managed the divorced bit without admitting to any kids.

The questionnaire provoked a snowstorm of correspondence over the next couple of days, white drops landing on my desk or lap at every opportunity.

'Debbie Finch is a lucky girl, I'm jealous, luv T.'

'I know someone who doesn't care about being friends with boys, luv T.'

'Divorced dads are sometimes the best kind, luv T.' I had forgotten she had personal experience of a father leaving, but it was too late to change my answers now.

The birthday question had its point as the girls were great ones for sending cards, something that had never occurred to us at Grammar. It was regarded as dodgy, if not plain queer, even to know your mates' dates beyond perhaps the month. The bumps in a concrete playground could be painful. In fact they were banned after bloodlust took over with Trevor Slater, who tried so very hard to ingratiate himself with staff and fellow pupils alike. As the boys grabbed his arms and legs, with only token resistance (he was after all momentarily part of the group) and bumped his arse hard on the playground

– one, two, three – coins spilled from his pockets. I'm not sure we even got to ten. Let fall from shoulder height, as he crashed to the ground everyone piled in, leaving him with black eye, swollen lip and cracked ribs. Steel toecaps were also banned after that.

One reason I was careful every evening to remove any notes from my blazer was that Mum would periodically empty it out for ironing, washing or whatever. Anything she found was considered public domain, so she had no scruples in saying at tea one night how pleased she was to see that Valerie Anderson had invited me to her party (Tina had made it clear I owed this to her personal intervention). 'We shall have to have one for you when it's your birthday.'

Before I could resist this proposal, Dad – always a step behind – put in his two-penn'orth. 'Anderson? Isn't that the one you always used to say you hated, because she was cleverer than you?'

The men in my family had only one joke, and they worked it hard. 'It wasn't that – she wasn't anyway – it was cos she was such a fat bit… bird.'

'And now she's not. Welcome to the wonder years, mate.'

He again felt the need to comment on party night when I came downstairs after my bath wearing a new purple and yellow shirt, with a white cravat. Smoking under his golden canopy as the dirge of *Coronation Street* sounded, he called to Mum in the kitchen. 'Aggie, get in here, he's only tied a snot rag round his neck with a curtain ring.'

'Leave him alone, Pete. He looks… have you got Valerie's card and present, love?'

'I've got the card. I thought you were wrapping the present.'

'You'll be wanting me to give it to her next. Wait a minute then, aren't you going to comb your hair?'

It was pitiful. I was spared further harassment by the arrival of Omie and Carl, who thankfully refused the offered cup of tea. 'It was too boring to stay at the big house, more like a kids' party, thought we'd get a smoke and a pint first.'

That had not been in my plans. 'Who's there?'

'Jambo, he told us which house was yours. Lady Val didn't seem to know. I tried to get Lesley Carrick to come down and show us being as she's from round here, didn't I Omie?'

'Yeah it's mainly girls, spose you've got to expect that, Jambo's like a pig in shit with Susan Tierney, Maureen Wheatley, smart Jane and plain Jane all there. That's why he wouldn't come with us.'

'He'll be wearing jamrags next. Mick not there then?'

'Would you be at a party if you could be alone with Caroline Peacock? Imagine wiping your helmet on that hair.' Carl treated Mick with the proper respect when he was around him, respect which did not extend to our mate's girlfriend. I was shocked yet also pleased at his image of Caroline. Not so pleased when he turned his attention to me.

'Course you and Omie will be thinking more of Gibbo. It was hard to get him to come for you, Ray. Even though you couldn't get near her for Roarer on one side and FA's lugs on the other. At least she'll have something to hold on to with him. Wonder if Roarer will be there watching.'

This was unwelcome news. FA didn't even have the grace to be ashamed of his elephant ears. I wanted to know more about Tina, but wouldn't show too much interest. 'No other boys there then?'

'Pukemore sniffing around Val and Tubbo sniffing around for some nosebag. Oh, and Jason with Vicky and her puppies. I'm going to ask her for a dance later and see if I can get a cheeky stroke.'

'Good luck with that, Carl. Her and Jason stick together like jizz and bog roll,' Omie answered as we closed my back door behind us. He was as pessimistic as me about chances with girls.

Dad had occasionally taken me in the Oak for a mid-afternoon game of pool, when he had for some reason been charged with looking after me. Omie and I followed in Carl's slipstream, though it was at my guidance he turned left from the main entrance rather than right into the public bar. My new shirt and cravat, so perfect for the party, did not seem quite as appropriate for the Oak, not even its lounge where the pool table was.

You didn't see the landlord's feet very often to check, but Ted always gave the impression he was shuffling around in carpet slippers. He came through to us in his own time, perhaps breaking off from a game of crib across the bar. A roll-up was glued to the corner of his mouth.

Apparently unfazed by the lack of any greeting from the slope-shouldered, cardiganed old man, Carl asked confidently for three twos and change for the pool table please.

'You've got till half eight,' Ted observed, squinting at the smoke rising from his fag as he pulled three pints, mixing each from two different pumps.

As we carted them to the corner by the pool table, Carl muttered, 'Flat as Gibbo's tits, but at least we've got 'em.'

80

Always less shy of showing ignorance than I was, Omie gave our mate the chance to explain, not without a hint of condescension, that 'twos' was the approved term for mild and bitter. Carl was a deal quicker than either Omie or me in drinking the vile mix. Perhaps he wanted to ensure we all got a round in. Omie came out of the traps faster than me on the second, so I ended up buying the third. I had no fears of approaching the bar by that stage, though I still didn't use the bell to summon our host.

'This is the last one, Ray. You're not leaving the village tonight, are you?'

His tone made it plain any thought or mention of doing so would not be well received. Surprised he knew my name, I gave too much information about only going to a party at the Andersons you know across the road top of Winfield.

Omie boked on the grass verge between road and pavement twenty yards before reaching Valerie's, luckily a respectable distance away from the Oak and not in the shelter where Mum would be waiting for the first bus to Washtown the next morning. It could have gone either way with me. I was pleased to join Carl in chaffing him about not being able to hold his booze rather than join Omie, barking up pure black liquid along with his tea.

'You'd better hope Val's granny's around tonight, mate, cos nobody else is going to snog you now.'

'I don't know, Roarer might still be grateful.' I took up my customary position of kicking a man when he was safely down.

My thoughts had already turned to snogging Tina Gibson, which seemed a far more likely proposition now than it had before our visit to the Oak. I was perhaps a little too effusive in thanking Carl for his brilliant idea of going there; definitely a little premature.

I knew Mrs Anderson in the same way I knew various women from around the village, by osmosis from early childhood waiting on them gossiping in the street with Mum, while I might be scuffling with or studiously ignoring (depending on gender) their own children. As she opened her front door, I realised for the first time that in certain lights, or perhaps by the power of twos, she was not unattractive. Looking a bit surprised when I shoved at her Val's gift and card, she sportingly took them off my hands before showing us through the hall into a room as big as our two downstairs ones combined.

I focussed at once on Tina, in the far diagonal corner of the floor space cleared by putting various settees and armchairs around the walls, along with a few beanbags between them. She was gratifyingly quick to raise a palm and wiggle her fingers at me in greeting, to which I responded with a curt nod. There could of course be no question of approaching while buggerlugs was at her side.

Apart from the guests my mates had already mentioned, Pat Wilson and VD were there to be ignored, which was harder in the case of Val's little sister – Mandy, was it? – and a friend of hers. They were busy toting around plates of sandwiches, crisps and the like, no doubt the price of their being allowed to attend the party. 'I love your cravat, Ray.' She giggled. 'Doesn't it look nice, Sally?'

Did every fucker in the village know my name? I was in a funny mood, on the one hand feeling well-disposed to all my great schoolmates, on the other quick to stand on my dignity or take the hump at the slightest thing. I barged into Jambo's group, putting my arm around his shoulders as he pretended to listen to Susan Tierney, the two Janes and Maureen witter on about something or other.

'Hello mate, thought you'd've come up the Oak with us, but now I see you got your hands full with these lovely ladies.' I wasn't joking. With the obvious exception of plain Jane it was surprising how much sexier they looked out of school uniform. Maureen especially, bit on the short side but not bad at all.

'Brassic to tell you the truth, Ray. Else I would've.'

We had discovered rhyming slang in our second year. Although we no longer tried to hold whole conversations in it, inventing our own where (as often) cockney wit failed, we still used odds and ends from time to time. 'You berk, I would have seen you all right. Would you believe that, Maureen? This wanker wouldn't even count on his mates. Sorry' – as I saw her shrink back – 'I didn't mean to swear, what position do you prefer? At hockey, I mean.'

I was feeling good from the drink, yet not as disappointed as Carl that Mrs Anderson was enforcing a strict no-alcohol policy. What the girls were calling sangria was Ribena with a few chunks of fruit bobbing about in the pitcher. There were various big bottles of coke, Fanta and other pops but even in the fridge – while Omie kept an eye out for parents – Carl couldn't find any beer.

I don't know how long I talked to Maureen, or Mo as I was already calling her without knowing if she went by that or not. Long enough for Tina to feign jealousy as she contrived to coincide with me in the kitchen. 'You seem very busy tonight Ray, are you going to save a dance for me?'

'Nobody's dancing. Anyway, you're well seen to by the looks of it.'

'Steven, you mean? He's sweet, and he was here when there were no other boys around.'

I thought she meant Omie for a second, so long was it since we had referred to Steven Barnes as anything but FA. 'So it doesn't matter who it is, any old boy will do. Put a packet of peanuts in your pocket and Tubbo will follow you round all day and night.'

'Don't be silly, Ray. Can't you be nice? I was so looking forward to tonight. I put this skirt on specially for you.' She stretched up to whisper in my ear. 'Mum nearly wouldn't let me come in it.'

The slight stretch to my ear was probably enough to give everyone a view of her arse, so short was the skirt. It was also the first time I'd seen her wear tights. 'Yeah, lovely, mind you don't let "Steven" come in it, or on it more like.'

I surely wanted to wound, so perhaps should not have been surprised when she burst into tears, after opening her mouth very wide then clapping a hand over it. She floundered till the tug Roarer got a grip on her arm and, after a quick word with Val, led her to the safe harbour of an upstairs toilet (we had been given to understand the whole upstairs was out of bounds).

'Nice one, Ray.' Carl grinned. 'I feel a six-pointer coming on in the roaring league. Shame she took the table-topper up to the bogs with her, otherwise you could have slipped up yourself in a few to console her.'

'I hardly said owt to the stupid bint, Jesus Christ.'

The girls' conversations gradually morphed into a kind of dancing in twos, threes and fours. Mandy and her little friend joined in enthusiastically until Val enlisted her mum to banish them. They missed accordingly the regal procession of Sarah Wallingham. The last to arrive at the party, she stayed only twenty minutes or so before being whisked off up town by Gloss Taylor. He had become captain of the school first eleven in the lower sixth and now, in the upper, was already driving not even his folks' car but one of his own. He had noticed us on occasion at football and didn't seem a bad bloke, but beyond ensuring we all saw him at the door – letting a hell of a draught in, as Dad would have said – Sarah had no intention of letting him join us. Of us fourth-formers she took little notice on her arrival beyond a chilly smile at Carl's hello, remaining nearly as aloof from the girls as the boys. After giftlessly greeting Val, she disappeared up the stairs in short order, perhaps scenting blood. Roarer came down alone almost immediately, dabbing at her eyes.

Although I would bet – always excepting supernova Sarah – that no such fluids were exchanged during the evening, the night of Val's party was seminal for male–female relationships in our year. She herself made the most of home advantage to snare Pukemore, if you could call him any kind of catch. Carl, perhaps looking for an excuse to come back to the Oak, made some headway with Lesley Carrick who lived across the other side of the village creek from me. Jambo boldly advanced on several fronts before achieving a significant beachhead landing with Susan Tierney. Omie began to work to an agenda of his own when I sent him to find out from Roarer what was the matter with Gibbo.

Sickeningly enough, Pukemore was the first male to take to the dance floor, not even hanging onto Val but in a casual, shuffling group that also included VD and Smart Jane. For the rest of us, dancing had about it the same potential for embarrassment as singing in front of Old Ma Crossan, with the same idea that it was a bit sissy. How many of us had ever seen our dads dance?

Unfortunately, it had to be done. It was the way to girls. As there came a point at the Clarkson sports-centre pool when – however much fun bombing and pencil-diving was – you had to take a header off the side to maintain your self-respect, so you knew you would have to graduate from clumsy verbal joshing and ham-fisted grabbing to leaden-footed movement while music played before you could be taken seriously.

Before that, a lot of standing around was to be done. Abandoning the kitchen to encamped Tubbo and visiting girls who would always chat to him – how come they were so much *nicer* than us? – Omie, Carl and I stood against the wall holding glasses of pop and passing would-be satirical comments on our fellow partygoers. I was constantly aware of Tina once she rejoined us, arm-in-arm with Sarah. The two of them huddled together until Sarah's carriage bore her off. Tina was briefly alone. Then Roarer and fucking FA closed in, before I could go over.

The music was initially up-tempo stuff, giving way as the evening wore on to slower tracks. The trick seemed to be getting your feet moving while pretending to be chatting normally, then zeroing in on someone as a recognisable smoocher began. The next stage would be sitting down with the girl, the boldest step of all to nab a beanbag because then you were practically *lying* down.

Omie and I were the last men standing alone, Carl having insinuated himself with Lesley. 'Come on then mate, let's go get our feet wet,' I said randomly.

Under pretence of having a word with Jambo we infiltrated the group that also included Susan, Maureen and the two Janes. The attention of us both was more on the trio next to us, of Tina, Roarer and FA. He was affable as ever in greeting us. I wanted to smack him. Tina wouldn't meet my eye and I couldn't quite manoeuvre myself to face her.

Things went from bad to worse. No wonder Val had wanted her sister away. She and Pukemore moved rapidly through the gears to beanbag and even beyond, hand in hand to another room altogether. 'He'll be dipping his wick tonight,' I grunted to Omie, not in envy as my ancient prejudices against our hostess still endured to some extent.

Jason had Vicky on his lap, despite there being a perfectly free seat next to him on the settee. Carl was hanging on to Lesley even during the faster numbers. All that I could bear, but it was bitter to see FA corral Tina into his arms. She caught my eye then all right, a challenging look over his shoulder.

I fancied I had made a good impression on Little Mo during my earlier beery ramblings. Whether or not, as Jambo faced off with Susan, I had to take steps to ensure it would be Omie left with Roarer.

Any hope of cutting in between FA and Tina vanished when they began to snog, during *You've Got a Friend* from that poxy hippie James Taylor. I hadn't even got my arms round Maureen, but soon did after that.

I had been right about her skirt. When they were lying down on the beanbag recently vacated by Val you could see the top of her tights over yellow knickers. She and FA were stretched out face to face, legs into the dancing area.

My earlier sparkling conversation had petered out. Maureen was becoming less enthusiastic about picking up with me after each track. I had to plead that *Tired of Being Alone* was a particular favourite to keep her with me.

She only came up to my collar, so I could see clearly enough to steer her towards the tighted and trousered legs, which were at least not getting entangled. When she realised she was about to back into Tina and FA she made a sharp turn to avoid doing so.

I kept right on going. I didn't care how convincing an accident it looked. Maybe I hadn't been quite steady on my feet when we arrived at the party, but a slip of a girl like Maureen could hardly have pulled me off balance even then. Nor had I lifted my feet from the floor while dancing, until now when I brought the right one crunching down on unsuspecting shinbone and ankle.

Chapter Four

The hurricane season had been a busy one, as evidenced by the fact that in the first days of September they had already reached M for Martin in the alphabetic listing prepared in advance for a six-year cycle, alternating male with female names. The women got their way in that, Ray would comment, nagging until the perfectly serviceable system of having them all as women – Betsy, Camille, Dora, Inez – had to be changed by the pussy-whipped NOAA boys stateside. There would never be another Hugo, if only because the names of the biggest disasters were retired, but Martin looked as if it might become a Hall-of-Famer off its own bat.

'Jan's getting worried about us, wondering if I've gone queer or you were born that way.'

'Thanks for the offer Ray, but no. I wouldn't have minded time in the office myself. I do appreciate you involving me in the meeting with Erik though.'

Eddie's involvement in the trip to Curaçao the week after the one to the Virgin Islands had been very much *not* Ray's idea; nor in fairness could he blame it on the Dutchman. He regretted having mentioned to Ken that he was heading there, to be reminded that Jemson was on their steering committee pointedly enough to secure his ticket. Horstwald had made his own suggestion, that Jan might accompany Ray 'so that we can mix a little pleasure with business, maybe have a dinner at my home.'

'I think he's a swinger, wanted you to come along for a bit of wife-swapping. You know what the Dutch are like, all pot and porn.'

'Right up your street then I should think. Of course Ray, I can leave the kids here alone midweek, they'll find their way to school and keep house for us. Shame though, I don't see how I could lose in a swap for you.'

'You could do a lot worse, believe me. Maybe we can get away to Barbados in the new year, the two of us.' Without wanting her to go, for tactical reasons he had made the offer for Jan to shoot down.

Her attitude towards him had thawed a few degrees since his intervention (however belated in her eyes) with Den. Bless the boy, he was doing his part, had somehow managed to mollify his mother without hogging all the credit. Ray hoped he was not as good an actor as he feared he might be.

Although the Dutchman was acting as host, and might be viewed as senior in terms of his breadth of responsibility and number of reports, Ray's premium income was higher because insurance cost more in his islands with their greater exposure to windstorm. He would in any case have felt obliged to suggest amendments to the first proposed schedule.

'I'm not taking you along just to show you Happy Valley,' he told Eddie. 'You and Jonno can earn your corn in the presentation on our operations, and the "blue-sky brainstorming" on "potential synergies" between our shop and theirs is definitely more your thing than mine. We'll get there Tuesday night, keep that one to ourselves then do the work straight off the bat on Wednesday before the piss-up that night. You can use the operational plan presentation with figures updated to half year as a basis.'

'I can probably put figures to end of September if you like.'

'No, third quarter's light, use half year then times three for annual projection. Fourth quarter's heavy.' He smiled. 'Show the opposition a strong hand, mate. We'll talk about next year's figures as and when, with or without the boost to Jonno's from the government account.'

'God, what a dump,' Ray announced at the tiny honour bar of the Gasthuis Margritt in Willemstad, not caring if any of the staff were within earshot. 'If you're going to bow, bow low. I'd rather have put the Marriott at the beach on Sovereign's tab if I'd known they were going to stick us in a B and B. He must be showing off their expense control, what a tight ship they run as he'd probably say, the cliché-fucking-monger.'

'I don't know, we're pretty central here, and it's all very picturesque, the bright colours on all the buildings.'

'Come off it, Eddie. Reminds me of the drawings Kimmie used to bring home from school when she was five years old. Anyway, since I used rehearsals for tomorrow's sing-offs as an excuse not to meet the Dutchmen tonight let's be hearing what you plan to say. Jonno, I expect you'll be winging it, but if you want a run through before we hit the town, no problem.'

In fact Jonno had gone to some trouble to put a presentation together, or adapted one he was already using to tout his operation to potential buyers. With Eddie's help they added another, rose-tinted slide on the assumption of acquiring the government business. Ray had cause to compliment Eddie on his draft for the totality of their operation.

While he may have given the others a different impression, this was Ray's own first visit to the Dutch Caribbean. He found much to like about it. The relaxed atmosphere of the bars Jonno showed them was reminiscent of Tortola, but with a more attractive female population. It seemed to do the ex-soldier good to be back in some of his historic haunts, the happiest Ray had seen him since the loss of his wife. Eddie stayed on at the fifth bar they visited when the older men pooh-poohed his notion of getting something to eat there.

'Looks like you've made a conquest, Jolanda,' Jonno said to the long-legged, short-shorted girl behind the bar with light brown hair cropped above her ears. 'If you can't persuade him to come home with you make sure he gets a taxi back to the hotel, will you?'

'No problem, sir. Might run him back myself if he keeps batting those big brown eyes at me.'

'You're in there, mate.' Ray clapped him on the back by way of goodnight. 'Enjoy your fish pie, but remember we're on parade tomorrow. Be in that cubbyhole they call reception by ten to for nine. I don't think our new friends are the type to arrive late.'

'Nice lad, keen to do well,' Jonno ventured once they were back in the four-by-four they had rented for the evening.

'Yeah, he's a good kid, probably a bit nervous about tomorrow.' (Though Ray had not detected any sign of that.) 'He can outdrink you when he's off the leash,' he added with a sudden access of loyalty Eddie would probably not have understood or thanked him for.

At their eighth bar, sensing Jonno was beginning to flag and might be reaching the stage when the pictures of his dear Sally would start to surface from his mind and wallet, Ray raised the topic he'd had in mind all evening, not to say since the possibility of visiting Curaçao had first arisen. 'So what about the whorehouses you used to live in over here then, mate?'

'The Dutch are sound on a lot of things, Ray, including legal brothels. Prices government-controlled, women checked regularly for crabs or worse, can't go wrong. Many years since I've been to Happy Valley. You after getting your weasel waxed then? There's plenty of willing girls on this island, you don't necessarily have to pay.'

'I find you do, mate. Always. Like getting a haircut, I'd rather pay a fair price for a good job – and not to have to get in a fucking conversation.'

'Fed up with running the clippers over your own head? I get it. Probably won't be many out there on a Tuesday night but we can look in if you want. Curaçao's most popular tourist attraction, and they don't even rip you off too much on the drinks.'

Had he been alone in a taxi, Ray might have had a moment or two's anxiety as they turned off the airport road, leaving all street lighting behind, a two-lane then little more than a cart path, albeit worn flat and smooth enough by the passage of many vehicles. Jonno drove it confidently enough. As he instructed, when Ray paid an afroed attendant the entry for both at a booth where you could also order your first valley beer, he declined to buy 'valley dollars'.

'US or guilders will do fine, you get ripped off on the exchange and I've known people get in trouble for having that currency in their trouser pockets ready for the wash.'

'Don't tell me. You was that soldier.'

He hadn't been expecting a stamp on the back of his hand, and couldn't stop himself consulting Jonno: 'Hey, I hope this washes off, don't want to be flashing it to our new partners tomorrow.'

The older man glanced at the imprint on his own hand, beside the blue swallow tat on the pad between thumb and index finger. 'No worries. They don't want it lasting too long, otherwise they'd have degenerates like you getting in for free night after night. You'll need to show the stamp if site security come checking on you. Don't have it then and the price of admission is whatever you have on you. Don't mess with them either, they're able for dealing with Dutch marines on shore leave. And I shouldn't worry about your insurance oppos. This is a legitimate business, wouldn't be at all surprised if they've taken out a policy: fire, theft and all risks of not getting your jollies.'

'Not forgetting business interruption. You've got a good memory if it was all them years ago, Jonno.'

'All sorts of people come out here. You see someone you know you nod politely, don't stop to engage in conversation, and neither of you ever mentions the meeting outside the valley.'

'Like being in the audience at a musical then?'

Ray had correctly decoded 'all sorts of people' as all sorts of the people who would be in drinking dens or whorehouses knocking midnight on a Tuesday. He didn't imagine many had come for the dancing, not even the three or four women languidly disrobing as they chatted to each other under strobe lighting on a small stage in the main hall. The rest of the space was occupied by leatherette chairs and sofas around small tables and a long bar, tended by the only fully clothed women in the place, if T-shirts and shorts counted as fully clothed. Ray couldn't help sizing them up too as he and Jonno took stools, side on to the bar so they could watch the floor show. The Asian-looking one who came to them was certainly worth cash money.

It was only when they went strolling down the village streets, wooden chalets terraced on either side, that Ray could name the memory that had been nagging at him since they entered the complex. It was pure Pimpinland, the holiday camp on England's east coast where he had worked one summer years ago. If anything, the women here were more discreet in signalling their sexual availability: some sat outside their chalets chatting demurely to each other, except that as a stranger passed they might tug out a nipple in salute, or uncross their legs to provide a peep at bare shaven flesh; others promenaded arm-in-arm, occasionally snogging and snuggling, flashing only the wooden discs on which their chalet numbers were clear.

It was all very civilised. It was true that women appeared surprisingly often between him and Jonno, finding it necessary perhaps to touch an upper leg to help them better reach the counter, or brushing them with almost totally bare buttocks as they leaned in to ask for a napkin or toothpick, but they were not importunate. Ray supposed they had needed to become more inventive in their patter since indoor smoking was banned, an otiose law strictly observed even here.

He was slightly put out when Jonno said he would not be making a pick, fearing he might be trying to take the moral high ground. 'I'm not sure I'm ready for it, that's all, Ray. I've started seeing someone in Road Town, only coffees and chat so far – never thought I'd miss that – but it's a big step for me.'

'Yeah, I understand. Sally was one in a million. Time passes though. If I was you I'd give it a go, make sure everything still in working order, risk-free environment and all that. You know I'm a tomb.'

'Me too. Go ahead, take your time. I'll wait for you here.'

Already informed at the entrance booth of the fixed tariffs, Ray approached a young lady sitting alone at her chalet door, brushing long black hair down her back in a way that stirred him as more overt displays had not. It was hardly Pocahontas bathing unawares; she must know that the stroking showcased a great pair of tits.

Introducing himself to Marcela, as she chose to call herself, he reflected at least there would be no clock-watching. He had never been able to work out whether it was better to arrive back first at the bar, sitting waiting for your mates to return, or to rock up after, as they sat blearily ready for kip and no longer quite so interested in the luscious temptresses hovering around. In practice, arrivals tended to be in the region of the thirty minutes typically paid for plus walking time, unless you had been unlucky enough to fall asleep on the job and be rooked for double fare. Woe betide anyone who rejoined the non-combatants within ten minutes, facing derision as either a two-push Charlie or someone who had simply turned tail and run.

'You dirty little tart.' He chuckled gleefully. 'Whatever will your girlfriend back in Blighty make of this?'

Eddie had clearly not expected Ray to be finishing off the hotel's best stab at a full English at eight in the morning, at a table to boot with a view of the street exit at which he had just parted from Jolanda.

'Needed something hot to set me up for the day. From your fond farewells there I guess you were ahead of me.'

Eddie seemed about to protest, or explain, but finally said only, 'Give it a rest, will you?'

'No need to get snippy, thought it might have relaxed you a bit to get your rocks off. I'm going for a sit-down before we head out, Jonno's already headed up. Sorry to leave you to eat alone, or did you already stick the Dutch for room service? How much did she charge by the way. I hope you weren't ripped off?'

'Fuck off, Ray.' The kid was learning.

It was a long day at the office, even from nine thirty to three thirty including an hour for a sandwich lunch, disappointingly alcohol-free. After coffee in Erik's office, which Ray was pleased to assess as smaller than his own in San Juan, came a quick tour of the open-plan workplace, shaking the hands of a dozen or more staff, the women all smiling brightly but only one worth the effort of remembering a name, Erik's personal assistant Diana.

'I've told them all who you are and what the purpose of today's meeting is, so hopefully now they've greeted you they'll be able to settle down to a day's work without thinking their fate is being decided behind closed doors.'

'Are they nervous about the merger then?' Eddie asked politely. There had not been much chat from him or Jonno on the way in, with Ray shotgun in the boxy car driven by SRG's manager for Aruba, William van Hek.

'It's natural, even though like yourselves we are spared having the other company as a direct competitor on our islands. I am nervous myself.' Erik laughed, giving every appearance to the contrary.

At their main meeting in the boardroom, apart from William they were joined by Erik's Finance Director, a saturnine fellow from Suriname with a pencil moustache by the name of Frank Erkelens, and the younger Underwriting and Marketing Director Martin Pietercz. Ray quickly drew a blank there; the guy had never heard of England World Cup winner Martin Peters, let alone been named after him.

Diana did not leave the boardroom once the systems were set up to provide a clear enough projection on the wall of the various presentations. She had supervised a blue-coated old woman, needlessly introduced also by name, to bring hot drinks if desired and supplement the bottles of still and sparkling water in front of them with notepads and pencils, then took the eighth seat herself.

Ray began with a few words of thanks for the invitation and other banalities, safe in the knowledge he could stop talking at any moment and pass the ball to Eddie. If he should then lose it, for instance dry up in the course of his presentation, Ray might make him wait a bit for rescue, teach him to tell his boss to fuck off.

In fact everything went swimmingly, both Eddie and Jonno talking confidently and well, with the older man the one to begin if anything a little more shakily. While Diana was disappointingly high-necked and trousered, Ray was able through the day to indulge at least his mind's eye with flashbacks from the previous night, flashbacks for once not of the gnawing remorse for drunken behaviour stamp. While Frank Erkelens droned on as only a finance director could about SRG's USP in the ABC islands, he was remembering fondly Marcela's own unique selling proposition.

'Do you like this?' The girl, who was from Barranquilla on Colombia's Caribbean coast (she would have no reason to lie about that) placed his hand again on her carefully trimmed bush.

'You kidding, course I do. Didn't I just prove it?'

She resisted his fingers trying to move lower. 'Not that, unless you want to go again, I can give you a repeat discount. I mean the hair. You don't think it's a bit *asqueroso*?'

'It's not disgusting at all, it's great.' He had no need to lie. Pubic hair, often much denser and more extensive than Marcela's landing strip, was the norm in his sexual youth, right back to Gloria Carney, whom he liked to remember as one of his earliest girlfriends.

'Nearly all the girls here take everything off, so I thought that would help me stand out a little bit from the rest.'

'I see you're a great businesswoman, like Shakira. Sexy as her too.' Now he *was* lying, but what the hell, he had no doubt she was too when she'd earlier complimented him on his skills as a lover ('*Usted sabe MUCHO*'). He left her a good tip and vacated the premises without too much fuss when she unabashedly told him his time was up. He had to wait at the bar for Jonno to return from an assignation of his own, about which neither of them ever said a word.

'Ray?'

'Yes, Erik. Sorry, I was wool-gathering there.'

Eddie bailed out his woken boss. 'We were talking about underwriting philosophy for the islands under our stewardship. I was saying we try not to sell our capacity cheaply, while recognising we have to operate within the realities of the different markets.'

'That's it, Eddie, thanks, spot on. We have to make sure when we eventually come to pool our resources, subject to regulatory approval' – he signalled quotation marks for the conventional cautionary phrase – 'that one plus one comes to equal more than two, not less than it.'

William and Martin nodded sagely at this blather, while Frank remained rightly unimpressed. It was unfortunate that the Surinamian's (Surinamese's? Surinaman's? Surinamanian's? Ray idly wondered) presentation, largely a recitation of tables of figures admittedly too small on the wall for his audience to read, had come after lunch when Ray's biorhythms were at their lowest. If his eyes may have momentarily closed – he had not come to the meetings from an early night – he was at least reasonably confident he had not snored.

'Well, lady and gentlemen, I think it has been a very fruitful day so far,' Erik said (at last) as their 'blue-sky brainstorming' session – how Ray envied Jonno to have been spared that, even at the cost of leaving before the evening cocktails –struggled ever more feebly to get off the ground. 'You will have seen that Diana has been very busy taking notes. I do not of course propose a lengthy minute of all our deliberations, but perhaps you could pick out for us the main action points you have jotted down.'

'Certainly, Erik. Please feel free to correct me on any point, gentlemen. I shall put them all into a document by the end of the day. I would also be grateful for the opportunity to clarify one or two items individually offline.' She then gave an excellent summary of their discussions, on which Ray was the first to compliment her.

'Did you see the cheap fucker, serving up the left-over sandwiches from our lunch?'

'True, but they did bring in the hot stuff as well, the meatballs were great.'

'Hot stuff that Diana too, I mean in a purely professional capacity of course. Why couldn't Ken have sent me someone like her instead of a hairy-arsed Forest fan.'

'Yes, Erik runs a professional outfit. It will be good working with them on the merger.'

Ray looked at Eddie sharply over the drinks grudgingly provided by one of Margritt's staff. Amstel Light was not a favourite, but a continuance of the only beer on offer at the staff shindig they had left to 'freshen up' before the evening cocktail party. 'Professional outfit compared to Fred Karno's Circus I ringmaster in San Juan, you mean?' Despite his never-sleeping paranoia, Ray was feeling fresh again and ready to forget his junior's rudeness that morning. 'You did well too, I have to say. You can stand down tomorrow, apart from say an hour before lunch to prep me for the last round with Erik.'

'Fill you in on the bit you slept through, do you mean?'

He started as Ray's glass slammed down on the bar, hard enough for a few suds to slop over its sides. Whether from that or the empucement of Ray's face, he shifted back a little in his seat as well as trying to retract his barb. 'I'm sorry Ray, that was a joke. I have to say I wasn't impressed by your crack about Jolanda this morning. I'm sorry if that made me overstep the mark now.'

Ray also drew back from the full-frontal assault he had been planning, though his hand trembled as he scribbled a close to their tab in a booklet on the bar in front of him. 'No, you're all right. I may have grabbed a few zees at one point. Don't think it's easy to catch me napping though.'

If he had been running a tight ship earlier, Erik showed every sign of pushing the boat out for their evening activity. Passing through an imposing stone archway, part of the city's Rif fort, they joined at *Le Clochard* on the waterfront Erik, William and Martin, loosely grouped around a massive, pink-faced fellow sitting with his back to the wall at the end of the bistro's bar. All the others were suited and booted, while he wore a guayabera. When Erik introduced them to his chairman, Bill Turnham, the big man offered a friendly smile and a ham of a hand but made no effort to rise. 'Good of you to come a bit early, we can have a chinwag before our other guests arrive and we're on display to the market.'

Bill was on secondment to the Curaçao bank, SRG's joint venture partners, in which his own Canadian one was a relatively recent majority shareholder. 'I don't know what their attitude is to us as an insurer,' Erik had confessed. 'We were part of the acquisition of Banco Bon Bini, but they may be prepared to cut us adrift, especially with the Sovereign merger coming up.'

Ray's initial impression of a boorish lardass softened considerably when Bill turned out to be a long-transplanted Englishman and United fan, noticing immediately the Devils' crest on Ray's necktie. After some general conversation he did unwedge himself from his prime location, impressing Ray further by addressing the barman in what sounded like the local mongrel language, Papiamento. The result was that a few minutes later, as the two men sat gazing out over St Anna Bay, they were brought not only beers but a glass each of the whisky Bill had been drinking at the bar, poured generously in front of them. Ray would normally have resisted any attempt to impose a drink on him, but since Bill had joined him on the beer and the whisky was his own preferred brand (Jameson's) he did not demur. He also followed Bill's lead in accepting one of the proffered Montecristo cigars.

'Seems a long way from Toronto' – which he pronounced Tranno in the Canadian fashion – 'and even further from Salford, but I'm not complaining. I understand you've knocked around the world a bit yourself, Ray.'

How was everyone so well-informed about him? No matter, he was happy enough with the day's work at an end to talk about himself, feeling he had enough material to impress. He would later reflect that was the first sign of his drunkenness, though Bill listened with every appearance of interest. 'We may want to think about bringing you on our board, it would be good to have people from both sides of the fence in your own merger process – which I don't envy you one bit, by the way.'

Ray was not far enough gone to take the polite musing for a done deal, especially as he was still waiting to hear from Ken about joining the board in Barbados. There was no opportunity to pursue the topic, since other guests were now arriving. Bill pitched his cigar over the rails into the dark water. Ray's had shown no spark of life for some time, so he slipped it into his inside jacket pocket.

Insurance salesmen are not notably shy of a drink or two. Ray made various new friends as the party grew in numbers, the volume of chat soon rendering the lounge pianist inaudible. White-jacketed staff circulated with canapés and drinks, the latter mainly whisky with which Ray therefore continued, to avoid – he told himself – putting the waiters to any extra trouble. He did not feel the need to eat.

By half past nine, only a few men were clustered around the piano, now attentive to its player who clearly wanted to be elsewhere, Ray pleading for *Mi Viejo San Juan*. His tie had gone, pressed on Bill as a parting gift – 'Come on, mate. One Red to another.' His jacket was around somewhere, discarded when smoke began to rise from an armpit, the tenacious Montecristo's death fart. He ran its hot end under a cold tap before putting it this time into the outside pocket.

Erik had been sipping white wine before himself leaving, something about seeing his kids before their bedtime. Whether at his instruction or by coincidence, Ray always seemed to have one of the SRG management team at his elbow. Diana, in a green floaty kind of dress which hinted at good legs and said outright good breasts, was one of a handful of women present, a careless sawmill worker's handful at that. Ray's heavy banter did not keep her long, but Martin and William both put in solid shifts by his side.

The night's timeline became lost to Ray soon after his failed request for the sentimental reminder of Puerto Rico. He would not remember spreading his smoky armpit across the back of the driver seat so he could try to see up Diana's skirt in the back, before William dropped her home. Eddie was there in the back with her, and an agent whose name would turn out from his business card to be Berry rather than Barry as Ray had called him all night.

Ray would not recall being blanked by Jolanda at her bar where they left Eddie. He would have only the vaguest memory of telling William what a great idea it would be for him to switch jobs with Eddie. He would learn from his wallet that he had paid three admissions to Happy Valley. He would have been mortified to see himself lumbering around the dance floor, lunging at passing whores whose initial amiability soon wore out. It was better that he never heard why he and Berry had fallen out. He would have been pleased to know he at least parted well from William, assuring him many times they were mates now but he was fine alone.

Ray did not remember the indignity of being frogmarched towards the exit after he fell over a second time, nor his inspirational passing of two twenties to his escorts, making them understand finally. 'Room 51. Room 51.'

'I remembered you. From all the rest.' As far as he could with both arms under restraint, he spread them out to her. A moment of puzzlement, a brief nod to the minders flanking him and Marcela let him lurch through the door and into her arms.

Chapter 5

'Aaaaargh, for fuck's sake.' FA was on his feet momentarily, then on one foot as he hopped and rubbed the injured area. 'What the hell was that for?' He was nearly roaring.

'Sorry mate, didn't see you there. You must've had your feet sticking out.' My tone was bland, but I had my eyes right on him.

Val had quickly rejoined the party from her private one with Pukemore, perhaps fearing the row would attract her parents. 'What's going on, what's happened?'

'Nothing. Ray tripped over one of FA's lugs, that's all.' Carl had been an amused onlooker, ready to pitch in if appropriate.

FA decided not to make a thing of it, and knew enough to keep out of my way for the next few days back at school. I failed to respond to the treacherous Tina's first few notes, except in my own head where ones like 'What's Maureen Wheatley got that I haven't?' provoked various stinging retorts, mostly one-worders: tits, brains, tits, loyalty, tits. Nevertheless, however much I might have railed against fate, my heart was already lost to Tina. Why else would I have been such a bastard to her?

I took to tagging along with Jambo in his hockey groupie role. While they were not exactly going out yet, he was definitely growing closer to Susan Tierney, who was attractive with dark curly hair but so defiantly unflirty that she didn't quite make it to the front rank of sexy girls. I was annoyed at being pushed away and called a dick by Little Mo after FA had got his stupid foot in my way, but if anyone had heard it at least nobody had laughed. One of the problems with girls was that you couldn't lump them if they had a go at you. Another was finding anything to say to them.

'Did you enjoy Val's party then?'

'It got a lot better after you left.' Maureen's face wasn't too bad either, though that pinched-lip look did nothing for it.

'It was all over by then anyway. Thanks for the dance, I enjoyed that, especially our last one.'

'I don't know what I… what anyone sees in you, you're nothing but a… a lout. And a bully.'

'I'm not a good dancer, I grant you that, not light on my feet. I didn't mean to land on Steven if that's what you mean, hard to avoid him. He was sprawled all over the fucking floor.'

'No need to swear. Was it really an accident? You looked as if *you* were going to hit *him*, when it should have been the other way round.'

'Him hit me? I don't think so.' I marvelled at how she appeared to *want* to believe it might have been an accident. I wished I'd broken the twat's ankle. 'Anyway, what do you mean it got better?'

'I was only saying that to get at you. But we did have a nice time after, those of us who stayed over.'

'Did that include old Retchless?'

She laughed, nice white even teeth, by no means a given in our class. 'He wishes. Val had fancied him for ages. No, just me and Sandy and Nicky.'

'I didn't realise you were that friendly with Val. So what, did you have a pillow fight and spiffing fun like that?'

'I'm more Nicky's friend. I was supposed to be staying with her, then she got the sleepover invitation so I was included. Only thing was, once we'd had the pillow fight, how did you guess, all bouncing about on the bed in our undies, me and Nicky had to share a single one and we'd both forgotten our jim-jams, so we had to sleep kind of scrunched up together in the nuddy. Why have you gone so red, Ray?'

Bitch.

All these sophisticated high school tarts, maybe what I needed was a country girl. A bit later than I would catch my bus each morning, most Feltwell kids were walking or cycling in the other direction to Lockwell. I didn't see as much of any of them nowadays, except for Jake either round and about the village or walking through Washtown of a Saturday. He was usually then, crombied in winter, with a girl hanging on his arm, her head coming up hardly to his shoulder. She never spoke when we chatted or even raised her eyes to me. I hoped she might be a child cousin, but he soon disabused me.

'Yeah, a couple of years younger than us, but she's grown up a lot lately. Birdie's little sister, Helen her name is.' Jake was leaning on his bike after stopping to talk at the top of my road one night when he was passing by chance as I got off the school bus. 'It started off with me kidding around with her, but I think she knew more than me. Nearly got caught with her in a dyke one day, down the Brambles, some snouty old fucker walking his dog.'

There had always been an element of rivalry between Jake and me, mainly relating to football but including all other games, of which girls were now becoming the biggest. It hurt to think he was getting ahead of me, even with a kid. 'Is she even on the rag yet?'

'Yeah. Not much tits but I'd rather have 'em big somewhere else.'

'Where?'

'Down there.' He nodded towards his crossbar. 'Where do you think? I don't go all the way, mind.'

'What, only finger?'

'No, I mean I pull it out before I come me mutton. That takes some doing, don't it?'

'Too right, mate.' I agreed enthusiastically, guessing. Luckily Jake was more interested in reporting his own progress than enquiring closely into mine. I allowed it to be understood that I was, if not beating high school girls off with a stick, at least having to exercise a more modest form of self-defence against them. 'What about girls in our year?' I tried to move on, not without filing young Helen's name away for future reference.

'Best ones all taken, mate. Sally Pritchard – we call her Prick-hard now – she's off with some old boy from Mere's Reach... picks her up in his car every night. They want ones already working who've got money to spend on 'em. Nobody's had her drawers down since first year.'

'What about Debbie Finch?' She lived down Jake's road but they had never been close, some long-standing feud with one of her brothers I think.

'You missed your chance back at Well Creek there, Ray. If they don't want married men they want to play at being married themselves. She's been with Charlie Mercer since first year, like fucking Siamese twins they are, always together.'

Jake's description of Debbie brought to mind the nauseating image of Pukemore promenading his various women – except, small mercies, his mum – around the school grounds. I had to be fair to Tina, she appeared to have grown tired of that soon enough. The problem was in the other direction, her gadabout personality engaging with any number of boys, all to my darkest imaginings. This went into overdrive as her own birthday hove into view. It seemed the whole pissing fourth form was going to be invited.

I benefited from her volatility in that she never seemed able to hold a grudge against me for long. While it pleased me to tease her that I might not be able to attend the party, I would not have missed it for the world. She lived on the edge of Washtown, almost in the country, a good but doable walk from Omie's, with whom I was able to wangle an overnight stay for that Saturday. I was determined not to be among the early leavers this time, ready should Tina invite me to stay over at hers. My fantasies had their romantic as well as sexual side.

Uncle Dan, still living in his one-bedroom flat in Washtown, may have had his moment in the sun with Tina's mum. Much as I loved the man, I had to admit he could hardly have offered what her current husband obviously did in terms of real estate. Set back from the road behind a heavy wooden gate, obligingly flung open for us so that you heard the dogs baying before you could read the sign to beware of them, was a big old looming house like something from a Hammer horror film. It was off to the side of a driveway big enough for an artic to do a three-point turn, but there was an obviously later addition in some kind of conservatory giving onto the drive.

We were not to be allowed to penetrate even the castle's outer ramparts, with a reception party waiting for us outside the conservatory. Two big dogs – Rottweilers, by Christ – were tethered to a table that looked solid enough to have held them, even if it had not been laden with birthday parcels and a selection of bottles and cans. Condensation drops on these suggested they were new to the neighbourhood of the free-standing brazier.

Carl Walters was also staying at Omie's tonight. 'One day, my son, all this will be yours,' he said to me with an expansive gesture and none too quietly – we'd drunk half a dozen Carlings from an accommodating offie already, huddled around a bench in the dark and empty park near Omie's house.

Tina was soon all over us, a little bit more all over me than the others I had to think. Did she take a nip at my ear with her teeth while she was whispering to me? 'So glad you could come, you won't regret it.' Roarer, close by as always, hung back a bit, but what the hell I gave her a hug too, hoping to encourage or show up Omie, I wasn't quite sure which.

The six adults around the table were neatly divided by gender on their choice of drinks, the women with what I assumed to be white wine, the men with what I could see to be cans of lager.

'Evening lads, this is where you get your hands stamped, one return allowed if you want to go to the White Hart but no later than nine thirty.

102

Bruno and Max will be reserving the right of admission.' The dogs pricked up their ears at the one word each recognised.

That dippy cunt Omie held out his hand to have it stamped, as if we were at some poxy disco up town. Fair play to him, the man didn't show him up about it. Jack Smeaton was a big fellow, dressed in jeans and a checked shirt. After he'd smoothly converted Omie's gesture into a handshake, when it came to my turn I found his was one of those so firm as to border on the aggressive or piss-taking. I said nothing but my name.

'So this is the legendary Mr Roden. I hear I may have to keep an eye on you.' He had made a point of looking us each in the eye as we shook, and there was nothing soft about that look either.

'Don't embarrass the kids, Jack.' Tina's mum put one hand on his left forearm and looked to give him a dig in the ribs with the other. 'Hello Ray, how's Dan surviving?'

No embarrassment there then. 'Oh he's... er, fine thanks. He sends his best.' I used the adult formula as insincerely as I had heard them do it.

'Yeah, I bet,' she said without smiling. 'I'm Julie, Tina's Mum,' she was on to Carl.

There were rows of plastic cups with what looked like orange juice in them, Tina and Angie trying to press them onto us as 'Buck's Fizz'. Perhaps the stepdad caught Carl looking at the lager. 'You know how your breath freezes in this weather, it's a little-known fact that steam gives away the last thing you've drunk. If it was up to me I wouldn't mind sharing my lagers with you so you could have another, but it's not my party. I won't pretend the women's piss has got real champagne in it, but it's got sparkling wine, which is why it's out here with us. Strictly one cup each. Soft drinks are in the marquee.'

I don't know about my friends, but I'd never tasted wine *or* champagne. Since it was alcohol, we had it anyway. It was crap.

We'd been at pains (and at our lager) not to arrive early, despite my secret fretting that Tina would have already copped off with some random bloke before we got there. It seemed she was bound to the mixed welcoming committee until the last possible guest had arrived, since she and Roarer didn't stay once they'd got us settled in.

If the house looked like it had been around for hundreds of years, the flat-roofed single-storey industrial units behind it were very much of our time. We were briefly introduced to cowled banks of machines – sewing? Surely not typing – as Tina showed us a coatrack at the entrance. Carl, the only one of us to be wearing an overcoat, hung up his Millett's East German Army-surplus with various others on what it pleased him to refer to as the chapel hat pegs.

Behind the units was the promised marquee, outside which amazingly enough stood a burger van. 'There's sandwiches and nibbles inside and if people want a bit later they can get chips and stuff if they like,' Tina was gabbling.

'You'll be wanting a bit later, Radar,' Carl told me before addressing the girl and the land stretching away to a stand of trees and more outbuildings. 'Some spread you've got here, Tina.' It only lacked for him to be standing flat-footed, thumbs hooked in braces, feet at ninety degrees, straw in mouth. 'How many acres?'

'Only down to the copse and paddocks there, it all belongs to Jack not us.' Tina sounded almost apologetic. It was never good form to show off wealth at our school, especially when it self-evidently existed.

Inside the tent it was more like a disco than an intimate party, strobe lighting and all. Despite the DJ's enthusiasm there were only a few girls up dancing, from a sizeable crowd including a few younger kids as at Val's party. At least there didn't seem to be any adult infiltration. Seeing Mick and Caroline over by a stanchion, his arm loosely round her shoulders, we went over to pay our respects, as it was increasingly becoming with him from the younger, more relaxed days of our Grammar friendship.

Caroline was in an eye-poppingly short skirt, but we followed convention by pretending she was not there. She was probably the reason for their joint presence tonight, Mick having more than once expressed a degree of scorn for 'fucking kids' parties with ice cream and balloons.' Caroline's family might move in the same horsey, countrified circles as Tina's current one appeared to.

'Stephen, Ray, Carl.' Mick acknowledged us in what I suspect was the order of affection he had for us. Despite being in the same House, and the two of them its only half-decent footballers, he was generally cool towards Carl. It was as if he somehow sensed the Washtown St Peter boy's asides, however carefully made outside his earshot, even the odd use of the P word.

'You fancy coming up the Hart in a bit, mate?' Carl was always polite, occasionally verging on the obsequious to Mick's face, though he did not lack a rep as a bit of a hardman himself.

'Might not bother. I've got everything I need here.'

It was not like Mick to brag on Caroline. He must have realised from our embarrassed silence that we thought he had shown a severe lapse in taste, because he burst out laughing.

'Not Caro, you fuckwits. Show 'em what I'm on about, babe.'

Wordlessly the girl held out her handbag to us and teased it open. I could see a flattish silver tin in a welter of tissues, tin foil, lipsticks, hair stuff and other mysteries before she snapped it shut.

'And I don't mean the pack of three, Stephen.' Mick laughed again at his primary school friend.

'Nice one, Mick. How'd you get a hip flask past the Gestapo at the gate?'

'Same way you've seen it, Walters. Nobody's going to search sweet Caroline's handbag, are they? She's well in with all this lot.'

'Tight cunt, would it have hurt him to offer us a nip?' Carl said a few minutes later when Mick and Caroline had strolled/teetered away from us, in his words 'to inspect the estate'.

'He'll be getting a nip all right, and not of vodka,' I tried. Carl's language and attitude were catching. 'Will you look at them legs? Has he shagged her yet, Omie?'

'What do you think?' Then, as if he had presumed too far on his standing with Mick, 'Don't think he tells *me* everything. I'm like you, hardly see him now.'

'No offence Omie,' Carl put a hand on his shoulder, 'but if it was a choice between you and hot legs you wouldn't be seeing me either. He's nearly as bad as Jambo, look at him over there with the hockey whores. He's gone queer I reckon.' Wanting sex with girls was natural. Liking, or appearing to seek out, their company was something else altogether.

Accused outright of poofery, Jambo only gave the infuriating grin of his that made you feel like smacking him. Without showing the signs of possession with Susan Tierney that Mick did with Caroline, he did not stray far from her all night. Pukemore and Val were even tighter, sticking together like a nun's knees as Carl put it. He ostentatiously invited me and Omie to go up the Hart with him and Lesley, but we both stayed in the marquee. 'Hope he gets back past curfew and Max or Bruno bites his balls off,' Omie said with uncharacteristic waspishness.

Tina was like my poor imagining of a society hostess, going around the tent talking to everyone, albeit less in the manner of a *grande dame* than an eight-year-old on a sugar rush. I could have told you at any moment where she was, for all that I carried on conversations with Jambo and Omie and Little Mo. Tina did keep coming back to me too, taking me outside at one point but only to queue with her for burger and chips. It was cold, right enough, but despite her standing very close to me in the line I couldn't quite make that step of putting my arm around her.

Although she had not been over attentive to any particular one of the boys there – believe me I was keeping a close eye on that wanker FA – it seemed the evening would end in another blank for me too. It was only right at the end when she insisted, grabbing me by both hands after virtually shoving Roarer into Omie's arms, on having a dance. It was some hippie shit about Woodstock, but slow enough to smooch. I don't remember if I said anything to her, but she whispered 'naughty' to me before lifting my hands a bit higher off her arse. That didn't stop her snuggling in even closer, and much though I'd like to claim the palm I have to say she kissed me first.

And I'm sorry Debbie, but that was my first kiss.

Then the balloons came down. I hadn't noticed them somehow rigged up in the roof of the tent, nor whatever mechanism released them. At least one popped on the massive cake bloody Jack Smeaton brought stately in, with (presumably) fifteen candles dotted around the shape of the horse. Tina was now the centre of much hugging and kissing, people patting balloons to each other as I grumpily tried to stomp one or two underfoot. Omie was snogging Roarer, poor sod, a lot of people were paired off, though I couldn't see Mick around to have his worst fears about kids' parties confirmed.

It all broke up quickly after that. Smeaton and Tina's mum were solicitous to see everyone safely off the premises, offering umbrellas and to call taxis if necessary – it was raining hard all of a sudden.

I didn't care about the rain, or the cold. She had kissed me. We had kissed. I had kissed her. Omie was more practical, but then he'd only been with Angie. As Carl pulled on his massive greatcoat he pointed to a nondescript blue mac on the rail. 'Take that, one of you, nobody will miss it and if they do you can always give it back to Gibbo in the week.' Omie grabbed it.

We didn't get a chance for a goodnight kiss, not a proper one, with watchful Jack still hovering around, but never was a peck on the cheek – as close to the lips as we dared – more memorable. 'My boyfriend,' Tina whispered.

Chapter Five

'Asqueroso! Me estás meando encima.'

Ray was propelled at once into wakefulness and the chilly morning street of the whores' village, fumbling instinctively at his Y-fronts to save them from further soaking. He managed to direct the final spurts from his semi-erect penis into the solitary plant pot giving a pathetic welcome to Marcela's chalet, another brave USP. There was nobody about to see him. He would hardly have cared if there was. He was still drunk to the wide.

She did not answer to his first knock, but when he increased the volume, perhaps fearing a scandal she let him back in.

'Sorry about that, darling. I didn't really piss on you, did I?'

'Pretty much.' She was scrunching up a sheet, revealing a rubber one underneath. Probably needed that for some of her clients, Ray reflected, without including himself in their number.

The great thing, or one of them, about working girls was that you could sort out most things short of murder or permanent scarring at no cost other than money. He knew – from Marcela's blandishments on the happier evening before last – the all-night rate, which he was happy to double even though he doubted anything billable beyond the accommodation had happened since his unexpected return to her door. He thanked his stars he'd been mainly on whisky, otherwise he might have flooded the cramped quarters. He was equally grateful he had not made it back to his hotel.

She still looked rather sulky, like a fifteen-year-old, sitting on the side of the bare bed in a long T-shirt, when he emerged from the small shower space that served her and customers. He searched for a conversation piece but there were no family snapshots and they had already talked about each other's tattoos.

'Look, sorry, you're a great girl and you've got me out of a jam. No harm done and here's an extra tip for yourself alone, US dollars. Can you chuck them away for me?' he nodded down at his sodden underpants by the shower curtain.

The extra money was enough to cheer her up. 'Normally the guest asks to keep my panties, not give me his.'

'I'll have a vodka and tonic, VAT as we say in England, ta very much Erik, a large one.' He was not confident of negotiating a full mug of beer without a degree of spillage until he had taken a swift steadier, a shame since they were in a kind of micropub, the Curaçao Brewing Company.

He had not had to wait too long for a taxi at Happy Valley, scoring a coffee among the cleaning staff in the meanwhile and making it back to town before 8 a.m. The desk clerk did not seem unduly surprised to be asked for an alarm call at 10.30 a.m., and he had sat down with Eddie half an hour later as scheduled, once again fully dressed.

'She's more than a cracking pair of tits, that Diana,' he ventured after reading his copy of her meeting notes. She had apparently brought them round at breakfast for discussion, which Eddie had handled. Ray thought better of asking whether that had put Jolanda's nose out of joint, then regretted his forbearance when Eddie went on the offensive.

'Let me know when you make up your mind if you want to swap me for her here in Curaçao or William in Aruba, won't you? So's I know, like.'

'Oh you've been talking to him as well, have you? Seems like you might be more at home here than in San Juan. Come on, I was only joking, you know what happens on tour stays on tour.'

'I know you a bit by now, Ray, but they don't.' Eddie was making a great fuss of putting the papers into his smart briefcase, ready to be off. 'God knows how you can still appear to be talking sense even when you're pissed as a fart. For some reason William was flattered. He was going to mention the idea of an exchange to Erik today.'

'Was he, by Christ? No question then, I'd pick Diana every time, he's too slack-mouthed.'

Whether William had in fact mentioned anything to him of their peregrinations the night before, or their career development interview, Erik was not letting on. Ray vaguely remembered also some disagreement with an agent, so thought it best to get in an early disclaimer to avoid being blindsided later on.

'That chairman of yours, Bill, he's quite a character. Certainly led me astray last night, getting me started on the whiskies far too early.'

'Yes, he's good value.' Erik sipped at his lime and soda.

'I'm sure he's already discussed it with you, he mentioned about me maybe coming on the board here. Of course, if that *should* happen I can tell you right off the bat I wouldn't be trying to second guess any of your insurance decisions. I'd definitely be interested though, and I've been floating myself the idea of an interchange at a lower level.'

'You didn't mention it in our blue-sky session yesterday.'

'Well no, it's not one for the official minute. I didn't want to name names then either, but your William looks a smart guy, and I'm sure you've formed your own view on Eddie.'

'Yes indeed.' It seemed that was it – like pulling teeth to get anything out of the Dutch prick today, Ray thought – but eventually Erik continued. 'A very favourable one, as it happens. What you say is interesting without doubt, but I feel we should see what happens at the top – if I may speak of ourselves in that way – over the next months, before considering other levels.'

'Sure, fair enough, I hear you.' I hear you loud and clear, it's you or me you bastard.

Ray knew that the time remorse, regret, a feeling you'd rather be dead typically set in after a heavy session is after you've failed to eat something around lunchtime the following day. He had tried to insulate himself against this by pouring down a couple of pints of craft beer – the first nearly came straight back up – after his second VAT. Still, the flight back to San Juan was not a happy one for him. He would normally have necked a couple of miniatures then trusted to the restorative powers of a good night's sleep, in his own bed. That was not an option tonight, as a slew of missed calls and texts had reminded him over the last twenty-four hours.

He had told an incurious Jan he would not be home until Friday. He would have called to say the plans had changed and he would be back tonight after all, except that Emilia Rosso was keeping him at the stake on commitments he had made to her, at a time when he thought it would be nice to celebrate a successful trip to the Dutch islands.

The upcoming Christmas season would mark the first anniversary of their affair. Opportunities to spend a full night together had been limited, except for occasional business trips such as one in Guadeloupe where he had gone to end Sovereign's relationship with a small agency. The fact that Jan's summer break in the UK with the kids tended to be longer than his leave allowance had also helped, though he had been careful never to bring Emi to their home. Jan was

109

not inquisitive, but she was sharp and ferociously jealous. He did not want to give her cause for grief or grievance.

After declining a lift from Eddie, he waited nearly half an hour for Emi to pick him up at the airport, with only a couple of kiosk cans of Medalla for company. There was a brief glimpse of an alternative life as he stowed his small case in the back of her red Mitsubishi Mirage, kissed her as he entered from its passenger side and enjoyed also a brief glimpse of red panties exposed by her mini skirt as she leaned towards him.

'Sorry I'm late, sugar, the traffic is brutal this time of night.'

'You're always late. Don't tell me you've been to work dressed like that?'

'Like what?'

'Like this.' He ran his hand all the way up her right leg, without meeting any resistance.

'I've come from the office but I did get changed there, told everyone I was on a hot date.'

'You'd hardly be going to a prayer circle dressed like that. I only hope you keep our thing quiet amongst your friends.'

'Our thing? What's that then?'

How soon the sands could begin to shift under your feet. 'I'll tell you later. I was hoping we might have a quiet night at your place, maybe order in pizza, but I guess that's not going to happen.'

'Damn right it's not, save that for the wife.' She removed his hand from her thigh as his fingers were starting to get busy, giving it a consolatory pat as she plumped it back into his own lap. 'It's kinda nice that you want to spend so much time in bed with me, but a girl needs to be entertained in other ways too. I'd hate to think you're ashamed to be seen out with me.'

'Never that,' Ray answered honestly. 'I'm highly delighted and flattered for people to see me out with someone as sexy as you, except San Juan's a village and you know how everyone in our industry gossips.'

'True enough, your friend Nelson most of all. It's too late to keep things secret since that time down in Ponce when we double-dated with him and that local tramp.'

'Tut tut, jealousy my darling.' Although what she said was all too plausible – Sovereign's Sales VP Nelson would think he was boosting Ray's image by retailing such information – for form's sake he replied that any leak was more likely to have come from one of *her* friends.

When she told him they would be dining at Morton's Steakhouse in the Caribe Hilton he realised he would indeed have to charge the evening as a business expense, right down to the tip for the valet-parker he privately considered sufficiently compensated by the view as Emi got out of the car.

He knew some of the head honchos in her brokerage routinely took Emilia along on major deals for more than her physical attributes. She was a sharp businesswoman and brought the conversation back to their own case early in the meal, as Ray gingerly sought to reintroduce his stomach to food (if not yet solids) by way of a tomato soup.

'Have you spoken any more to Mr Johnson about the BVI government account?'

'Not yet. I haven't got it cleared from London either, they'll be worried about the aggregates, the sheer number of properties that could blow down in a hurricane. They love the premium, but expect to get it without any risk.' He reached across to pinch a prawn from her plate, hoping it might stimulate some semblance of appetite.

'You know we have a relationship with B & M. If you don't think your English buddy's up to it we could maybe try to run the account through them.'

'Who said Jonno's not up to it?'

'Look, he's a nice guy but he obviously hasn't got any experience of putting a major slip together.' She shoved the plate with the last remaining prawn and scraps of rabbit food across to him. 'We have. I'm going to level with you, Ray. My bosses will feel more comfortable dealing with Joe Makepiece than him. And we already agreed your head office would take more kindly to a submission through a correspondent of a big worldwide producer like Fawkes Fordham, didn't we?'

'Feel under more pressure to accept the business, right. But you'll be in it whether it's with Jonno or B & M. And I want him involved.' He told himself it was personal loyalty to Jonno that made him insist, not that he needed the premium in his BVI account rather than through the USVI agents who now reported to Jaime.

'I love it when you stand firm, honey. I wanted to give you a heads-up, that's all.' There was nothing wrong with her appetite, a juicy sirloin and chips for the lady before the waiter put a miserable mushroom risotto in front of Ray. 'We can help you and whoever to put the information on aggregates together as well as the schedule to sell the deal in London. I'm sure there'll be a lot of work needed from you and me personally on that, a lot of late nights in the islands.'

Twelve hours later the prospect of further late nights together seemed much more remote. By giving himself a bollocking and switching to rum, Ray had managed to maintain a sociable front through the evening, allowing himself to be manoeuvred around the Hilton's dance floor a couple of times. Back at Emi's condo his tiredness caught up with him.

'Sorry about last night, hope that made up for it.' He was nestled up against her naked body from behind, left arm slipped under hers and around a breast. He was surprised at the bitterness with which she responded.

'Had to wait for the tanks the Dutch *putas* emptied to refill, did we? I was so looking forward to seeing you last night, that's when I wanted you. I'm not here so you can throw a fuck into me whenever it suits you.'

'What a lovely way of putting it. I thought we made love. If that's how you feel, maybe it's better if we call it a day.'

She hoicked his hands off her, turning to face him. 'What? You come here and five minutes after dumping your load you want to dump me? What is it, afraid you might have to buy me a Christmas gift...? Or looking to pick up some new piece of tail in the party season?'

His attempts to respond were batted away, with more aspersions cast on his reliability and desirability as boyfriend and lover. He did not like confrontations with women at the best of times, and Emi was beyond all reason. 'You're proving my point. If you think so little of me surely it's better to part.'

'Spare me your prissy flowery English, man. I can do a lot better than you, believe me. Someone who'll talk to me occasionally before the third drink, someone who'll at least pretend to care, someone who'll show a bit of passion.'

'I can get all this at home. I don't need it here.'

'Fuck off home then, see if I care.'

By the time they had showered and dressed, separately and tiptoeing around each other in the small apartment, her temper had cooled. 'How about we dip off the highway on the way into town, have a juice by the beach, baby? Talk things over.'

'I'm surprised you've got anything more to say.' Under cover of running water he had managed a quick phone call to Jaime, who had not left for work yet and agreed to take him in (he didn't seem to need directions to Emi's home). 'If you'll let me get my case out of your boot – sorry, trunk, I won't insult you with the English language – then you can be on your way, and I'll be on mine. Thanks for the bed and... well, thanks for everything.'

Then it was tears, worse than anger. He had never been so glad to see his friend when Jaime parped up a few minutes later. 'Another of your asshole buddies knows about us now then.' Emilia came out for another round. 'Don't you hold me responsible if other people you'd rather not find out a little bit about us before too long.'

'You look like shit on a stick, mate.' Larry pushed back the seat beside him in the corner of Frankie's for Ray to join him. It must have been still before noon, as he was on vodka and grapefruit juice.

'You're not the first to notice.' Jaime, who had of course already known there was something going on between Ray and Emilia, had not commented directly, but Marta had wondered aloud if he was ill. Seizing on the idea, he let it be supposed within his own small unit that he had perhaps picked up a touch of food poisoning in Curaçao, glad Nellie and Carmen did not press him for details so he had to invent an actual meal taken there.

Larry's presence did not bode well for the quiet lunch he'd envisaged, a couple of beers tops and perhaps a plate of rice and beans, in the safe company of Luz Angela or Sandra. One day he intended to surprise the girls by walking in and ordering an iced tea. Not today.

'I mean you live with a Puerto Rican woman, does she give you the sort of hassle I've been getting?'

'Number one, Rita owns a bar.' (The Crazy Horse was where Larry would normally conclude his drinking sessions, having ranged through vodka, beer and whisky in distinct time zones at Frankie's). 'Number two, she's amazing in bed. So the perfect woman, right? Wrong. She busts my balls like you wouldn't believe.'

'Yeah, but to be fair she's like your missus by now, I mean you expect it the longer you live together. You wouldn't believe how much Emilia reminded me of Jan this morning. I mean gimme a break, surely you expect something a bit different from a girlfriend.' He signalled Sandra for more drinks, wondering again why sitting beside Larry always increased his speed of consumption.

'Not necessarily, mate. You're like a hamster on a wheel, you run after the things you like, why wouldn't you want the same type as you married? How Janet puts up with you I have no clue, by the way, that lady's a saint.'

'You don't know the half of it. Hamster in a cage, it would be great if life was that simple. Get tossed a few treats every now and then, what do the little fuckers like?'

'Lettuce and shit, I expect. If you want red meat, a red-blooded woman, you've got to expect them to have teeth. However long you see them only in a big old smile, they always bite in the end.'

'Ta for the advice, Dr Ruth. Never mind bitten I feel savaged, this last ten days I've been kicked out of their beds by my wife, my girlfriend and a … another one. Chewed up and spat out. Listen.' He lightly rapped his knuckles against Larry's breast pocket to reinforce the message. 'It shouldn't come to anything, but if somehow Jan should find out I was back in San Juan last night, it was too late for me to disturb her so I crashed round yours, all right?'

'It's a mug's game, shitting on your own doorstep. And I'd hate to deceive your sweet wife. You listen.' He poked a finger into Ray's chest, hard. 'If women are so much trouble, why do you always want more than one?'

'Because they make me feel so fucking good.' Ray laughed. 'Give it a rest, Larry. You know as well as I do women are made to be lied to, it's the rules of the game they play themselves. I don't imagine it will ever come to the crunch, only if some nosey bastard who knows Jan might have happened to see me in the Hilton last night. Are you my mate or not?'

Larry was not convinced by the argument or the appeal. 'Don't you mean fucking them makes you feel so good? And how do I explain the tart I suppose was hanging off your arm in the hotel, to Janet or to my Rita for that matter if I was supposed to be with you?'

'You'll be able to invent something, I trust you. I know you've had the practice, mate. Don't you fucking deny it.'

Jan showed so little interest in his landing time or indeed his whole overseas trip as to make him almost resentful, giving him no chance to parade his carefully crafted alternative version of the last seventy-two hours. He knew better than to volunteer any information, answering only direct questions – and even there it was surprising how often women passed on regardless if you kept quiet for only a moment or two. He found he was blaming her more and more for the way he felt about himself.

Perhaps he had less need of an alibi on arriving home around eight in the evening after his session with Larry, half in the bag, bellowing for his dinner, because it was standard operating procedure for him to tank up on spirits whenever he was flying. Jan did, however, spark into life at his claim on Saturday morning to be fully refreshed after a good night's sleep.

'A good night's sleep? I'm glad that's how you remember it. You were up and down like a yo-yo, every half hour, muttering to yourself in Spanish, putting the bathroom light on every time, no consideration. I know you're full of shit but I wouldn't've believed you could have that much piss in you.'

'All right I'll piss the bed next time, see how you like that.'

'You're disgusting.'

Weekends were increasingly the only time Ray found any respite from drinking, which he did his very best to sell to his family as an integral part of his job. His attempts at abstinence were however not always acceptable or welcome to his contrary wife. 'Here's an idea. Try laying off the booze Monday to Friday, then you can perhaps enjoy a civilised glass of wine with me and the kids on a Saturday night.'

So he would end up having a drink at family dinners too. His suggestion of an impromptu one after Eugenio Hostos' end-of-term fundraiser and PTA was received almost cordially by Jan, who had heard there nothing but praise for straight-A's Kim, and no mention from the faculty of Den's transgressions – he too was more than holding his own academically.

'I didn't know the Prestwick lad was leaving your school, Den, you never said,' he threw out after his second beer, once Jan had satisfied Kim's exhaustive enquiries on what her teachers had to say about her as the two females tucked into the Ponderosa's bottomless salad bar.

'Didn't think you'd be interested. Mum knew.'

'Was it to do with that run-in you all had with the authorities?'

'Dunno.'

'I expect that did have something to do with it, but Mary Ellen had been saying for a while they weren't happy with the quality of education here. How would you feel about going to school in England, Denis?' Jan fired that one in out of left field.

'What?' Impossible to tell from his tone if Den was astounded at the question or had not heard it.

Ray could not recall any mention of the possibility to himself, but knew he might be wrong on that. 'Come on, love, you know he's been doing better since that business, why punish him? Besides, if he went anywhere with proper academic standards he would be nearer the bottom than up around the top of the class, where he is now.'

'That's right, *Father*, give his self-confidence another knock. And don't tell me you were only joking. I've heard that once too often.'

'I'm not sending him away to boarding school, and that's that.'

'What, doesn't fit in with your working-class self-image? We know you grew up in Feltwell, we don't all have to be stuck with you there for evermore.'

'Is that where we're going to be spending Christmas, with Nanny?' Kim asked brightly, whether because she had not been following the early part of the conversation or because she had, and wanted to break any rising tension between her parents. They exchanged one of those glances of the long-married, indicating that the subject could be shelved but was far from closed.

'Yes darling, we'll be going down there for Christmas, then perhaps on to Aunt Lucy's where you can see Louise for New Year. I suppose you'll be going into the office, Ray? We can call on my mum then.'

'I may not be. HR have all got their knickers in a twist' – how the kids grew, a couple of years earlier any mention of the word 'knickers' would have set Kim giggling – 'about the merger, so I haven't had the usual leave form. Waste of time going round all the departments bullshitting – sorry Kimmie, bullpooping – to people who might not have a job next year. I suppose I could find out when the Christmas party is, maybe go in to see Ken and for that.'

Maybe not, Jan's look suggested. Obviously she still remembered the party much earlier in their marriage that had cost him his shirt. 'You needn't think I'm washing this, stinking of cheap perfume,' she had announced by way of good morning the next day, theatrically binning it before he could suggest she stop using the cheap perfume then. She did not mention that occasion now, but did ask if he might not be one of those jobless.

'Ta for that boost to *my* self-confidence. I expect Ken will look after me, and if he doesn't we won't have to worry about boarding school for Den. We'll all be back home at Mum's and he can go to Washtown Grammar.'

'Number one' – hearing his friend's characteristic emphasis, Ray wondered briefly if Jan had been seeing more than she should of Larry – 'it's great to hear you still referring, after all our years together, to your mum's council house as home. Number two, you go "home" by all means. It will be without me and the kids is all. And number three, hasn't the school gone private since your day? Surely Sovereign won't pay fees if they chuck you out?'

'Way to go, Jan. The power of positive thinking. Unless it was for gross misconduct they'd have to give me a pay-off. That would go a long way in Feltwell, especially if you got yourself a job with Mum to look after the kids.'

'Do you guys have to keep on arguing? Can't we have a nice quiet dinner for once?'

'You're right, darling.' Ray laughed at his daughter suddenly playing the parent. 'Long as you stop referring to us as "guys". Let's order one of them massive slabs of chocolate cake they do here to share with your mum and then we can all be quiet.'

If their flights home had not already been booked, Ray would have been tempted to change them to avoid Sovereign Puerto Rico's year-end party. Last year's held happier memories of hooking up with Emilia, but her presence would not be so welcome this time around, particularly after a tip-off from Nelson one night in Frankie's before the party season got fully underway.

'Ray, can I have a quick word with you, excuse me.' His arm round the shoulder brought him close enough to smell on his breath the port that had been passed willy-nilly between them all at the Bankers where they had just finished the board Christmas lunch. 'Sandi, bring me a double Cointreau on the rocks, whatever all my friends are drinking and the check, please. Ray, let's go over here a sec.'

A standing space near the toilets in the Christmas-crowded bar hardly seemed to afford much privacy, which Ray would have welcomed as soon as he realised his friend was talking about Emilia. 'I saw you with her last year, brother, of course, but none of us dreamed you'd get serious.'

'Come on Nelson, I wouldn't say I was serious. You know how it is.'

'I do, and that's why I'm talking to you now. You may not have been, but she's as serious as a heart attack, let me tell you. Way back, when I was still a broker myself, with Johnny Mangano, she and I had a bit of a thing. It nearly cost me my marriage.'

'Which one?'

'This one, with my Miriam.' The Puerto Rican could clearly not see the relevance of the question.

'Not so very way back then.' Ray's retrospective jealousy was redoubled.

Nelson bounded on, oblivious to the drunken sarcasm. 'And I don't mean she found out by accident, or because I got careless. That bitch was spreading it all over town, even started calling us at home. She's a great lay, takes it up the ass and everything – well, you know all that – but she's a nutjob too.'

'What happened then?'

'The usual, Emilia threatening to kill herself, Miriam threatening to kill me, take my kids away, her mother on my case, believe me I don't want anyone to go through what I had to. That's why I'm telling you she's starting to get loud again, all over the place she is like – what's that phrase you taught us? – like a madwoman's shit.'

'Lucky Jan's not part of the market, she doesn't mix much. Let's hope Miss Rosso can pick up someone new this season.'

'Miriam isn't part of the market either. Women always have a way of sniffing out bad news. Finding someone else won't be a problem for Emi, she can land on anyone's dick in a heartbeat, but I'm telling you brother, so as you know, she don't care where she makes a scene when she's in this mood.'

'How did you get out from under then?' Ray really wanted to know.

'I had a word with her boss at the time, a *pana* of mine as it happened. That was before she moved to the double-barrels. Micky told her she was being unprofessional and it had to stop. Cost me a cruise to the Bahamas with Miriam into the bargain, her old woman having the kids to drip poison into their ears about me the whole time we were away.'

'I'll have Jan out of here within a fortnight anyway till after Three Kings, hopefully it'll all have blown over by then.'

'Most likely. And be careful she don't get chatting too much to Miriam at the ACODESE dinner. She's not malicious, my wife, you know, but she can forget who she's talking to after a few drinks.'

'So Miriam knows about me and Emi as well then?' Recalling his sometime girlfriend's words, Ray wondered who was really the blabbermouth in Nelson's household. He took his friend's warning as seriously as he could take anything at that stage of the day's drinking, while also wondering if he might yet contrive to fuck Emilia up the arse without making things worse.

As it turned out, the shitstorm was coming anyway.

Chapter 6

'We won't be able to do anything like that, you do realise, Ray love?'

'Nobody's asking you to. All we need is a few sandwiches and some cans of lager.'

Still on a high from the Saturday night at Tina's or the six-pack split with Omie and Carl the next morning before catching the bus home, I'd made the mistake of answering Mum's questions about Tina's party. It never occurred to me that she would start getting competitive, or worry about not being able to put on as good a show as my classmates' parents. It was she who had insisted on me having a party at all. I thought it seemed a bit sissy, to be starting again after something like ten years since the last one.

If I was shy of being a host, I was even more so of being a 'boyfriend'. I soon made it clear to Tina that I wouldn't be spending my breaks strolling hand in hand with her. Although it hardly seemed justifiable as a bus ride to me, much closer than Carl or I lived to school at any rate, she sometimes did catch a bus from the same Cattle Market depot as us.

'You want to walk with Gibbo from now on, that's fine mate. But don't expect me to tag along as goosegog and don't even think of double-teaming me with Roarer.'

'What's up, Carl? Thought you'd be walking down there with Lesley Carrick from now on anyway?'

'Lezzer Carrick, you mean. She's frigid.'

Clearly the excursion to the Hart hadn't gone quite as well as planned.

After an awkward Monday when Tina and Angela constantly baulked our progress to the buses, which we liked to make at a steady pace (not clutching each other's arms and cackling every few steps), they got the message and kept a respectable distance. Apart from the hoped-for sex with her, Tina as girlfriend was a bit like I imagined having to look out for a younger sister would be – OK at home but embarrassing at school.

It was Wednesday or Thursday when Omie got smacked. It turned out that Mick Turner had not left Tina's party before us as we'd supposed. He and Caroline may have been somewhere in the works unit even as Omie was there nicking his raincoat to walk home in. He might have got away with it if he hadn't brought it back to Tina at a moment when Caroline happened to be around. 'You're for it, mate,' was all she said.

It wasn't that Mick had got wet. Caroline had taxi money. It was a question of respect, someone messing with his property, even unknowingly (Caroline herself perhaps missed the admiring glances she used to draw from everyone before she started going out with him). Omie might suffer less for it than some, but he would suffer.

There was a bigger group of kids on the Cattle Market than usual. The ones who caught buses of course: Val (with Pukemore), Lesley and Jambo for Feltwell, Gibbo and Roarer, Caroline for Mere's Reach where the inhabitants mostly had webbed feet. Other onlookers of both sexes, including various hockettes and the wanker FA, had no real business there.

As Omie had not said a word to either of us, we did not know what arrangement had been made. Lounging as usual on the crash fencing separating the terminus from the dual carriageway, we greeted him without any sign of surprise when he turned up on his bike. He propped it against the two metal bars, without sitting down beside us.

Mick came walking across the broad open space at the centre of the market, where the red double-deckers would swing round. I had never seen him there with Caroline. He had no need of the raincoat today.

Omie walked a few steps to meet our other mate. Mick said only 'Stephen', raising his head slightly as if to acknowledge an acquaintance on the street. He casually swung his right fist into Omie's face, making him stagger sideways, without quite falling. Mick did him the courtesy of standing ready for any response, though we all knew none was coming.

'Show's over,' Omie muttered to the assembly, grabbing his bike and launching off on it towards his home. Turned out it wasn't, not quite.

Carl and I had stood up from the railings, without any intention of intervening. There was nothing to say to Omie, who had at least fronted up. Roarer was living up to her nickname at some volume, being consoled by Tina.

Mick had turned and begun walking away towards town. When he stopped and came back, I thought it was towards Caroline. Instead, he approached us.

'Mick,' we said as we had a few minutes earlier, but that couldn't have been what he meant by 'What did you say?'

There was more intent behind the punch he drove into Carl. 'Here you go you snidey cunt, Walters.' Carl was propelled backwards by the force of the blow, doubling over with a hand to his stomach.

'What the fuck? I didn't say nothing...' he wheezed, incapable of any physical comeback even had he dared. Mick glanced at me with no great affection but it was Carl he spoke to once more.

'I thought you did. My mistake.' This time he did leave.

'What the fuck was that for? If Omie said anything he's getting another one.' While Carl's reaction was understandable in his humiliation and pain, neither of us really thought Omie had anything to do with the second assault. That was pure Mick. 'It fucking *hurts*,' Carl gasped. It was not until that evening at home he would begin to cough up blood.

'I don't care what you say, or how much you try to get around your dad, I'm staying and there'll be no booze.'

The party was becoming a nightmare even before it started. Apart from insisting that she would not abandon the house to a group of teenagers – a decision of which Dad approved, though he would be going to Grandad Will's to watch *Match of the Day* and probably stay the night – Mum was even asking me what sort of food and drink had been served at other parties. She flatly contradicted me when, disclaiming all interest in the food, I said there had been crates of Manns Brown. Seems she'd had a word with Val Anderson's mum.

Invitations were another thorny issue. I didn't have any qualms about not inviting Jake, Kev or other village mates. The school world was a separate one. We obviously didn't have a marquee, or a marquee's worth of space, but neither was I as much a part of the social whirl as Tina or Val. And now there was the prospect of bad blood if Mick and Carl both came.

There was no problem between Mick and Omie. The raincoat thief accepted his punishment as just. I saw Mick have a friendly word with him at school the next day as if nothing had happened. The situation with Carl threatened to become more complicated. He had a couple of fractured ribs, and his mother wanted to know who to blame, we heard from Tony Wilson in the year below, who lived in his village. 'Carl said he fell over. His old man said, "What, fell over on to some cunt's fist?" But he wasn't going to grass anyone up.

Did you see that punch though? They say Mark and Geordie, Carl's brothers, they say they know and they reckon Mick's got a hiding coming to him.'

'Good luck to 'em,' I said. 'Mick's got brothers of his own. Not that I've ever seen him need 'em yet.'

Carl ended up having a week off school before coming back tightly corseted, somewhat morose not only because it was an agony for him to laugh. He wasn't even allowed to play football. He needed some persuasion to come to my party the following weekend, the fact that Mick was also invited finally tipping the scales. 'That arsehole needn't think I'm scared of him, it was a sucker punch, you saw it, no warning or fuck all.'

'Lezzer Carrick's been asking after you.' (She hadn't.) 'You can get her to tickle your ribs better.'

'She can kiss my cock better.' He cheered up a bit.

I know that didn't happen at my party. No more than spoken word of oral sex had reached our part of the young teen population of Washtown and environs. We would all have known if anything beyond snogging was going on, with up to twenty people crammed into our living room and kitchen. Upstairs was out of bounds except for the toilet, in theory reserved for the girls while the boys used the one in the passageway beside the coalhouse. In the back room, Mum amused herself somehow, when she wasn't popping through to the kitchen to check there were still enough sandwiches, sausage rolls and trifle to feed fifty or more.

There were more girls than boys, partly because there was more obligation from invitations already accepted or expected to their own parties, but also since I was keen for them to see me with Tina as mine. Jason was invited anyway which meant Vicky Cooper, while Pat Wilson and VD were an acceptable level of collateral damage to encourage the presence of Cathy Strain (who could not hide her surprise when I asked her, since it was almost the first time we'd spoken). Caroline Peacock came as a package with Mick.

I was surprised to find my first arrival Sarah Wallingham, dropped off by her mother, who turned out to know mine. They even had a cup of tea together in the kitchen, leaving Sarah and me somewhat awkwardly alone in the living room. I had my eight-track tape playing at lowish volume as yet, though later the music would have been too loud for Mum to watch telly next door if Dad could have been arsed to move it out of the living room for her.

'So you and Tina are an item now, I hear.'

The phrase was new to me, but I agreed we probably were. There was something about Sarah that made you unable to think of anything but her, or more specifically her in a sexual context, whenever she turned full beam on you.

'You like little girls then?'

'She's in our year. You like old men do you, like Gloss?'

'Who? Oh yeah, that's your silly nickname for my Matt, isn't it? I must tell him, he'll be coming to take me away from all this' – maybe Sarah did have a vestigial sense of humour, unlike most girls – 'as soon as Joan buggers off. I'm only messing with you, do you fancy a smooch? Get off, you dickhead, I was joking. You stay with Tina for now, look after her well and if I hear good enough reports we may talk about promotion for you one day.'

I knew she wasn't talking about football. Otherwise I was floundering. Jambo's arrival, with Sue Tierney, Maureen Wheatley and the two Janes, saved me saying something lame like you weren't a grown-up because you called your mum by her Christian name. I was glad my mate hadn't come in a few seconds earlier, when I'd been literally wrong-footed by Sarah's apparent invitation to dance.

Jambo was in charge of music, a choice between my tapes – I'd made an effort to record the whole of that week's Top of the Pops but couldn't be sure I hadn't also picked up my old man's sarky comments throughout – and any the others might bring. There was also Mum and Dad's cabinet gramophone for records, singles or albums (I'd checked Mum had kept her promise to move elsewhere her Mantovani and Dad's oompah shit).

I persuaded Agnes (slightly surprised, no doubt, when I addressed her thus) to move herself also to the back room as the other kids began to arrive: Pukemore elaborately having Val precede him into the kitchen; a welcome kiss of greeting from Cathy Strain; awkward hugs with her acolytes Pat and VD; disappointment from Carl that there was no beer ('thought I'd have a swift one 'fore I went for Lesley, we'll be back later from the Oak then'); and Gloss Taylor.

'All right? Sarah's in here waiting if you…'

'No, he won't want to come in. You nearly lost me to this charmer, Matt.' She linked her hands through my arm and nuzzled up to my face, planting a brief kiss on my cheek. 'I may be back later, enjoy your party and remember what I told you about playing with little girls. Your secret's safe with me.'

With a minimal nod from Taylor they were off, crossing on the garden path (shared with two neighbours) Tina, Roarer and Omie – so that was why the sly git hadn't come down earlier in the day as invited. There was some hugging and interplay between Tina and Sarah before she let them come through. Taylor had also closed in to embrace Tina (but not Angela), so evidently she was not such a child as to be beneath his notice.

'You could have gone off with them in his car if you'd rather, you know,' was my less-than-friendly greeting. She had clunked me on the back of the head with a solid gift-wrapped package, so keen was she to get her arms around my neck and kiss me happy birthday. She couldn't find anything to say to that. I felt a bit sorry at the look I'd brought into her eyes, but eased her aside to greet Angela – I could be a gentleman, even if that ponce Taylor couldn't – and josh Omie about his new travelling companions. On balance Mick had done him a favour. Other girls as well as Angie had viewed him as the innocent victim of bullying and therefore a source of some interest, while none of the lads felt he had behaved badly. Unlike Carl, he had not even been particularly hurt, because Mick had pulled his punch (so we all said, though none of us would have wished to be on the end of it).

In the event, Mick and Caroline did not grace us with their presence. My rudeness to Tina led to an awkward period of reproachful glances and keeping our distance, which would have allowed me time to mingle and attend to other guests, if I had had the slightest idea of what being a host meant. There had never been a party in our house.

'I'm sure I saw him kissing a girl, but he didn't think to introduce me,' Mum told Dad over Sunday dinner. She had indeed come bustling through at one point when I was snogging Tina, half across her on one corner of the settee (seating space was at a premium), causing me smartly to draw back. I was still stuck a tiny bit in Well Creek Primary, fearing ridicule for having anything to do with girls, yet none was forthcoming even from Dad now, as usual face into his roast. My schoolmates seemed to accept Tina and me as a couple – we had been together most of the evening after the first half hour, hardly speaking but building on that first kiss at her party once we had reached the second at mine.

It probably helped that the other lads were busy playing themselves, rather than looking on from the stands. Jambo still seemed uncertain which of the hockettes to go in hardest on, or was perhaps unable to cut one loose to bring down. Whenever I came up for air, I would see Omie getting what I insisted was a sympathy snog from Angie. Carl seemed to have struck out yet again with Lesley Carrick. We never found out if she had gone with him to the Oak or kept him waiting an hour at her house. Whichever, after arriving together at mine they hardly spoke to each other for the rest of the evening. On the other hand, he did seem to make some progress with Cathy Strain, who as the fittest unpaired girl at the party perhaps felt she needed to have a male dancing attendance on her.

Omie had stayed the night and was able to provide Mum the reassurance she sought that her catering had been exemplary. We never had desserts, but today there was trifle in abundance. Dad was probably relieved not to have to take Omie back to town, his offer to do so vetoed by Mum because of his pre-lunch visit to the Swan. We left him asleep on the settee after *Match of the Week* for Omie to catch the last of the sporadic Sunday buses back to town.

Neither of us had spoken much about the party. I didn't want to embarrass Omie in case he was ashamed at having copped off with Roarer, or appear to brag on myself with Tina. Standing against the cold in the wooden bus shelter, itself the scene of various village courtships and even occasional consummations, he had a sharp enough reply to my innocent enquiry: 'What's it like snogging Roarer then? Does her 'tache tickle?'

'At least she's got hairs.'

We were both innocent of any intimate knowledge of the female body. My look at Gloria's stupendous bush had grown stale in the telling, and that hardly amounted to a close examination. Since first year at Grammar we had been used to passing through communal showers as a group, stark naked, except for one or two boys with mysterious exemptions. There was never any horseplay or mockery of other boys' genitals – a teacher always lurked outside to count us all in and count us all out – but you could not fail to notice some lads had much denser pubic hair than others. Generally they were from the darker-haired of our entirely white Anglo-Saxon population, though at some point Marcus 'Ginger Nut' Williamson became 'Ginger Nuts'.

Tina's blondeness and lack of breasts, plus Sarah's then Omie's comments, had put a doubt in my mind about her body's physical maturity. It was more than an academic question, a matter of honour as well as desire to progress as far and as fast as possible to the next step beyond snogging, or rather the next-but-one as the worn joke had it. ('Gloss was in the pictures with Sarah Wallingham and stuck his hand right up her skirt. She slapped his face. "Tits first," she said.')

Parties were all very well, but you tended to be in a group of other kids with areas of potential privacy likely to be cordoned off or patrolled by adults who were all too clued up on teen sex. Living out of town as I did, it wasn't even possible for us casually to drop by each other's houses or go walking outside them. Besides that, it was November. Jake had complained to me that the dykes were no longer so congenial a courting ground for him and Helen. Anxious to provide her with a little more luxury, a failure to pay enough attention to his dad's shift patterns did for him.

'It was the first time I'd ever had her stripped right naked, mate, in our living room, and I thought I'd take her up to my bedroom. There was her little arse bobbing up the stairs in front of me, right at the top the old man comes out of the bog scratching his bollocks, in the scod hisself. How was I to know the fat fucker was there getting his head down for a couple of hours?'

In principle we tended to avoid out-of-hours school activities. What could be more fun than sitting around Omie's on a Friday night, playing cards? Sitting in the Royal Standard three streets away playing cards, it transpired. Still, we thought we might give TNT's 'youth club' a try.

Richard Thwaite was in his probationary year of practical experience, he made the mistake of telling us the first time he took us for English. He put his surname up in block capitals on the board, before laboriously sponging out three letters: 'So that's "THWAITE", not "TWIT" please.' His icebreaker was surely straight from teacher training college, perhaps illustrated there by a more tractable name than his own. By his second class he was universally known as TNT ('twat not twit', as we would wearily have to explain to the girls).

A legend quickly bloomed that Old Ma Granger, Head of English as well as Deputy Head, was determined that TNT would not survive his teaching practice, or at least not well enough to achieve tenure. At the same time, he was crazily lusting after Jackie King. It was thus with Old Ma Granger's cynical blessing that he was allowed the folly of a Friday night 'youth club' (TNT was the only one to use the phrase unironically), with Jackie needed to ensure nothing untoward occurred in areas out of bounds to him such as the girls' toilets. It would be an area free of the Clarkson Secondary Modern town kids who frequented the genuine youth club in Oliver Street, by the picture house, though the Ollie held little fear for most of us. There may even have been something faintly Christian behind TNT's initiative.

At the counter from which our dinners were ladled out, a selection of confectionery and soft drinks was available, while the hall which doubled for assembly and meals was the main area for the non-sporting elements. Some sixth-form loser or predator was prepared to spend his Fridays supplying the music. Basketball was the main activity in the gym, at which the hockettes were predictably engaged with a smattering of boys, just as predictably including Jambo. He was as crap at that as at other sports, but of course could easily hold his own with the women.

TNT doing his rounds found Omie, Carl and me playing sergeant-major on one of the two ping-pong tables in an upstairs room with a view down to the gym. 'Want to play, sir?' Carl gave a friendly invitation. 'Do you like the cards?'

As well as supposedly being desperate to get into Jackie King's knickers, TNT was also widely scouted as being gay (we did not use that word). He did not rise to the fact that we were playing with a deck of nudes, or at least topless women, their hairstyles suggesting the poses had been struck a decade or two before. 'I bet they belong to Mr Roden,' he said, possibly fancying me an ally because he knew I was at the top of the class in English.

'No, sir, we found them in the corridor outside the staff room.'

'Maybe I'd better confiscate them then, or rather seek to return them to their rightful owner.'

'They're good for strip poker, sir. We always play three of hearts wild, cos she looks super wild.'

'I'm sure she does, Walters.' The use of surnames unadorned or with an arch 'Mr' was another sign of how out-of-step TNT was. Even Monkie had grudgingly learned a few Christian names over the course of the term. 'Don't let me hear any complaints from the girls or else I'll have to take them away.'

'Like to see him try, the tosser,' Carl muttered once TNT had moved on. The cards belonged to an elder Walters, perhaps father rather than brother from their vintage. Like the routine homophobia – and racism too, had there been anyone on whom to exercise it – they belonged to a more innocent, pre-internet age. We were practically porn-starved.

Generally sex-starved too. When eventually we came to the real point of the evening, and I was outside against the gym wall with Tina, she responded enthusiastically to my kisses, at least initially. 'Ow, you're crushing me!' As indeed I was, drawing back briefly to free my hands from between the wall and her back. I had no idea how to undo a bra, even if she would have let me, even if she would have been wearing one.

'I'm sorry but you must know what I want to do to you.'

'Of course I do, silly.' She cupped my face and gave me a quick kiss on the lips, before drawing back to look me square in the eyes. I felt like a dog being muzzled, and I wasn't so far wrong. That serious look, that earnest tone, how well I would come to know them over the years. Now it was all new.

'Ray, I like you an awful lot, you must know that. I want to be with you, and I think we could have something really special, even… well I won't say the word, it's too early yet.'

'What word? Sex?'

'No, don't be naughty.' She gave me a flat-palmed push against my Levi breast pocket. 'I already l-u-v you, but l-o-v-e… well, let's wait and see.'

'I thought you couldn't spell was all.' I was growing uneasy.

'We can have a lot of fun together, and I do mean physically too, but I have to tell you I made a promise to my father not to… er, not to go all the way till I'm eighteen,' she finished in a rush, burying her head between my shoulder and neck and pulling me at the same time towards her. 'I hope you can understand.'

'Understand? I should fucking coco. Three fucking years?' the vigilant Mrs King's arrival stopped me saying out loud. Shepherded back inside by her, all I had to show for the evening was a watch face severely scuffed from the gym wall. I would keep that watch in a bedside drawer years after it died.

Chapter Six

Puerto Rico was not in the most heavily trafficked windstorm path but had been hit on a number of occasions in the past, most seriously during the twentieth century by Hurricanes Hugo and Georges. Sovereign had generally come out of major and minor events ahead of many of its competitors for its prompt and efficient settlement of claims. Jaime's performance during earlier crises was noted and had given him a significant career boost. Ray found it difficult to imagine Martin doing the same favour for him, even without yet knowing the extent of the damage in Tortola.

The previous year had proved hurricane-free as far as Jaime's and Ray's portfolios were concerned, though they had suffered turbulence enough from the takeover of Sovereign by SRG. In what might be its last year of operation under that name, Sovereign had its usual table for eight at the ACODESE black-tie ball on 15 December in the Normandie Hotel, presided over by Jaime and his wife Gloria; Nelson and Miriam Cano always attended, while Underwriting Director Hugo Ramos fought it out with Finance Director Pedro Hernandez over the fourth pairing. This year Hugo had lost and was there with his wife Soraya.

There was the usual chuntering beforehand from Jan. 'They're so *glamorous*, Puerto Rican women. I get dressed up once a year, always feel out of place.'

'You've got nothing to worry about, darling.' Ray put a hefty rum and coke down beside her at the bathroom mirror. 'I don't care how glamorous you think they look, I've never been anywhere you're not the most beautiful woman present, and that's not going to change tonight.' He nuzzled up to kiss her bared neck. She shooed him away but he could see she was pleased. He was not lying either.

It was not only in deference to Jan they spoke mainly English at the dinner table. Gloria and Soraya were Nuyoricans, born and raised in the Bronx, more comfortable in their American-English than Spanish. Miriam would not speak at length in anything but Spanish, having grown up in the small inland town of Aibonito. 'My little *jibara*, my hillbilly girl.' So Nelson would often introduce his pretty young wife, in a way she did not seem entirely to relish.

Ray was properly mindful of Nelson's tip off. Over dinner the women were seated alternately with their husbands, leaving no chance of intimate chats or damaging gossip. Any danger would likely come after the coffee, the tables largely abandoned for the dance floor but occupied willy-nilly in any break. Ray had no intention of dancing so planned to keep an eye on things.

While all the men at the ball were with a woman, naturally enough they were not all married couples as they were at the Sovereign table. Those present as principals were generally at a senior level within their firms – the cost of tickets saw to that, tax deductible or not. Carolina Perez, a junior underwriter at Sovereign greeted warmly by all its executives present, was seated with a coming young man of Martinez y Asociados in her capacity as a stunning redhead.

Emilia was not with the Martinez gang. Ray noticed her presence partly because he was always on the alert for breasts and legs, of which she had two of each largely uncovered, and partly because she was with one of the market's more flamboyant characters, Gerardo Borja.

As an inveterate drunkard if not an alcoholic – no one cast stones on that subject in the San Juan insurance fraternity – it was fitting enough that Gerardo derived a comfortable living from the island's Don Pepe rum distillery. Its insurance programme was his main source of income, even on a co-brokerage basis with the Martinez boys. He left them to do all the admin work, while the fact that the long-term CEO and leading shareholder of the brokerage was in an equally long-term marriage with Gerardo's sister meant he had no fear of them taking the account off him completely.

Perhaps Gerardo had dealings with Emilia in that or some other account, perhaps he was revisiting an old relationship from between or during one of his several marriages to date, or perhaps he had met her in a bar that afternoon and invited her to come along with him. Ray had not seen them at dinner, and some people did arrive after the meal. Gerardo was the only man in an open-necked shirt, under a plaid sports jacket.

Emilia acknowledged Ray with a smile and a friendly wave, so maybe she had no mischief in mind. She could hardly complain of a lack of eyes on her from both men and women in the Peacock ballroom, whether drawn by her own outfit or Gerardo's energetic and eccentric dance moves.

The first trouble came from nearer at hand. Gloria had been a big help to Jan in settling into San Juan, where her daughter Sandra had also been an early friend to Kim. Tonight, Ray thought only later he might have noticed her a little quieter, drinking a little more intently over dinner. He was surprised when she seemed at first reluctant to take Jaime's hand for a dance the moment the band struck up its first merengue. Although he did not socialise much nowadays, Hugo had apparently in another life been a prize-winning ballroom dancer and was not averse to showing off his prowess. While Nelson checked in on Miriam from time to time at the table as well as dancing with her, he was also part of an all-male community at the bar.

'All hands on deck guys, who knew Javier Mantillo had a thing going with our *colorada* Carolina?' Jaime's tone was accusatory.

'He's been around the office a lot lately, but I thought he was more in love with our new business package product.'

'It's her personal package he's after. You wouldn't know, Ray, but Gloria's got a crazy jealousy about me and Carolina going way back.'

'What, did you...?' Ray trailed off, knowing better than to complete a question which would most likely not be answered, and did not need to be.

'That's all history. Thing is, Glo's on the scent of something else going on right now. She's trying to pick a fight with me even though deep down she doesn't want to know.'

'So what do you want us to do, boss?' asked the ever-attentive Nelson.

Jaime looked bleakly over at their table. 'Oh Christ, now Soraya's gone back to join them. She'll have a whole year's gossip to catch up on, and Gloria always drinks at twice her normal pace when she's around. I don't know. I suppose Jan is a bit out of all this anyhow, but Nelson if you can put in a word with Miriam, and talk to Hugo too. Maybe he can do his fucking Patrick Swayze bit to keep all the women happy and apart from each other.'

It worked for a while. 'I could fancy that man.' Jan laughed as she returned breathless to the table. 'You have to get out there with me next, Roden, I won't have people saying I only dance with other men, not my own husband.'

'All right, let me know when. I can't tell when one number ends and the next one begins. You enjoying yourself? Is Gloria all right? I thought she looked a bit...'

'Yeah, I'd forgotten how great it is to dance with a man who not only knows what he's doing but seems to enjoy it. I think Gloria will be OK. Is Jaime playing away? I wouldn't trust any of you further than I can throw you, I told her that. The other girls agreed.'

'I bet you did,' he said sourly, yet relieved not to detect any real suspicion in her tone, no more than the usual bad-mouthing of him and all his kind. It was unfortunate that Gerardo and Emilia should choose precisely that moment to swing by their table. Jan knew the broker from the regular Sunday parties at his beach house in Cerromar, where they would sometimes drop in with the kids on returning from the club. Gerardo kissed her hand with his usual overblown bullshit courtesy the women lapped up, not letting it go till she agreed to take a turn with him. That left Ray sitting at the table with his head on a level with Emilia's breasts, her dress split to the thigh on both sides showing off her legs as she moved lazily to the music. She stood very close to him, without speaking. Equally she showed no inclination to talk to Miriam, who had thrown her a rapid, almost fearful, look over her shoulder before returning to the fringes of a heart-to-heart between Soraya and Gloria.

'Thought you'd never ask, baby,' Emilia leaned closer to whisper once he'd decided it would look more natural to have a dance with her than continue sitting with his head in her tits.

'I thought you were well busy. I see you didn't let the grass grow under your feet. Or is that too much of an English saying for you?'

'Gerardo and I are old pals. You know why I like him? Because he doesn't give a shit, he goes after what he wants. And I know you want me. Want to go outside for a smoke? I've been told I'm smokin' tonight.'

'Emi, Gerardo may go after what he wants, look where it gets him. Any number of broken marriages, kids all over the place, and here making a fool of himself with a woman, what, twenty years younger than him?'

'I thought your wife was nearer his age than that. You know, that's exactly what you sound like, a wife. Gerardo's probably the happiest man here tonight.'

'Are you sleeping with him already?'

'Jealous now, baby?'

'No, I want to give the old guy a warning. He may be the happiest man here tonight, thinking about getting into your panties – if you're wearing any – but boy is there a hefty tab to pay after.'

132

'You saying I'm a *puta* now? Work out how much every fuck you get with your precious wife cost you. I could take you away from her as easy as I'm going to take Gerardo now, you see if I can't.'

Before he could retort she was shimmying away from him. She said something to Jan as she eased between her and Gerardo, in a way that seemed natural enough, leaving Ray to face up to his wife.

'What did she say to you?' he asked, perhaps too sharply.

'I couldn't hear, something snide probably for all that fake smile on her mug. What did she say to you, more to the point? You know, when she had her tongue in your earwax for the last five minutes?'

'I couldn't very well leave her standing there while you waltzed off with Don Sweet Pi-Pi, could I?' He barely stopped himself from raising a hand to check the inside of his ear. 'You know you can't hear anything unless you get as close as we are now, see.' She snapped her head away from his as if he had been trying to insert his penis under her dress on the crowded dance floor, rather than a cheeky tongue into her ear purely to illustrate his point.

'You're drunk, Ray. Why am I not surprised?'

Why not indeed? They had all been drinking steadily for several hours, and Ray was not as used to wine and spirits as his Puerto Rican buddies. Even Hugo was knocking them back, but at least he was sweating a good deal out on the floor. 'I've gotta hand it to you, mate, where'd you learn to dance like that?' Ray was seeing a new side to the man, far removed from his ISO rating manuals.

'Growing up with lots of sisters, bro, I used to charge to show 'em how. Used to show 'em what moves to watch out for from the men, too.' He laughed.

'Why don't you get Gloria on her feet, she looks as if she could do with cheering up?'

'You kidding me? The boss's wife? With annual reviews coming up, I'm not risking my bonus.'

'Why would you be? Looks like he might thank you.'

'He might at the minute, but then when he thinks about it after he might not. He's a crazy jealous motherfucker you know. Then there's Soraya.' He sighed heavily in mentioning his own wife. 'If he don't hang me out to dry, you can bet she would. Don't get me wrong, she's not insane, she don't mind me dancing with your wife, but when it comes to her own close friends, *tu sabes*. I mean not that your...'

'Don't worry mate, I get the picture.' Ray patted the underwriter on the back, feeling his white dress shirt clammy with sweat.

The band, led by a big name on the Puerto Rican scene Ray had heard referred to as Gilbertito, was on a break before the last set of the evening. The Sovereign male contingent was standing at the bar with Gerardo, the drink he was fetching for Emilia forgotten on the counter as she stood alone across the room. Ray was going boss-eyed trying to keep track of her without losing sight for more than a moment of his wife. Didn't either of them have any friends here he could rely on to engage them in neutral?

Gerardo was the only relaxed one of their small group. Hugo and Nelson were both nervous as their boss grew increasingly morose. Jaime was best left to himself at such times. His wife was the centre of attention at their table. Head bowed, she had Soraya's hand apparently massaging the back of her neck as the fellow New Yorker spoke earnestly to her. Miriam and Jan were on her other side, both also leaning in close.

'Holy shit Hugo, can't you go in and break up that clusterfuck? If you won't dance with your own wife, go take her out for a stroll in the moonlight or something.'

Jaime's outburst checked even Gerardo's flow. Hugo was already heading to the table when Soraya moved away from it towards the bathrooms, arm around Gloria's heaving shoulders. At the same time Emilia approached the bar.

'Uh oh, looks like you're in trouble, Gerry.' Nelson tried to lighten the mood. 'You shouldn't be neglecting a girl like that.'

'Neglect? I'll be nuts deep in her before the night's out. Happy days.'

Nelson shot a look at Ray, who was furious with jealousy at this comment. Gerardo had surely trodden on a few men's toes over the years without letting it bother him unduly – he was a big fellow – but there did not appear to be any crowing here. His remark had been addressed to Nelson without so much as a glance at Ray.

Emilia came up between Ray and Gerardo, linking an arm with each. Ray thought of a boxing ref about to ask for a good clean fight. 'Who's a girl got to bang to get a Cuba libre around here?'

Gerardo was reaching for her drink when Jan invaded the ring on Ray's left side, so that he was between her and Emilia, whose hand fell swiftly away from his upper arm.

'Right. I'm leaving now. You please yourself.'

'Why? What's the matter, love? If you're thinking of taking Gloria home…'

That was when Emilia made her mistake. 'Surely you're not going to take this lovely man away from us already, Mrs Roden? It's still early yet.'

Jan elbowed Ray aside. She stood shorter than Emilia, who had the advantage of higher heels. 'I don't care if he comes or not. How about you have a drink on me? Oops, I mean on you,' as she watched her full-on splash of rum and coke trickle down Emilia's face. Gerardo had caught a share too, but luckily the ice cubes had not hurt anyone.

'Ooowwww, *perra*!' Emilia gasped. Gerardo had her right arm, as Ray stood too stunned to intervene. Jan looked more than ready to go in both senses, and spoke again only when it was clear Emilia was not going to fight back physically. While fully appreciating the gravity of the situation, a tiny but insistent part of Ray's mind pictured him licking up the drops of Cuba libre already trickling down her boobs.

'I ever see you near my husband again I won't just spoil your slutty dress. I'll knock your fucking teeth down your throat.' She turned and marched away.

Gerardo wiped his wet forearm across his mouth. 'Definitely Bacardi. You should get her onto Don Pepe, Ray, it's a lot smoother.'

'They get better every year,' Eduardo Hurtado said as he showed them the photos in Jaime's office.

'More like you're a bigger *corrupto* every year, Eddie, that's what it is.' Nelson laughed as he took in almost the full expanse of Glorimar Salcedo's bosom, snapped as she bent to talk to a friend at Sovereign's staff Christmas party. In a briefly tense conversation there, Nelson had vehemently denied that his Miriam had spilled any beans to Jan about Ray's relationship with Emilia. 'She felt bad being left there on her own after you followed Jan out, and then it turned out Soraya had taken Gloria home. Man, I suffered for Hugo when he had to break that to Jaime.'

'What did he say?'

'He said Hugo would have to get a taxi then cos he wasn't giving him a ride. Miriam swears she didn't say nothing but she was upset too, didn't stop crying till I told her at least she got to take the table decoration.'

'Good for you. I doubt if a big bunch of flowers would have helped me out much.'

Ray was now in a double bind. He could not recall what he had said on their white-knuckle ride home from the Normandie, throwing himself into the car before Jan screeched off in it. Had he assumed she knew everything, spilling his guts, it wouldn't happen again, a moment of weakness? All to no purpose if her jealous tantrum had been generalised rather than based on specific information. By the next morning he was already concrete-set in the wrong and unwilling to ask his wife for an action replay of the fight.

The Sovereign party in the Zipperle restaurant, at which he and Emilia had first sparked the year before, was the last do he attended before their home leave. He left early in case she had the brass neck to turn up along with other invited brokers (though there was no warm welcome at home). He was now seeing what he had missed, another Christmas tradition.

Eduardo was an agent of the company who also ran a photography shop, everything from first communions to weddings. He was happy enough to run off a collection of shots at the Sovereign party which would appear as a montage at the New Year's Eve closing drinks on the office premises. If staff wanted to buy prints of themselves in full party mood and finery, they were available for purchase at mates' rates. What were not on general display were the snaps he was now showing to Jaime, Nelson and Ray, the ones of female staff caught unawares by his prowling lens.

'Wow, purple panties if you can call 'em that much. You can nearly see her moustache.'

It was good that Jaime had cheered up a bit, particularly at an unexpected bonus in this year's collection. 'Wait until you see the Sharon Stoner I got, the new girl, Alicia is it? I don't know what the parties were like where she worked before but she came to this one ready for action. You could definitely see her 'tache if she weren't clean-shaven, *la cabrona*.'

The temperature in the Roden marriage was still well below zero by the time they flew to England for their Christmas leave. He had managed to carry Christmas and Boxing Day in Feltwell, or rather not see their established plans cancelled, sandwiched between visits to Jan's mother and sister. Let her bitch to them if it would help, was his view.

He liked to think he had a good relationship with Jan's mum Grace, already separated from her dad Eric when they first met. He'd seemed all right, rest in peace, though Jan never had a good word for him, no doubt loyally following her mum in their estrangement. Ray had seen other men with Grace before she settled to a comfortable berth in Blackheath. Her not-so-new old man, David, was something not insurance in the City.

Ray spent a day trailing round the Kensington Museum Parade, largely abandoned by the two women to the mercies of his children. He only managed a couple of swift bottled beers in the Deep Blue Diner at the Science, which he secretly agreed with Den was way boring, Kim's enthusiasm to the contrary. He understood he had to do penance, and was on the alert for a chill in the mother-in-law's attitude that evening, sitting round their big fake farmhouse table pretending to like lasagne. He detected no change, taking limited comfort from that. One reason he was not forced to spend more time with Jan's side of the family was that she and her mother had a limited tolerance for each other. Jan was much more likely to confide in Lucy, who was a sweetheart and would surely not give him a hard time.

He had body-swerved a formal visit and schedule of meetings at the International Division's offices in Cornhill, to Ken Thompson's evident displeasure when he had caught him by phone virtually on the way to the airport in San Juan. 'All right, go ahead and hang yourself if you want, but you're coming in to see me, and you can buy me a pint as well. Fix it up with Hilda.'

Apparently immune to any kind of masculine attentions, Ken's long-term secretary had grown to tolerate Ray, though it had taken him eighteen months to graduate to calling her Hilda from 'Miss Carrington' (she was furious if anyone thought to address her as 'Ms'). She had ignored his attempt to sound out Ken's mood when arranging the meeting over the phone. When he came to see her at the beginning of Christmas week, however, she seemed almost flustered.

'I'm sorry, Ray' – it would normally take her a couple of 'Mr Rodens' before loosening up to that extent – 'I had no means of contacting you. I hope you haven't come far. Mr Thompson is not in today. Please accept his apologies. At his request I have arranged for Mr Mackieson to see you.'

'No harm done, I'm in London at the moment. For a day or two,' he added so she would not try to reschedule. 'I hope he recovers soon,' he shot in the dark. He had never known Ken to be ill, but Hilda's pursed lips suggested he might have hit the mark.

Alan Mackieson, from the graduate intake a year or two ahead of Ray, was well enough pleased to see him, waiting coated and scarved at the lift when

Ray descended from the rarefied air of the executive floor to the Reinsurance Department.

'Macca, I was going to check if you could bunk off this afternoon once the Big Man was done with me. Where is he, by the way, I've never known him break a meeting before?'

'Lord knows, he's living on a plane nowadays. Poor bloke probably hardly knows what time zone he's in between AsiaPac and the Americas.'

'He's all right though, yeah?' Ray caught Macca by the arm as they left the building to ensure he gave the question due attention.

'Some say he's lost a bit of weight, I don't know, I can't even tell when my missus claims to have dropped a few ounces. Still a moody bugger, though.'

'Ken or Margaret?'

'Good question. The both of them. How's Jan, still putting up with your shit and nonsense?' Macca and Ray's wives had always got on well together on the few occasions they coincided at company functions.

'She's fighting fit, I'll tell you over a bevvy. Have you booked anywhere or can we go to The Cock?'

'I've booked, but The Cock it is.'

Macca ordered them pub grub at the Fleet Street bar along with Ray's first pint and a bottle of wine for himself. 'Before I forget, Eddie was on the blower from San Juan yesterday, asked if you could give him a call this aft.'

'Shit, I wasn't planning to go back to the office. What did he want, do you know? You can't get the staff nowadays.'

'He was a bit cagy – I see you've trained him not to give anything away to head office – but he was wondering how to reflect a big new account in the Virgin Islands. Show the insured limit or the total values at risk? You got something interesting in the pipeline?'

Ray took a good drink before answering. 'In the pipeline, exactly. It's the BVI government business, or what we're trying to persuade them to insure as a package. Early days yet, and I'd eventually have to run it by the Big Man – above my pay grade – but it could be a major boost to income. Young Eddie may have been giving it more thought than I have up to yet, but yeah a first loss cover on locations across the island would probably be it, so that whatever the damage we couldn't lose more than the limit. You'll be the one presenting for the worldwide programme, what do you think?'

'We could probably follow what's decided at regional level. I'd need to see some figures to say more. If you're treating it essentially as one risk, wouldn't you need to get sign off from Reg Cowley nowadays with all the kerfuffle over underwriting licences?'

'Every time I come home I hope they'll have pensioned that old fart off. Surely Ken trumps him if the Big Man wants to do it? You know what Reg is like, by the time we get a submission detailed enough for him to turn down it'll be June.'

'I hear you. I'm only saying.'

'It's time you got your arse overseas, mate. Only risk you have at the minute is getting splinters in it from sitting on the fucking fence all day.'

England never seemed more attractive to Ray than when he pulled their rental off the M11 back into the Fens on each leave visit. By the end of them, he would usually be ready to return to the airport. He remembered when his mum had the two downstairs rooms knocked into one, how massive the space had seemed. Now he felt almost claustrophobic in it, with only the five of them.

Christmas Day passed quietly, between a heavy session in Washtown the day before while the women and kids shopped and the renewed appetite for booze of Boxing Day. The Oak with Den on Christmas morning hardly counted; even Jan did not get indignant and put the kybosh on that. Maybe the gold bracelet he'd given her when all the other gifts had been opened, neatly and festively wrapped for an extra couple of quid by the shop girl, was already working its magic.

Christmas Day opening of pubs was nothing like the novelty it had been in Ray's youth. Landlords had to scrabble nowadays for every penny they could get. Ted had long been called to the Great Snug to play crib against the angels without the distraction of punters wanting a pint. The current landlord greeted Ray with only moderate cordiality. 'You know we close at two today? On the dot.'

'No problem, Jacky. You've got the football on all day tomorrow though?' Since he was now on holiday whenever he came into what he still considered his local, the cockney guvnor had often found him reluctant to call it a night.

'Yeah, that's it. Do you want me to bring 'em through, your mate's in the back room?'

It was an unexpected bonus to see Jake, with two of his own sons playing alternate pool shots against him. 'Finally found some players at your own level then, mate?'

'They'd like to think so, but not yet. Cheers for letting us know you're home.'

'Flying visit this time and she's got me on a choke chain. What brings you to the village anyway, don't you live up town no more?'

'Picking up the Old Dear to have her Christmas pud with us.' He took without hesitation a shot that snookered his younger boy, leaving the two of them to confer on the best way out of it. 'Here you go, mate. You can play our next shot,' he handed his cue to Den before turning back to Ray. 'You at yours, I suppose? You still slumming it in the Caribbean?'

'That's about it. How's your work?'

'Slow.' Jake was in the building trade and as habitually gloomy about the sector as farmers were about theirs. It did not help him that no sooner had he built his dream house than he was having to give it away. The boys with him today, younger than Den to whom he had casually introduced them as Bryan and Eric, must be from his second marriage, to a woman from outside the village Ray had yet to meet. Probably never would now, as Jake was on his third.

The extent to which the two of them would have a full session during Ray's trips home depended on how flush Jake was and the current state of his love life. Such matters would only be discussed after the fourth or fifth pint, beyond either of their remits today.

Ray was heading out the door at five to two, to the closing strains of 'American Trilogy', pausing only to hold it open for a woman incoming. 'You'll have to be quick if you want to get a drink, Jacky's looking to shut up shop.'

'I wasn't sure what time they closed, only coming in to get a bottle of Warninks to take home if I can. Snowball's my one Christmas tipple and my old man can't even set it up for me.' She nodded her head backwards to a car pulled up rather than parked behind her. 'How are you doing, Ray?'

'Oh not too bad… Lesley, sorry I didn't realise it was you for a second. You're looking well.'

They compromised on a half hug, a handshake too formal for one-time classmates and a kiss dangerous ground for Ray at present with any woman (not to mention the bloke he didn't recognise at the wheel of the car). Lesley had indeed worn well, he thought, despite the hippie floor-scraping skirt and chunky pullover. He didn't express his doubts about Jacky having a bottle of Advocaat handy, not a drink he'd ever seen served or requested in the Oak.

140

Their brief chat could surely not have delayed him enough to justify the frosty reception from wife and mother. It was not as if he was going to carve the meat or anything like that. He did not realise until Jan was warding him off in bed that night that she had not been impressed by the school reunion Lesley had mooted for the following year.

'Want me only cos your village girlfriend reminded you of the old days?'

'What? You're batshit crazy, there was never nothing between me and Lesley. Ask Agnes.'

'Agnes always says she couldn't keep track of you and your girls, as if she's proud of you for that. Maybe she'd like to hear about you and your San Juan floozy.'

'I gave Lesley my business card, said I'd be interested if we're in the UK.'

'I bet you did.' She was already talking with her back to him, as much distance between them as the bed allowed. 'Who has a business card in their pocket on Christmas Day, by the way? I'm surprised you didn't fish out a packet of three you took up the Oak with you on the off chance.'

'Come on, she said wives and husbands would be welcome too.' He was not revisiting the condom issue. He had already told her the ones she found in his bag for an island trip must have been from one of their own holidays together – which would account for the packaging being intact, he made sure to add.

Jan ignored that. He knew she would have been shouting if Agnes had not been sleeping next door and Kim in their own room. 'If it wasn't her, I expect it still took your mind straight back to your first love, that little scrubber who hurt you so bad and gave you all your commitment issues. Very handy she was. That's it, keep quiet about her. Good night, Ray.'

And a merry fucking Christmas to you too, he thought. He would keep quiet, but she could not stop him thinking about Tina.

Chapter 7

Love, however you chose to spell it, was abroad in our family as the Christmas holidays approached. Mum had managed easily enough to get Tina's name and serial number out of me. It was no big stretch to talk of the girl I thought about all the time. Mum would give any member of our clan or indeed her bingo friends and village acquaintances the 'Ray's got a girlfriend now' routine, as if there was something to marvel at in the fact. I'm sure if one existed, she would have liked to show around a photo of the two of us together, as documentary evidence.

Supporting evidence of a different kind was less welcome to her. She would bring a cup of tea and poached egg on toast to my bedroom each morning before she went off to work. She would then put my crisps or chocolate into a side blazer pocket as she took it out of the tallboy, hanging it on the outside door ready for me to put on. One morning she pulled something from the outside breast pocket behind the school crest, squeaking, 'What's this?'

Knowing instantly, I kept my head down in bed and face away from her. 'What?'

'This... oh, er nothing.'

It was one of those things every boy at school somehow absorbed without having to be told by any individual. In a side street near the Clarkson memorial was a barber shop with a service window onto the pavement. Whether designed for the purpose or not, it was the place to go to buy johnnies, rubbers, Londons, nodders, dunkies – they were called anything but condoms in those days.

Although we all knew the code of 'something for the weekend, sir?' it was not a question invariably put to fifteen-year-old boys. While few of us would be insouciant enough to ask outright while farmers and assorted buffers sat waiting for their short back and sides, it was more comfortable to make the transaction through a small sliding glass window. Still far from easy, mind, and not without embarrassment or the potential for it.

'Packet of three, please,' I tried to breeze, without quite the confidence to add 'mate'.

I'm sure there was no malice in the barber's bored enquiry, nor particular interest. Radio Two was coming through the window. Inside it was hard to distinguish anything much through the fug of cigarette smoke. 'Which ones?'

I was pleased with my presence of mind, not having expected any such question. 'Medium, please.'

He shook his head briefly before naming three different prices. Again I chose the middle one of the range.

I suppose Mum had also shown a certain presence of mind, overcoming her initial shock almost at once to avoid what I can only think would have been a horrendous conversation for us both. She never raised the topic again. I found out the next weekend she had, unusually, referred it to Dad, who never mentioned it to me either.

'Come on then, I hear you've been banging in a few for the under-fifteens, let's see if you can beat Dan "the Cat" down at the playing field.'

I had been mildly surprised to see him arrive around eleven that Sunday morning. He would normally pull up outside at between ten and five to twelve, if closer to five finding Dad already walking up the path to meet him. While the invitation did not have the appeal, almost the magic it would have only two or three years earlier, I was happy enough to go along with him.

Trying to impress, my first few efforts at beating him were alternately tame or wild; soon though, he had to discard his cigarette and back me up from the penalty spot to outside the area to take my shots. He did not move from the goal line, leaving me to retrieve the ball whether it hit the back of the non-existent net or went wide.

'Not quite ready for the Robins yet.' (He claimed to have starred for our village team about a century ago.) 'Next season I might put in a word for you.' We were walking back through the village, me wondering if it would be too childish to ask him for a can of coke from the post office.

'That's if I'm not in Washtown Reserves, our sports master's talking about putting me and Fid up for trials.'

'Washtown, get you. You're growing up fast, boy. I hear you're even buying rubber johnnies nowadays.'

The sudden change of subject caught me totally by surprise. I couldn't stop myself – who ever can? – from turning bright red, nor come up with any answer.

'Nothing to be ashamed of, mate.' He ruffled my hair in that gesture he knew I hated, then kept his arm loosely draped round my shoulders. I was nearly as tall as him now. 'You've got your dad to thank for calming Agnes down about that, he told her surely better to be sensible than sorry, if you can't be good be careful, all that jazz.'

'Why didn't he talk to me then?'

'Didn't fancy it. It was a hospital pass to me, tell you the truth. What do I know about bringing up kids? I suppose they still think of you as a baby, but I know what a little bugger you are. I'm to find out if you're using them responsibly, your mum said. I said I'm not sure I want to know. Buying them seems more than they could expect from a boy your age. Look, if you want to tell me anything about it, that's fine, and if you want to ask any questions about that sort of thing, feel free. I mean look at my track record with women. I must know everything, right?'

Maybe I could have used some advice, but in Dan my parents chose exactly the wrong person to talk to me. He felt more like my own generation, where you had to find out things as you might, but above all without ever displaying any sign of ignorance, innocence or naivety. He seemed to be expecting some kind of answer, so I gave him a comradely pat on the lower back: 'You're all right. Ta.'

'Any time, you know.' His relief was obvious. 'If you can buy 'em I suppose you can hear a joke about 'em. Why is a rubber like a wife?'

'Go on.'

'Because it spends more time in your wallet than on your prick.'

Dan's own current sex life turned out to be a matter of interest to Mum, which might have accounted for his invitation to stay on for Sunday dinner as much as his commission to talk to me. In the circuitous way of our family, perhaps she had been charged by Nan to investigate. He allowed that he was seeing a woman called Kate – 'Katiuska actually,' he added almost shyly.

Mum was on that like a rat up a drainpipe. 'Katooshka, what's she a foreigner?'

'No, it's Katiuska Berlinovskaya, surely you know the family from Mere's Reach? Only joking sis, don't rack your brains, she's from Hungary originally and I may not have got her surname exactly right.'

'You be careful Dan, she probably only wants to get married so she can stay over here.'

'Who said anything about marriage? Ray knows what I think wives are like, don't you boy?'

I had no wife or indeed wallet to judge if Uncle Dan's joke was based on sound observation. The first condom came out of its wrapping smartly enough, a curious thing slimy and unpleasant to the touch. I did not want to be caught fumble-fisted in front or on top of Tina (ideally, but any other girl would do), so had fetched the packet from its new home in my Subbuteo box to try it for size. Not for the last time, I found you needed a decent boner to get it on properly, one slow in coming in the middle of the day, on rather than in my bed, but eventually putting in a brief appearance as I had the only posh wank – involuntary – of my life.

Tina proved frustratingly as good as her word in that her virginity was not up for grabs, but equally so in that we did have a lot of fun together, and she did mean physically too. I was entranced, randy as a puppy dog and just as timid at first.

With Christmas coming up, teachers relaxed a bit their regular pattern of lessons. So it was we came to hear 'La Marseillaise', when old Toulouse lugged in an antiquated tape recorder, translating the Frog anthem's words for us then giving us a chance to sing along, as he did rather stirringly himself.

Hoss Jenkins was even more ambitious in adding visuals, with a science film. It wasn't about reproduction – we realised by now we'd have to work that out for ourselves – but to be fair he was standing in for his physics colleague Now Then, who'd bunked off early for his Christmas break. Hoss shifted us from lab to lecture room, green banquette seating rather than wooden chairs, and Tina rather than Omie sitting beside me. She made sure of that. We were a row ahead and slightly to the left of the teacher as he grappled with the projector and its big spool of tape.

No sooner had he ordered Colin Bale to turn down the lights – 'Not yet boy, blast your eyes, wait a minute, right, that's it. Now. NOW.' – than Tina grabbed my hand. What was it about girls and holding hands?

Was it photosynthesis, osmosis or some other deeply uninteresting process we were observing in these pictures about the life of plants, some of the girls oohing and aahing at speeded-up shots of flowers opening up or rotting away? Thank God the moving images weren't slowed down. It was already like watching paint dry, nearly as bad as a normal science lesson. Perhaps Tina was bored too, because she suddenly placed my hand between her knees, clamping them tightly shut on it.

Maybe she's cold and wants me to warm her legs on my hand, was my first idiotic thought. And they *were* cold, still bare in December, compared to the hand I'd been holding.

Once she was sure I wasn't going to remove my hand, she grew quickly impatient that I wasn't moving it either. As if settling herself more comfortably in her seat, she pulled it up closer to her immodest hemline, at the same time relaxing her legs' grip on it. Perhaps her movement was not as natural as she'd hoped, or perhaps he caught my startled eyes, since Hoss rather rudely half rose from his seat to peer down at us. I guess he couldn't see exactly what was going on over Tina's shoulder, for as we froze again he eventually subsided.

Not for long though. I may have been slow, but I had at last grasped what Tina wanted me to do. The insides of her legs felt so soft, not cold at all now. I inched my hand gradually up between them. Roarer, to her right, shot us one glance then looked away in embarrassment or complicity, sharply enough to attract further attention very likely. Stevie Thomas to my left was sound asleep.

'Roden, concen— Oh Christ.' There was an almighty crash as Hoss, standing up fully, knocked the projector off its perch and into the solid head of Alison Bright, sitting beside Roarer and until then enjoying the film. The room was suddenly full dark. A moment earlier Tina had sunk down a bit further in her seat, with a little moan that nearly made me come in my pants. At least I was spared that embarrassment as Hoss hollered for Bale to put the bloody lights on boy. When he did, Tina and I were sitting demurely side by side, not even holding hands.

Between making sure that the school's audio-visual equipment was undamaged and checking that Alison didn't need to go to sickbay – 'So sorry my dear, unforgivably clumsy of me' – Hoss didn't immediately pursue whatever he'd been about to say to me. Without attempting to restart the film he limped to the end of the period with the help of some of the science nerds prepared to engage in a stilted question and answer session. He had moved to the front of the class and for a second I thought it was all going to start again. This time though, without looking at me, Tina gave my hand only a quick squeeze.

As we trooped out for lunch at the end of class, Carl anxious to know if I'd got my fingers wet, and was that what set Hoss off, the teacher asked me to stay behind for a moment.

'What did he say, how much did he see?' Tina grabbed me straight after lunch. As we walked away from the main block, I firmly detached my hand from hers, spotting an opportunity. 'Look at the trouble that's got us into, we ought to cool it a bit.'

'Us? He didn't ask me to stay behind. Come on, what did he say, tell me.'

'Said he was all for boys and girls getting on, then mentioned a big "but".' I grabbed at her arse and it was her turn to disengage promptly.

'Now I know you're lying cos my butt isn't big, not like Cathy Strain's. I suppose you prefer hers, do you?'

'Well, now you mention it... no, I'm only joking you, I love every little thing about you. As far as I could make out from the forty-year-old virgin, he's got his eye on us all right but he wouldn't come out and say we'd done anything wrong.'

'And we didn't, did we?' She took my upper arm between her hands and pulled me towards her to have a nibble on my ear. 'It was lovely, Ray, wasn't it?'

'It was, and there's so much more...'

'Don't start that again, you're not going to get me into trouble.'

While she did not exactly get into trouble over the episode in the lecture hall, Hoss had not entirely neglected his pastoral duty (on which he had laid heavy emphasis during our chat) to Tina as well as to me. Whether fleeing his own embarrassment or following standard procedures, he did not speak to her himself but ensured that Jackie King did so.

'Thank God it wasn't that old cow Granger, Mrs King – she even lets some of the sixth-formers call her Jackie you know – at least you can believe she's had sex a few times in her life.'

'Lucky her. Did she say it would be all right for us to have it a few times as well?'

'Don't be silly. She may know how a girl feels with her boyfriend, but she's still a teacher. She told me off in a way, once she'd made sure you hadn't been attacking me – "making unwelcome advances" she called it. I could have dropped you in it big time, trust me.'

'She knew my name then? Hoss must have told her.'

'I suppose. Well, I might have mentioned it. I told her you were my boyfriend and we were a serious couple, and I didn't see it was wrong to be holding hands in class. I told her that's all it was and it wasn't even a proper lesson, more like being at the pictures really.'

'And she bought that?' Even at second hand Tina's spiel sounded almost convincing, and I knew how persuasive she could be at first hand.

'I think I convinced her. I couldn't bear it if they said we couldn't be together at school, Ray, could you? We get so little time outside it.'

'And none at all over the holidays.' If I was spiteful to remind her of her upcoming trip to see her father in the States, that was surely less hurtful than saying I would trade all our public time together for those frustratingly rare and brief occasions when it was the two of us with nobody else around. I'd been sulking ever since she told me she would be away for Christmas and the New Year, and not because she would be going to Disney World. That in all honesty I could not picture her as part of the Roden family festivities was not the point. The point was, she should be as desperate for me as I was for her.

Carl was out of his rib strapping in time for the fourth and fifth form Christmas disco, the inaugural such event, since nothing could have been sadder than a boys-only party in the former grammar school. Armed by the hole-in-the-wall barber, he had high hopes when we gathered in the Royal Standard to get in the mood for love with four rounds of headless beer. Aiming for Lesley Carrick, he was dreaming of Joanna Richardson.

'But she's a fifth-former.' Omie, last to arrive though he'd only had to come two hundred yards, seemed a bit subdued for some reason.

'That don't matter. You know her mate, Sally Ann Something, has been asking about Ray. Your reputation as the science-class shagger is doing you no harm at all, mate.'

I tried to be modest about it. Carl himself had probably been responsible for spreading a luridly embellished version of what had happened during our film show. The incident appeared to have had a see-saw effect, sending my stock soaring while Tina's reputation had plummeted. 'They all think I'm a total slapper now, thanks to your mates and their lies,' she had wailed, at least having the decency not to accuse me of promoting my own legend. It was all very flattering, but Sally Ann Farthingdale? Surely not. Some of them fifth-form girls were old enough to have sex *legally*.

Gloss Taylor had no business being at our disco at all – the one for sixth-formers was the next night. Not too many fifth-formers appeared to have turned up – I could not see Sally Ann, for instance. Still, the hall and dance floor were nearly full when we rolled in. My eyes would never rest until I had located Tina in any gathering, and there she was, inevitably with Roarer, head bent and whispering something to the shorter girl, so that she didn't clock me at first. Sarah Wallingham was beside them, looking rather stern, with Taylor beside her, sporting a shit-eating grin.

'Mr Rudy Roden, that's Rudy as in Valentino not rude boy though I hear that too, isn't it Sarah?' He was giggling and for some reason wanted to hug me. Stiffly, I allowed it. He had never taken this much notice of me before, and it was still gratifying that he didn't take any of my three friends now.

I greeted Tina with a kiss, which she did not return as hungrily as usual. She hadn't had four pints to loosen her inhibitions. Rather than take my coat off, I suggested she might want to put her own on and come outside for a breath of fresh air. Promisingly agreeable, she went at once to the girls' cloakrooms and returned wearing a bright red thing cinched tight around her waist but broad at the shoulders.

'Where have you been, Ray? We've been here over an hour waiting for you, you know this is our last chance to go out together this year. And you've been drinking.'

'Christ on a bike, are we married already?' Jocose to bellicose was only a short step. 'You knew I was meeting the lads first, we had to wait for Jambo to get his round in. Only man I know who can peel an orange in his pocket. And anyway, whose fault is it this is our last night?'

'Don't start that again, please. I wanted everything to be perfect, and now I've got the curse, and everybody's looking at me, and then there's that creep Taylor.' She grabbed my broad lapels as if about to stick the nut on me, but only pulled them apart to snuggle her head in between coat and shirt. I felt that getting wet before I realised from the muffled noises and hitches of her head that she was roaring.

'What, you're on the rag?'

'Do you have to be so crude? Yes, it's come on a bit earlier than I thought, must be all the stress.'

'No reason for you to be late, is there? What stress anyway, what you on about?'

'Oh yeah, Mr Big-Shot now,' she flared, 'with Fanny Ann Farty-arse saying she might take you as a toy boy, it's all very well for you, everyone thinks they can treat me like dirt.'

'What do you mean?' I was genuinely puzzled. I pushed her back a little bit so I could see her face, blotchy red. 'Hey, you've got a conk like Coco the Clown,' the beer made me say, before I tried to be more concerned and caring. 'Who's treating you like dirt?'

'I told you, that... that *arsehole* Taylor. I thought he was a gentleman till tonight, so I didn't mind when he asked me to dance, you weren't here, and Sarah seems kinda spaced out, not as bad as him though, she said "be my guest" and it was that old Rolling Stones song, not a slow one.' She paused, for breath perhaps. 'I didn't come on to him one bit, but he put his arms round me like it was a smooch, so low down I had to move them and I wanted to break loose anyway, and then he was saying all sorts of things to me.'

'What things?'

'How he'd heard lots about me lately and how he could properly give me some satisfaction, soon as I realised he wasn't even joking I pushed him away but I should have kneed him right in the googlies.' Now obviously wasn't the time to correct her. 'His girlfriend standing right there, she was grinning like it was funny, and she's my friend as well and what must he think of me to do that? What must everyone think of me?'

'Hush babe, we'll give him something to think about, don't worry. He thinks he can fuck with what's mine he's got another think coming.'

'You *what*? What's yours? So you think I'm your property do you, to play with whenever you like. This is all your fault anyway.'

I would grow more than accustomed to these leaps from females, not following any logical stepping stones but jumping right into the river to splash you with all the blame. Sometimes they were right, even if they couldn't explain exactly how or why, which gave you a chance to deride their intuition as superstition or unattractive suspicion. There was usually a way out, their hearts were kind after all, but my blood was up (raised already somewhat with beer) and I felt insulted too. 'My fault is it? I wasn't the one smooching with the twat. I'll sort it out all right though.' Leaving Tina to follow me or not, as she chose, I returned to the disco. 'Where's Taylor?'

'Gone.' Omie laughed. 'TNT grew a pair and chucked him out.'

Fiona Price had been chatting to her Mere's Reach friend Caroline Peacock. Taylor, perhaps thinking the dwarf would be a total wallflower and he was doing her a massive favour, bowled over and literally swept Fiona off her feet, raising her to his face level and starting to spin around the dance floor. When Mick saw her struggling in his arms, Caroline could hardly stop him doing what I'd been planning. Later legend would have him saying to TNT: 'Sir, either get that prick out of here right now or call an ambulance, cos if Half-Price don't do him herself I'll put his fucking lights out.' Mick would only say to that version: 'What, me call TNT "Sir"?'

So I had arrived late to the party a second time. Instantly convinced I would have put Taylor down with no bother, I may even have said as much to one or two people. Tina didn't disagree with me, and seemed glad that I'd been prepared to stick up for her.

The ejection of Taylor presented an unlikely opening for Carl. The sixth-former had shown himself up and Sarah, far too cool to want to be associated with that, had not left behind him. It was unthinkable that she should be alone, so – at least until she could bag a fifth-former – Carl was in pole position. Lesley had blanked him and there was no sign of his fifth-form fantasy Joanna and her pal, so credit to him for his opportunism. He got Sarah outside an' all.

The evening went quickly flat after the initial flurry of excitement, or perhaps I finished sobering up. Omie left early, escorting Roarer who apparently had a headache.

'I shouldn't bother walking her home, mate, the headache probably means she's on the rag like Tina. You know they get synchronised with their mates, like in women's prisons?' Omie, intent on his mercy mission, ignored my well-meant advice.

Tina remained in a fragile, teary state. There was no point in taking her outside again, though she herself suggested it at one point, saying we needed to talk. I didn't like the sound of that. The only thing I wanted to say I already had, that it was up to her over the Christmas holidays to find a way out of that bullshit promise she'd made her father. I didn't have any arguments to help her convince him to release her, only naked self-interest.

As long as I knew she couldn't be off with anyone else from school, a part of me was not displeased at the thought of a little break from Tina. She was like a kid really, we didn't have much to talk about. There were also so many other girls around. With typical perversity, they only fancied you when you already had a girlfriend.

Having made Tina promise to write me every day, I was delighted to start receiving her letters and postcards almost before I thought she could have reached her father's place in Miami. They were inconsequential, frothy, affectionate. I pored over them as if they contained the answers to all life's mysteries. I did not write back to her, despite increasingly frantic pleas at the close of her letters for me to do so, until a couple of days after Christmas, saying I'd had no news till then.

The gifting season began a week earlier, when we drove to Uncle Jack's for what had gradually become the only time each year we would see Dad's brother and his family. If Mum could hardly wait to tell Aunt Margaret that I was courting now, proof of Janet doing so was a spotty four-eyes beside her on the settee. 'Mervyn, this is my favourite cousin Ray, the one I told you I've been planning to marry all these years.' She gave me a hug, and a peck on the cheek. I told her no need to change her plans yet.

Dad's parents had died when I was small, Grandad Roden falling stone dead from a heart attack on his potato field while his wife was already losing to cancer. In my memory we had always been at Grandad Will's on Christmas Day. Dan was an intermittent figure, never failing to leave me a decent present even if he was not always there to see me open it. Today we arrived almost simultaneously with him and his Katiuska, making her debut with the wider family.

'And they say he might be getting *paid* to shag her. Jammy bastard,' I would echo my cousin Tom in explaining the residency question to Omie. While I had not given Dan's fiancée much thought, I was not expecting to see what might have been a superfox sixth-former if they had been allowed to wear fur boots and jackets. Her hair was all blonde ringlets, cascading down over big hooped earrings. She was hardly out of Dan's car before she was hugging Dad and a tight-lipped Mum. 'And you must be Dan's handsome nephew. Ray, isn't it?' Delightedly she squeezed my cheeks between her gloved hands.

'No, it's the other one. This is ugly Ray.' Dan was evidently pleased at the impact his girlfriend had made. She was rather more sedate in greeting Nan and Grandad, shaking his hand quite formally having removed her mittens before astonishing the older woman by taking her hand to her lips and kissing it. 'Such a pleasure to meet you at last, my Daniel's dear mother. I thank you so much for inviting me into your lovely home and family.' Nan looked at Grandad, gobsmacked.

'You coming, Father?' Dan asked, as he and Dad prepared to leave for the Oak, where they felt bound to support Ted's initiative of opening for the first time ever on a Christmas Day. 'Father?' he repeated as Grandad Will blanked him.

'Me? No, no fear. Shouldn't be allowed to open today.'

Getting into the car before anyone could tell me no, without thinking that my haste to get away with the other men might be a blow to Grandad, I heard Dan sounding off to Dad. 'Self-righteous old fart, like he's never been in a pub in his life. Some of the stories I heard about him from his brother Marcus, God rest him, they'd make your hair stand on end. I know things change when you're married, look at you, but at least you don't get smug about it and I *know* you still miss the old days sometimes.'

I knew that Dad was some years older than Mum. A few caustic comments from her over the years led me to think he had a somewhat adventurous life as a bachelor, insofar as I thought of him as anything but my boring old man. I saw another side to him that Christmas morning, not only insisting on a couple of his own choices from the seven he allowed me on the jukebox – the first time I ever heard Elvis' 'American Trilogy' – but revealing unsuspected talent as a pool player. I would never have thought he could beat Uncle Dan, but neither of us could knock him off the table.

That hour or two in the pub was the best part of my Christmas. We didn't even get in trouble for it. Mum and Nan were often red-faced from cooking by the time we sat down to dinner, but today a little Hungarian cherry brandy might have added extra colour to their cheeks. 'This is delicious, love.' Mum beamed. 'What did you say it is Katie...? Parlinka, that's it. Try some Pete, it's delicious.'

Later, some years later, I would realise that Dan and Katiuska had either been drinking that morning before arriving at Grandad's, or were perhaps still what Mum would call 'half cut' from the night before. Over the turkey Dan proudly explained how he had honoured Katiuska's traditions by allowing her to prepare a feast for him on Christmas Eve afternoon – something about fish soup and stuffed cabbage, didn't sound like much of a feast to me, but my fifteen-year-old cynicism told me he wasn't with Katiuska for her cooking.

The afternoon was generally spent in a state of torpor – verging on stupor today as far as Dad was concerned – by the men of the family. I was kicking a ball against Grandad's garage doors when the last of his children arrived with her family to inject fresh energy into the day. Aunt Rose, between Agnes and Dan in age, had married younger than Mum so that my two cousins were older than I. Tom, working with Uncle Mike on his farm, was at twenty already married with a child. Paul was the first in our family ever to go to university, apparently staying with friends in Leeds over the holidays.

There was a further round of opening presents, and much cooing over Ellie Baba (I was inordinately proud that I had given Tom and Glenda's daughter the nickname adopted by the whole family). Dan pretended to put into her pudgy paws a small, untidily wrapped gift. 'Here sweetie pie, can you give this to Auntie Katie from Uncle Dan, please. There's a good girl.'

Of course it was a ring. The females formed a huddle around it, while Dan explained that he had given it to Katiuska the day before, no way he was risking a refusal in the middle of his family. She'd made him wrap it up again.

'Ray, do us a favour will you, go and fetch that tray of drinks out of the kitchen for us.'

I was happy to do so, a dozen proper shot glasses rather than the mishmash of wine and pop ones the women had been drinking from earlier. When Dad, still elated from the lunchtime session, proposed the 'panini' toast, fixing the bride-to-be's family name forever as Katie, she and Dan took their drinks in a strange way she must have showed him, kind of crooking their elbows round each other so they were almost bumping noses as they raised the glasses to their lips. Before I could be challenged, I grabbed an untaken glass, gulping down its contents and thinking for a second I had splashed acid on my tonsils.

Only Glenda, not much older than me, noticed my participation, without concern. 'Are we supposed to throw the glasses into the fire?' she asked doubtfully.

'No, that's the Greeks, darling,' Dan clarified. 'Besides, they're an extra little present for Mum.' He put his arm round Nan, who barely came up to his chest. 'Sorry I had to take 'em out of their box and you'll have to wash 'em up first.'

I didn't mention the tears I saw in Nan's eyes in my letter to Tina. I also soft-pedalled a bit on Katiuska's extreme hotness. I invited her to the wedding which would romantically – coincidentally, Dan tried to insist but no one was buying it – be on Valentine's Day. Until then Omie had generally been my plus one at family gatherings where Mum feared I would otherwise be isolated or bored, but he accepted his relegation with good grace.

'I expect you'll be out having a candlelit dinner with Roarer – I mean Angie – on Valentine's anyway. She over the blob now, did you see her at Christmas?'

'She wasn't on the blob at the disco. I took her home, but we came back here first. Mum was out.'

I would normally have prompted him for every last detail, but suddenly decided I didn't want to know. 'You dirty dog,' I managed. It was bad enough that Jake should be getting sex before me, but Omie? Omie, for fuck's sake!

If I had not already posted my letter to Tina, I would certainly have reinforced in it the need for urgency in negotiations with her dad. I'd gone round to see my mate mainly to confirm our New Year's Eve arrangements, when we planned to attend a disco at the Washtown poly together. I had a terrible sense of time passing. Now more than ever I needed to end the year with a bang.

Chapter Seven

Hearing on the radio the roll call of the Sovereign islands already affected, in some cases devastated, by the passage of Martin – Dominica, St Kitts, Antigua, St Croix, Tortola, St Thomas – Ray wondered if the company's policy of spreading its exposures across the whole region would survive the event. SRG's focus on a narrower range of territories which were generally safe from the major storms would undoubtedly look more attractive short term, and short term was increasingly all that mattered.

He could not claim the Sovereign strategy as his own, but he had been tasked in recent times with implementing it. They could point to successes too, with substantial income from the Bahamas and Barbados which met the SRG criteria without them having operations there. Too timid to leave their Dutch colonies, he thought uncharitably. He had been personally prepared to spread the Sovereign word to every spit of sand where a house or a motor car might need insurance, under Ken Thompson's benevolent autocracy. The last time he had seen Ken was in Barbados, seven months earlier. Looking back, that was when the lights had started to go out.

'There you go, darling. This is the life, isn't it? Happy Valentine's Day.'

He couldn't claim any credit for the red rose Starburst Airlines – a Puerto Rican venture surely already heading for bankruptcy – had handed out to every female in its first-class cabin, but it was his air miles that had upgraded Jan and himself to those seats. She did not instantly remove her hand when he sought it out amongst their cocktail glasses and ramekins of mixed nuts. That was progress of a sort.

It had been a tough couple of months since the ACODESE dinner. Having survived Christmas, Ray had been careful not only to forward to Jan but mention over dinner (she tended to ignore his messages) the January email from Lesley Carrick, saying they were looking to arrange an autumn reunion and she would be in touch nearer the time.

'Yeah great, we can take the kids out of school for a week.'

'No need to be sarky. It might fall at half-term or something. If not, no bother.' He felt no need to mention his reply to Lesley, asking if she could give him an early heads-up before they fixed a date. He was interested in attending, but it was too far ahead for him to have grown obsessive about it. He was still hoping for great things, personally and professionally, from their trip to Barbados.

The way things were between them, Jan might not have agreed to accompany him to Bridgetown except that Ken's wife Elizabeth would also be there. He suspected the women might have spoken over the phone. Ken's call to him had included no apology for leaving him hanging at Christmas. Perhaps he thought he was being generous enough in offering the extra ticket, however ungraciously: 'Willie is going to pick up your hotel bill – room only, don't get any ideas about marmalising the minibar – so you can charge Janet's flight to the company. Economy naturally, it's only a short hop.'

'Does Elizabeth normally travel with Ken?' Jan was fiddling with the label on her bottle of Banks, as they sat outside in the warm Bridgetown evening, waiting for their pub basket meals to arrive.

'I think at his level it's a standard perk that the wife can go on one or two trips a year. I bet the tight old bugger's not paying for it himself. I've never known him take Elizabeth, but then he did used to work here. Maybe they were already married then, or perhaps still young and in love and have some happy memories.'

'Do you think our happy times ended when we got married?'

He barely heard her. He reached out to take her hand away from the bottle.

'No darling, I don't think our happy times have ended yet. Look, don't take this as an invitation for a fifteen-minute rant, but I know I may have – all right, I have been a bit of a prick, I admit it. You and the kids, you're everything to me, I want you never to forget that. Maybe we should try to do this sort of thing more often you know, get away, the two of us.'

'The two of us and your boss and his wife and the Barbados bosses and their wives.' She squeezed his hand before he could bite. 'Well, all that starts tomorrow, let's enjoy tonight, you're right.'

Separated by status, Ray had no regrets about being in the Radisson rather than the Hilton where Ken was staying. He even had time the next morning to enjoy with Jan what Malcolm Walsh, the Sovereign Barbados general manager, called a sea-bath. Under the hotel's own pier leading out to the restaurant where they had breakfasted, he left her enchanted, fussing over a big brown thoroughbred its groom had led into the sea to cool down after its morning canter.

William 'Willie' Chamberlain, the local operation's chairman, like Malcolm had a son occupying a management position in the company, into which they had by all accounts not been parachuted but reached after a rigorous apprenticeship. The younger generation had spent time on secondment to Sovereign in England while taking their Chartered Insurance Institute exams.

'I knew your lad Billy when he stayed in London,' Ray said to Willie as they entered the Sovereign box at the Kensington Oval. 'The company cricket team was very sorry to see him pass his exams and come back here.'

'He would have come back even if he failed his exams, boy,' Willie replied. 'But he wouldn't have come back to a job with us, and he would have had to repay our loan for his studies.'

After a board meeting in the Broad Street offices, which began at eleven and was over by noon, an undemanding affair not unlike those Ray was used to in Puerto Rico, an adjournment had been called to the Test match. Ray was now formally an alternate to Ken on the board. His boss must have missed the dress-code memo as the only one to attend in a tie and jacket. The latter seemed to hang off him. His reluctance to take it off might have been due in part to the braces he was wearing. No affectation, they had a job to do in keeping his suddenly baggy trousers up.

In his boyhood, while football was his first and always major love, Ray had followed most sports with some degree of interest. As a student he had enjoyed cricket in two modes: live at grounds which might have a bar open beyond pub hours; or all day long recovering from a hangover, lying in front of the telly with a newspaper or book – odd times also a sick bucket – to hand.

As a Yorkshireman, Ken was contractually obliged to have a crushing full bore on about cricket. If England were playing a series in the Caribbean he would even go so far as to pay his own money for some of the matches, if they should take place on islands where the company was not represented. Today he was able and willing to root with his hosts for the West Indies against Australia.

Willie and Ken sat at the front of the box, watching every ball with personal service by the white-jacketed barman, Heavy.

'Bit tasty is he, doubles as a bouncer?' Ray asked Malk of the cheerful nine-stone attendant.

'I'm sorry? Oh, Heavy, no we call him that because he drives the heavy roller.'

The two younger men, quicker over their beers than Ken and Willie, did not risk missing any of the once-an-hour action by sitting at the bar, behind which a large TV screen was also showing the Test.

'So, good to have you on board, Ray.' They clinked glasses. 'I guess maybe Ken's looking to take things a little easier from now on.'

'I don't know, Malk. To be honest I haven't said more than hello to him yet, did he tell you that last night?'

'No man, we didn't see him. Correction, *I* didn't see him. It's possible he and Elizabeth went out with Willie and Rose, they go back to when Moses was a boy. Maybe they chilled out to recover from the flight though, he doesn't look quite his normal self to me.'

'I haven't seen him for a few months but you're right, he's lost some weight for sure.'

After leaving time for Ray to elaborate, which he had no means of doing, Malk continued. 'I can't speak for Willie, but I for one am glad that if there is a change it will most likely be yourself, someone we know from Sovereign, not that gentleman from Curaçao.'

'Who's that? Horstwald? Erik Horstwald? Was that a possibility then?' Ray was suddenly all ears.

'Maybe. He swung by here for a couple of days, anyway. I didn't take to him. I believe he thought I was born in cucumber season.'

'You what?'

'A saying we have, because a cucumber is mainly water I guess, I reckon he thought my brain was the same. It won't do him any favours to go kissing Willie's arse either. We may use the Sovereign name, but with majority local shareholders – you saw George and Rohan at the board – we don't have to kowtow to either Sovereign or SRG.'

'Yeah, you're well set. I'm glad it's not only me as doesn't trust the Dutchman.'

For all Ray's insistence that she did not have to glam herself up for their dinner at the Brown Sugar restaurant, that Bajan women were far more relaxed than Puerto Ricans in that regard, Jan still contrived to cut into the hour they were scheduled to have at the Hilton bar before joining their hosts. Ken was not impressed, as he made clear to Ray while their wives were exchanging compliments on their dresses.

'I said an hour, there's things to talk about. Or are you ducking me like you did the rest of the office at Christmas?'

'Sorry, Ken.' Now was not the time to joke about his mania for punctuality, or the unreliability of women. 'I did come in to see you at Christmas.'

'Yes, because I bloody called you in. You need to learn to play the game a bit, start making a few friends around the place, and on the SRG side of the table. For all they keep crapping on about a merger, don't forget who bought who. Anyway, sorry I wasn't there to make a few introductions at the time. What's the latest on the BVI?'

'All set to go. Long as you're comfortable with it.' Only as he spoke did Ray realise how much he was counting on the Big Man's approval. 'I'll tell you now, with the transfer of the USVI business away from us, premium income is going to look pitiful unless we can give it a boost like that. It's in our revised budget, unless you say different.'

'Ah... budgets. Operational and strategic plans. I'm assuming you haven't lost all your underwriting skills since you've been in the Caribbean. Still, do make sure you clear it with Reg Cowley, everything has to be done by the book nowadays.'

'I've still got my own underwriting authority, isn't a nod from you good enough?'

'A nod's as good as a wink to a dead horse.' Ken laughed. Ray wondered briefly how many G and Ts he'd put away during the Aussies' interminable second innings. 'You have my blessing, for what it's worth. I will say be careful though, not for the first time I believe.'

Although Ray had spoken of Barbadian women being more relaxed than their Puerto Rican sisters about dressing up for an evening out, neither of their hosts' wives at an outside candlelit table were originally from the island. Willie's Rose retained an English rose complexion along with her cut-glass home-counties accent even after thirty years or more away. She sat to the right of the table head occupied by her husband, with Jan on his left, then Ray then Elizabeth, to the right of Ken at the other end of the spotless linen. Opposite Ray was Malk, promising at least some male conversation.

The final place at table, between Ken and Malk, was the latter's wife Lorena. Darker-skinned by several degrees as well as over a decade younger than anyone else of their company, she was a beauty. Although her bare arms and strapless dress drew Ray's eyes more than was necessarily good for him to a fine bust, her manner was not in the least flirtatious. She said very little once she had admitted to being from Guyana.

Perhaps she was bored, Ray reflected over his Trout Amandine. Although the head waiter had tried to jolly them up – 'Now ladies, when you see dolphin on the menu please don't be concerned, it's not the mammal but a fish of the same name. We won't be serving you up Flipper!' – the women may have talked themselves out in the Bridgetown malls, as the men had drunk themselves sober at the Oval. The atmosphere of the restaurant was decorous rather than rackety, the service attentive rather than insistent. Elizabeth and Rose, both no doubt practised from years of business entertaining, kept a general conversation going as well as bringing the quieter women out on occasion.

While utterly uxorious, Ken could usually be relied on to show off a little to a good-looking woman and had a fund of stories from all around the world. Tonight he said little to his own wife let alone Lorena, and appeared to eat hardly anything. If Ray had not seen him give the order to their waiter, he would never have suspected him as the source of eight glasses around a bottle of Mount Gay.

Conversation had grown so desultory that Ken had to make no special announcement to hold the floor, nor particularly raise his voice. 'Willie and Rose, Malcolm and Lorraine, Ray and Janet.' He looked throughout only at his own wife. 'I'm sorry I've been poor company tonight. I didn't want to put the mockers on the evening. Maybe it would have been best to speak earlier rather than stew over it. We can serve ourselves, thank you.' He dismissed the hovering waiter. 'Ray, do the honours with a round of shots, will you?' He waited to see Ray launched on the task before continuing. 'Exemplary hospitality as always, Willie and Malk. It's great to be back with you, more years than I care to remember when we were setting up the Sovereign operation here – before your time certainly, young lady.' As he nodded at Lorena, Ray noticed his abundant eyebrows were as reduced as his waistline. 'I have to say this will be my last time here with you.'

'Nonsense man, I don't...' Willie tailed off as Rose's long painted fingernails curled round his upper arm. Ken turned to smile at Ray.

'We talked about networking earlier, a bit more than a fancy name for gossip I hear. I'll count on you, given my pretty plain weight loss' – he thumbed his braces at the assembly – 'which would have delighted Elizabeth up to a slightly less dramatic point. I'll count on you to squash, and especially not to start, any rumours that I'm dying of Aids.'

Ray wanted very much to drain his glass, but knew he would have to wait until some kind of toast was proposed. He found himself unable to return the smile.

'No, it's pancreatic cancer come for me. So we'll be saving on Christmas presents this year and Elizabeth can order a smaller turkey.' Ken offered a smile and a short laugh to which no one responded in kind. Malk was a doer, not a talker. Willie, head bowed, was not going to say anything. Jan had given a little gasp and exchanged a look with Ray, from which she must have seen the announcement was as unexpected to him as to her. His hand gripped the bottle of rum. The lovely Lorena wordlessly put a hand on one of Ken's, which were both planted on the table in front of him.

Malk in the end was the one to break the silence. 'But Ken you've got to get it treated, there must be something, I mean…'

'Yes, Malk, it's treatable,' Elizabeth interposed calmly. 'Just not curable. We're still coming to terms with what that means, the doctors won't set a time, every case is…'

'Liz, don't do this,' the boss said harshly; perhaps more harshly than he meant, for he was quick to put an arm around her as she shrank away from him. 'I won't be seeing New Year fireworks, though there'll likely be plenty of fire where I'll be. I wanted you all to be among the first outside my family to know, at the cost of being a major party-pooper. My appetite's not so great nowadays, but at least the medicos have stopped nagging me about the booze. So let's have a toast, then maybe a proper drink.'

Ray stood up instinctively. Perhaps his instinct was wrong, since Ken looked fleetingly surprised before rising to his own feet. He looked at each of the group in turn, ending with his wife. Facing the table again, he raised his glass. 'Here's to life's greatest test – Test cricket.'

This time he did elicit some smiles as they all joined him in the echo.

Chapter 8

Omie's dad was flaky. We all knew that. When our mate talked excitedly about weekend plans, we would never ask on Monday how they had gone. He would tell us if they had happened, and if they hadn't it was better not to push it. When we were younger I had sometimes, accompanying him and his dad – 'call me Bill' – to the pictures followed by a McDonald's, wished my old man was divorced and offering me such treats instead of sat there every night of my life in front of the telly.

Mrs Newnham answered the door to me on New Year's Eve. 'I'm sorry Ray, we couldn't get in touch with you. It was only last night that ex-husband of mine came through, tickets for Chelsea.'

'Yeah? That's right, they had Everton at home today.' A live football match, especially for your own team, trumped everything, fair enough. I clutched at straws. 'That was a midday kick off, couldn't they get back in time?' It was not worth telling Mrs Newnham the result, a one-nil away win. There would be time enough to piss on Omie's chips about that.

'I suppose they might have, but it's always the same, famine or feast. They're going on to a show then to see the fireworks in Trafalgar Square at midnight. I expect Bill's got some new girlfriend in tow he wants to impress.' She sounded cheerful at the thought. 'Won't be back till late tomorrow. So sorry, Ray, you're not the only one he's let down. Come in and have a cup of tea or something.'

Without the presence of mind to be on my way I walked past her, knowing already beer would not be among the somethings on offer. I was surprised to see Roarer sitting at the kitchen table, all dolled up, looking none too pleased with life. I guessed that wasn't from disgust at the Chelsea mug in front of her.

'I expect you were surprised to see me at Stephen's?' she said on our half-mile walk to the poly.

'Only because I thought he might have played the white man and gone to pick you up, instead of the other way around.'

'You knew then…?'

'Knew you copped off at the Christmas do? Course I did. I'd seen you at my party already, remember. Me and Omie are best mates, you don't think he's not going to tell me everything, do you?' I tried to put a goading emphasis on that 'everything', but she neither bit nor disgorged.

'I get tired of hearing about you from Tina as well. She's so missing you. I spoke to her at Christmas. Couldn't you have arranged to be at a phone to take a call from her?'

'Ar, we country folk don't hold wi they new-fangled contraptions. No, the village booth's been kicked in and Grandad seems to think it costs him by the second to take as well as make a call, don't even mention an international one. Is she enjoying herself out there?'

'She's enjoying being with her dad, even if she hasn't got him all to herself. She idolises him. I keep telling her she's got a terrible taste in men though.'

'So you're the one who's been poisoning her against me. I see I might have to buy you a drink tonight, get on your good side.'

'I'll take a drink off you. Tina would only think I'm jealous if I tried to put her off you. I'm all over that, even if I do remind her sometimes I saw you first.'

'I'm not sure about that.' I remembered the TB clinic. Angie was easy enough to talk to, a bit more to her than I had realised. Maybe Omie had got a better deal than I'd thought.

The same could be said of the greasers who'd booked a raucous local group by the name of Shitehawk for the end of year event. So were they billed on the early flyers for the dance, and they might not have compromised their artistic integrity to change for a few tech students their calling card all around Washtown and the five villages. When a surprise hit propelled them onto *Top of the Pops*, however, their drums had been hastily repainted to show SCREECH – HAWK.

Naturally everybody in town turned out to be best mates or family of one of the five Shitehawks. If not for the influx of out-of-towners – some from as far away as King's Lynn, it was whispered – most of the tickets would surely have been comped rather than sold. Walters claimed not to have paid for his and Sarah Wallingham's. At the bar when we arrived, he handed me a pint in a plastic glass. 'Fucking double VATs all the way that Sarah mate, but you better believe she's worth it.'

Unfortunately, I had no problem in believing that. Angie asked only for a coke, which Carl, updated on the situation with Omie, grudgingly provided ('I'll get the money back off the twat next year'). The crowd was three-deep at the bar as the warm-up act, some hippy-dippy pair singing about peace and love, meandered on. Perhaps the student organisers had tried to cater for all tastes, since apart from having the same shoulder length of hair, the Hawks were at the other end of the scale. While Jason and Mary's faces were wholesomely smooth, the Shites' ranged from gooseberry stubble to full rotting blackberry beards. Their sudden glory was due in part to a factitious, tabloid-fuelled public protest at the possibility of their self-penned 'Satan's Child' being the Christmas Number One.

We were among the younger people at the gig. Nobody had asked for proof of age when we bought our tickets and it had looked like the attendance might be as low as at a women's football match. There were no free tables left, but one in the furthest corner from the bar was colonised by assorted hockettes.

I could hardly believe the plastic cups contained a full pint. Mine was nearly empty by the time I got to Jambo, hovering behind the seated Sue Tierney and Maureen Wheatley. He had a comfortable position there, back to the wall commanding a view of the room and down Sue's cheesecloth shirt. Maureen shifted up in that way girls do to allow Angie to join her and Sue on two seats.

'How long you been here, mate?' I got my own back to the wall beside him.

'Up town all day, at Sue's, here about half an hour maybe.'

'Up Sue's, I bet you have been an' all. You're a fly bastard Jambo, talk about a fucking stealth bomber. Anyway, get some dosh off her and the other jolly goshes and we'll go get a round in before Balls-to-the-Wallingham can finish hers.'

While the crowd were not exactly storming the stage, there were a respectable number in front of Jason and Mary. Some of the saddos not planning to drink all night were perhaps reserving the spots where they could count on getting their eardrums burst by the Shites. Others might have been enjoying Mary's stagecraft. I couldn't judge if she could carry a tune in a bucket, but she knew how to work her pristine pink knickers. They were not on constant show despite the shortness of her pink one-piece dress and the elevation of the stage. She brought them into play mainly getting on and off her stool, using her guitar at times as a baffler. Jambo had to move me along to the bar eventually.

'Hey, Ray. Ray Roden, that's it, don't forget about me.'

Squeezed in at the bar, with an elbow on it at last and ready to place our order, I could not see at first who was hailing me. Sally Ann Farthingdale was not very tall.

'Can you get me a drink please, handsome? I'm afraid I'll get crushed if I try to get through there.'

More likely couldn't be bothered and preferred to cadge, but she had me at handsome. I tried to play it cool, as far as you can when nearly shouting above the scrum. 'Yeah sure, glad to. What you on?'

'Vodka and tonic, please. Large one if you like.'

'No problem.' I was modestly flush with Christmas money. It would have been no use trying to cop a loan off Jambo, and sadly I would have to take the hit even if Sally Ann should offer to pay. Having dispatched him back to the table with a tray of mainly soft drinks (without consulting her I had switched Angie's to half a lager and lime – 'Make sure she knows I paid for it'), it took me a minute or two to locate Sally Ann again in the shifting mass.

I suppose it would have been too much to hope she was alone.

'Hello Ray, thank you so much you sweet man. You see, Jo, I told you he'd come through for us. Sorry to hit you up for a double but me and Jo can share it, cheaper than two singles.'

'No bother, I would have been glad to get her one as well.'

Joanna Richardson was the tug of the two, albeit with a fuller figure someone like Walters might go for in preference to Sally Ann's prettier, blue-eyed face. While neither of them were top four players, they were respectable enough even in their own form, and especially so to us looking up from fourth to fifth.

'Doesn't your girlfriend mind you buying drinks for other women, then?' Jo nudged her friend as she spoke, as if she had said something so witty it must not be missed. Sally Ann spared me the need to reply.

'He's probably got more than one girlfriend Jo, you know what a rep he's got.'

'What about your boyfriends anyway, where are they?'

'Right behind you. Ha, got you, did you see the look on his face, Sal. Hey, looks like the Shites are about to start, let's get over there.'

> *You ain't no devil in disguise,*
> *Cos when I look into your eyes,*
> *I see you plainer than I oughta*

An' you a proper devil's daughter.
I was a bit surprised they'd launch right off with their hit,
Satan's Child, drive me wild,
Satan's Child, Satan's Child
not realising we would be hearing it many times during their set, whenever the audience attention showed signs of flagging at some of their weaker material or during uncertain covers. Sally Ann and Jo were moving side by side in front of me, no chance of further conversation in the din and crush, for which I was not sorry.

Sally Ann was not quite a Half-Price, yet I could easily have rested my pint on her head if I had not finished it before following them into the melee. I let the plastic drop to the slickening floor behind me. I didn't know the form in situations like this. Although she could not possibly be seeing much of the group, I didn't think my relationship with Sally Ann was quite at the point where I could offer her my shoulders, to clamp her legs around my neck and sway above the crowd as a few other girls were happily doing. I was going swivel-eyed trying to keep tabs on the fitter ones, since I'd heard it was the done thing for them to flash their boobs at the boys in the band. I tried a hand on Sally Ann's shoulder, which she did not shrug off after confirming with a backward glance whose it was.

Volunteering for bar duty during one of the Shites' slower numbers, when the mad pounding of the mob briefly eased, I found Carl standing at it – no problem getting space or served now – with a pint and a shot in front of him.

'What's up, mate?' He looked as if he'd just taken another punch from Mick.

'That bitch. Fainting my arse.'

He was not concerned that Sarah, literally carried off backstage by some of the band's mates who were riding the unscheduled gravy train as roadies and security, might have really been close to passing out when she'd signalled her distress to them from the front row up against the crush barrier. 'Bastards wouldn't let me go through with her neither. Soon as the Shites go offstage she'll be getting herself screwed in the poxy changing rooms, I know her.'

He only brightened a bit when I told him I had Joanna Richardson's arse within grabbing distance in front of me. 'Let's go then mate. Great band!'

It would have been rude not to neck a quick shot with Carl at the bar, so I had maybe gotten a bit over-confident from booze when I misstepped with Sally Ann. She didn't seem to mind when both my hands were on her shoulders, nor eventually when I moved them around her waist. She would even lean her head back towards me at times, though between worrying about the pint between my feet and patrolling my eyes for potential tit-flashers I was never quite sharp enough to move in for a snog, which I assumed she was angling for. Carl seemed to have progressed to the same stage as I had with Jo, without the need for any conversation, let alone the cost of rounds of drinks.

It was already the third reprise of 'Satan's Child', the crowd singing along with the verses as well as the thumping chorus

You look as sweet as Rosie's baby,
But all you do is drive me crazy

when I made my mistake. She was a fifth-former, so I expected her to be a bit more up for it when I tried to slip my hand from her side – bare skin between blouse and jeans – under the waistband at the front. She instantly conjured up the space to whirl and slap me in the face, hard for a littlun. 'What's your game? Leave me alone you creep.'

Satan's child, drive me wild

Beyond an amused glance from some hippie standing behind me, and one of puzzled sympathy from Carl as Joanna turned to stand four-square with her friend, the focus on the music was such (I rationalised later) that nobody much noticed my shot-down-in-flames dive to the edge of the throng. People made way readily, perhaps thinking I was rushing off to puke. For a moment I thought I might. I went to the toilets anyway, as some sort of explanation for anyone who had seen my flight.

Angie came to join me at the hockey whores' table. There were plenty of empty seats, all of them but mine in fact. Maybe I had my head down a bit. She came and knelt in front of me, putting her forearms on my legs so she was looking up at me when I raised it at her. 'Are you OK?'

'Yeah yeah, I'm fine. Wanted a bit of a break from all that head-banging. I was hoping you might come back to base at some point. Look, I've even got you a drink.' I didn't expect her to believe me, or to accept my own vodka chaser, but she smiled.

'Lager first, now vodka. If I didn't know better I'd think you were trying to get me drunk, Mr Roden. I can see you don't need it anyway. Maureen had a little bottle in her handbag, not vodka, what's the other one, so we were consoling our lack of boyfriends with that – gin, that's it. She likes this band, even before they got famous. To be honest – and please don't tell anyone, promise me – I thought Jason and Mary were better.'

167

I let slide her insult that perhaps I'd already had enough alcohol. She was the one rambling on, even if not quite slurring her words. 'You have got a boyfriend, don't forget poor old Omie.'

'And you've got Tina, also not here tonight. They're on holiday, why can't we take a break too? I said I'd keep an eye on you for her, so that's what I've been trying to do. I bet Stephen didn't tell you to keep an eye on me.'

'Too right, fucked off without a word, he did. But I'll keep an eye on you if you like.'

None of our schoolmates reacted with mirth or derision as they drifted back to the table from time to time to find me hunched over and snogging Angie, still on her knees between my legs. I couldn't believe it was Omie who had taught her to kiss so well. I wondered if she and Tina practised on each other.

The Screechers took a break, leaving a DJ with the thankless task of keeping up the momentum – Jason and Mary had perhaps cleared off to a Young Christians' evening to see in the new year. Angie asked me if I wanted to stay for the second half of the headliners' set.

'What, and hear "Satan's Child" another twenty times? It's worse than sitting through the whole box set of the bastard *Omen*. Seems a pity not to get our money's worth, though.'

'Maybe I could make it worth your while if you walked me home.'

That sounded like a promise. I remembered how she had dragged Omie out early from the school disco. Admittedly he'd had his own place to take her to on the way. I could hardly go first-footing at Mrs Newnham's and ask to use her facilities. Still, it seemed a good idea to go. One of the reasons I hadn't stirred from our corner was fear of running into Sally Ann again.

I hadn't been able to drink at the same rate after hooking up with Angie – I was nearly out of money for one thing – so I wasn't staggering enough to need her support along the road, for all she tucked herself in tight at my side. I did wonder about trying to back her up out of sight if some convenient cut or natural cubbyhole should present itself. Then again, I thought I might wait till we reached her house. If she were to react as childishly as Sally Ann had, I did not want an argument in the street.

Bateman Avenue turned out to be an upmarket estate off the road out of Washtown towards Feltwell. Number seventeen rose behind a deal of shrubbery separated from the pavement by a low wall. It appeared to be in total darkness beyond a porch light that came on automatically as we approached up the garden path. She turned a Yale and we were falling over ourselves in a dark hallway. Instantly a female voice came from upstairs. 'Angela, is that you? Did Stephen bring you home, love? I must come…'

'No Mum, don't worry. I'll come up to you.' She bundled me through a door to our right, reaching round me to turn on a light. I was still standing in the doorway when she returned, speaking quietly without exactly whispering. 'She thinks you're Stephen, said I should make you a cup of drink against the cold. Do you want a coffee?'

'I'd rather have something else hot.' I tried to pull her close to me but she resisted.

'Maybe she's left some wine in the fridge if she got on to a second bottle, which it seems like she did. I'll see what I can do. I daren't touch Dad's beer. Have a seat, I'll only be two shakes of a lamb's tail.'

The phrase, one of my mother's favourites, turned the dial of erotic promise down a notch or two, as had her turning up of the dimmer switch when she came in. The room was revealed as one for family relaxation rather than entertaining, a big TV, some shelves with more ornaments than books on them, a desk in one corner and a music system in another.

Angie came back with a glass of white fizzy liquid in one hand and (my heart sank even lower) a mug of what must surely be something hot and non-alcoholic in the other. I'd optimistically positioned myself on half of a two-seater settee in front of the telly. 'Your mum and dad in bed then?'

'She is. He won't be back from the pub for hours yet. Mum doesn't like going out, and she doesn't like to be up when he gets home.'

'Fair enough.' I was not touching that one. 'That where you do your homework then?' I pointed my chin at the desk.

'Sometimes,' she answered absently. 'Do you want to listen to some music?'

'Got any Jason and Mary?'

The mug of Horlicks and her undimming of the room were my first two clues. After I'd tried the awful wine and persuaded her to lay her own drink aside, my third came in her reluctance to be kissed, and her manner of responding when I did find her lips. She pushed me away before we'd hardly started.

'Ray, I'm sorry, I don't think this is such a good idea.'

'You did half an hour ago. Or was that angling for some twat to walk you home?'

'That's not fair. You could tell I enjoyed it. If you knew how I used to fantasise about us being together you wouldn't say that. I didn't mean to mislead you or lead you on.'

'You know there's a word for girls who do that, don't you?'

'Don't be horrible. I know you can be, but you've been so sweet to me tonight. I admit I was thinking differently at the dance, that we were a proper couple or could be. It was like the cold air shocked me.'

'It's called sobering up.' I gave her all the weight of my experience. 'Come on, don't start grizzling... there's no need to roar, worse things happen.'

'Like with Sally Ann?' She dared to say it with a kind of smile. That was it, the instant you drop your guard they're in with a knife to the ribs.

'What do you mean?' I tried to throw the line away, addressing the terrible wine again.

'I saw you were all over her at one point before you suddenly came back to the table.'

'Bought her a drink, that's all. I bought you more than one.'

She tucked her legs under her on the settee and settled back from me, picking up her cup again. I realised she was moving definitively from snogging to talking mode: time to go.

'It seems a long while since I knocked on Stephen's door, thinking I'd be seeing in the new year with a boy for the first time. Tina did ask me to keep an eye on you, and it was Sally Ann Farthingdale she was worried about. You and me was something I thought I was over even thinking about. She can't have dreamed I would betray her. I feel so bad about it, I'm not that kind of girl at all.'

'What about you cheating on poor old Omie?' She ignored me, another mad idea catching her. Maybe she wasn't sober yet.

'I know, why don't you stay here till midnight' – so that had not been the general plan, then – 'and we can call Tina. I've got her dad's number and it's like five hours earlier there so we should catch her, we can – no, *you* can surprise her, wish her Happy New Year.'

'Yeah, lovely surprise, me and you together at midnight. Look Angie, if you're blowing me out let's not prolong the agony. I won't say anything to anyone if you don't.'

'But all the others saw us. And didn't you want... a part of me doesn't want to deny what happened between us because I know something did, and didn't you...?'

'Angie, get a hold of yourself.' I got a hold of her myself in no amorous way, hands on the sides of her shoulders, keeping her at arm's length. I wouldn't have minded giving her a good shake, but tried to keep calm. 'What happened happened, we'll always have our Jason and Mary moment, but others don't have to know. We can swear blind you were drunk, you had something in your eye, you were feeling ill, it was an early New Year's kiss, Christ, you think of something. And do it before we meet up with them on Saturday when she gets back. What fun that'll be now.'

'Oh my God yes. I'd forgotten about our double date, we were both looking forward to it so much. And I do feel bad about Stephen, I do honest.'

'Yeah, I bet.'

'What about if Tina calls me before that?'

'Tell her you were with me all night and nothing happened. Not much of a stretch, is it? Is her old man made of money, to be calling you?'

'We sort of said we might talk tonight.'

'Jesus wept, so that's where your idea of me wishing her Happy New Year came from. I'd better get out of here and leave you to it. As a matter of interest, would you have turfed Omie out, if he'd been here?'

'I'm not turfing you out. And it's different with Stephen. He's my boyfriend.'

'Is he the fuck, well glad to hear it.' I took another snog off her on the doorstep, was momentarily tempted to give her a love bite to mark my presence until I realised I depended on her goodwill even if I couldn't count on her good sense to keep the lid on things. And then I didn't want her squealing and waking the neighbours.

I couldn't expect a lift home till people had done the 'Auld Lang Syne' shite in town, after which some should be heading out to the villages. I set myself walking, taking my mind off what everyone would say to everyone else and how many ways it could all go tits up by composing some better lyrics for the Shites.

Your every drink cost me a quid
That's how I know you're Old Nick's kid

would do for Sally Ann. At least I had the memory of my fingertips in her pubic frizz. Walking past the brightly lit Flying Horse on the other side of the road, I imagined Roarer's dad in there getting bevvied up.

Are you the child of Lucifer
Or a stupid little prick-teaser?

was perhaps a little harsh on her, and again there were positives. I felt confident now that Omie hadn't popped her cherry after all. As the fireworks started to go off for midnight in the town behind me, and in clusters across the Fen villages around me, I began to feel more cheerful, maybe even singing along a bit to the featureless land.

Satan's child, devil's kiss.
Satan's child! Suck on this!

Less than sixty hours later at Omie's, Angie was notably affectionate towards him, clingy I would have complained if it was me, but he seemed to lap it up. Apart from giving him a bit of stick for disappearing at year end and leaving me to keep his girlfriend out of mischief, I had my hands full with Tina, who was in one of her hyper moods. We could probably have each safely made her a lengthy confession without her noticing, so much did she have to tell us about Disney and Miami Beach and how she could sunbathe every day, as well as telling us frequently, me especially, how much she'd missed us.

There was evidence she had indeed been thinking of me in the big bag she lugged into Omie's. I was soon glad I'd forgotten to bring her Christmas box. The pair of earrings Mum had got for her would surely have to be supplemented in the light of the sweatshirt, T-shirt, basketball shirt, sunglasses and baseball cap she produced one by one (I suspect she had got me two caps, but gave Omie one so he wouldn't feel totally left out). I had no idea who the Heat or Dolphins were; all I knew was the Yanks were crap at football. Still, I was touched by her bounty. 'And I've got an extra little something for you when we get to the pictures,' she teased.

I wasn't a fan of the Bond franchise, but its latest was the only game in our one-screen town. We'd arrived early to be sure of those prime seats that were not overlooked (if they still had a projectionist in the back, we counted on him being more professional and focussed on his own business than Hoss had been). We needn't have bothered. The fleapit was half empty.

The lights were down, the adverts and trailers still on when Tina pulled back from our first clinch to produce a little red box.

'What's this, an engagement ring?'

'I may be bold, but not that bold.' (I would have to let her know gently sometime that it was not pronounced 'bald' as in Grandad Will.) 'That's the man's job, but I like the way you're thinking.' She went in a breath from giggly to grave. 'Ray, I know you're not religious but it's such a lovely story, I hope you like it.'

I could see on the bed of cotton wool a small medallion on a chain. The big stick, the apparent two-headed figure of which the larger one was heavily bearded, probably ruled out a Virgin Mary. In Tina's gabby mood I didn't need to ask for an explanation.

'It's a St Christopher, he's the patron saint of travellers so Mum gave me one as an early Christmas present before I flew off to the States. I thought how lovely it was, yours isn't exactly the same as mine, I'll show you that later when you can see better. You know the story, do you?

'There was this traveller, Christopher his name must have been and he came to a river where a little boy was sitting on the bank. He didn't dare try to cross because the river was too deep and strong for him, but it probably wouldn't be for a man. Anyway Christopher let him hop on his back and started to cross, but the water was running super fast and the bottom was rocky and slippery, so it really wasn't safe at all. Then the boy started getting heavier and heavier and the old man nearly drowned but he didn't let him go. He only just managed to reach the other side with the boy weighing like a ton, and threw himself down on the bank, exhausted. But when he looked up it was the Christ child standing there, and he rewarded him for carrying him across and passing the test by making him a saint. What's the matter, Ray? Don't you like it?'

I hugged her tight as ever I could. 'Nothing, Tina. I was listening. It's a great story, and a wonderful present. Will you put it on for me?'

'You do like it then.' She brightened at once, having mistaken my emotion for disapproval. I had a knot in my throat. It was the closest I came to saying I loved her, you know the whole three-word solemn declaration deal. She put the chain tenderly around my neck. As she clasped it at the back her face was so close to mine I knew how to take it from there. I had to enjoy how great it was to have her back, not worry about how I might have screwed things up in her absence.

Chapter Eight

Although Puerto Ricans were not as obsessed with the weather as the English, for many it became the major topic of conversation throughout the hurricane season. Hugo Ramos would hang in his office every year the Friday before Memorial Day a wall map, so that he could religiously pin and string the path of each named storm as it developed off the coast of Africa and crossed the Atlantic. One drunken afternoon Ray had twitted him about his charting. 'Nine out of ten of them don't make landfall anywhere, let alone anywhere near Puerto Rico. If any do get close there's plenty of warning, time to hunker down without your pincushion on the wall. It's different with earthquakes. San Juan could be at the bottom of the sea without time for a last Medalla.'

'I know, and that's what I'd prefer. I don't care about earthquakes because there's nothing you can do except clear up the mess afterwards if you're still alive, please God. Hurricanes you can see the motherfuckers creeping up on you, you may have time to get ready but it's the waiting that kills me, not knowing if they're going to hit or not.'

Hugo would not give houseroom to Ray's idea that a big map looming over him every day from the end of May through to Thanksgiving, the blue painted sea black in places from so many pin-stickings, was only intensifying the anxiety. 'I like to know exactly where them sonsabitches are, I got two families and a book of property business all over Puerto Rico, not to mention in the islands that should by rights still be yours.'

The passage of Martin's eye was through the narrow channel separating the US Virgin Islands' largest land mass, St John's, from the biggest island in the British VI, Tortola. Biggest was a relative term, twenty-one square miles entirely engulfed by that eye, so massive was the weather system. Despite some hefty values in luxury resorts, Tortola was the only significant population centre of the islands, inlets and cays making up the BVI, almost a hundred of them rather than the 11,000 unlucky maidens supporting St Ursula after which Columbus had originally named the archipelago.

St John's was basically one big nature reserve, with little in the way of insurable property. There had been substantial losses in St Thomas and St Croix, as Hugo confirmed. 'It's not pretty, Ray. We thought at first it wouldn't be as bad as Marilyn but now they're talking storm of the century shit. I've had Frank and Joe both on to me, looks like Jaime wouldn't take their calls, can't say I blame him. From everything I hear you're right to worry about Jonno's book. The storm's up to Category Four, sustained winds of 150 miles an hour would cane Road Town.'

The evening in Bridgetown when Ken announced his terminal illness had become unexpectedly convivial after his toast to Test cricket, any tendency to hysteria tamped down by a second bottle of Mount Gay. Ken drank sparingly, but Malk and Ray had his share and more. There was affectionate rather than maudlin reminiscence of his earlier years in Barbados, talk of everything but the heavy bass note he had put in everyone's mind.

'I didn't want to bother him with that shit,' Ray had responded sharply to Eddie's enquiry as to whether he had got the Big Man's signature on the form detailing their acceptance of the BVI government account. The truth was he had forgotten, though it would have been more comfortable in some ways to talk about insurance than listen to Ken's assessment of Ray's career and personal prospects at their one-to-one meeting in the Bridgetown Hilton the morning after the night before. He took in the need to raise his profile with new faces at head office and above all turn in a good set of figures. He was prepared to accept the wisdom of 'you hang on to that wife of yours lad, you'll do no better'. It was only when Ken bluntly told him he needed to get a hold of his drinking that he closed his mind.

'I understand. It's a terrible business.' Eddie kept his maddening calm. 'Ryan is in bits about it, I'll go see them on my summer leave. Only I don't have the underwriting authority to accept it myself, and I thought you said you didn't either.'

'I probably don't but here's the fucking form, I've signed it so you'll be in the clear, don't worry. Whatever he says, I'm betting on the Big Man making it through to next year and I won't fail to meet budget for him. Speak to that prick Cowley though will you, see if you can unload say twenty-five per cent of the risk to him fac, we'll be all right then.'

* * * * *

Although he had not been able to raise him the previous day, Ray was not worried for the personal safety of Jonno. He had seemed harassed but resolute when they spoke thirty-six hours earlier. Professionally, as an agent rather than an insurer, as long as the Scouser had done right by his clients in planning their covers, and by his principals in ceasing to accept new business once a hit became a certainty rather than a risk, his long-term financial stability should not be threatened. The same applied to insurers vis-à-vis their reinsurers in many ways, except there Ray had a growing sense that he might not have done right, at least in one important respect. Hence his first question to Eddie on the morning of Martin's expected evening arrival was not about Jonno but whether he had been able to raise the brokers' boss, Jorge Martinez.

'He's not getting back to me, Ray. I was hoping you might have a go. We need that schedule of values. I think Tortola probably got hit harder than the USVI, being on the north-eastern side of the eye.'

'Who's been listening to the weather channel then? Thing is, it's like being hit by Iron Mike's left or right, either's going to put you out for the count. And what's that about schedule of values? I meant about the security sheet. Who cares about full values, I thought we were declaring the first loss limit, that's the most we can lose?'

'That's what we did declare, but Macca's asking for the underlying schedule so they can try to work out if their top layer acceptance is likely to be hit.'

'You can tell them to count on it being toast. On another day I'd say it serves that cherry-picking bastard Cowley right, you should never have let him have ten per cent top end at the price he quoted, made the balance a whole lot harder for Jorge and his boys to place in Miami. Look, I've got to go to the exec meeting now, we'll speak when I get out. Talking of getting out, you might want to be away from that beachfront walk-up of yours this evening. Jan says you're more than welcome to come round ours. The ice will start melting as soon as the power goes off, so it will be a race against time to finish off all the cold Medallas. I could use a hand.'

Jaime and his executive team, veterans of various storms, were calm and businesslike when Ray joined them as Hugo was finishing a presentation. 'So, we've already been closed for new business for forty-eight hours, which didn't stop Enrique Martinez calling me to see if we'd hold cover on the Condado Treasure Isle.'

'Since they rent it by the hour I suppose they think they can buy insurance the same way. I guess Kike was only asking you as he's one of their VIP clients. He'll be trying you next, Ray' – Jaime welcomed him to the meeting – 'don't need to ask if you know the joint. Seriously though, looks like we'll have to put the worst-case emergency plan into operation, Code Five. Pedro, how are things with the staff?'

Finance Director Pedro Hernandez doubled up as HR manager. He spoke in his usual measured tones. 'I've already told the staff they can leave at midday. What is it now, twenty after eleven? I expect there'll be more empty seats than at a Ricky Martin concert since he came out by the time we're done in here. Ray, I'd appreciate it if you could get your guys out the door too so we can make a final sweep – don't let that countryman of yours get any misguided ideas about working late. We've got until what time before the storm starts making itself felt, Hugo? Four o'clock?'

'About that. Count on it getting dark early tonight. And all due respect to everyone's intelligence and experience, let me say that on current projections the eye will pass right over San Juan. If the wind drops in the night, don't be tempted to go outside and check for damage, the second half may be tougher than the first.'

'Yeah, I can't see Ray getting out a ladder during the eye and inspecting the shingles with a mouthful of nails like Ken did, crazy guy got away with it too. At least he won't be worried about Martin.'

That was the first time Ray had heard Jaime mention Ken's name since he had delivered the grim news on his return from Barbados. It had been received tight-lipped before a lunch at Che's that saw them ceding their table only to his dinner crowd. Ken was now officially on sick leave, from which everyone knew he would not return.

'Always time for you, Ray,' the smoothie Jorge Martinez said as Marta waved goodbye in transferring him the call. 'Tell your young assistant, whose keenness I admire by the way, I was on the point of getting back to him. As I'm sure you all do at Sovereign, we have plenty on our plates at present.'

'Enough to say grace over, that's for sure. So I'll cut right to the chase. I need to have the paperwork in order on the BVI government case, not today of course but it struck me I don't recall seeing your fully completed placement slip for the big chunk between our retention and the top layer.'

'I wouldn't have been on the same page as you there, except my brother-in-law was bending my ear about the self-same case not two days ago. I had to remind him, and I'm sorry to have to tell you, that it's not an account on the books of Martinez y Asociados.'

'Hold on, Jorge. I never said a word to Gerardo about it. The liaison point was Emilia Rosso and last time I checked she *was* on your books.'

'You obviously haven't checked recently then. She is so no longer. This is off the record, but one of the reasons why is that she and Gerardo thought best not to involve us. She had effectively become his, his employee already, although I understand she may not be by now. If you did the business with her – excuse the expression – then you must check the placement with her.'

'So Martinez y Asociados, which is you George as we all know, are washing your hands of it completely. Have I got that right?'

'Ray, would you be interested in writing the Treasure Isle account?'

'Come on, you know very well I have no acceptance authority in Puerto Rico. In any case it's an almost certain loss, I'd be crazy to take it on.'

'I understand. My son told me the Sovereign attitude. So please understand my position on the BVI. That is not *almost* certain, it has certainly already happened. Martinez y Asociados was not involved in the placement, much as we would have wished to be, and frankly I have no time to consider other people's problems right now. I wish you and your family a safe passage through this storm, Ray.'

'You too, Jorge.' Ray choked back 'you slippery bastard' and a threat to take him to court. He recognised his own slackness, and the merciless efficiency of the broker's response. There was only one more call to make.

Eddie had organised their small team into stashing the computers, cowled, underneath desks. The two of them joined Jaime, Hugo and Pedro in ensuring that all the external windows were tightly shut and shuttered. The building could be expected to perform well, with wind-resistant as well as anti-seismic features, but if Martin could find a way into the shell he could tear the roof off and attack everything beneath it with a heavy charge of water.

'Are you coming to ours then, Eddie? We'll get hit like everyone else, but at least we're not right on the seafront.'

'No thanks, Ray, and do thank Jan for me too. I won't be at home, I've volunteered to help out at one of the shelters in the Condado.'

'Good call, mate, should be plenty of streetwalkers pitching up there. You do realise it won't be all sitting around a campfire singing Kumbaya, don't you? Them bums must stink something fierce, and you can bet they won't have any bevvy either. You sure? Don't leave it too late to change your mind, and stay safe. We'll have a shitload of work to do as soon as we can set foot outside once the storm passes. You've got your emergency pack?'

Sovereign had gifted favoured agents the previous Christmas a fire-engine-red plastic chest containing emergency items against natural catastrophes. Nelson naturally reserved a few for friends within the company. Ray had never opened his own – there were much better gifts coming from around the Caribbean at Christmas – but had it ready for his car today.

'I knew I wouldn't need it, so I gave it to Carmen.'

'They were reserved for management,' Ray snapped, pausing in a struggle against a window that had somehow warped and wedged itself ajar. 'You shouldn't even have had one yourself, by rights.' He raised a hand to vizor his forehead and looked at Eddie. 'Get the dazzle off that halo. Don't think I'm not telling Nellie though.'

'They tossed a coin for it.' The little shit had an answer for everything, and didn't even sound smug about it. Jan was hearing none of this, Ray decided, rather that Eddie was going to be riding out the storm at a pool and pot party with the other denizens of his condo. 'Take a break from being Mother Teresa and shut this fucking window, will you? I'll pick up the BVI file off your desk. I doubt I'll be getting much sleep tonight anyway.'

After making his excuses to Jaime for not joining him and Nelson immediately at Che's, Ray drove the fifty yards to Frankie's. The sky was totally grey already, except for a WOSO traffic helicopter. Feeling harassed and sorry for himself, Ray imagined the chopper pursuing him as in Ray Liotta's *Goodfellas* paranoia, brightening only at the thought of the ordnance *Sopranos'* Melfi would be able to get down her knickers compared to the single shooter wiseguy Ray's younger wife could manage.

'You going to sit out Martin in your passion-pad then, Frankie?' he greeted the bar owner. Apart from the kitchen facilities there was a small private room where Frankie would sometimes spend the night, alleging work pressures to his wife without mentioning these might include the interviewing of prospective waitresses. The restaurant area, like the car park, was nothing like as crowded as usual.

'No sir, the second you leave I'll know it's time to shut up shop and get the hell out of here, not like Hugo when we had an all-night poker session with Larry and a few other regulars. He called this morning, I told him he'd pussied out by being in Phoenix, nobody believes that story about his daughter's graduation or engagement or whatever it was.'

'Granddaughter's more likely,' Ray said mechanically.

'If I can sell fifty plates today I'll be happy, most of them probably carry-outs. I'm glad I've got my freezer contents insured with a reputable company – La Nacional.'

'Yeah, you can even claim loss of profits from them for that two-for-one special you've got on Medallas – give us a couple.'

'Can I? With the power likely to be down for Christ knows how long, and the emergency generator at full stretch, I thought it made sense. Who wants to drink warm beer? Oh, I forgot, you British assholes. Can I really claim?'

'You can try. Give us a large house white will you, and leave us in peace, there's a good lad.'

'Do you want me to turn the lighting down a bit for you?' Frankie called after Ray as he shepherded Emilia to a corner table. Superstitious as he was, he could have wished she had furled her umbrella at the threshold rather than making such a ham-fisted job of it as they crossed the room.

The absence of any natural light in Frankie's had never bothered him – if anything, it was another positive feature of his local. Only now did he realise, with a pang of envy directed at the Hugo poker-night stags, what a good Alamo the place would make.

Messing with her brolly, Emilia had hardly looked at him until they sat down. He soon found she was far from timid or cowed, however, boldly raising her glass and looking him right in the eye: 'Salud. I thought you'd lost my number, baby.'

As usual she had not stinted on the make-up the umbrella had probably been brought to protect as much as anything. It was all too easy to remember why he had so fancied her, even though she was dressed modestly in trousers and a jacket over a non-transparent blouse.

'I'm hardly going to chase after you when you're with that fat fuck Gerardo, am I? Is it right that all ended in tears?'

'You mean you were too scared of your wife to come anywhere near me again. Don't forget you were there with her when I showed up with Gerardo, did you expect me to go on my own?'

'I never expect you to be on your own. Good luck to you, but don't insult my intelligence. Don't tell me Gerardo was a friend, he doesn't go in for that.'

'Don't judge everyone by yourself. He likes women. I don't have anything to confess or deny to you, but I did think we were friends, yes. As to ending in

180

tears, it cost me my job. I'd be really struggling if I didn't still have my broker licence and a few faithful clients.'

'And unfaithful husbands? No, I'm only joking.' He had seen the hurt in her eyes. 'I'm not here to score points or fight, Emi, it's business I wanted to talk about.'

'Business? Must be serious. You know Ray, this is the first time I've ever seen you with a file in front of you.'

It did not take long to establish that the case was as bad as he had feared, somewhere between SNAFU and FUBAR. Jonno had not distinguished himself in pressing the BVI government for a full schedule of values, or in a clumsy pass at Emilia if she was to be believed. Apart from the lack of underwriting information making it hard to sign up blue-chip reinsurers, there had clearly been an almighty row over placement protocols and the commission to be expected from such a chunky account.

'I can hold my head up.' Emilia did exactly that. 'I placed a good ten per cent or more even with what we had, with Gerardo and the Martinez crew trying to cut me out all the while, saying it wasn't my personal account but a corporate business one. I had to let it go in the end, can't you see I've lost twenty pounds with all this stress?'

She made a gesture of sweeping both hands down over the front of her body, palms up so that the little fingers must have practically brushed her nipples. 'I'm sorry how the deal worked out in the end but it's Sovereign behind you, not your own money.'

'Not my own money, but it's my own career.' He was trying to look mournful, play for sympathy, but couldn't resist adding, 'At least you don't seem to have lost the weight off your boobs.' She smiled and they were friends again. He called up another two-for-one and large wine.

Most people had already left the bar when the door banged shut behind someone shorter than the wooden partition which prevented casual gawpers seeing the dining area. Ray withdrew his hand in a hurry from Emilia's when he saw his daughter come skittering towards him as soon as she had clocked them in the corner.

'Daddy, come on, you've got to come, Mummy didn't want to bring me to fetch you but we've got to find him, you've got to help.' She was tugging frantically at his sleeve.

'Hold on Kimmie. This is Mrs Rosso by the way, where's your manners? What's going on?'

'It's Sanjo, I was with him all day honest like you said but I had to go to the bathroom and he was gone and the Hurricane Martin's coming so we need to look for him with both cars, you've got to come.'

'Of course, baby, I'll come right away, you go and tell Mummy, tell her to take the area turning right out of our house, I'll go left, he's probably still on the *urbanizacion* somewhere, don't worry.'

On the occasions Jan picked him up from a bar if he was without a car she would normally stay outside and send in one of the kids. Not today. Frankie, already stirred from behind his counter by the frantic arrival of Kimberley, succeeded in steering her towards it. Only when she re-emerged with a carton of cigarettes, a bag of ice and a six-pack of Medalla did she turn to look at Ray.

'Kimberley. Come with me. NOW.' Counting on her child's obedience, she thrust the beer back at Frankie and left the bar without looking back.

'Go on, darling, go with your mum. Tell her what I said and I'll be along soon as I've settled up here.'

'Hurry Daddy, please, it makes me cry to think of him being out in this, it's raining so hard already.'

It certainly was. Somehow it was already gone half past three. Emilia disappeared to the toilet. Ray couldn't quite bring himself to leave without saying goodbye to her. He had to settle their tab anyway, including Jan's purchases.

'Sorry, I tried to keep her talking, she said she hasn't smoked in years but thought she might need some tonight, what do you guys call 'em, faggots? She laughed when I said I was only selling ice to people who bought at least a six-pack. You might as well take it, she didn't exactly suggest you drink it when she shoved it back at me. Bad luck, mate.'

'Martin will have nothing on her now. Jesus, what a mess. Emi, I'm going to have to go. Listen, you take care, stay safe, let me show you to your car.'

There was the interminable business with the brolly again, though at least he managed to hustle her to the building's outer doors before she began it. He held it for her as she folded herself behind the wheel of her car, couldn't work the mechanism to fold it up again so ended up thrusting it still open through the back door. He ducked his head to give her a quick kiss goodbye and didn't like what he saw in her eyes: no affection, a mixture of pity and scorn. She had not said a word since her smiling *Hola, linda* to Kimberley.

His own car was the only one left in the park. The minute he started reversing he felt a clanking lurch on the front passenger side. The tyre was floor flat. He took a thorough drenching in retrieving jack and spare from the boot then changing it, taking off his suit jacket but soon giving up on any attempt to keep his soaked trousers clean.

The entrance to their *urbanizacion*, a gated community, was normally manned, but not now. The barriers were up and open to all, the guards presumably settling themselves in at home to see out the storm. 'Fucking dog,' he tried to focus his rage on Sanjo. His exertions with the tyres had sobered him slightly. He had a can of Medalla in the cup holder beside him and was thinking Frankie needn't have stuck Jan with the six-pack, he'd already met the consumption requirement.

'Fucking dog, you fucking beauty.' That gimping left rear leg, the bat ears erect, the take-on-the-world attitude, that could surely only be his boy. Like a kerb-crawler, he pulled up carefully beside the mutt – crazy little motherfucker was dumb enough to throw himself under the wheels to spite him – and reached across to push open the passenger door. 'You coming home, boy? Come on. Up.'

Although the *sato* was as wet as Ray himself, he still took his Sanjo, muddy paws and all, on his lap at once. Fussing him he took a celebratory swig from his can. 'Who's a good boy then, who's his daddy's best boy? You knew I was coming for you, didn't you, didn't you? I may be a hero yet.'

Chapter 9

Tina brought back with her gifts no revocation of the papal bull as I called it, the bullshit pledge of chastity (or at least virginity) to her dad, though she spared me that news until well after our trip to the cinema. 'He'll be coming over for my next birthday, he wants to throw me a *quinceañera*. He says he's prepared to talk then, once he's met you.'

'A kinssy what?'

'It's like a sweet sixteen party, I know they don't have them so much over here.'

'Tina, don't you see how creepy it is him wanting to meet me and everything? He's trying to control your life. If he cares that much he should have stayed with your mum.'

'He does care, he cares more for me than you do I bet.' She ran off, probably to continue crying to her friends.

It did not seem to have done me much good to get away with New Year's Eve, since Tina and I were fighting all the time anyway. I was on edge thinking Roarer or one of the hockettes might blab and drop me in it, on purpose or not. I thought I could count on my own mates, Jambo despite his predilection for long conversations with girls, and Walters who had fell in the Forty Foot and come up with a salmon in his mouth.

Sarah Wallingham was no longer talking to him, not because she had one of the Shites for a new boyfriend but because she'd spent the rest of New Year's Eve in hospital with what they finally sorted out as severe dehydration. 'Like I was supposed to know. I said I tried to go backstage with her but the arseholes wouldn't let me.' He was now seeing Joanna Richardson. It galled me that he thought he could give me advice on women. 'Mate, you have to take it slow, inch by inch, with old Sally Army Annie you probably startled her diving straight for the muff like that. I'll see if I can get you another shot at her sometime if you like. If you're going to two-time Gibbo, surely better to do it with her than Roarer. That's borderline perverted.'

It was only a couple of weeks to Dan's wedding when things blew up. I came up behind Tina talking to Jambo as they queued for dinner, with a knot of third-formers around them. The lines were typically three or four thick. A teacher was always supposed to be on duty to keep order. The civilian dinner lady was quite incapable of doing so. It was in the spirit of comedy rather than lust that Roger Dodd, a sick fifth-former, grabbed one of her boobs to make the traditional car hooter sound. Word was he would have been expelled rather than merely suspended had the matronly old dear not shown forgiveness.

The shakier our relationship grew, the more need I felt to assert my ownership of Tina, so I gave her a quick kiss and took her hand, nodding at Jambo behind her through the crowd of little kids. Physical contact of any kind between boys and girls put the staff on alert (nobody dreamed that same-sex touches – a boy with his arm around another's shoulder, two girls walking linked – might have any sexual content). Still, as we had already discovered, hand-holding was not viewed as the worst crime.

Except today it was.

Tina seemed faintly distracted, but it wasn't until we came to the right-angled left turn to sniffing distance of the dinner hatch that I saw why. At the corner was a double-doored, barred fire exit giving onto the rarely used way out of school past the staff room. The throng of third-formers parted momentarily so that I could see Tina, back to the wall and coming up to the turn, was holding Jambo's hand with her right even as she gave her left to me.

I dropped it in a hurry. She tried to block me off but I was already scattering the little kids to get to that snake and punch his lights out. With nowhere to run, he ducked so that my wild left hook only connected with air. It would probably have smashed into the double doors except that he was charging my body back from chest level. Trying to lever myself free by pushing my right hand down on his shoulder, I pulled the left back to have another go and felt that elbow connect with something behind me. There was a muffled cry and one of the third-form girls started screaming. Then someone had me by the hair above my left ear while an arm came across my chest, a foot booted the bar to open the doors and I was outside still flailing.

It was Monkie's trademark move of course, the hair grab. He'd probably been skiving somewhere, arriving only to see Old Ma Sealey take one on the snout for trying to intervene. I heard later there was a deal of blood around, none of it unfortunately from that prick Jambo.

'The more you struggle, Roden, the more it will hurt,' Monkie gloated. The old cunt was surprisingly strong. 'Have you gone mad, boy? I know it's chips today, but surely that's not enough to be fighting to jump the queue.'

'I wasn't jumping the queue.'

'No, you were assaulting a member of staff.'

'I didn't even see you, I was trying to get Haslett, that's all.'

'Ah, thank you for identifying the other party. I thought you might be bullying third-formers. And why would you want to 'get Haslett'?'

'That's between me and him. Sir.'

'Oh dear no. That's between you and him and the headmaster.'

So it proved. Outside Uncle Joe's office I swore softly at Jambo. 'I didn't mean to grass you up, you fucking bastard. Redmist tricked your name out of me.'

'I don't care. So long as we keep Tina out of it.'

'Always the gentleman. Don't worry, you're still going to get yours. You must take me for a right twat if you think you can get away with that.'

'I'm not scared of you, Ray.' He said it in an offhand kind of way, as if it had never occurred to him I might think he was. 'Whether you believe it or not, nothing's happened between me and Tina. I may have been a shoulder to cry on for her at first, but I tell you I've got higher hopes than that now.'

'We'll see about that. I don't call holding hands nothing, by the way. Who do you think you are, haven't you got enough on your hands with the hockey whores? *And* we're supposed to be mates.'

'I thought the field might be clear after you got off with Angie on New Year's Eve. And talking of mates, what about Omie?'

'Boys, I hope you'll be as talkative when Dr Hiller is ready to hear your explanations.'

'Sorry, Mrs Metcalfe,' that lick Jambo said. She was new since the last time I'd been up before Uncle Joe. As she sent Jambo in first, I whispered, 'It was all about football remember, stick to that.'

The head was farting about with his trademark pipe when I went in, less than ten minutes after Jambo. He had not re-emerged, but everyone knew there was a separate exit from Uncle Joe's office, the escape route he was firmly believed to use every Friday to bunk off for golf. That was why I had not been surprised that our summons to his room came only on Monday afternoon.

He had a different reason. 'I hope the weekend has given you occasion to reflect that your behaviour on Friday was totally unacceptable. Stand up straight, boy, even if you may well hang your head.'

I raised my head. I wondered if he was keeping me on my feet to make me sweat on the prospect of a caning. A standard punishment for serious misconduct at the old school, that was rumoured to be no longer allowed: sex equality and stuff.

'While I realise you and Haslett may have had time to collude in a story, it was more important to take Mrs Sealey to hospital. I hope you will be pleased to hear that poor lady's nose was not broken. Pleased not for your own miserable skin, but from common decency boy, if that's a concept you can grasp. For allow me to assure you' – he was working himself up now – 'even if she had not been touched, if I thought you went to strike her deliberately the consequences would be grave. I mean expulsion.'

'It was a total accident, sir.'

'You are lucky that I don't have only your word to take for that, Roden. Mrs Sealey herself – to whom, by the way, you will make a full and abject apology when she returns to duty – accepts that you caught her by accident when she became involved. Bravely but misguidedly, I had to tell her.'

He stood up behind his pristine desk, palms down on it as he leaned towards me. '*However*, Roden, and this is no small matter, you were at that point engaged in attacking another boy. This is not the first time I've seen you for fighting, even though at the old school, in an all-male environment, we were perhaps a little more relaxed about scuffles between pupils. Here and now we have a greater standard of care and respect to the ladies, whether staff or students. I will not put up with bullying of any kind.'

'It wasn't that sir, no way. You've seen Haslett, he's as big as I am.' I was stung at the suggestion I would only go to smack kids I knew wouldn't hit back.

'You should know he did not accuse you of it. Although you were clearly the aggressor, he even accepted a degree of blame. Nevertheless, bullying is not always physical. Your academic record, and I understand also your sporting one, is excellent, Roden. That means other pupils may look up to you, but don't get above yourself.'

So that was the message, the one every kid hates most: stop showing off. 'I understand, sir. I'll try to make allowances that Haslett doesn't know enough about football to bother arguing with.'

'That's very big of you, Roden,' Uncle Joe said in a belittling way. 'Thank you for reminding me of the beautiful game. You will not be kicking a ball anywhere on school property for the next two weeks. You will not represent the school during that period. Which does not mean I buy your explanation that football was entirely the cause of this sorry incident. I have heard some noise around you on girls. Don't let me have to see you separately on that topic, any more than I expect to see you in here again for fighting.'

'You won't, sir.' He would.

Jambo had pulled a one-week suspension from football, which would not matter a jot to the little shit. My two-week ban would take me through the weekend of Uncle Dan's wedding. While the loss of my dinner-hour game pained me, at least it did not mean I would have to spend more time with Tina, from whom I had turned my face away.

I had told her plainly to fuck off when she tried to approach me on the day of the aborted fight itself, suggesting she could hold hands to her heart's content with the cunt Haslett whenever she fucking wanted. I had stayed away from Washtown and Omie's that weekend, knowing she had no way of contacting me in Feltwell. On the Monday and Tuesday I caught her looking at me many times but never softened. I was waiting for her to get together with Jambo so that I could blow my stack, this time outside the school gates. She gave me no cause.

I had two problems. Mum was already pressing me to confirm that my girlfriend would be coming to the wedding, and were we to pick her up and take her home and all the rest of it. She clearly wanted to show Tina off to the rest of the family, and so did I. How to get her to the wedding yet continue to make her suffer was my first poser.

The second was how badly it hurt without her. I wouldn't have believed how much I'd miss her silly chatter, her pet names for me, her displays of affection I'd so often shrugged off in public. Worse yet was not having private time with her. Worst of all was the fear she liked Jambo better than me, the fear she could like anyone better than me.

She had given me plenty of reason to be jealous though, hadn't she? Could I be so weak as to make up after catching her double-handed? Could I trust Jambo that things hadn't gone any further between them? Should I smack him anyway? Were my mates laughing at me? Surely the volume and the content of her notes to me, which I took out again and again in our back room as my mind slewed away from homework to these questions, surely there was proof of her love in them? I didn't know what to do.

I could not play football. I briefly considered offering to play in goal – hadn't Uncle Joe only mentioned 'kicking a ball'? – before deciding if he found out he might consider (not without justification) that was taking the piss. I still had my apologies to make to Old Ma Sealey, without letting her or other staff get me into more trouble. So I turned to chess.

It was not compulsory to be outside during breaks whatever the weather, as it had been at the boys' school. The big, airy second-floor art room was turned over to approved indoor activities, the meetings of different clubs, as was the room the girls – and Pukemore – used for home economics, into which I had never set foot. At least one teacher was always present in each room, more if they were trying to interest kids in their own boring hobbies – there was even a lick of stamp collectors, for chrissakes.

It still rankled with me that in a multi-disciplinary house tournament at the old school I'd lost my leg at chess to a super-nerd who supposedly played with his dad in some proper club. James 'Shadow' Scott had his nickname from a rate of beard growth, visible well before five o'clock, totally at odds with his general low-testosterone demeanour. He rarely saw the light, and didn't seem displeased to lure someone from it when I challenged him to a best of seven, one game each dinnertime. He said he'd bring in a spare set from home so that others' games would not be disturbed by our match. I drew the line when he suggested using a clock.

Shadow did me up like a kipper in our first game. That same Wednesday afternoon Tina flicked me a note. Without any intention of replying, I still had to pick it up to prevent anyone else from doing so. I expected some pleading, then suspected mockery as I read the single sentence: 'Will you teach me to play chess?'

I didn't answer that or the succeeding flurry of one-liners, including 'Please help me learn from a grand master' and 'I really want to play with you'. I wasn't even moved to correct her evident confusion with draughts, as shown in such purlers as 'Don't be in a huff' and 'Let me king you'. On Thursday afternoon, however, knowing I needed to sort out the wedding plans before the weekend and another bout of nagging from Mum, I received her emissary, Angela.

'Ray, why are you being such an idiot?'

'Whoa, what's all this about? Has that bitch sent you just to bad-mouth me?' I had just gone two down to Shadow and had the board as it was when I resigned in front of me.

'She's not a bitch, and for some reason she doesn't think you're an arsehole. If you knew how upset she is. Why can't you at least talk things over with her, that's all she's asking?'

'*She's* upset.' I waved Shadow's queen (that had done me such damage) at her. 'I catch her holding hands with that dickhead Jambo, I nearly get expelled, I get suspended from football and *she's* upset. Give me a break, Angie.'

'You already got a break. Remember New Year's Eve.'

'What? You mean us? She was in the fucking USA, away with Mickey Mouse. She was holding twathook's hand AT THE SAME TIME AS MINE. That's like me trying to snog you while she's sitting on my lap.'

'We did go a bit further than holding hands if you recall. And you know I still feel guilty, her being in the dark about it all.'

Her voice was low, at least compared to my shouting. 'Oh I get it, Christ I'm slow, so you're after grassing me up are you? Well don't forget your precious Omie, cos if *she* knows, he will.'

'I don't doubt it. I hate the thought that he *doesn't* know, deep down. I honestly think we're strong enough to survive it together.'

'Good for you, Romeo and Juliet. Can you excuse me a sec while I go boke into the bushes.'

'You make me sick as well, believe me.' She grabbed a handful of the black pieces I was studying from the chessboard. 'Will you listen and answer me with the truth for once, preferably without swearing. Why should you care if she knows, if you don't want any more to do with her anyway?'

'I never said that.'

'You're acting like it. Look, nobody's threatening you, God help me I can even see you've got a bit of a point in your own twisted mind. I know it's breaking Tina up this whole thing, don't drive her into James Haslett's arms – I'm not sure he's any better than you are – unless that's what you're trying to do.'

'Course it's fucking not.'

Angie brokered for Tina a chance to make her apologies to me the next night at TNT's youth club, which I had not realised was still limping along. She didn't say much, didn't have to once we were outside and she'd flung her arms around me. We didn't mention the dinner-queue fracas. Things seemed like they were before. I was so dizzy with relief to have her back, and at her confirmation she would come to the wedding, I even agreed to go with her the next day to Peterborough to buy her clothes for it.

It would keep me from thinking too much of the Under-15s match I was missing, coincidentally at Orton Longueville, on the outskirts of Peterborough. The lads were probably boarding the coach to return to Washtown as Tina and I were travelling in the opposite direction, in a service bus. We worked hard not to complain to each other at the extreme slowness of our progress, meandering through all the villages and hamlets between the town and city. It wasn't the huge number of stops, more the time it took each pensioner to get on or off. We would never be old like that.

The bus station was central, in an area with plenty of shops, various of which I visited for the only time in my life as Tina tried to find a suitable outfit for Dan's wedding. Not the wedding itself, a registry office do we wouldn't be attending, but the reception at Aunt Rose's farm. Hard as I tried to insist that a mini skirt would be ideal, Tina was stubbornly set against it, while sportingly allowing me to see her try a couple on until the maungy assistant began to tut. I finally left her to it, while I scouted a venue for lunch. I was seated with a pint at a window table in the Old Monk when Tina joined me with a garish bag into which I could have fitted my whole social wardrobe.

I had a great time. With her bag of shopping between us, her burbling about how she was so looking forward to seeing Uncle Dan again, and meeting the rest of my family, her constant grabbing at my hands in hers, her feeding of my face with her chips and kisses, I could almost believe we were the soon-to-be weds, or at least engaged. I was caught somewhere between a rosy future and memories of our first innocent day at the seaside together, good things already behind us and better ahead. Maybe it was partly due to my second pint of Abbot, a beer chosen confidently at random which I would only realise later was stronger than the normal Greene King we drank at the Standard. 'You know, I think this is the first time we've really been out together, just the two of us,' I mused.

'I know Ray, we must be telepathic, I was thinking the same thing, isn't it wonderful? Angie's great and I know what good friends you and Stephen are, but it is lovely to be on our own. Let's promise not to let other people come between us' – she stopped her mouth in a way that was almost comical – 'don't put on that face, honeybunch, give me your hand back, I didn't mean that, you know I didn't.'

I let myself be mollified, dragged out of the Monk to the cinema. Although she gave me first pick of the flicks at the multiplex, once you'd winnowed out the kids' cartoons and the films aimed squarely at teenage girls there wasn't much left. We saw in the end a kind of teen film, one where the actors as usual were pushing thirty: *Streets of Fire*, a bit of fighting in it, gangs, some biker trying to rescue his girlfriend and one great soul number. It wasn't as painful as *Grease*.

Straight after the pictures it was time to head for the bus depot, me carrying her bag, hooked at the wrist of one hand so I could keep both in my pockets. She clung to my arm with her face tight against the shoulder of my greatcoat, nose red under a white bobble hat. For once I didn't feel hobbled at all.

We had the whole top deck of the bus to ourselves. For all I tried to explain to Tina that the big wing mirror was to help the driver see roadside and overhead hazards, she would not be convinced he couldn't use it to spy into the cabin. It was a point of honour to have the front seats, feet up on the railing before the big double windscreen, so I couldn't suggest we take others she might accept as a blind spot. Still, we were very close. I should have known when I was ahead. Maybe I'd inadvertently swallowed some of the hokum from the film, which naturally had a happy ending.

'Tina, I want to tell you something.'

'You don't have to tell me anything, my sweetheart. We don't need to talk, that's always when things start to go wrong.'

Even so warned, I ploughed on. 'After today I can almost believe you didn't know how much you hurt me when... no, don't try to shut me up, I'm not going through the whole thing again. I'm sick of thinking about you with him, believe me.'

'Ray, it's you and me here now, only us.'

'I know and that's why I want to be honest with you, without all the bullshit.'

'What is it Ray, you're scaring me now? You're not going to break up with me, are you? You've not given me this day before chucking me, please say you haven't.' She was sitting upright staring at me now, both hands on my arm.

'Course not. I'll never let you go. I want to say sorry to you for something.'

'I hate violence, you know I do, but I understand why you lost your temper and...'

'Fuck's sake Tina, will you listen! It's not about Jambo. It's that Angie and me... well, I walked her home on New Year's Eve.'

She was quiet now.

'It's a long story, but listen nothing much happened. I was trying to look after her, she'd had a few drinks.'

'Nothing much? And she doesn't drink. Angie doesn't drink. Her mother—'

'She did that night. Maybe that's why it affected her, if she's not used to it.'

'Did you kiss her then?' Her hands were digging into me now.

'Yeah sure, course I did. If you could see your face Teens, course I did, I mean it was New Year's Eve. Everyone has a New Year's kiss.'

'Just one? Was it only a New Year's kiss? I shall ask *her* you know. That sneaky cow.'

She had pulled away from me, shrinking against the side window. If the driver really could see into the upstairs seats, and if he could give a fuck, he might have been concerned that she had been attacked. 'Don't be like that, Tina. Come here. She's your best friend and I hope she can be a good friend to me too. That's all it is, you've never seen me look twice at her when you're around. Come on, don't start.'

'Don't start? Don't start? You've only gone and ruined our day, our special day, not to mention probably screwed my best friend, why should I mind any of that?'

She turned her back on me completely to stick her face against the cold glass. Not sure how much was getting through to her, I blundered on. 'Don't exaggerate Teens, who's talking about screwing, even Omie hasn't... I mean I don't know, it's not such a big deal for some people, whatever you and your dad may think. Listen to this, listen Tina... darling' – that put the snuffling on pause – 'do you think I'd be crazy enough to tell you if it was something I thought might come between us? I've had a great day too. I didn't want you hearing things from other people and jumping to conclusions, that's all.'

'I shall find out exactly what happened, even if I have to choke it out of her.' (So much for her hatred of violence then.) 'But do you swear it was nothing serious between the two of you? And there's me been trusting her with everything, to talk to you for me.'

'How serious is holding another boy's hand right under your boyfriend's nose?'

'You *git*, so it's all back to that again. I don't know how else I can show I'm sorry, so sorry, but if you can't forgive me maybe we *should* finish.'

'Maybe that's what I'm trying to say – no, not that, not that we should finish, ever, you've got me all muddled up myself now. I mean how about we both try to forgive and forget a little bit? Let's start again. Let's pretend we had this conversation on the bus out, or last night or whenever, so we can remember all the good things about today, remember it as a new start. How does that sound? Come on, give me a kiss, a proper one, I don't care if the fucking driver *can* see.'

Jack Smeaton was waiting for us at the Cattle Market. He looked at me a bit sharp as he asked Tina if she was all right. Why is it always so obvious when girls have been crying? She reassured him, as she had me during the last stretch of that interminable bus ride, that she was fine. Politely declining his unenthusiastic offer of a lift home, I waved them off before walking through town then thumbing it. I abandoned my idea of going round Omie's to give *him* my New Year's Eve when it occurred to me he might be with Angie. I couldn't stand that much drama in one day.

Tina was sunnier and friendlier than ever during the next week at school. I was glad to have her come and watch my championship chess match with Shadow. 'If it looks like I'm losing, let him see your knickers accidentally on purpose and the poor dipshit's head'll go.'

I'd spent a deal of time at home on Sunday over my own chess board, discovering that *Chess for Children* didn't contain stratagems sophisticated enough to trip up Shadow. Uncle Dan, who had taught me the game years before and only stopped playing when I started to beat him regularly, came for a pint but wouldn't stay either for dinner or to let me work a fianchetto out on him. 'Get used to it, mate,' my old man laughed, 'this is his last week of freedom. He's too nervous to concentrate on chess or anything else for now.'

'I doubt he's as nervous as you, sweating over a two-minute best man's speech,' Mum intervened tartly.

By Wednesday, after a slow start to the series, I was only 3-2 down, without having needed to play the ace of my girlfriend's underwear. I could tell Tina's presence among us made Shadow and his little gang nervous, all the same.

While we had not returned to the topic of Saturday's bus ride home, I could not fail to realise the extra time she was spending with me was time she was not spending with Angie. That either meant they had sorted things out satisfactorily and were dedicating some quality hours to their respective boyfriends, or that they were on the outs. On our way to Wednesday's match (so that the conversation could not be prolonged if it went bad) I asked her, as if idly, 'You and Angie OK?'

'Sure. Why wouldn't we be? I'm not speaking to her, but we haven't fallen out. Do you think I should speak to her? You getting bored with having me around?'

'No, no I mean speak to her if you want, I wouldn't want *you* getting bored watching chess, however much it would upset Shadow's pussy-cat posse not to see you there. I just thought – oh, never mind.'

I had to lean hard on my opponent to persuade him the draw was the right decision that day, when the bell caught me in serious trouble but not yet mated. We both knew I should have resigned, as Tina did not and nobody else dared say out loud. That meant the best I could do within the seven-game format was draw, and that only with a win the next day.

I played well on that Thursday and definitely had the better of him, but it was a lot closer than the day before when the bell went. As if it had triggered a Pavlovian reflex in him, Shadow instantly knocked over his king and held out his hand. 'Well played Ray, three and a half points each, a draw.'

I eyed him suspiciously. Was he taking the piss? He wasn't looking me in the eye, so no change there. I didn't delay long, mind, in taking his hand. 'Yeah, thanks Scottie. Maybe we should play a decider, tiebreaker or whatever they call it in chess, tomorrow.'

'You're all right, Ray. You were getting too strong for me. Let's leave it as a draw if you don't mind.'

'Suit yourself. Thanks for the game. See you next time I get suspended.

'Smug git, you'd have thought Shadow won instead of lost the way he held his mitt out at the end,' I grumbled to Tina during afternoon break as we played on a portable magnetic set she'd brought in. I had tried to do a fair job of teaching her the game, yet this time I was ripping her to bits, my queen savaging her minor pieces and both my rooks well advanced.

'You did really well considering you hardly ever play and he's at it all the time.' She could be loyal in some things at least. 'You should keep at it even after you can play football again.'

'No chance. I mean, I kind of enjoyed it, and I was glad of your support. I suppose it was only fair you should serve the time with me being as you did the crime.' I was one move away from mate, impatient to be done with it.

'You said we wouldn't talk about who did what, and I've kept my part of the bargain. I think that's checkmate, isn't it?'

She wasn't talking about mine. She had caught me with the most blatant sucker punch, one even *Chess for Children* warned against. In my haste to attack and do damage, after castling and moving both my rooks forward from the first rank I'd left my king on g1, blocked in by three pawns on the second rank with no escape when she brought her only remaining rook up to c1. That was the last time we played chess.

Cousin Tom had been deputed to come for me on Saturday while my parents and grandparents were occupied at the registry office. Grandad Will had fought a hard, ultimately losing battle with Nan Joan to be spared that buttoned-up part of the day in favour of driving us himself. We would pick up Tina on our way back through town to Tom's farm in Harpole St Andrew's, less than ten miles the other side.

'Sorry I was a bit late Rayburn, I stopped for a livener with Uncle Dan at the Angel. He wasn't too bad but it looked like one or two of his mates had been there all night. I said to him about Katie – can you believe it, she's going to be our *aunt* – I said, "Are you going to be a man, Dan, and do it tonight, or a mouse and do it tomorrow?" He said, "I was a rat and did it last night."'

'I doubt it. Katiuska spent the night at ours.'

'Wake up, it was a joke. Hey, did you drink her bath water? I would of.'

Tom waited in his mum's car – 'She wouldn't let me bring mine, said it was too much of a tip between Ellie Baba and the dogs' – as I went to knock for Tina. It was Smeaton that came to the door. After a minimal nod to me he turned to yell back into the house: 'Tina, are you going or not?' Then he was suddenly right back at me, hardly reducing his volume. 'I don't know what you've been up to my lad, but sobbing her heart out she was last night. I was nearly round your house to give you a bloody good hiding.'

Chapter Nine

Ray had planned to enter the house with Sanjo cradled in his arms – pity in a way the dog didn't have some further injury than those inflicted by his hard early years – like a San Juan Fire Department officer rescuing a cute kid, himself weary and bedraggled from the heroic effort. As soon as he opened the driver's door though, under the shelter of their carport, the treacherous little sod was away and into the house, back door wide open. Kimberley was ecstatic, Jan less so.

'I found him then.' His wife was sitting out on the covered patio watching their small rectangular pool fill up with rainwater, for all that the landlord had advanced its cleaner's weekly visit by a couple of days to drain off a foot or two against the expected deluge.

'Bully for you.' She was smoking. The liquid in the glass beside her looked too pale to be straight coke.

'I might have been home sooner if I hadn't had a flat outside Frankie's. Funny how that could happen between leaving the office and getting ready to follow you?'

She appeared neither contrite nor triumphant, saying nothing. Maybe it had been an accident, a coincidence. He had not inspected the tyre closely, the garage would eventually tell him if it had been slashed, punctured or deflated. He would have to let it go for now.

'I know what you must think, I do honestly, but it was all business today. The government account in the BVI, we've got a big problem with it.'

'Have we? Have *we*? I asked you not to go there today and you lied in my face. The worst thing is I was still kidding myself you might *not* be there. You had to put the cherry on the cake, didn't you, sitting with your floozy bold as brass while your daughter's sick – I mean physically sick – with worry because she lost her dog and Daddy told her specially to look after him.'

'All right, Jan. Look, we need to get through these next twenty-four hours. I'm sorry if you don't believe me but we need to work together, now more than ever. Give us one of them fags.'

He had to take one himself. He had given up even longer ago than her, had to struggle alone to do so while she still smoked. Never mind that she tried not to do so in his presence, to keep the cigarettes out of his sight, the fact that they were in the house had not helped. He worked to dredge up a little of his aged resentment at that, before conceding she was entitled to her little mardy for the moment.

'Kids, looky here, not quite a goody bag from the company golf tournament but let's see if we've got anything we can use in this hurricane repair kit. Your dad could have used a tyre repair kit at Frankie's today, in case anyone's interested.' Jan was still studying the falling rain. 'Who did the windows, by the way?'

'I helped Mum, but we couldn't see what difference it would make.'

'Well, you've marked the spot nicely anyway, Den. When I told your mum to tape up the French doors, I didn't mean with Sellotape. You're dead right, that may not help too much, but if we use this' – he produced from the chest, with something of a flourish, a reel of masking tape – 'we can make the same criss-cross pattern, only stronger.'

'If the wind's going to be like a hundred miles an hour, will even that tape really stop the glass breaking?'

'You wouldn't think so, would you Kim? It's not the wind so much that breaks it, it's what the wind might blow. Like that heavy old ashtray Mummy's got out there.'

'Why is she even smoking, Daddy? Is she afraid we're going to die?'

'What, the condemned man – or woman's – last cigarette? No darling, come here, give me a hug, nobody's going to die. Look at Sanjo, he's probably survived worse storms than this in the open air, remember where we found him at the Reef? That whole bar may have blown away, right on the sea, but he's still here safe and warm with us.'

'Why *is* she smoking then? And I saw you having one too.'

'Do you know what the temperature at the end of a cigarette is? It's like a thousand degrees or something – and don't ask me Celsius or Fahrenheit Den, cos I don't know. *Anyway*, the point I'm trying to make if you'll let me is that's why people can smoke in the rain. We're probably going to lose electricity later on, maybe when you're already asleep, so we bought some cigarette lighters to go with the candles we've got ready. I guess we thought we'd get some cigarettes to go with them.'

'That sounds a pretty feeble excuse, Dad.'

'He's got a million of 'em, Den.'

'All right Janet, how about you tell Kimberley why *you* bought the cigarettes? And maybe an early dinner wouldn't be a bad idea before the power does go.'

'You won't be smoking in the Alamo, will you? You know I can't stand it and it's not good for you either.'

'You're right, baby, of course we won't smoke in the bedroom. I doubt very much if we'll need to go in the Alamo except to get to the toilet, and we'll only need to go there if the potty bucket gets full.'

'The what? Don't be gross. Tell me he's only joking, Mom.' (Kimberley liked to use the American variant when she remembered). She flew outside to Jan.

'So as I was saying Den, the idea of the tape is to keep the glass more or less together if it does go. Modern glass is designed not to tear into big jagged lumps but I don't know if this is modern glass. The little splinters and fragments can cause a lot of damage.'

'If the tape keeps it in bigger chunks, wouldn't they be even more dangerous?'

'You've got a point.' Ray lowered his voice. 'Look, between you and me, some people nowadays say it's not worth putting tape on windows, it might actually make matters worse like you say. But your mum's going to be sore as hell when she has to try and peel off all that Sellotape tomorrow. Let's look busy and make sure we put the proper tape over the top to avoid double work. We won't be in this room anyway.'

'What are you two whispering about?'

'Men's work. Can't we have our little secrets?'

'You love your little secrets, don't you Ray.' Jan had bestirred herself to pass through to the kitchen. She put her glass at the ice-dispenser in the fridge before setting the cubes acrackle with a generous shot of Ray's prized Barrilito rum. She added a little caffeine-free diet coke before serving the kids glasses of that. She offered Ray nothing.

'I heard you asking your mum about the Alamo this morning, darling, as I was leaving for work.' He did not know whether Kim would remember her brother's scaremongering or not. 'She doesn't know as much about history as I

199

do, so she probably couldn't tell you.' Ray was doing his best to keep the tone light, despite Jan's provocation. He served himself a beer, resolving not to start on the rum until the worst of the storm had passed or everyone else was safely asleep. Much as he admired Jan's drinking capacity, he could see her crashing out early at this rate. Someone had to be the responsible parent.

'The Alamo was a place of great heroism that is still talked about today.' He could almost feel the energy draining out of his voice at the general lack of enthusiasm his lecture was drawing. Only Kimberley had a morbid interest.

'Was it like Den said though, Daddy? That all the Americans got killed like rats in a trap?' So she had not forgotten.

'Denis knows even less history than your mother, darling. If you look into it, Den, I think you'll find there were more foreigners than Americans killed there. And I'm not talking about the Mexicans, I mean defending the place, including Englishmen. In any case Kimmie, all the women and children were OK, none of them got hurt.'

'Yeah, but Hurricane Martin won't know the difference between men, women and children like the Mexican soldiers did, will it Dad?'

'No it won't, smart-arse. I'm talking to your sister but since you mention it, it won't be firing bullets either. It was only an example I thought your mum would understand, we can call it our safe space or panic room instead, whatever the hell you like. I'm going to watch the film again definitely when everything's back to normal, you can join me or not as you like. John Wayne's in it.'

'Whoop-de-doody,' Ray pretended not to hear the boy say.

'Did you get the recipe from Gloria? This rice and beans is even better than hers, I have to say Jan.'

'Stop creeping. She still cooking for Jaime then, is she?'

'I'm not creeping, I was only trying to be nice. It's not as good as hers if you really want the truth. And you might remember Kimberley plays with their Sandra, leave our friends out of it even if you've copped a chinker with me.'

'Maybe not for much longer.'

'I'm glad to hear you're getting over your paddy, since we're going to be cooped up here till the storm passes.'

She spoke with more emphasis. 'I meant the kids may not be playing together much longer. I think we might be better off back at school in England.'

'Lord, that same old song. Put it on pause for twenty-four hours Jan, that's all I ask.'

They kept to their usual schedule of early evening TV, a couple of American syndicated shows: a middle-class black family with small kids in a half-hour sitcom; a middle-class white family grappling with teen problems that could all be resolved in an hour including ads. Ray secretly enjoyed this part of his day, sprawled on the settee with Sanjo on his lap and their own kids on either side. The difference tonight was that the TV sat on the floor rather than its usual table, already in a blanket which would be wrapped round the screen too when they had to leave the room.

Ray was keeping in touch with Martin's progress through the radio-alarm plugged in at his and Jan's bedside, saving the battery-powered transistor for later though he fully expected the WOSO local signal to be cut off during the night.

The storm's expected path was one that would impact every municipality on the roughly rectangular 100-mile-long and 35-mile-deep island of Puerto Rico, making land near the south-eastern tip and exiting near the north-western. San Juan might not be dead centre but that was little consolation since the eye was almost broad enough to cover the whole island.

There were always some numpties who rushed to the most exposed coastline to greet an oncoming storm with cases of beer, video cameras or even surfboards. Any fatalities were normally amongst them, or people suffering heart attacks and the like which may have been lurking in wait for such a moment when emergency services, like all others, were suspended. Shelters for the homeless and displaced, like the one Eddie would be manning, might on other occasions serve as polling stations and in daily life as schools.

Jan was suddenly businesslike. 'Why don't we all get ready for bed, while there's still power and water to brush your teeth? You can hear the wind howling outside now.'

'Yeah, come here Kim, look at the rain it's going straight across nearly and look at the trees bending across the road at Mr Garcia's.'

'You come away from those doors right now, Denis.'

'All right Jan, easy does it. Glad you've woken up, but it's natural they're a bit excited. How many kids in England can say they've lived through a hurricane?'

'I'd just as soon mine didn't have to either. You make it sound like a treat.'

'Not a treat, love, but an experience for sure. You know the saying, what doesn't kill us makes us stronger.'

'Are you putting that to the test with our marriage? I know, I know now isn't the time, now never is the time with you though. I'm sick of it all. If you knew how I felt when I saw you this afternoon.'

'I know darling, I've tried to explain, come on don't start bawling. Don't worry kids, Mum's had a bit of a stressful day, come over here and join us – come on, group hug. Yes, you too, *cómo no* Sanjo, little buddy.'

The big picture window in the main bedroom occupied (nearly always) by Jan and Ray had contributed to their decision to use Den's room as their sleeping quarters that night. Potential flying objects had been removed, of which there were alarming numbers. Ray had even lugged out the metal bed frame, leaving only the mattress on the floor alongside one for Kimberley they had dragged in.

'Is all this really necessary?' Jan had asked that morning when they were still on speaking terms.

'Probably not. I work in insurance, remember. If things start flying about in here, I'd rather have as few sharp edges around us as possible. Besides, it gives us a bit more room. It's going to be a tight squeeze as it is.'

It seemed to have been a very long day. The storm had brought an early nightfall but it was still not even nine o'clock, as Denis was quick to point out. 'Why should we get ready for bed? Even if we should miraculously survive till tomorrow, there definitely won't be school. And shouldn't we keep our clothes on anyway, in case we have to evacuate the house in the night?'

'It will be miraculous if you survive the night without a slap, that's for sure.' Ray's patience was wearing thin to out. 'I know you're only trying to frighten your sister, don't bother, she's too sensible for that, aren't you sweetheart? You're getting into your jim-jams, both of you. If water starts coming into the bedroom we'll go to the Alamo, that's the worst it can possibly get.'

'What if the roof blows off?'

'Don't be silly darling, we're a long way from Kansas. I mean this isn't like *The Wizard of Oz*, or is that another classic movie you haven't seen? No I'm not being sarcastic, yes I do know that's the lowest form of wit, I'm trying to keep a sense of reality is all, a sense of proportion here.'

'You're the one who turned the house upside down and put the Alamo into the kids' heads, Ray. No, I'm not having a go at you, you're right, your dad's right children, we're going to get through it but we have to be careful. That's not Postman Pat's windy day out there. Now go get in your pyjamas unless you want to have to undress in front of each other in Den's room.'

No yoga practitioner, Ray felt keenly the absence of chairs and a table as they played knockout whist on the mattresses and a couple of beanbags in Den's room. The kids were naturally supple enough to cope, and Jan could still easily assume the lotus position – a legacy of her hippie youth, he thought sourly – while he had to fidget and shift before finding a half-comfortable position on his side, propped on one elbow, kneeling to deal as everyone but Den expected him to do for them. Jan had been reluctant to join the game at all, finally giving in more to the kids' pleas than his.

The lights went out about ten. They were ready with candles, matches and lighters (the cigarettes, at Kimberley's insistence, had been left in the kitchen). Ray always had a powerful torch under the bed, wide-beamed and heavy enough to use as a truncheon if necessary, with which he made a quick final tour of the house. They had unplugged the television and other appliances, so that they would not be blown when power returned, and switched off the lights other than in the Alamo. He turned off Den's bedroom light but left that hallway one on, so they would know if and when power did come back.

The rain was lashing hard against the French doors. Only close to them could the sound of their rattling in the frames be distinguished from the general hullabaloo. The radio had confirmed earlier the storm was approaching Fajardo as a Category Three hurricane. While a welcome drop from its former status as a Four, this still ranked as a major event with sustained winds up to 129 miles per hour. Crossing the island it might be expected to weaken, but Ray placed no great faith in the east to west 'mountain' range. Its highest point between the east coast and San Juan, in El Yunque rainforest, was only some 3,500 feet.

His insistence on the various measures they had taken around the house was mainly to instil a sense of occasion, of respect for the storm, amongst the family. It did not hurt to keep them busy during the long hours awaiting Martin's arrival (travelling as it was at the average speed of a Santurce bus, no more than 20mph), even if their activities were not likely to be effective against a major blow. Spitting into the wind at least helped stop your mouth from going dry.

Their landlord had told them not to worry about a lack of hurricane shutters on their home, it had survived Hugo – the benchmark for older Puerto Ricans in talking of major storms – and was well insured, with Sovereign as it happened. Ray had no concern for the property as such, and it was too late now to check its previous claims history. It was his business to know, however, that its construction – basically a one-storey solid concrete bunker – and its location – well away and slightly upland from the beachfront – put it in a better position to survive unscathed than many others. He knew that Nelson, for instance, would be riding out Martin at the house of Miriam's parents. His wooden chalet-style home, built from a kit, was at risk not only because of its structure and material but its rural location, with more trees around to cause damage of one kind or another. Unlike Sanjo, more than comfortable amidst the soft mattresses and quilts with his family, Nelson's two German shepherds would be locked into a shed on his plot and left to their fate.

Thinking of sneaking a cigarette before returning to the bosom of his family, he briefly envied Eddie, with only the welfare of strangers to worry about. The organisation around the official shelters, from what he had heard of earlier events, might well be unrehearsed and chaotic, but his assistant would only have to follow instructions. On the other hand, he was unlikely to have a fridge well stocked with beer at his disposal.

Having popped the top on another Medalla – they were warming by the second, he reasoned – and provided the rest of the family with drinks in plastic cups (a bowl for Sanjo), he was ready to settle beside his wife on a bed of beanbags, quilts and pillows. They had shared worse over the years. 'Are you ready for me to blow the candles out, kids?'

'Can't you leave them, Daddy?'

'No, darling, there's always the risk of one starting a fire while we're asleep. Not a big risk, I grant you, and OK if you like I can leave it a few minutes more, then blow it out before I go to sleep. How's that?'

'Will you read to us? You can use the torch, can't you?'

'Aren't you a bit old for bedtime stories now, baby?'

'It doesn't have to be a children's book.'

'I don't think I've got *The Perfect Storm*. Any other ideas? Your mum mentioned one earlier, remember?'

'Not *Postman Pat's Windy Day*, please.'

'And what do you call Postman Pat when he retires?'

'Pat,' his wife, son and daughter replied in unison, with varying degrees of enthusiasm.

'You all right with the idea of reading, Den? I can't remember the last time we did it.'

'Yeah, I don't mind. We can't read to ourselves anyway if you're going to hog the torch.'

'Den, I only took it off you earlier because it's not a toy. We may be without power for more than one night.'

A quick trip to the bookshelves and Ray began to read, by candlelight after all, because he found the torch too bright and broad-beamed in the small room rather than from any desire to preserve its precious batteries. 'Marley was dead, to begin with. There is no doubt whatever about that.'

He heard Jan whisper to Kimberley that no, her dad wasn't reading *Marley and Me*. Both of them, and Denis too, were asleep before the first ghost clanked up. It reminded Ray of their trip to Disney World. They had a three-day pass, and every evening they were all gone before he pulled their rental out of the car park to return to the hotel. He went on reading a bit for his own pleasure, knowing he would not be asked to continue aloud for theirs any time soon. Most likely never.

He noticed from light coming under the door to the Alamo that power was restored within an hour of going out, but its return was short-lived. By midnight there was no longer any signal from local radio either. As he fiddled with the transistor, he thought of tumbling into the luxury of his own double bed, then thought better of it. He did not want to be discovered well-rested by a Jan who had woken alone with the kids, stiff-backed to add to her already stiff neck.

When he woke momentarily disorientated on the beanbags, she was no longer beside him. Suspecting her of giving way to the temptation he had so nobly resisted, he went to check their bedroom. Finding it empty, he used the en suite to rid himself of some processed Medalla. The torch left everything outside its broad beam in absolute darkness. Returning to the living room, he caught a glow from the kitchen. Jan was smoking at the counter by the sink, looking out the window across the street. She did not turn as he approached.

'Want me to freshen that up?' He served himself a Medalla from the fridge, surprised for a nano-second that the ranks of cans were not lit up when he opened the door.

'No thanks. I've had enough.' She swirled the ice round, the main thing left in her glass.

He laid the torch on its side with a tea towel over it to muffle the beam. He didn't want a cigarette, but that was their remembered beauty. Even when you didn't want one, you had one. At the sputter of the lighter, he suddenly realised there was no other sound. 'Wow, I hadn't thought, how long has it been quiet like this?'

'Don't know. I've been up maybe quarter of an hour. Perhaps it was the stillness that woke me. I can see some trees down across the road but no dead bodies floating down the street.'

'I never said there would be.' Why did she make everything sound like an accusation? 'It's not over yet though. This must be the eye going through. It's right what they always say about the calm at the centre of the storm then.'

'When did you stop reading to the kids at bedtime?' This one sounded like a genuine enquiry rather than a barely disguised bitch.

'I was wondering the same thing. I don't know if there was any exact stopping point. I never expected to do it again till maybe we had grandkids. It's funny you know. I was nervous before I started reading tonight, wasn't sure I'd be able to do it, like a kind of stage fright.'

'You sounded all right. Do you remember when you'd record cassettes for them so I could play them when you were on a trip?'

'I do remember that.'

'You were doing all the voices in them, getting into it, then I realised you must have been half-pissed when you recorded it.'

'Here we go again.' Did everything with her nowadays have to lead back to drinking or other women? 'I don't recall them complaining. I mean I wasn't slurring my words or nothing. At least I cared enough to do the tape in the first place.'

'Were you cheating on me even then, Ray? Did you care enough to keep it hidden a bit better? Alex warned me, what was it he said, them Feltwell boys are all mouth and trousers.'

'Christ on a bicycle Jan, how do we get from reading to the kids to me suddenly cheating on you? And since when was our brother-in-law a source of marriage guidance? Look how well him and Angie are doing. Maybe he warned me about them Roper girls as well.'

'What did he say about me?'

'Less than your face just told me.' For once it was she who had to look away. He did not cut as deep as he might have. 'It was always like he wanted to keep some kind of monopoly on you all, but I thought he was mainly bullshitting, typical Washtown wanker. Why don't you tell me yourself what he said about you? Come on, let's have it all out for once. I'm tired of being the bad guy all the time.'

'Well don't work so fucking hard at it then. If I spill out my past to you it will burn you like battery acid, and you're still the father of my children.'

'One of them anyway. Sorry Jan, that was a cheap shot. Throw the ice over me this time if you like.'

'You're cheaper than ice at the North Pole. I wouldn't waste it on you in a hurricane with the power off. Soraya was reminding Gloria of a Puerto Rican saying at that wonderful ball we all enjoyed so much, since you bring it up. It's better to be alone than want to be alone. I might do you that favour. You won't drag me to the past, that wasn't a great place for me a lot of the time.'

He longed to take her in his arms and have an end to all the fussing and fighting, at least for this one night. He managed only the slightest move towards her before she put up a hand in the universal stop sign, at the same time turning her head towards the bedrooms and their children.

'If you want to behave like a single man, or not a man, like some cuntstruck teenager back living in Feltwell, go ahead. What, surprised I know that word Ray? Sometimes there's only horrible ones that do the job. Or if you'd rather be a cheating bastard, why not settle down with your tart out here and find another idiot to take her job. Cos I won't have it. I won't be here. Nor the kids.'

'My past wasn't that fantastic either.' Her flip-flops stopped slapping on the tiled floor. She had already been past him when he spoke, might not have caught what he said despite the hush around them. He turned from the sink and spoke to her back. 'Look, it may sound funny but I've enjoyed tonight. We should do things together as a family more. Once we get through the second half of this storm, let's talk about that. Maybe we should take the kids to Disney again, how about the one in Paris? I know it's supposed to be poxy, but we could maybe do it when we go home for Christmas. Hey, hey, whaddaya say?'

She turned only her head to look at him, shaking it slowly. 'I think you do sometimes believe your own bullshit. I was standing here before you came in, smoking at three in the morning, with a headache from drinking too much rum, and I decided this isn't what I want. I don't want to be here.'

'Fair enough. We are in the middle of a fucking hurricane.'

'It's not the hurricane, Ray. Though I *was* thinking of that in one way. All right Jan, we've got to see out the second half and pat ourselves on the back as survivors in the morning. But a marriage isn't like that. I can get out right now, in the eye.'

'Whoa, you're losing me. I don't know what you're talking about.'

'It's not that complicated. Will you go back to the kids?' she asked.

'OK, let's do that. No more words.'

'No more words.' But she did elaborate. 'I'm going to our bed. Alone.'

'What about Martin?'

'Martin's shot his bolt. I know the worst is over.'

Chapter 10

I had backed up a step from Smeaton's front porch as he loomed over me. I heard the Astra door slam behind me. Then Tina's mum was between me and the big lump, smaller than both of us but clearly in charge. 'Try giving his Uncle Dan a bloody good hiding if you like, don't think I don't know what this is all about. Ray love, come on in, don't mind him.'

'I'm fine here Julie if you like, my cousin's waiting for me.' I turned now to see Tom sitting on the bonnet of his mum's car, like an adult side-saddle on a Shetland pony, thick arms folded across his chest.

'He's welcome to come in too if he likes. Come on.'

It was practically an order. I followed Julie into the house, Smeaton shutting the door behind us.

'Go put the kettle on Jack, there's a good lad. I fancy a coffee. Ray?'

'No thanks.'

'Tina's getting ready, she'll be down in a jiffy. Jack may be a bit over-protective, but better that than the other way. And he's right, Tina was very upset last night.'

How lucky was I? A girlfriend whose dad would have clapped a physical as well as a psychological chastity belt on her if he could, *and* a psycho stepdad looking out for her. Although Julie had put him down briskly enough, her own attitude towards me had been warmer on other meetings. Their kettle must already have been on the boil, as Smeaton returned to plonk a mug down beside her before I could have answered, supposing I had something to say.

'Sobbing her heart out she was, said she wasn't going today, wanted me to let your parents know...'

'Sit down Jack, you're making the place look untidy. Ray, I think you're a nice boy at heart, and I've never believed girls should only always be in the company of girls. On the other hand, however much she'd hate me for saying it, Tina is young for her age, if that makes sense. And she is a year younger than all of you. I'm not sure she's ready for a big steady relationship.'

'I'm not her first boyfriend. And she's older than me, her birthday was first.'

'Except she was only fourteen this year. She took her eleven-plus a year early, I thought you knew that. As to not being her first boyfriend, you have a bit to learn about gallantry I see. Whatever you may both think now, the odds are stacked against you being her last. That's not the end of the world, it is the world. You shouldn't be in each other's pockets all the while, you should spend time with friends of your own sex too.'

'Next week I can play football again.'

'That's good. And I was glad when Tina went round to Angela's for tea last night, she was the first real friend she made when we moved here.'

Now I saw where it was going. What had that poisonous little toad said? And what was all this about Tina only being fourteen? FOUR more years.

'As I said, Tina *was* very upset when she came home last night. Luckily, she seems fine this morning. She may be a bit of a drama queen, but don't forget she's also our little princess.' There was a friendlier look at Smeaton at that point. He reminded me of a pathetic old dog waiting at a table for scraps. 'Don't think we won't watch out for her interests above all else, because we will. Talk to her today, Ray. Try to have a proper conversation so we don't have to sit down like this again.'

There was a tremendous clatter as Tina came down the stairs at speed in what sounded like hobnailed boots but turned out to be stack-heeled clogs. 'Hello darling, sorry to keep you waiting, I hope they haven't been giving you the third degree.' She made a point of coming over to give me a kiss, no chaste peck either. 'Are you all right?'

'Yeah, I'm... you look great. So grown-up.'

She wore a black skirt not too far above the knee, plain tights and a white blouse under which I could see the outline of a white bra.

'She does look lovely,' Julie endorsed my involuntary compliment. 'As to grown-up, appearances can be deceptive. Enjoy yourselves today, kids. Don't forget the wedding present, Tina.'

'Don't you want to send the groom your best wishes?' Jack muttered.

'Thanks for reminding me. Not to send Dan my best, though please do that for me Ray, but that you and me need to have a talk about growing up as well.'

No treats from his missus for old Jack then, but a surprisingly affectionate parting hug from Tina, as he looked over her head and tried on one more silent snarl at me.

Tom gave my attempt to get in the back with Tina short shrift. 'I'm not your bleedin' chauffeur mate, excuse my French young lady, you need to teach this yobbo some manners. Even our Uncle Dan will have to start behaving now. I saw him this morning and asked if he was going to be a man…'

My cousin was clearly having a day off from his responsibilities as father and husband. I wondered if he had taken more than a single livener (even as I wondered exactly what a livener was) with our uncle earlier. When we reached the farm, he was told firmly that the marquee wasn't open for booze until the wedding party arrived, but we were welcome to help lay out the food if we could do so without touching any of it.

Although Tina's apparently sincere offer to help out Rose and the bustling, busty Glenda in any way she could drew a 'Bless you' from my aunt, I didn't feel I could presume to push her straight into the kitchen. Tom heard me ask if she wanted to come over to the pub with us even if she would be the only woman there, and decided the matter for us.

'Course she should come, she can meet Mary. You don't want to let this one out of your sight for one minute, Rayburn. I never thought you'd get so spawny.'

I was not averse to having Tina with me, only a little shy at the prospect of the serious conversation her mother had suggested we have. While to ask Tom for advice would have been nothing short of suicidal, I might have welcomed a bit more time to work out exactly where to start. Tina herself seemed far more relaxed than I felt, showing no dismay even at the dinginess of the Butcher's Arms right across the road from the farm.

Apart from a clacking domino school of old gaffers and one man hunched at the bar over a folded tabloid crossword, our family had the place to itself. My cousin Paul was already occupying the pool table, playing a stocky young bloke with short curly hair he introduced as Mario. 'You know Paul, never let a dago by,' Tom interjected with a pint into my hand as his brother was explaining how Mario was a fellow student.

'Of course he hardly has to work at the language side at all, has the gift of tongues,' Paul tittered, 'brought up bilingual, but he still has to crib my literature essays.'

Mario was friendly enough and I would hardly have placed him as a foreigner from his accent. I was not keen when he took Tina's hand and kissed it, but thought I'd better make allowances. They probably did things differently wherever he came from.

For all my and Tom's prompting, Tina would not take an alcoholic drink – 'maybe later' was the most she would allow. We doubled up at pool and Tina proved better than Paul (always a bit rubbish at sports, but he still should have been ashamed of himself).

Only when we found ourselves sitting out did I decide I might risk a private word with Tina. Paul spent half his time, even when supposedly playing, away from the table at the ancient jukebox, asking Mario what he wanted to hear. His presence overlooking their table and the eventual choices both seemed to displease the domino players.

'So why was that lairy bastard Smeaton right in my grill then?'

'He's not a bastard. He really cares for Mum.'

'Good on him, but don't mean you have to like him. I fucking don't.'

'I didn't expect you would. Who *do* you like, Ray? I often think you don't like me.' There was a sudden challenge in her voice.

'You kidding?' We were sitting side by side and I had been talking down into my pint; now I turned to face her. 'Is that a trick question, so I say no I don't like you – but I love you. All I'm saying is, he was out of order.'

'You don't see the best of him, he can be a bit loud at times I admit. He wouldn't have hit you though.'

'Whoa, hold on a minute, you don't think I was *frit*, do you? You didn't see me run away, did you?'

'Nobody's saying you were scared, why are you always so touchy? If he was upset it was only because I was.'

'So then he wanted to make all three of us upset. Well it didn't work. Why were you, anyway?' I knew I had to be careful now. I mustn't condemn myself by volunteering reasons. Her spiteful little mate had probably stitched me up well enough already.

'Are you sure you want to hear?'

'Go on, spit it out.'

'I went to Angie's last night and we had a long talk. You know her and Stephen are probably splitting up?'

'News to me.' I ducked sideways to retrieve the white ball Paul had screwed off the table. 'I suppose he'll be wanting to punch my lights out as well, will he? In his dreams.'

'Why does it always come down to fighting with you?'

'Cos that's the only way anything ever gets sorted out. I didn't know you cared that much about Omie to get upset yourself. Or wait a minute, did he dump *her*, was that what set you both off roaring? I hope this isn't all taking us back to New Year's Eve. I thought we'd agreed to put all that behind us.'

'Did we? That was a lot easier when I'd only heard your side of it. I wasn't happy about Angie, how could I be, and I let her know, believe me, but what about Sally Ann Fartface? You didn't mention her, did you?'

I shook my head as if in disappointment, in reality caught unawares and needing a moment to think. 'No, I didn't. Probably because NOTHING HAPPENED with her. Have you ever seen me anywhere near her even? And by the way, thanks for telling me you're only fourteen, only *just* fourteen. Talk about immature.'

'Immature? I never made a secret of it, I'm not the one for secrets. I guess you never cared to ask. I did make a decision last night, after a lot of tears.' Her eyes were a bit shiny now, but she had no trouble looking at me full-on in a way I quickly found uncomfortable. 'I think I will have that drink now if I may.'

I had used her age as a distraction for the present, thinking I would have leisure to revisit it. 'That's more like it. Result! That's my girl.' I kissed her on the lips, ignoring Tom's prompt advice from the pool table to get a room. The fact she was here with me at the wedding proved which way her decision had gone. As a special bonus I didn't even have to buy the drink myself. Uncle Mike chose that moment to fill the door frame and pause like a sheriff come to sort out trouble in the saloon.

'Right you lot, good man down today, time for the rest of us to pay our respects. I don't suppose you've got a bottle of champagne on ice, young Derek? Good. I'm glad of that. All right then, one two… six Grouses, large one for me and a pint. No, no pints for the others, I've been sent to gather the family home.'

Suited and spotlessly black-shoed half an hour later, Uncle Mike raised his glass – now indeed champagne, or at least sparkling wine – as enthusiastically to the 'happy couple' as he did, flat-capped and muddy-wellied, in the Butcher's Arms to his own toast of 'another one bites the dust.' He looked vastly more relaxed than Dad, whose moment had come at last.

'Right, er sorry, if you can give me one more minute before you all hit the bar and get even more drunk.' Mum loyally struck a knife to glass behind him. 'I remember the first time I met Dan, well over twenty years ago now. He said I was a brave man to take on his sister. Then he invited me to have a pint. Or perhaps I should say he invited me to buy him a pint. I'm still waiting to get one back from him.'

Good-humoured though the crowd was, if Dad had been expecting belly-laughs he did not get them. His opening had been delivered in a single breath. For a moment he looked at a loss as to how to continue, despite the much-folded sheet of paper in his hand. Mum nudged him from behind with another glass of champagne, which he glugged down gratefully before continuing.

'I'm sure Will and Joan must have been wondering for years when they'd get their only son off their hands.' (Poor old Aunt Jackie, was I the only one who remembered her?) 'I'm telling you now, Ray' – he must have known exactly where I was standing as he lasered right in on me – 'I'll expect you to be getting hitched a lot earlier than your uncle, don't follow his example in everything. Don't look so scared Tina, love, I'm not putting any pressure on you, we can all see you're well out of his league.'

There were laughs at that all right, the old man recovering his confidence at my expense. Tina drew even more laughs when she stood on tiptoe to kiss my flaming cheek, refusing to let me get into a sulk about it.

Like Tina at mine, Mum was right at Dad's shoulder. She probably knew the speech by heart from all his rehearsals. I had heard her claim more than once that she might as well have written *and* delivered it for him, the fuss he was making.

'I double-checked with Agnes beforehand, and although I'm definitely up for it, if you'll pardon the expression, she tells me we will not be having a daughter, a little sister for Ray.' ('Shame,' hollered Uncle Mike.) 'I didn't exactly walk Katie down the aisle today, but I was proud as a dog with two… tails, when she asked me to stand in for her father, as unfortunately none of her family can be with us today. I'm sure they soon will be, though.'

That last sentence must have been Mum, a stiletto smuggled into the bouquet. Katie was either oblivious to any insinuation that Dan might be a passport for her family – and Dad I could tell delivered the phrase in perfect innocence – or confident enough to disregard it. She looked almost demure in some cream and brown outfit, a fedora in the same colours at an angle on her head the only hint of raffishness.

'I can only say, Katie, that once you're in this family you're in it for life – no time off for good, or even bad behaviour.' (How had Aunt Jackie escaped then?) 'You've asked me to thank Will and Joan, and of course your new sisters as you called them, for this marvellous spread they've put on. Thanks to you and Dan also for putting the first drink behind the bar for everyone – hold on, Tom, it's not going anywhere.

'Maybe this shouldn't be part of my speech, but I'm going to say it anyway.' He was no longer looking at his piece of paper. 'It's a big thank you to my dearest Agnes. I don't know if I was brave or not. I do know marrying you was the best thing I ever did. Dan and Katie, may you be as blessed with each other as I have been all these years.'

Mum had not seen that one coming. For the first time in my life I saw her as a beauty, a much younger woman looking at Dad. With the room's full attention at last, he had the sense not to milk the moment.

'And so... I'm sure nobody will mind a second toast. For those who don't like champagne I know there are a few bottles of Hungarian brandy, paraquat I think it's called, no only joking' – he made an elaborate consultation of his script – 'palinka, that's it, just as dangerous to drink as paraquat. So whatever your tipple, and mine's a pint Dan thank you very much, here's again to the bride and groom... and to family.'

'What a sweet speech by your dad, Ray, you must be so proud of him,' Tina said as we queued at the bar.

Even knowing women got sentimental at weddings, I was still pleased to hear the compliment for him. I answered gruffly, 'He's changed his tune, that's all I can say.'

'How do you mean?'

'You weren't there on the day of their twentieth wedding anniversary. Caught him down the bottom of our strawberries, sobbing his heart out.'

'Whatever for?'

'That's what I asked. I'd never seen him cry, and like I say he was sobbing. He put his arm round my shoulders. He said, "Son, you're old enough to know now, I once had a very big decision to make. It was either join the army or get married to your mum." I didn't have a clue what he was on about, so I said, "But if that was twenty years ago, why are you crying now?"'

'And?'

'He started crying again. He said, "Today I would have served my time and be leaving with a pension."'

215

'What? Oh, I see, he was joking you.'

'No Teens, it never happened. I was telling *you* a joke.'

'Well I still thought it was a great speech.' She stubbornly declined to laugh. 'I never thought I'd see your mum tearing up. Don't let it give you any ideas about buying me a ring though.'

'No chance. I'll wait till Katie throws Dan's back at him then beg that one for you.'

I must admit her reminder was timely, because never mind about women, Dad's speech had put me in a bit of a mushy mood. I could not help thinking of what it would be like to be married to Tina. One in the eye for old Smeaton, for sure. I was getting tired of the constant teasing on how far above my weight I was punching. Nobody needed to tell me that.

Though Katie may not have had any family with her, she had brought along a couple of friends who were nobody's idea of matrons of honour. I wondered if the names given us on introduction, Lin and Lou, were like Katie a fenlandisation of something longer and less familiar. 'Such a shame that you are already taken by this young beauty Ray, you are as handsome as Katiuska told us,' said Lou (or Lin) in an accent and a clear enunciation that were definitely not Washtown.'

Relaxed by the drink I had already taken, I apologised for my unavailability but referred them to my unmarried cousin Paul and his friend. The girls giggled at the suggestion, so I guessed I might have done the lads a favour.

My family was out in force. I felt like Michael Corleone introducing whatever Diane Keaton's name was to a gaggle of great-aunts, second cousins and friends from Dan's louche past (I had conveniently forgotten to pass on his invitation to Julie), though Grandad Will was not dispensing favours to anyone on this day of his son's wedding. He sat nursing a shandy on the only table marked 'Reserved', shared with Nana Joan, their three children and spouses. He was often the only man left at the table as the others held court at the bar, Dad basking in whatever plaudits he was receiving for his speech and looking like he was on a mission to get shitfaced. Maybe his extravagant compliment to Mum had been a pre-emptive strike, to reduce her predictable anger at him by the end of the day.

Tina seemed content enough at the table nominally shared with Tom and Glenda, Paul and Mario, Lin and Lou – women who certainly knew how to drink – and Terry and Pam. Terry was a long-time Washtown drinking buddy and sometime workmate of Dan's, his wife Pam known to the wider family because she had put in a season or two picking strawberries at Grandad's.

The late afternoon and early evening passed uneventfully in the marquee, except for a groom-led exodus of menfolk – Dad, Uncle Mike, Tom, Terry and me included – between 4.30 and 5 to catch the football results in the house. I had never heard Grandad Will say a single word about the sport but he was there as he was every Saturday at home, checking his pools using the stub of pencil as a cigarette-substitute when he was not writing down the scores. United suffered a rare defeat to some bottom feeders, which Dan was keen to rub my nose in. Marriage didn't seem to have changed him much.

Between the pub and the toasts I had had a good number of unmonitored drinks. In the warmth of the house I nearly fell asleep during *Final Score*. When we returned to the tent I wished briefly that I could delight in an extra glass or two of coke, but there was no going back to childhood. Continuing to reassure Mum I was on shandy, I continued to drink beer.

There had been little acknowledgement by the adults that it was Valentine's Day. Perhaps the wedding did fall on it by pure coincidence, as Dan had always maintained. Tina had shyly handed me a card when we arrived at the farm, as she passed over the wedding gift and a bag of her own to Aunt Rose for safe keeping in the house. I had pretended to be embarrassed at not having one for her. There was no way I was risking Tom seeing the oversized box, much less the teddy-beared and pink-satin-hearted card it contained, so Mum and Dad had brought it via the registry office. In a mood of great bonhomie, Dad insisted on coming with me to retrieve it from the boot rather than simply giving me the keys (which I suspected would not be in his charge much longer).

'Great day, son. I don't care what people say, I think your Uncle Dan's bagged himself a winner there. And you too, by the way. When you find a good girl like Tina, you make sure you always treat her right.'

That was the only advice about women Dad ever gave me.

The evening's music was to be provided by a local man with a karaoke set-up long before these became popular, contracted on the strict understanding – so Mum had told me earlier in the week – that he would keep the tunes coming like a conventional DJ if the wedding guests did not want to 'stand up and make fools of themselves'. A shaven-headed bloke with a couple of mates arrived, behind long-haired Derek from the Butcher's to take the evening shift at the bar, whom I greeted like an old friend. I was feeling pleased with myself and Tina's gratitude for the card, for all she had seemed momentarily doubtful of it.

The opening song, to which Dan found himself obliged to take the floor first, with his new wife, was that old 'You Say It Best, When You Say Nothing At All'. Unimpressed by the emotional freight of the lyrics, Tom laughed. 'That was probably what Dan thought before Katie could speak any English. I wouldn't mind teaching one of her mates a few words either.'

'Why didn't you get in to dance with one of them then, you should have been a bit quicker off the mark than Big Terry?'

'No, you've got to be canny, Rayburn. Glenda could come back any minute from putting Ellie Baba down with her nanny. I might try to get a number later, mind.'

The nanny in question was not an employee but Uncle Mike's mother. Nana Joan was out on the dance floor with Paul, who had been organised into it by Aunt Rose while Terry's Pam sat with Grandad Will. It was unthinkable that he would dance and I was one or two drinks shy of doing so myself, despite Tina's voluble wishes. Her slim figure looked a good fit in the arms of Mario, with whom I'd cheerily waved her off even as my heart went black inside.

Lou or Lin with Terry was in contrast almost like a child dancing with her dad, while her oppo was already deep in conversation with the DJ. Dad and Mike were on parade with their respective wives, following Dan's lead. It would most likely be Uncle Mike's only turn of the evening. There was no telling in his present mood *what* Dad might get up to.

The village football team had arrived at the Butcher's a few minutes before we left that afternoon, more than happy to join us in a round of shots to celebrate a derby victory over the hated Harpole St Jude's. Whether they had been formally invited by Mike or Tom – Paul hardly seemed to know any of them – I recognised one or two amongst an influx of new guests arriving for the wedding's evening session. Perhaps stirred by this injection of youth, Tina had a few faster dances with Lin and Lou before returning laughing with them to our table.

'I'd almost forgotten Ray, I've got a surprise for you, if you like it will you promise to have a dance?'

'What is it?'

'It won't be a surprise if I tell you.' (Was everyone to address me like a child today?) 'Give me a couple of minutes, I need to fetch it from the house.'

Surely she had no way of trumping my boxed Valentine which was propped up against her folding chair in the tent? I'd refused to let her display it on the table. She didn't force a commitment from me to dance before dashing off, but agreed to a rum and coke for when she came back. I had no fear of not getting served it by my pal Del, and the money was not a problem since Dad and my uncles had a tab going for the immediate family.

At the bar I fell into conversation with Terry about the afternoon's football results, as we had not been able to do at the time for Grandad's peremptory 'hold your noise' while he checked off the results being read out. I was alerted to Tina's return by Mario standing behind me, of whom I was half aware seemingly bickering with Paul about something. 'Wow, the little girl's grown up,' he said.

Tina had changed her clothes. I had to revise my immediate unfocussed feeling of lust to accommodate the fact that it was my girlfriend standing in the entrance to the tent. She did not seem entirely sure of herself, clutching a shiny black handbag, matching in colour her new, towering heels. The only other item of clothing visible was a canary-yellow micro mini skirt, one I instantly remembered having admired almost on her in a Peterborough teen fashion shop.

Mario was obviously taking his own close look, sharing his view with Paul. '*Mira corazón*, she's even taken her tights off, for easier access do you think?'

Chapter Ten

After Jan took her separate turn off the Alamo, the torch Ray was holding found Den's bedroom door ajar. Kim was stooped at it, her hand in Sanjo's collar.

'Daddy, it's so dark I couldn't see and I heard Mummy shouting and I think Sanjo wants to go out for a wee.'

'Hush darling, you'll wake Den. Don't worry, you go back to bed, give me Sanjo the Ninja Sato, I'll take care of him. Mummy was having a bit of a nightmare, but everything's all right.'

'Has Martin gone? It seems quiet now.'

'No, darling. This is what they call the eye. It's like he's holding his breath for a bit but he'll start blowing again, perhaps even harder, soon enough.'

'I know what the eye is.'

'Excuse *me*, my bad, I'm glad of that. There should be enough of a breather to let the wee man out for a wee though, give us him here. Do you need to go yourself by any chance?'

Jan was at his shoulder. 'Let me light a candle quickly for us girls to use the bathroom while Daddy takes the dog outside, precious. The worst is over now, don't worry.'

Jan was right in terms of Martin's direct physical threat. Although its windspeeds slackened during the passage across the island to around 100 miles an hour, that along with thirty inches of rain dumped by the storm was enough to damage or destroy 100,000 dwellings as rivers overflowed and beaches were eroded. It robbed 96% of the population of power, 75% of water and sewage facilities. The eventual cost would run into billions of dollars.

Within the Rodens' *Urbanizacion Santa Teresa* all was quiet the next morning. It was not the quiet of massive trauma or mourning. The only apparent damage to their own house was a ripped patio awning. While Jan was preparing a list of chores for them to bring the interior of their home back to normal, Ray took the children and an eager Sanjo for a walk around the streets.

The company Volvo and Jan's Plymouth appeared untouched by any flying debris under their shelter which led away from the kitchen door. With Sanjo choking himself on his lead and Ray keen to cast an insurer's as well as householder's eye over their neighbourhood, it was as well that Den spotted a booby trap left by Martin that might yet have brought the whole flat roof of the carport down on the vehicles as well as anyone who happened to be in or around them. When his attention was called to it, Ray could see a sag of at least a foot in the middle, such as a very big arse might make in a bed you happen to be hiding underneath. The roof looked to be of solid construction, masonry or concrete.

The floor of their garden shed was inches deep in water when Ray fetched the collapsible step ladder from it. The swimming pool was brimming over. The quantity of water buckling the carport had no means of escape since the guttering was choked with leaves and other debris. Low-tech clearance of this by the fistful led quickly to a gratifying jet of water from the run-off spout at the end of the roof. Warning Jan not to venture out to the cars without a hard hat on, they set off on their delayed walk. When they returned, water was still running off but the roof had more or less regained its original shape.

The sky was not yet its usual bright blue, and it continued to rain lightly. It quickly became clear they would not be using the cars today, as they could not walk more than a hundred yards in either direction from their house without finding the road blocked by fallen trees and power poles. While the kids could clamber over these obstructions, and Sanjo could worm his way through, they would take a little clearing. Ray knew all such official services would be fully occupied on more important roads. The children, initially subdued, found some amusement in taking photographs of the scene, with which they planned eventually to impress friends and family back in England.

The number of deaths in Puerto Rico did not reach double figures, and those were attributable to human error more than the direct effects of wind and rain. Fires were caused by candle flames, there was at least one electrocution and more than one case of carbon monoxide poisoning as people failed to appreciate the dangers of gasoline-powered generators in the absence of public supply. Jan was cooking on a portable gas grill Ray had won in the raffle at a golf tournament as their days without electricity ran on, though thankfully water was restored within forty-eight hours.

In strengthening again before hitting the island of Hispaniola to the west of Puerto Rico, Martin finally claimed more than 600 lives. Sovereign's interests in the Dominican Republic and Haiti were limited, and Ray's greatest concern remained the British Virgin Islands. There were a score of deaths there, again mainly from indirect causes though some drowned at sea as the storm struck. The standards of construction were, however, much lower while Martin had been stronger than in Puerto Rico, so that the insured losses would prove to be much higher in proportion to total values at risk.

It was the busiest time of Ray's working life. The offices were open on the second day after the storm, initially for a limited number of hours each day, when the emergency generator was switched on. Still without power at home, he would go to bed earlier and wake at first light. He attended Jaime's executive committee meetings at seven thirty every morning, concluding on alternate days with phone conferences to London. They both missed the steady hand of Ken Thompson at that end. An SRG apparatchik from the Group Finance Department, one Malcolm Hyett, chaired the calls with Reg Cowley and Alan Mackieson there to cover the insurance and reinsurance angles respectively. Ray of course knew both of them, though not the SRG Claims Manager Peter Drake.

Because Martin had not touched the mainland USA, they could count on the group's US catastrophe response team of experienced loss adjusters. Most of these, as non-Spanish speakers, were happier dealing with the Anglophone Virgins than Puerto Rico itself, so Ray had no problem getting a good man on the BVI government account. Unfortunately, it was the underwriting more than the claims adjustment aspects that worried him.

Head office was insisting on estimated final loss numbers despite his and Jaime's repeated representations that it was still too early to come up with anything that could be treated as reliable. Ray suspected the driving force behind this demand was the finance guy Hyett. Macca, whom he would call informally outside the scheduled teleconferences in an effort to soothe his paranoia and find out what was really going on, had a slightly different view.

'He's pushing all right, but I think he's being pushed himself by Van Houden, you know, SRG's Caribbean supremo in Amsterdam. He was taking over Ken's responsibilities in theory but not getting involved much until this shitstorm. I can tell you, Ray, there's been a serious sense of humour failure over here at the initial figures the modelling firms are coming up with for your markets.'

* * * * *

Jonno's house, where Ray was overnighting in the absence of any viable hotel accommodation on Tortola, had been carefully and solidly constructed into the slope of a hill to the former soldier's own specifications. Ray had visited before, but only now saw the custom-built Alamo within it, where the agent and his Jack Russell Shanks had waited out the passage of Martin.

'Twelve hours we were in here, and this little hero didn't take so much as a pee, even though I'd put some earth down for him in the corner if he needed it.'

'Our boy was good as gold too,' Ray lied. 'And a proper chemical toilet for you, I'm surprised you didn't have half Road Town beating a path to your door for shelter.'

'People here are resilient. They make a proper effort to protect their houses and businesses and get them back to normal as soon as possible. They won't fail to claim on their insurances but won't necessarily rely on them or the government for a total bail out.'

The two men were sitting outside on the terrace with a view down to Road Town and its bay. There were more lights from the vessels in the water than the properties on the land, with power not yet generally restored. Ray had enough to occupy his hands between fussing Shanks, smoking one of Jonno's Romeo y Julietas and sipping at his whisky and water. Luckily both men preferred that as a mixer to ice, for which across the islands affected by Martin old ladies were being mugged after standing in line for hours to pick up a bag or two.

'I think this will probably be my last hurricane,' Jonno mused.

'What, you think B & M will want to take your portfolio on right now? With all the claims to settle?'

'No, I'll stay on to manage that side, but it would be a smart move for them to do business right now. I'm not greedy in terms of the price I'd ask, and Joe will know as well as anyone that insurers will be gouging. Higher premiums may mean more income – unless you lot slash commission rates – but they definitely mean more stress in explaining things to your clients.'

'You can call it gouging. I'd say looking for a little honest payback with more realistic premium rates. Apart from the business side, surely you'll miss all this though' – Ray swung his glass in a tight semi-circle – 'compared to your Croxteth council estate?'

'Well done Ray. I'm surprised you can name a suburb of Liverpool, never having been north of Coventry. No, I'd probably keep this or another place on here for the winters – I grant you it can be a bit chilly on the Wirral. Leave the hurricane season to tourists paying an extortionate rent.'

Ray knocked his glass against Jonno's, to toast the proposed venture and discreetly indicate that his was about empty. 'You could make great money right now putting up adjusters. I'll expect an introduction fee for any of our boys, mind. For me too if I end up coming back here next year as a tourist. I'll probably cop the blame for underwriting the losses in the USVI, some scary numbers coming out of there Jaime tells me. And when London hears what we were talking about earlier for Tortola they'll not hang me out to dry, they'll crucify me, the full Spartacus. Can we shave anything off it?'

Jonno poured another giant measure for Ray and a marginally smaller one for himself. 'You can do what you like with the figures as long as all my clients get their claims paid fairly. That's what we've been selling them all these years, what was the slogan you used to have, *Sovereign Remedy*? You asked me for the maximum possible loss, that's what I tried to give you.'

'So could we trim the overall estimates down?'

'That has to be your call, Ray. With the government account representing seventy per cent or more of the total loss, unless you don't agree that's totally blown – and it is a first loss cover, remember – any dickering with the rest won't have a major impact. I mean apart from that it's still finger in the air stuff. Don't they realise that?'

'Ken would, which is not to say he wouldn't have been pushing us hard for figures as well. The SRG arseholes have hardly anything in the way of hurricane exposures so they don't have a fucking clue.'

'Yeah, it's a bad business about Ken.' They clinked glasses again before Jonno resumed. 'I was pleased to get a call from Erik in Curaçao asking how I was and if there was anything he could do to help. I thought that was a nice touch.'

'I hope you told him to manage his own business, not mine.'

'It was a personal call, he mentioned he'd been trying to get through to you. It was a nice touch, whatever you say. The call from the minister I told you about was a different matter. They're already looking for an advance on their claim, and it will go badly for Sovereign in terms of publicity if they don't get it, especially with the island's hospital one of the properties trashed.'

'Yeah, I thought they'd be a bit quicker asking for a payout than they were with the underwriting information.' As a guest in Jonno's house, Ray didn't tax him on his own role in the placement process, much less mention his possible go at Emilia. He saw the main fault was his as clearly as he knew that was the way it would be seen in London.

Claims from a major hurricane were always high multiples of a company's annual premium income, but Ray could not point to a bank of profits built up in previous years from the new government account to cover this. As Jonno had mentioned, it was huge by the standards of the BVI market as a whole. Sovereign was not the only insurer of the account, which was placed amongst US and European players, with heavy involvement of the international reinsurance market. *Mal de muchos, consuelo de tontos* was the Spanish saying that harm to many is the consolation of fools; nevertheless, if for example Lloyd's had taken on the risk at the same terms he had, it might help justify his underwriting decision. He did not want to argue that pressure from Ken Thompson for premium growth had forced him to seek new sources of income, particularly as the Big Man could not be asked to back him up on that.

He needed to prepare whatever case he had since his planning and reinsurance visit scheduled to London pre-Martin was being enforced by his masters there, despite his argument that he was more needed working from San Juan on the fallout from the storm. The London session had been ominously rechristened as a 'stewardship meeting'.

An uneasy truce had held between Ray and Jan since the night of the hurricane. If not notably supportive, at least she wasn't adding to his problems. Things had been no picnic for her either. They were more fortunate than many people in their escape from serious damage to their home and belongings, as too in the fact that water and sewage services were restored within forty-eight hours of Martin's departure. Still, it was now approaching ten days since that and they remained without electricity.

Jan cooked as best she could on the portable gas stove, relying more heavily than usual on barbecues and takeaways though neither Ray nor the children uttered word one of complaint about that. He was wearing his stock of polo shirts (many of them gifts from reinsurers when he had still been their darling) to the office, where the dress code had been relaxed from suit and tie, so he did not have to notice any difficulties she might be having with washing and ironing. Perhaps deluding himself, he put her refusal to indulge him in any kind of sexual activity down to the lack of air-conditioning.

'Yeah, so it'll just be a week. They're hauling me into the office for Martin as well as the more routine stuff we'd already planned, then I'll probably go see Mum for the weekend.'

'I might come with you.'

'Really? I thought when we talked about it before you said the kids were in school or something.'

'So they are, but half the kids and some of the staff haven't shown up since Martin according to Denis. In any case they're not as arsy about taking kids out in term time as they are at home.'

'I should hope not considering the amount we – well, Sovereign – pay in school fees. You realise Den has been known to exaggerate on occasion, especially if he thinks there might be a holiday back in England for him.' (Lately Ray was careful never to refer to the UK as 'home'.)

'What, don't you want us to come? After we pop in on my mum in London I'll take them to Lucy's then maybe join you for the weekend. Or is that a problem?' Jan's tone suggested it had better not be.

'No, you know it's not. Mum will be made-up to see them. She can babysit if you want to come to my old school reunion. Long as I'm going to be in Feltwell, I thought I might as well take that in.'

Jan's face darkened but before she could answer there was a knock on their back door, sending an enraged Sanjo to investigate. Gathering him into his arms, Ray opened to Eddie.

'Hi Ray, sorry I know it's late but I thought I should come round.'

'Yeah we've already lit the candles to show us the way to bed. I'm guessing it's not good news, though honestly I'm struggling to see how things could get any worse. What's up?'

'It's Ken. Ryan called to say his dad passed on.'

'OK. That is worse.'

Ray's paranoia spiked to an historic high when he saw Erik Horstwald chatting amicably to Alan Mackieson and Reg Cowley in the meeting room to which he had been directed on arrival at the former Sovereign and now Group head office in the City. He hardly had time to apologise for not returning the Dutchman's calls since Martin before two more men entered: Malcolm Hyett, the Group bean-counter in chief, was a jowly character who introduced himself in what sounded like a Midlands accent; the SRG Claims guy Peter Drake, an older man, offered a more friendly smile.

'It's good to meet you finally, Ray,' Hyett began when they were all seated. 'I know there was some talk of cancelling your visit in view of the workload locally, but we felt it important to see you. I understand it now also gives you the opportunity to attend Ken Thompson's funeral, which of course we will respect. I gather you worked quite closely with him over the years so I'm sorry for your loss.'

'Thank you.' Ray nodded to a supportive murmur from the others round the table. Hyett seemed relieved to have got the human business out of the way, proceeding more briskly.

'I have called in Erik to provide me with personal support and insight into the situation post-Martin, liaising between local regional management and group exec. As his own operation was not involved in the loss yet is a major part of our current Caribbean structure, I believe he can take a dispassionate and informed view of matters.

'It's no secret that the underwriting approaches of SRG and Sovereign to the Caribbean have been, if not diametrically opposed, then somewhat different. In a nutshell, SRG have looked to avoid entirely or at least minimise exposures to the risk of hurricane, whereas Sovereign have, perhaps embraced is too strong a word, certainly accepted those exposures across a large part of their portfolio. Going forward those strategies may be seen as incompatible. I've been asked to submit a draft report on the Group's future philosophy to Mr Van Houden. Again, I've asked Erik to help me distil this from the collective wisdom you and other colleagues represent.'

Ray, trying not to be impressed by the Brummie's fluency, wondered if he was reading from the papers in front of him. He knew his own role today was mainly to sit and listen.

'While I am very glad to hear your strategic views,' Hyett flowed on, 'they are in the next couple of days a nice-to-have. What I *must* have from you – with any support you require from friends around the table – is an operational report on Hurricane Martin. You probably know there has been a degree of unwelcome noise around one or two aspects of this event, particularly the alarmingly disproportionate loss we appear to be facing from the British Virgin Islands. Please address this in detail, and in particular the underwriting, reinsurance and likely loss amount of the government account which appears to be – well, we're no longer allowed to talk about woodpiles and what might lurk in them, but I'm sure you know what I mean. Are you clear on what I'm asking of you, Mr Roden?'

'I think so.'

'Good. I don't want to cut into a couple of days leave time for you later in the week, including attendance at Mr Thompson's funeral, so if you can let

Erik have your paper by close of play tomorrow that will be fine. I'm sure he will be prepared to give you input or guidance as you work on it too.' (Eager nodding from the Dutchman.) 'Good luck.'

'"You're going to need it," the fucking yam yam might as well have said,' Ray vented to Macca over their second bottle of wine in The Cock at lunchtime. 'You can see the SRG boys trying to get one up on Sovereign to carry their own strategy through and save their own people's arses, so the timing of Martin couldn't be worse. I miss Ken, God rest him, for a million reasons. One big one is that he would have been in our corner.'

'I can't disagree with you. Jaime's been asked to provide a similar report. Word is the Puerto Rican operation may be merged into the US, if it survives at all.'

'What about the USVI? Are they blaming me for the losses there too? If I was Jaime, mates though we are, I'd be saying I only inherited that account, nothing much to do with me.'

'I don't know. The BVI's the hot topic.'

'Hot enough to fry me, you don't have to say it, Macca.'

By nine o'clock that Monday evening Ray had his paper ready for submission the following afternoon. He had received no more comfort in the office one-to-one from Messrs Cowley and Drake than from Macca in The Cock, barely restraining himself from giving Cowley a slap. That turd was behaving as if he was now, or always had been, an SRG employee.

Having purposely not taken up Erik's offer to sit down with him at any time, Ray was all the more vexed to find him alone at a table in the Crosse Keys when he walked into it for a sleeping draught. Cursing his luck – the man was drinking coffee and might have been leaving any minute – he bought him a Baileys to go with it before joining him.

The Dutchman's greeting was hardly effusive, from which Ray allowed their chance meeting might be equally unwelcome to him. 'How are you, Ray?'

'Not too bad, Erik. Putting the finishing touches to my suicide note.'

'You are joking? I hope so.'

'Christ yes, things aren't that bad.'

'But they're not that good?'

Ray decided to tell him. Everything would come out eventually, and he had the professional pride not to lie to his employer or seek to minimise his guilt. They talked for over an hour, the Dutchman switching to schnapps on which Ray accompanied him as chasers to his own pints. The man had a fair head for liquor after all.

'If I understand you right then, Ray' – even in drink Erik still followed good business practice of summarising discussions before moving on – 'the main issue for you is the gap in the placement which will increase the Group's net loss?'

'That's the chap. I hadn't raised it earlier because I wanted to check with Macca if the Group's EML-bust cover – that's estimated maximum loss, sorry Erik – would pick up involuntary shortfalls in cover as well as ones where the event loss exceeds reasonable expectations. He said nobody would have the front even to ask reinsurers just because we didn't get the fac we needed. That will substantially increase the Group's net loss, and that news I know will be as welcome as shit on a tablecloth.'

'It is news to me, as you say. I understood the issue to be more one of breaching the terms of your underwriting licence in accepting the risk at all.'

'Guilty again. I know I should've got Ken's autograph on it, but I don't regret not covering the topic in the last conversation we'd ever have. If that cunt Cowley had only backed me up and took the share for Group we offered him it would have been hunky dory. Instead he took only a part, and at a higher premium, leaving us to scrabble around to place the balance facultatively in the open market.' He had caught the look of distaste on Erik's face at his characterisation of Cowley. 'Look, I know I shouldn't refer to a colleague in those terms. I know all this probably sounds like sour grapes, and I'm not expecting you to take sides or anything. I know I fucked up. I could talk about the agency misleading me, I could talk about Eddie Jemson not screwing Cowley's balls to the wall like he should have. I can talk about the brokers in San Juan letting me down on the reinsurance placement, but I know it's my head on the block.'

Erik was silent for a moment or two, either to give Ray a chance to calm down or from reluctance to make his next comment. 'There was in fact some unpleasantness over here about that reinsurance side – not from anything Reg Cowley said or did,' he quickly added. 'Fawkes Fordham, who as you know are probably the Group's biggest business producers amongst the multinational brokers, approached Mr Van Houden himself on behalf of their local correspondent – Martinez and something, is it? There was talk about disloyal competition, about them being cut out for personal reasons and some nasty rumours which I don't believe should have a place in business discussions. Certainly not to be raised for the first time at the level they were.'

'What sort of rumours? Wait a minute, let me get another round in before they call last orders. All right, a bottle of water for you it is, good idea for the night sweats, I think I'll have one myself – as well as a last big one to hear this latest beauty.'

When Ray returned to their table, one of the few still occupied in the acreage of the Keys, Horstwald tried initially to close the conversation, or at least postpone it to the next day. Ray was having none of that.

'All right, as long as you accept this is totally off the record. I don't even think Group will want to pursue it. All I know is there were some allegations, or insinuations, probably nothing in writing, about sexual relationships or favours from a female broker who had no other reason to be involved in the account.'

'I'm glad you said female. I would hate anyone to accuse me of being gay on top of everything else.' Although Ray laughed, he felt a violent flush rising to his face. 'So it's all rumour and gossip, you get used to that in the Puerto Rican market but I can't believe that weasel Georgie Martinez would bring it to London. Am I going to get any chance to defend myself against this bullshit?'

'As I say, I don't think Group will go there. In fact I believe Mr Van Houden gave them a robust response, which didn't stop the word getting out, you know how these things are. The matter would probably never have been mentioned if the figures stacked up, but as you've said yourself they don't look good.'

'You got that right. I only hope nobody is suggesting I was on the fiddle. Of all the money sloshing about in that account, I'll tell you here and now Erik and any fucker who says different I'll swear it on my children's life, not one penny found its way into my pocket.'

'Calm down Ray or they'll throw us out of here before you can finish your drink. If it's any help, I believe you on that. I'm glad to have seen you tonight, I understand the whole affair much better now. Like you, I think insurance is a risk business. Our masters are increasingly looking for someone to blame whenever there's a big loss. That's true even if there are no, well aggravating factors as there clearly are here. Listen, do you want to meet here again for breakfast? I hear they do a good one and I'll be more than happy to cast an eye over your draft report before we submit it. I can't change what has happened, but I do admire your honesty this evening. Perhaps we can at least phrase the report in a way that will not make matters worse.'

'I appreciate that, Erik. I'm sorry again I didn't call you from San Juan. I keep thinking I'll be able to handle everything myself. Yeah, why not tomorrow, a Spoons fry isn't bad and you can get a pint with it as well.'

Chapter 11

'What did you say, you foreign fucker?' I barged into his back, spilling his beer over my cousin.

Mario had clearly been unconscious of my presence, but turned quickly. 'I'm sorry kid, I… calm down.' He put his hands up into some kind of kung fu stance but I didn't care. Big Terry proved capable of moving faster than he had on the dance floor, pinning my arms to my waist and lifting me off my feet to swing me sideways-on to the outsider. I was shouting and swearing.

'Easy, tiger. And you, Muscle Mary, you can put your paws down unless you want to try some of your fancy fighting with me. I don't know what you said or did, but it must have been bad to get my little mate's dander up like this. You might want to think about an apology, me old beauty.'

'Of course. I did not know he was there, I meant no bad, I would gladly shake his hand. Or maybe you should hold on to him a moment more.'

I wanted to spit in his face, except suddenly Mum was right in mine. 'Ta Terry, you can let him go now. What the bloody hell do you think you're up to? I hope you're not drunk like your father. Everybody's looking at us. Are you satisfied now you've ruined your uncle's wedding, how could you…?'

'Come on sis, don't get carried away. Good to see the lad's got some grit, going to take on a bigger man, even a… a Frenchman. Look, Katie didn't even notice, no harm done, wouldn't be a proper wedding if there wasn't a bit of aggro, and I could hardly cause it myself today. Terry, top man, get us all a round in will you, I think my credit's still good.'

When I had grimly shaken hands with Paul's mate as Uncle Dan's price of freedom, having refused to say what he had done to upset me ('He knows!') I went in search of Tina. At the door of the house I was met by Glenda.

'If you're looking for your girlfriend, she came in here like a hurricane, waking Ellie Baba when she slammed the toilet door behind her. I don't know what you've done, but I suggest you leave her alone for the minute. I'll let her know you come looking, and tell you when – if – she's ready to see you.'

232

There was something in the young mum's manner that made me understand why Tom had not wanted her to come upon him chatting up another girl. 'All right Glen, tell her I'm sorry if she's upset but it wasn't my fault.'

Barred the house, and not wishing to use either of the Portakabins, despite the fact I suddenly felt a bit queasy, I hung about in the crew yard. I did not want to slink back into the wedding party alone. I cadged a fag off one of the footballers, ready to palm or discard it if Mum should appear on the warpath. Tom brought me out a drink.

'Aunt Aggie said no more bevvy for you, but she's not to know there's a drop of the hard stuff in this. Come on Rayburn, get back in here with us, she's the only one thinks you did anything wrong. I don't know what the poof said, but I doubt it was as bad as what I've been telling everyone he did. Come on in, Katie's mates are worried about you, you jammy little sod.'

'So old Mario won't be getting off with them then?'

'Never any danger of that. Come off it.'

How slow was I? Only now did I twig Tom was using 'poof' as a specific rather than generic term of abuse. Surely Paul didn't know, I thought momentarily, before concluding he surely did.

Tom returned from the house, where he had gone to give Ellie Baba a goodnight kiss. 'Sorry Ray, it was all done when I got in there. Glenda only let young Tina use the phone, called her dad to come fetch her home.'

'You what? We were going to take her.'

'I know, but he's on his way. She said she'll see you now if you want to talk though.'

'That's mighty fucking big of her.'

His meaty slap to the side of my head knocked me sideways. 'Don't gripe about that twat dissing her then do it yourself. You don't have to see her but if you do, don't make things worse. I mean it. You hear me?'

I nodded my head into his chest as he gave me a bear hug.

I found Tina sitting stiffly at the kitchen table, dressed again in her daytime clothes. Rather than facing her across the table – I wanted no further confrontations tonight – I sat down beside her, not risking it but ready to put an arm around her given the slightest encouragement. I nudged my glass along the Formica top towards her. 'It's got a bit of a kick in it if you want.'

She did not bring the glass into the circle of her arms.

'Why are you leaving, Teens? It wasn't a fight, I was only sticking up for you, you didn't hear what he said.'

'I didn't need to, I don't want to, I could see him laughing, Mum was right about me not wearing that dress, I should have listened to her. What *did* he say?'

'Never mind. And the dress was lovely. I was totally… it totally blew me away.'

'I know.' She looked at me for the first time, with what I hoped was affection but feared might be pity. 'I could see you were… I thought my surprise had worked nicely, then you were flying at Mario like a madman.'

'I had reason enough. Is it right you called old Smeaton to fetch you home?'

'I can't go back in there.'

'Why not? Course you can, most people probably didn't even notice. Come on, how about putting on your new dress again?'

'Don't you touch me!' I hardly had, just reaching the top of her hand with my fingertips. 'I mean it. It was a mistake to come today at all. Perhaps I should be saying sorry to you.'

'Why? You've got nothing to—'

'No, listen Ray. Will you please listen? I started to tell you earlier, in that horrible pub, I suppose I chickened out. I must tell you now, it's only fair. Today was always our last date. I'd already decided that. I know now I was right.'

'Is this about Angie and Omie again? Or Jambo? What is it, Teens?'

'It's not about them, or anyone else. It's about us. I really really loved you, more than any other boy I've been out with and I thought… I don't know, it's not working out. Is it? Honestly? You never seem happy with me.'

'I am. I am except when I'm having to fight off other men. They're always around you, Tina, like flies on shit. I mean not that you're…'

'You've got such a lovely turn of phrase, boy. I thought I was a jealous person but you, honestly, you scare me sometimes.'

'Why? Don't be daft. I've never threatened you. I wouldn't even smack that little bitch Angie.'

'That's not what I mean. I know that, I… I don't even know how to explain it. I just…'

'You're just chucking me, right? Is that what you're trying to say?'

'Do you have to put it like that?'

'Pardon me, what other way is there? You don't expect me to beg, do you? Cos no fucking way.'

'I don't want you to beg me, I hope even that we might—'

Now I had raised my hand to her, palm out only though, not in threat. 'Don't you *dare* say you hope we can still be friends, cos that's not happening, no way. We were never friends before, why should we be after?'

Then I started begging. I might have cried a little bit. I could barely pull myself together when Tom tapped on the kitchen door, a rare gesture of delicacy in his own home, to let us know Smeaton was there. We went outside. She allowed me to put my arm around her thin shoulders as we set off towards the car, already turned around for her road home.

I broke off from her and went back to the marquee. Tom and Smeaton were looking warily at each other when I returned, toting the Valentine box. 'Might as well have it. No good to me.'

'Oh Ray.' She flung her arms round my neck, leaving me still clutching the wretched card. I gave her a proper kiss, not caring what Smeaton might think. I persuaded myself she responded, but of course she was the one to break off. She looked very pale as she sat, above me, in the passenger seat of the Land Rover, the card-box shut on her lap.

Three times Dan and Katie sent away the cab coming to take them to the fabled honeymoon suite of Washtown's Rose and Crown – each one with an excessive tip to the driver for his trouble – before closing the party down sometime after midnight. We were long since back in Feltwell, driven by Grandad Will. He found it hard to keep up with Dad's constant chatter in front. In the back we were largely silent, Nan Joan asleep, Mum affronted at me and Dad both, blaming us for Tina's abrupt departure.

'Behaving like a football hooligan, Ray, I could of died, and as for you Peter Roden that poor girl must have been scared stiff at the thought of getting in a car with you driving.' Mum had a licence and seemed sober enough to have driven us home in our own car, but part of Dad's punishment would be to bus back – Sunday service and all – to Harpole to fetch it the next day.

There was no escape from my punishment. I had lost Tina. During the first days of the next week at school my prime concern was that she was not mocking me, not suggesting I might have behaved in an unmanly way when she gave me her second surprise of the night. I was also waiting for her to make some move to come back to me.

My heart leapt when I saw the familiar handwriting on an envelope in our hall, only to find it addressed to Mr and Mrs Roden. 'Nice touch,' a still subdued Dad agreed when Mum cooed over Tina's thanks for Saturday and apologies for not having said her goodbyes properly. I looked at the note later. There was no mention of me. Over the next fortnight Tina did make attempts to involve me in general conversations with friendly comments in my direction, met by me with a stubborn silence. I wanted to be alone with her, and she showed no inclination for that.

'Course you can, love, it has turned cold again, but it's not like you to ask. Are you sure you're not sickening for something? Do you want a Haliborange?'

'Don't fuss Mum, I've got this French essay to do tonight and I was feeling a bit chilly. It don't matter if it's too much trouble.'

'No trouble at all. Shouldn't be needing a fire in March but it's bitter out. I hope you're OK, you seem a bit below par lately.'

'Leave the lad alone Aggie, give him room to breathe.'

So I got my fire in the back room. I wasn't cold. Times had moved on since all that Jane Austen crap about returning each other's love letters. I retrieved all the inconsequential notes Tina had flicked across classrooms to me. There must have been a hundred or more. Some were purely administrative: 'See you tonight at disco, can't hardly wait xxx' Others marked what she saw as major developments in our relationship, like the one where for the first time she signed off with a heavily underlined 'Love' rather than 'luv'.

Mum was for some reason obsessed with not throwing paper of any kind onto the living-room fire, not even sweet wrappers which crumpled and crackled in a satisfying way. She was sitting in front of that fire now ('If it's cold enough for the boy, it's cold enough for us,' Dad had convinced her), not in front of mine.

I read each note, some more than once, before burning them individually. I was tempted to put them to the flames with music... 'What Becomes of the Brokenhearted'... 'Someday We'll Be Together'... 'Maybe Tomorrow'... but it didn't take that long. I left the first till last: 'I suppose you know half the girls in class fancy you. Not surprising!!!!'

While I might not have fancied as many as half of the girls in our class, from the end of my relationship with Tina I set two iron rules: I would go out with anyone who showed the slightest sign of liking me, regardless of her age or looks; and I would not get burned again.

236

Naturally Tina soon started going out with Jambo. All through the fifth form and lower sixth they were inseparable, to my agony disguised by nasty comments about her whenever I was with my mates.

Tina matured physically in those years, losing a little of her coltish charm and developing some modest curves. Not of the opulence and promise of Sarah Wallingham's perhaps, but nor did she flaunt her beauty like Sarah did. She always retained something of the tomboy I remembered from our innocent day at Hunstanton. If she was aware of my brutal reflections on her to others, now for her childishness, now her sluttishness, I never knew her to respond in kind. The indifference was more galling than any degree of hatred.

I remained acutely conscious of her throughout our schooldays, still lusting after her as well as harbouring the most ridiculous romantic yearnings, both aspects kept firmly locked away from anyone else, and especially from Tina herself. Boys talked about girls, and girls talked a lot about boys. I once overheard her in a group where someone remarked on the number of girls I had been with. Before the conversation ended as they realised I was within earshot, Tina had answered, 'Yes, but he never seems to *get* anywhere with any of them.' It was her detached tone, a mild observation on a matter of no great interest, that hurt most.

It was true that girls were kind, already from that fourth year after Tina dumped me. Some of it was no doubt because Dad dropped dead in the Easter holidays. Although I never mentioned that to anyone at school, everyone knew and I could see how it might have made me more interesting. After the funeral but before we returned for the summer term, Jack and Julie Smeaton brought Tina to our house for an excruciating half hour with my dazed mother and me.

It was also true, as Tina had donnishly pointed out, that my relationships never lasted long. Their pattern was predictable: expression of interest; going out together to a disco, dance, party or cinema; pushing my sexual luck as fast and as far as I could, with strikingly different success rates; disgust, disenchantment, disentanglement, always leaving them to end it or just not seeing them again. I never had to repeat the scene in Aunt Rose's kitchen.

With girls from school, I usually waited for the expression of interest to come from them. Marianne Jarvis, for example, scored a bold proposal into the top of a desk where she must have known I would find it in a subsequent class. Like Count Dracula, I needed an invitation to cross the threshold, but then I could be a bit of a nightmare.

The fear of being knocked back, exposed to the ridicule of my classmates, was the main reason for my circumspection. With my village mates I was more outgoing, prepared to initiate contact from a standing start. Never a dry one mind, we would invariably have been drinking first.

I did not fall out with my schoolmates, though for a while there was an understandable coolness between both Omie and Jambo and me. They grew closer to each other. If Omie blamed me for him and Angie splitting up, he never said. She had nothing at all to say to me.

Carl had not lasted long with Joanna Richardson, but she did take him back for an introductory double date including me with her and Sally Ann Farthingdale during that fourth-year summer term. I was not bothered if their motives included pity. I hoped to get a reaction from Tina on going out with Sally Ann, but that fire had long gone out.

Mick was one of the few kids to end his schooldays after the fourth year, leaving Caroline Peacock in a kind of limbo with nobody at school quite daring to approach her. She double-teamed with Sarah for a while but that was never going to last; they were both the pretty one. Through the fifth and sixth years Carl bagged and hung on to Cathy Strain, Pukemore and Val Anderson were still nauseatingly together, as were Jason and Vicky Cooper. If I occasionally felt a pang of envy as they all talked about their 'missuses', it was easy enough to disguise. What the fuck, did they think they were sixty years old and married for forty-five of them?

Sam Hopkins, sometime unveiler of Gloria Carney's seminal bush, had already had a proper missus, wed at sixteen, a father a couple of months later and lodging alone with an aunt in Feltwell a few months later yet. He was earning good money as a plasterer, and whatever else his brief wife Linda had robbed him of, he still had his car. I was increasingly allowed one of the back seats of the old Vauxhall, with Jake, Kev or whoever else of my age was hanging about hopefully in the early evening Oak. Shotgun was always reserved for Sam's best mate and brief brother-in-law, whom we all only ever knew as Fitz.

The price of those trips to pubs, legions and village halls all around Washtown was that we were sometimes egged on to start fights for the older boys' amusement. Sam and Fitz might finish them if we were getting a real hiding, or they might not. Another charge we had was to chat up girls on the monosyllabic Fitz's behalf. Sam was more than capable of attacking them himself, insisting they all loved a wedding ring. 'You know, shows them you're a proper man. And when I flash the Polaroid of Linda's brat, they can hardly wait to get their drawers off for me.' He also insisted, after offering some rough sympathy, that the loss of my father was potentially a trump card. 'A sympathy fuck is still a fuck, mate.'

Occasionally I would relapse. Was it the fifth or lower sixth year Christmas party when I learned (I could not hear her voice without listening hard to every word she said) that Tina would be spending the night at Angie's? Jambo was not around for some reason. I spent much of the evening drinking in the Eagle near the school, alone apart from the odd pint with people like Carl escaping briefly from the disco. Cathy by then had him so pussy-whipped he was only taking the time for a short, and getting started on them may have been my downfall that night.

It was acceptable practice for a Christmas kiss to be almost a proper snog in the many-eyed safety of the hall, even with girls you might not have spoken to all year. Many relationships got off the ground on that seasonal sentiment. I made sure I did the rounds before the disco's nominal closing hour of ten thirty. Angie's lips were pressed tight but I hardly cared about that. Tina seemed surprised at the invitation but agreed to dance with me when at last a slower tune came on. I clung to her tight without saying anything before at the end claiming my kiss. Cautiously friendly is about the best I could call it on her part, as if poised with a garlic mouth spray in one hand and a crucifix in the other. She certainly showed no inclination to prolong it.

'How about coming next door with me, you know, for old times' sake?'

'Is that where you've been all night? You're drunk, aren't you?'

'Come on, I can walk you back to Angie's later if you like.'

'How do you know I'm staying at Angie's?'

'She must have said. Come on, a quick one, rum and coke or something?'

'No, Ray. You can let go of my arm soon as you like. Please.'

So I went back to the pub on my own, furious at her strength of will and my weakness.

I came to myself well after midnight, in Angie's back garden, dick in hand. I had no recollection of a conscious decision to visit Bateman Avenue for the first time since New Year's Eve of our fourth year. My subconscious, drunken cunning or drunkard's luck had body-swerved the porch-light trigger. It was definitely the romantic rather than the sexual side of my love for Tina that brought me there. My penis was out not for any display or masturbatory purpose, only to satisfy an undeniable need to urinate.

I was looking around in the well-tended shrubbery for gravel chips or clods of earth to shy at an upstairs window when I came more fully to my senses. Which window? To what end? There was no balcony, and I was an unlikely Romeo waiting for Juliet to appear spouting poetry at my call. My presence was more likely to lead to arrival of the police than a heart-warming reconciliation. In my mind that would be less of a problem than the ignominy of being tagged by my schoolmates in such hot, futile pursuit of a lost love. To pretend I had been after Angie would make me look even more ridiculous. Zipping up, I only began to breathe freely again once I was back on the pavement then the main road to hitch home.

The running sore became a dull ache, I suppose, yet it was always with me. Over the years I might begin to understand in general terms how final the withdrawal of a woman's love can be, without ever accepting it in the particular case of Tina and me. One aspect of keeping her in my heart and my heart for her, convenient enough to arouse even my own suspicions, was that I was in no danger of losing it to another.

Jason and Vicky were only the most extreme example of a long-standing couple in the school, Head Boy and Head Girl in our final year. He and I were friends rather than mates. I asked him once, 'Surely you've had all you can get out of her now, mate, don't you want to move on?'

He chuckled in an infuriating, patronising way. 'You don't get it, do you Ray?'

Omie kept putting himself out there and was with Sue Tierney for a spell, though his longest relationship probably remained the one with Angie. We never let up on insisting he was madly, incomprehensibly in love with her.

Carl Walters' weakness in women was always Sarah Wallingham. He was never able to resist if she called on him when she lacked an older man, and more recently he had an added attraction for her as a driver sometimes able to borrow his brother's car. For all he tried to blame strands of Sarah's trademark long red hair in the car's passenger area first on a dog, then a girlfriend of said brother, Cathy Strain did not need forensic science to call him a cheating scumbag. With a promptitude Carl found deeply suspicious she was taken up by a lad from her own village, never again to be seen in school social circles.

Cathy's defection took her into a second group of pupils who had steady or serial relationships with people from other schools or in the world of work. Others had no relationships at all, or ever seemed likely to. Within this group, or indeed perhaps the other two, some may have been in deep cover or denial, but to my knowledge there were no recognised same-sex pairings.

Angie seemed to be settled with some hippie from the Washtown Poly, a relationship that would prove bad news for Jambo. Although the poor sap didn't know it at the time, when Tina broke off with him in the first term of our final year she already had an admirer from the same poly. I knew from bitter experience how careful she was to line all her ducks in a row, to avoid any possible accusation of two-timing.

It was generally known which girls at school were either having full sex with their current partner or had done so with one or more people in the past – 'confirmed sightings' was the phrase we used. Jambo had maintained the maddening discretion from his earliest days with girls by flatly refusing to get involved in any such conversations about Tina, whether to brag, modestly demur (another form of bragging) or regretfully concede that they had not 'gone all the way'. With my customary ambivalence where she was concerned, I was capable of believing both that she had given herself up to every kind of depravity with her boyfriend, and probably others on the side, *and* that she was still resolutely preserving her virginity out of some misguided sense of duty to her absentee father's wishes.

My obsession did not go quite so far as stalking Tina to Durham University. Our paths did cross once more, near the Clarkson Bridge in Washtown one summer holiday. It was a Saturday, so I had called at the Oak when it opened at half ten before heading into town to take advantage of market day's extended licensing hours. Without ever going near a market, we knew the days they were held in each of the towns within drinking distance.

She accepted to have one with me in the Clarkson Hotel, not the licensed premises I was heading for (that would have been the Lion) but one I thought she might consider a bit classier. Any hope I had of our session extending past midday and long into the afternoon was soon dashed when she ordered a coffee. You would not have thought there'd be such a palaver about getting one in a hotel, but the delay around it at least gave me time for a second pint.

I thought we were getting on famously. The barman had at least been able to provide pen and paper, and I had her address in Durham safely tucked away in my Levi breast pocket. She was wearing her hair long and it kind of masked her face when I leaned in for a kiss. She laughed in embarrassment, denying the moment. Although I did not persist or lose my temper, she could not be persuaded to a second, proper drink.

I did write to her at Durham, referring back to our meeting in the Clarkson but no further in our history, indicating I would be more than happy to visit her there if she or anyone else could provide me floor space. She did not answer that or a second letter, more modest in its request only for her to respond and stay in touch.

And that was that until Lesley Carrick's mention of the school reunion. While I had not seen Tina since that final disappointing taste of her hair in the Clarkson, she became the girl of my dreams in a literal sense: the only woman with a name and a known face I would dream of at night, sex of course featuring but also a reconciliation, a recognition on her part that we should and would be together. There always followed a melancholy undertow on waking, with short-lived fantasies about getting back in touch with her in some unspecified, non-desperate way.

I told Jan in broad terms about how my heart had been broken and tossed into an incinerator during my schooldays, along with way too much detail about my sexual history. What was in the early days of our courtship a charming little baton relaying everything about my past she cared to know (and much she might have preferred not to), became eventually a big stick I'd handed her to beat me with. I never told her I still had the dreams though. I never gave up Tina's name either.

My thoughts turned increasingly to her after hearing about the reunion. Without a clue where in the world she might be living, what she might be doing or with whom, I assumed straight away she would be there – there being, in my mind rather than what would eventually prove the case, the old school buildings.

Initially I saw a sexual opportunity. Naturally she would be available and amenable. I could fill in a missing link in my romantic CV, chase down and conquer the nemesis I had been pursuing for years, improve my personal sexual narrative – to some extent I was thinking revenge fuck. As things grew ever rockier between Jan and me, however, the sentimental, self-protective side of my nature began to make itself heard. I had missed out on one of my teenage life goals, that of being divorced with two kids by the time I was thirty. I had the kids. Was it totally unrealistic to think of presenting myself to Tina as someone ready to make a new beginning?

Chapter Eleven

'God Ray, it looks like you're the one fit to be buried today. Cremation wouldn't work, they strike a light anywhere near your breath and there'd be one almighty explosion.'

'While you look as fresh as a daisy my love, or at least a black orchid.' Ray wished his wife, in a dark trouser suit, might have prolonged their all-too-brief hug at the King's Cross platform waiting for the 9 a.m. departure to York. She had pulled out of it before he could give her a proper kiss. She was now fussing with the black necktie he had bought and put on a few minutes before.

'Have you been sleeping rough since we parted Sunday night? I know you didn't want to commute from Lucy's but did Sovereign not have a hotel for you?'

'Course they did, or at least somewhere to flop. I haven't been sleeping that well. It's been a stressful couple of days.'

'Tell me about it, travelling on British Rail or whatever they call it nowadays with two kids.'

The fact that Jan's invitation to tell her about it proved purely rhetorical and a two-hour-plus train ride gave Ray ample time to pick and gnaw at his recent performance, without having to edit any of it for her consumption. He supposed she must have made an early start to get in from Lucy's in Chelmsford, and did not begrudge her dozing opposite him in their pre-booked window seats.

He had not in the end met Erik for breakfast the day before, unwilling to rehash over hash browns everything they had discussed the night before that, much less let the Dutchman become aware that he could not remember its detail. What had shaken him most was the mention of his relationship with Emilia. Had Erik actually said her name? Was that bitch going to wreck his career as well as his marriage? Would the Hong Kong business rear its head again, had that too reached the HR files in London or would it be buried with his boss today?

In the airless meeting room on Tuesday he saw only Peter Drake, bringing without comment the latest claims figures as a damning appendix to Ray's report. He had been instructed to keep that brief, which was no problem. He added only one short paragraph to what he had substantially drafted the day before. He emailed Erik that he would deliver the paper by three thirty at the latest, without apologising for missing breakfast, hoping to suggest it had only been a casual may-see-you rather than a firm commitment.

By eleven he was climbing the walls ready for a drink. Macca cried off a second consecutive lunch, for all Ray's chiding of him as a pussy. He had been out of London so long he hardly knew anyone else to invite. In the end he called up an old reinsurance broker friend, one he knew would not have been involved in Caribbean business, to meet in The Grapes.

'When did you get to be such a lightweight, Briggsie? You do realise the pubs don't shut in the afternoons anymore, don't you?'

'Might as well. Things have changed in the City, they don't even serve spirits at our in-house dining nowadays. Time was you could sit down to eat already with a decent buzz on, now we get memos saying we're expected to be back at the coalface by three o'clock. Some of us are still tied to a desk, not swanning around like you expats on your expense accounts. I'm glad to hear things are going so well for you though, seriously mate.'

'Mustn't grumble, sure you haven't got time for one for the frog? Got to be back in the office half three myself.'

'I hope it's only for a kip. I see you still know how to cane it, but that doesn't play in London the way it used to, back in dear old Ken's day. Still the best boss I've ever had, I was starting out in the industry.'

'I'll second that emotion. Come on, we must at least toast his memory. Two large Jameson's guv, please.'

Back in his little den at Group head office, Ray suddenly did not feel like talking to Erik or anyone else. Hyett's secretary brought him in two hard copies of his report. He dared not sign them in front of her, in case his hand began to shake despite his sedative lunchtime session. When he appeared at her desk five minutes later, having scratched out a signature with left hand gripping the writing one, he already had his overcoat on.

'I don't know if they needed a signed copy, Claire, but here's one in case. I've sent one by email to Mr Horstwald, explaining I have to go meet my wife rather than see him in person. That's a change of plans imposed by my real

244

head office, know what I mean? Of course I can make myself available over the phone to discuss any of the finer points.'

'Are you sure, Mr Roden? I think Mr Hyett may have been planning to join you too.'

'Doubly sorry in that case.' He was already leaving her desk, taking five flights of stairs to avoid the possibility of meeting anyone in the lift. Back in the pub, having switched off his mobile in case anyone should have the gumption to call its Puerto Rican number, Ray decided a spot of lunch was in order. It was a near run thing but he managed to keep down a scotch egg and packet of cheese and onion, congratulating himself on responsibly switching to what could almost be considered a soft drink (lager and blackcurrant dash). Briggsie had obviously been right about some wage slaves returning to work, as the crowd was much thinner now; nevertheless, ashamed to occupy a spot at the bar while he was eating, he took his *Mirror* over to a table.

Shuttling between The Grapes and a bookies hard by it, Ray passed a pleasant couple of hours in his own company. Sentimentally he chose to bet on the meeting at York. He had to make one cashpoint visit to restock his wallet before clearing a monkey on the day's last race, the only one he would remember. *My Little Cracker* came in at long odds in the five thirty. He spent a generous proportion of his winnings on a pair of earrings for Jan, imagining fondly how pleased she would be and how he could say he backed the horse only because its name made him think instantly of her.

He could still order a pint clearly enough over the next few hours, but he was beginning to stumble and nod, so getting a second one in the same establishment was sometimes more problematic. The New Moon, White Swan and Red Lion all featured in his itinerary which somehow eventually took him beyond the City and the streets he knew reasonably well.

Feeling lonely, he failed to get an answer on calling Emilia in Puerto Rico. His phone had no London numbers for girls on it. Clearly none of the missed calls and messages he deferred for review the next day could be from any such improbable saviour.

The driver of the first black cab to stop for him seemed at first disinclined to recommend a club to him, whether 'down and dirty' as he requested or not, but eventually pulled up in Soho and announced his fare.

'The Windmill? Fucking hell, how old do you think I am?'

'I don't know mate, but this is as far as I'm taking you. You're on your own from here.'

'I'm always on my own. Keep the change, ta.'

The Windmill looked almost respectable. Fearing a tourist trap, Ray soon found somewhere more in line with his original specs, hardly crowded – it was still early in the evening by the standards of nightclubs – which suited him fine. He ordered a vodka and tonic at the bar as he watched the floor show, aiming for the metropolitan rather than overawed out-of-towner look, as if free market rules of sexual attraction might apply.

He soon found himself in a private booth with 'Valerie' from Bulgaria. She was all over him.

'All right, that's enough. I've warned you three times, now I'm calling security you nasty man.'

'Wait a minute, hold hard, what's up?'

'You know the rules, I explained them clearly. No touching.'

'No touching! If we were in Bucharest or whatever little shithole you gobbled your way out of I bet you wouldn't be saying that.'

'We are not in Bulgaria or Romania, sir. We are in this shithole. Now you can pay me and leave' – she named an extortionate sum and had the cheek to add a 'please' – 'or I go ahead and call security. I would recommend you do not use bad language to them.'

'Just for my information, how can you justify that amount for a private dance, cos God's my witness I've not had anything more than a dance.'

'You have had five dances.'

'*Five*! Sweet Jesus, how long have I been here?'

'I know you are tired, but you definitely agreed each time I asked if you wanted another dance. You nodded to say yes.'

'Would that be when you grabbed my head and shook your titties at it?'

'It is all on the CCTV if you want to review it with our management, sir.'

'Everything all right here, Irina?' Had she given some secret signal to summon the goon?

'You see what I mean?' pole-name Valerie said. 'Henrik must have seen what you were doing, which I told you was against the rules.'

'She's right, sir, the girls always are. It's closing time for you I'm afraid. Pay up nicely and get out or you'll still pay up and not get out so nicely.'

'Knew I should have gone to the Windmill, that fucking place never closes.' Maybe he really was too old for this game, the blank looks of Henry and Val told him. Ray paid up many multiples of what his love affair with

Marcela had cost him, adding a generous tip to show he wasn't on the bones of his arse and was a good sport to boot.

The encounter with the nightclub bouncer – no big deal, they had ended worse for him in the past – was his last clear recollection of the night. He had been glad somehow to wake up in a dry bed in Club Quarters, albeit late enough to put him in a rush to meet Jan at King's Cross. He only regretted he had managed, somewhere in his unholy pilgrimage, to lose the earrings with which he had intended to make everything right with her.

'Only Ken could ever get me to Stamford Bridge.'

'What?'

'Wake up Jan, it's the village where the funeral is. We won't have time to go to the house first, but it shouldn't take us long to get there by taxi.'

It was a big do. Ken's coffin arrived by horse and carriage, the brutes surely painted to be so neatly and fully contrasting, black and white. There was a proper choir in the Methodist church so that the organist did not have to rely on the congregation's feeble vocal support in the tunes of glory – 'Abide With Me' and 'Jerusalem'. As Ray glanced round from his seat near the back, he saw people standing in the entry porch for want of pew-space.

It was Macca, looking a bit desperate Ray thought, who had beckoned them to seats in the church beside him and Hilda. Ken's bereft personal assistant of so many years continued sniffling, barely raising her head throughout the service. Ray made sure to usher Jan to the seat beside her, taking the aisle for himself.

'Where's the boozer then?' After the service and committal Ray was feeling a bit desperate himself. His throat that morning was as parched as if he had been eating rather than smoking the cigarillos, of which he found a surprise packet with zippo in his coat pocket. They were not much compensation for the earrings, but he had not discarded the remaining ones before meeting Jan, even though she was touchy again about smokes around her since her cave-in on the night of Martin.

'The Swordsman? Should suit you Ray.'

He gave Macca a sharp sideways look before deciding his friend was not being unacceptably sarky. 'Hush your mouth, not in front of the missus.' Jan was baulking them ahead, arm-in-arm with Hilda.

247

'Proper old school village, church and pub practically next door to each other. Did you pick up the messages from yesterday?' Macca asked more urgently.

'Yes mate, I want to have a word. Let's pay our respects and get the women parked first though.'

Ray had never before seen Elizabeth without Ken. She was standing at the pub door with a dark-suited, short-haired young man Ray knew from the reading in church to be her son Ryan. He momentarily reminded Ray of a bouncer.

Ray introduced himself as Macca was hugging Elizabeth. 'Well done in the church there, it couldn't have been easy.'

'The vicar steered us to the text. I couldn't have managed a eulogy, didn't think it would be Dad's style anyway. He told us to get through the day with as little stress to ourselves as possible, cos he wouldn't be feeling any.'

'That sounds like Ken. Eddie Jemson sends his prayers and condolences. He would have liked to be here, but we couldn't leave the shop in Puerto Rico unattended. Your dad would never have allowed that.'

Elizabeth thanked him for making the effort to come up from London, which he assured her was no effort at all, the very least he could do, giving her a tight hug. 'Go on Ray, get yourself a pint and make sure you look after your Jan.'

'Free bar an' all, Ken must be spinning already.' Ray took the head off his first Timothy Taylor's Landlord in the cheerless smoking area looking over the deserted beer garden. 'Now what's all this bullshit about me having to go back to the office?' he asked Macca.

'Didn't you speak to Erik at all then?'

'No, I wanted to get the scoop from you first. He left me a voice message saying I was, what was it, "required to attend" a meeting with Hyett ten o'clock tomorrow morning.'

'That's all I can tell you myself. I'm only the messenger boy. They were wondering if they had to use carrier pigeons to reach you. I'm assuming it's for something in your report, thanks for showing me that by the way, it might have helped. Erik did ask me to make you understand they're not fucking about. He seemed more than a bit pissed off as a matter of fact.'

'I did you a favour not showing you the report. You don't want to be associated with it, trust me.'

Ray spent another night alone in the hotel where Hyett's secretary had rebooked him. Jan preferred to catch another train back to her sister's. 'You're pissed already, why do you think I wanted to get you out of the wake? I'm not going to spend tonight either watching you get more drunk or taking the blame because you're not drinking. I'd recommend you don't carry on if this meeting is as important as you say, but that's entirely up to you.'

'They did him proud. It was a sad occasion, and there was a lot of dignity, especially from Elizabeth – that's his wife, or widow I should say. But there was also a lot of laughter.'

'I'm glad to hear it.' Malcolm Hyett closed his opening enquiry. 'I know this has been a hard week, a hard few weeks I suppose, and I'm afraid I'm not going to make it any easier. It gives me no pleasure to advise you that the Group is today serving you six-months' notice of termination of your contract.'

Ray felt a sudden throbbing behind his eyes. 'You mean you're accepting my resignation?'

'No, Ray.' It was easier somehow to get the news in this flat Brummie monotone. While he could believe Hyett was not taking any pleasure in their conversation, it was clearly not causing him any great distress either.

'The final paragraph in your report came as a surprise, even to Erik with whom I know you had discussed the draft. If you insist on resigning then of course we must accept it. Personally, I feel it was a somewhat quixotic gesture, a product perhaps of recent strain as much as anything.

'You may not have followed the communiqués from Group HR – you've had other things on your plate – but essentially no member of staff in either Sovereign or SRG has a cast-iron guarantee of continued employment. It may not seem much consolation at this precise moment, but as a member of the expatriate management team your severance terms are quite generous. I have arranged for Dorothy Hooper from HR after this discussion to explain in detail the package, which I can assure you will leave you and your family financially better off than if you were to resign. Substantially so.'

'This is more than a formality, right? I mean you're not putting everyone on notice so you can move forward quickly after six months or whatever when you've decided who are the chosen ones?' Ray spoke more for the sake of saying something than in any real hope.

'That option was mooted but no, yours is an individual case. I hope with Dorothy's input and after sober reflection you will agree that what I have said is the best outcome for you. It is standard procedure for a full audit to be carried out after any loss event as big as Hurricane Martin. Without prejudging anything, if this should find you guilty of, let's take the harshest view and say gross misconduct, things could be rather worse than a resignation and very much worse than the termination I mentioned. You are a long-time member of the Sovereign management team, one who has given good service over the years. However, based on what we know as we sit here today, it does not look to me as if you would come out of an audit with your reputation enhanced.'

Seeing that Ray was not going to object to this analysis, Hyett continued. 'I do realise this must come as a shock, even if you had some inkling of what the tone of our conversation might be. All we ask of you today is that you sign a formal acknowledgement that we have served you notice of termination of contract.'

'And then what? Am I on gardening leave for the next six months? There's not a lot to do on the land this time of year, you know.'

'That depends largely on your own attitude. We hope that you will feel able to return to Puerto Rico and help us manage settlement of the Martin claims – there is obviously no shortage of work to be done. As is the case even in the best of times, your work will be subject to performance assessment and targets. It will be important for you to maintain a high level of motivation.'

'Even under the shadow of the Spanish archer. So let's say – let's just say, Malcolm – I work my bollocks off from now on, put in a real shift, is there any chance of me keeping my job?'

Hyett hesitated. 'I don't want to give you any false hopes. I would think it is extremely unlikely, but the circumstances of the merger are unique. I would suggest, if I may, you think of it in another way. Not only individuals but whole companies under the Sovereign/SRG umbrella may end up outside the merged group. If you do a great job over the next period, it can only improve your prospects, whether within the group, with a one-time group company, or in the open market.'

'Good politician's answer.'

Hyett rolled smoothly over the sarcasm. 'I'm sure your feelings at present include a significant amount of anger, probably directed partly or even mainly at me. I can only say, as I did at the start, I derive no enjoyment from this conversation. May I suggest you try to channel your energies constructively, to prove people wrong if you like. Take as long as you need with Dorothy, and indeed before seeing her if you want to gather your thoughts. Call your wife if you like. There is no need to tell any of your colleagues yet. In fact, if you are to continue working through your period of notice it might be better to keep matters confidential, avoid any chance of lame-duck syndrome.'

'There wouldn't be any leak from my side. I know how to keep a secret.'

'I can make myself available again later today to cover any points or concerns you may have. Even to let you have a bit of a rant, if that will help.' He tried a thin smile.

'All right. Well... it feels a bit odd to say thanks...'

'Of course, for sure. Any thanks would be due to Ken Thompson. He had a high opinion of you, which has been enough to influence the thinking of very senior people at Group in your favour. As I keep saying, you may not see it now, and nor would I expect you to, but things could be considerably worse.'

'Come on Greg, I'm only suggesting a couple of quick ones before we go home to face them Roper girls. Nice of my wife to come to the station to meet me, by the way.'

'No danger of that, chap. They've been on the Prosecco since lunchtime, and an early lunchtime at that I'd estimate. You all right, seriously?'

'Yeah yeah, I'm fine, no worries.'

It was true he did not feel worried about anything after a few hours of solitary drinking and strategic thinking in The Grapes, with windows on Kempton Park, Doncaster and Newmarket. He had resisted the temptation of an 11 a.m. livener before meeting Dorothy Hooper. A plump, middle-aged woman, she put him in mind of a dinner lady from his grammar school days rather than someone moving forward in the new sharp-elbowed world of the merged Group. From all she told him in terms of payout, pension and tax, he could almost believe he was better off taking the terms than continuing to work for what would soon no longer be Sovereign. He had never expected them to accept his resignation; he realised now in offering it he had perhaps been overestimating the fund of goodwill that remained to him.

His brother-in-law was sound enough, and judging from the number of different business cards he had pressed on Ray over the years might have known a thing or two about redundancy terms. He was, however, totally pussy-whipped. Naturally Lucy would feel free to pass anything she heard straight on to Jan. Having persuaded Greg to a pub round the corner before going home – 'No, don't drop off the car first, you wally, we'll never get out again' – he therefore kept talk well away from his own business. He had decided in The Grapes that Jan did not need to know anything yet. Told he had effectively been sacked, she might consider it a tad frivolous of him to attend the school reunion the next evening.

'So are you *sure* you don't want to come tonight, Jan?' She had considered him unfit to drive across East Anglia to Feltwell, taking her opportunity behind the wheel spitefully to stop for a fast-food rather than slow-drink lunch.

'You're really going then? That about says it all. No Ray, I don't want to go and hang out with your old girlfriends. See if any of 'em want you back, why don't you? I'll take you into town, but don't expect me to fetch you home smashed out of your head after midnight.'

'As if. Are you ready then?'

'Ready? At half past four? We've hardly got here. And don't you think you should spend some time with your mum?'

'There's all weekend for that, if she's interested. All she had to say was how fat I'm looking. She only cares about the kids nowadays. The do doesn't start till eight, but I might see Jake for a drink first, ease me into it. Don't you worry, go ahead and have another glass of plonk with Mum. I'll get a bus into town or call a cab from the Oak.'

'Don't you *dare* talk about *me* drinking. Leave me with the kids and your mum, that's fine, always plenty to do in this dump of a village. Go off and enjoy yourself, go on, get out of my sight you shit.'

PENULTIMATE

One

Jake was always late. Ray never minded waiting for him as long as it was on licensed premises, and today he had Kev for company.

The Lion's Den was a small room within the Golden Lion pub. The golden letters of its name had been freshly painted at its entrance in the men's teenage years. While the Den might still be a weekend gathering point for young people, on Friday afternoons it was more of a labour exchange for the informal economy.

'Remember when we had that girl from your school's pants round her ankles in here, off her tits she was, ready to take us all on. What was her name?'

'Was you there that night?' Ray laughed. 'Nobody was asking her name then. Janie it was, Janie Carlton or Carling or something. There's one in for you, mate,' he called across to Jake, arriving at the bar.

'Was you here that night, Jake,' Kev echoed, 'when we had that grammar school bird pissed as a parrot squirming around against the wall right here?'

'She was squirming around cos he had three fingers up her.'

'Fucking hell, let me take the head off this at least 'fore you start.' Jake grinned at the barman in 'What are they like?' indulgence, before pulling up a stool between his mates. 'Talking about fanny already? You out on the pull tonight then, Ray?'

'I told you Jake, this school reunion.'

'Oh yeah, what you going to do to the women there, shag 'em or try to flog 'em insurance?'

'I asked what he was doing in a suit and tie an' all,' Kev chipped in. 'Bit upmarket for the Den. I already told him I shan't be staying here too late either, promised to take a chinky home for Sal and the boys.'

'Living the dream. There's nobody waiting at home for me, that's for sure. I'm not joking Ray, if you cop off early and she's got a mate, give me a bell. Don't even need to be that fit.'

'You never were fussy. As it goes the one I've got my eye on always had a friend clinging on like dingleberries, definitely not that fit but…'

'If they're desperate enough to turn up to a do like that they might be ready for a bit of rough.' Jake brightened. 'You've got my number.'

2

I had wondered about the suit, and wondered some more as I crossed the Clarkson Bridge. Made to measure in Puerto Rico, it was a bit tropical, not much protection against a cold night in Washtown. I was also wondering if I should have stayed with Jake and Kev. I only saw them when I was home on leave, but we always picked up then as if we were all still living in Feltwell. Apart from Lesley Carrick, I couldn't remember the last time I'd seen anyone from secondary school. She had been moaning by email that our alma mater's current regime had offered zero support to our event, not even a room.

I don't know who might have gathered in the Assembly Hall before it became a popular venue for my classmates' eighteenth birthday parties. I was not invited to as many of these as I had been to ones in the fourth year. My behaviour had grown a bit erratic, though constant in that I would always arrive drunk or get drunk very quickly. No change there, I reflected, Kev with his Chinese curfew having set a fast pace.

Old Grammarians were crowding the Griffin bar a couple of doors down from the hall. It had the air of a reunion all right, shrill yelps from women and much manly hand-pumping and shoulder-slapping. At first I didn't recognise a soul.

'Ray, how you doing mate? Bit thinner on top, and dressed like a Latino pimp, apart from that you haven't changed much.'

'All right, Carl? You here looking to get back with your ex?'

'Lesley you mean, or Sarah, or Cathy? Too many to count, not that I heard about this from a single one of 'em, gutted I was. What you having? We're sitting over there' – he pointed – 'got here earlier than most.'

'Get us a Stella, will you?'

'Wifebeater? What do you call a woman with two black eyes?'

I pretended not to know, though I'd heard often enough.

254

'Nothing. She's already been telt twice. What's all this lager shit though, seriously, Greene King not good enough for you anymore?'

'Never was from the minute I tried anything else. Watered down piss straight out of the Nene.'

At the table were Omie, Jambo, Mick and an FA I only recognised from his ears, more prominent than ever without a single hair on his head. Only Omie was wearing a tie.

'Our man in Havana,' our Catholic Jambo greeted me with a broad smile. 'Shouldn't that suit be white, Ray?'

'Like the fucking scouse Spice Boy cunts,' Mick growled a less literary reference.

'What, to reflect your teeth Jambo? How many thousands did it cost to get them sorted? Or did they clear the whole lot out and put in a double-six dommie?'

There had been some debate about whether spouses should be invited to the reunion. If Jan had shown any serious sign of wanting to go, I had been ready to hit her with the committee's decision that only bona fide Old Grammarians should go. Some of these might naturally be married to other OGs, or have been, or were hoping to be. Our corner table was, for the moment, as stag as it had been in 3A.

Three

The Assembly Hall was an upstairs space big enough to have held a dozen snooker tables without the players getting in each other's way. Mounting the broad stairway with his friends, Ray had a flashback of coming down it at a greater speed than he would have liked, limping away into the night with a sprained ankle. Whose birthday had that been? Wah Wah's? Jason's? Was it the one he'd been asked to leave early for threatening a barman who declined to serve him, or the one for projectile vomiting on the dance floor?

As they entered they crowded upon Tina and Angie chatting in front of a table with Lesley. 'Hello, is this the welcoming committee?' Mick confidently approached the women, hugging and cheek-kissing each in turn.

'No fear, we just got stuck here talking. How are you all?'

Ray had forgotten Tina was at least a head taller than her friend. Lesley indicated the table. 'The last few name tags are here, boys. You might be legends in your own minds but trust me not everyone will remember you. If you don't see yours, it means even I forgot.' She pointedly handed a blank sticker and felt tip pen to Carl Walters. 'We went with school names, you'll see some of the girls crossed them out and put married ones. They'd like you to think that means you've got no chance, but hey the night is yet young.'

'I remember when you'd go spare at your mum for calling you Christine. And who's the lucky Mr James?' Ray nodded at the card stuck skew-whiff on Tina's polo pullover, then added in a rush, 'You're as beautiful as ever, though.'

'I don't recall you ever telling me that back in the day.' Her reply was hardly encouraging, its tone guarded, so he switched from a frontal assault.

'How is your mum?'

'Quite poorly, thanks for asking. That's why I'm back in the country. OK Ange, I'm coming. We'll catch up a bit later if that's all right, Ray.'

Although there were tables round the outside of the hall, most people were still using these mainly to park bags, coats and drinks, meeting and greeting on the dance floor. There was much peeking at name tags before committing to embraces.

'All right, I think you've had long enough to reacquaint yourselves,' the DJ in a plain white T-shirt and sleeve tattoos spoke into a mic from the stage. 'I was a couple of years below you at the good old WGHS, Martin Newnham is the name if any of you young ladies – cos we're all young again tonight – is looking for a toy boy.

'No takers? Right then, I'm gonna up the volume a little bit, with apologies in advance to the teachers I understand are here. With the marvels of modern technology I can probably locate stuff you haven't heard since our prehistoric schooldays, so don't be shy of making requests. Dedications cost nothing extra, or you can stay anonymous and make your own introduction to your lost love. I haven't seen mine here tonight but this first one's for the fantasy figure of me and all my mates in 3G back when... Miss Sarah Wallingham.'

'Christ, is that your little brother, Omie? You'd better watch out for him if old Sarah's here, Carl, she always did like the music men.'

'Fuck off Ray or I'll set Redmist on you. See if you're still shit-scared of him.'

4

I don't know where Carl got the idea I was frit of Monkie in our schooldays. If we were going that way, I could have suggested he might now be ready to take on Mick. I made a real effort to push the dark thoughts away, not just the fantasies of revenge violence but my unemployment, news of which I could not believe would be a shot in the arm for our marriage when I got round to telling Jan about it. On the bright side I had a bellyful of beer, plenty of money to buy more and a roomful of women I didn't have to go through the tiresome formalities of pretending to want to get to know.

We had replicated the table from the pub and I slung my jacket on the back of the chair next to Omie, stuffing my tie in a pocket. 'Looks like you might have had a lucky escape with old Angie mate, she's packed it on a bit since school – you could slap her legs and ride in on the ripples.' Having checked with him the identity of an elegant piece talking to Jambo, I approached the two of them with a lie. 'Now here's one who hasn't changed a bit. Mo, Little Mo, I had no idea you two were a couple nowadays, why weren't you over the pub with us? You might have been able to bully this cheap bastard into getting a round in?'

'We're not together, not unless I decide I fancy a one-night stand.' She was supposed to be talking to me but linked her arms round one of his and tried to get him to meet her eye. 'We were having a chat about old times.'

'So it's still Maureen Wheatley, does that mean I'm in with a chance at last or are you a feminist, won't take a man's name but happy to strip him of everything else?'

'Glad you're still taking an enlightened interest in the women's movement, Ray. One thing you are right about is dear James here, what was it you used to say, tight as a gnat's chuff. You can certainly buy me a drink if that's still how you like to start your courting.'

So I bought Mo a drink and we had a dance or two. I kept a constant eye on what Tina was doing and where. As I remembered it she'd always loved dancing, but she was hardly hogging the floor. She was sitting at a table with Angie and a few others, mainly women but including Mr and Mrs Retchless, the latter my one-time academic rival née Valerie Anderson. Ever the gentleman, that slippery smarmbollocks Pukemore was dancing in turn with each of the women.

Tina was more modestly dressed than in our schooldays, skirt not much above the knee and the high top, but it didn't matter. She was not running to fat like Angie or, even more blatantly, one or two others. She did not look like a middle-aged schoolteacher as did some of the one-time hockey players (perhaps that's what they were, fair enough). I could hardly remember which of them were supposed to have fancied me. It didn't matter. It was still Tina for me, my only innocent love.

'If you're really into one-night stands, maybe we could have something together you know,' I ventured to Maureen as she scrupulously bought me back a large vodka.

'I'm choosy. You'd have to drop nine or ten stone first.'

'Leave off, I may have a bit of a beer gut, all paid for by the way, but I'm not carrying that much timber.'

'I was guessing your wife's weight. Unless you've worn Jan down to skin and bones by now, which wouldn't surprise me. And don't insult me by saying she doesn't understand you, or that she's already left you, because I know that's not true.'

I didn't have the presence of mind to say that proved she had at least been checking up on me. Did she even know Jan? I let her go without saying anything nasty, to go make my music request to the gym-bunny.

'Hello mate.' I'd stumbled on my way up to the stage. 'Look I've wrote it down for you, if you've got the song can you say the dedication exactly like that? Is it all right if I give you the nod when I want it on, let me take up my position in the box and all that?'

'Not really, no. I've got better things to do than keep my eye out for you, and there's a lot of people already ahead of you. What's this?' He waved the note I'd folded into the request slip.

'I don't know the form, it's a tip or whatever, something for your trouble...'

'Still Bertie Big-Bollocks, the great I Am Ray Roden. It's a bit different now you're not two years ahead of us mate, flash your cash as much as you like, I still reckon you're two bob.'

Whatever, the bastard still trousered the money. I could understand him being upset if I had offered him two bob, which was about all his shitty disco was worth. Maybe he was still jealous of all the girls I'd bring round his brother's house back then.

I wouldn't have expected Mrs Jackie King to remember me, any more than Sarah Wallingham would ever have noticed the little arsehole who'd dissed me. The home economics teacher, young enough perhaps still to be employed as such at WGHS, had kept her good looks though her spectacular frontage had subsided. Some of the girls must have invited her, since apart from Brian Retchless her whole class in our year was female. He'd been the smart one as it turned out. Mrs King was sitting demurely at a table near the door with Vicky and Jason – he like Pukemore marooned amongst women, though the daft fucker was probably just as happily married to his childhood sweetheart and oblivious to all but her – Lesley and a few others.

I could not imagine who would have invited old Redmist, still short-back-and-sided, still with that poker-up-the-arse bearing as he stood at the bar waiting to be served. He was much shrunken since my schooldays, shorter and more slightly built than me. I wanted to say something cutting but didn't even know how to address him. I may have pushed in a bit to get beside him at the bar, and I may have stared a bit at his name tag: Mr Jackie King.

'Yes Roden, it's a kind of joke from some of the young ladies.' How well I recalled that testy tone of voice. 'Jackie and I have been married for ten years now. I don't expect congratulations, and I doubt you can come up with any new jokes or even variations on a theme. In fact, if you don't mind me saying so, you look considerably the worse for wear.'

I did mind, very much. 'No I'm fine, I was actually going to buy you a drink. Hey, matey.' The barmen had survived the early rush and weren't exactly overworked, yet the one nearer to me took his sweet time in coming over. 'Matey, I'll get the ones this elderly gentleman ordered, give me a pint of Stella and two chasers an' all, Jameson's, hope that's all right. *Sir.*'

'I've no intention of drinking whisky or anything else with you, Roden. I had to deal with you while you were at school but I certainly don't now. Once a lout, always a lout, it would seem.' He handed the barman a note. 'For the two drinks I ordered, thank you.'

'Lout or not, I've done all right for myself if you must know. If I turned out bad I'd blame my teachers. Are you still here, bullying the boys and letching after the girls?'

'Will you let me pass please? I retired three years ago, and was glad to.'

'Not so glad as the kids, I bet. Did they have to retire you when sideboards went out of fashion again? Nothing for you to get a hold of to do your levitation trick, you mean old bastard.'

'Steady on, Roden.' Mick put a heavy hand on my shoulder. 'Monkie's a bit too old to be offering outside. I could hear you having a pop right through the music. You shitfaced as usual? Do you want to go out for a bit of fresh air, it is fucking hot in here?'

'What, you offering *me* outside Mick?'

'If I wanted to chin you I'd do it right here. I was only trying to help keep things pleasant. Why don't you step away from the bar for a bit?'

'All right, I don't care about drinking on me tod. Here have a Jameson's, thanks for looking out for me, but you know how he…' Turning to point at Redmist, I found him gone. Course I wasn't really threatening him, I wasn't the bad guy out of the two of us.

Five

'I'm only reading this because I was paid to.' The DJ had not waited for a nod from Ray. If he saw him, he might have chosen a moment when he expected the request to be missed, as Ray gave every appearance of being asleep or passed out at the table beside Omie. He had been trying hard to plead forgiveness for having two-timed his best mate with Angie, though he did not get the message across very clearly. 'The dedication is "from a bad film and a bad boyfriend, a great number to a great girl". That's it, and whoever the lucky lady is I hope she'll remember the Sorels better than I do.'

No more timing each tear that falls from my eyes
did not wake Ray. When the volume rose to the title line he also rose, like a zombie, unsteady on his feet and dead-eyed but suddenly steady of purpose. He took a swig of his beer before lurching off with it towards Tina. He heard Angie's enquiry, 'Is he all right?' and did not turn back at Omie's reply, 'Frankly my dear, I don't give a flying fuck. He's out of his bonce. Somebody else can look out for him, telling me I'm his best mate when I haven't seen him since we left school. What planet is he on?'

'Will you do me the honour of this dance?' Ray managed to make himself understood.

'Sorry, I don't think so.' He could not read Tina's expression, was already past reading.

'Don't you remember the song? You've got to, surely? Come on, one dance?'

'All right, don't make a scene. Are you saying that dedication was for me? I had no idea. You can put that drink down though. I'm not dancing with you slopping beer all over me.'

'Do you not remember it? "I can dream about you"' he bellowed tunelessly into her ear well behind the band. 'When the three black dudes get out on stage in their shades and the whole crowd goes surging forward. Best moment in the whole film it was.'

'I think you'll find it was four. People in the group.'

'So you do remember it. Let me tell you something, no word of a lie, that day up Peterborough was one of the best of my life, is still, as I speak. You must remember it if you can tell me how many singers there were, right?'

'There was a pop video of the song. I may have watched it one or two thousand times. Yes I remember the day, calm down, let's go and sit, I'm getting fed up with supporting your weight.'

'Can I get you a drink first? How about a rum and coke?'

'No thanks, I'm driving.'

Ducking and driving, Ray thought. 'Where to? Angie's? You staying with her?'

'Why on earth would I be staying with her? She lives in King's Lynn.'

'Can I get myself a drink? All right, no, I'll come back to the table with you, sorry. I never was much of a dancer. It's so great to see you again.'

'Is that you or the beer talking?' Was that the trace of a smile he saw?

'We speak as one. No, it's me, Smee. I know I've made a bollocks of it again, but how are you? I did try to stay in touch.'

'How was that? Through telepathy?'

'In dreams. And you know I wrote Tina, you know I did. But how the devil are you?'

'I'm OK. As I said earlier, my mum is sick. That's why I'm back in England.'

'Yeah I heard that, I did hear you, I'm sorry.' He made a production of pulling out the chair for her, not quite daring to put his hand on her shoulder as she sat down. 'Is it the big C?'

'It's cancer, yes.'

'And is she… never mind, please give her my best. I remember when I first met her – and you as you if you know what I mean – that day at Hunstanton, do you remember that?'

'Ray, I remember a lot of things, and there are some sweet memories. A lot are not so good though.' She briefly covered her face with both hands, as if to shut out attack from the not-so-good ones. 'Christ, I suppose I should have expected nostalgia coming to a do like this.' She looked at Ray again.

He pounced on the word. 'Nostalgia! I'm not having that. I'm with Kesey on nostalgia. He had it pegged, nostalgia's just looking backwards with both eyes full of bullshit, that's what he said, but that's not what I'm talking about. I'm talking about the here and now.'

'I think I'm wasting my time. I don't know if anything is getting through to you. Listen, this minute, this couple of hours, is nothing *but* nostalgia, and however you want to define it, don't confuse this little bubble with the here and now. In the here and now I'm a married woman with three children and a dying mother.'

'What, so am I pissed right now, or only in the here and now? I shall be sober in the morning, and you will still be beautiful. You say back in England, so where are you living?'

'Nostalgia's not the only thing full of bullshit, is it? I live in the States, in Florida.'

'What, with your dad?'

'No Ray. I'm not fourteen, and I'm not Tina Gibson. Can't you even read?' She showed anger for the first time. 'Have you totally lost it? You remarked on my name tag when you came in, take another look at it.' She grabbed his arm, pulled off her tag and plastered the sticky side onto the back of his hand before waving his own fist in his face.

'Yeah. Christine James. Yeah, that's it.' He sank back into the folding chair against the wall.

She did not let him subside completely, probably not wanting him asleep at her table. 'Anyway, aren't you married yourself? I thought I heard you were.' She moved the knee on one of his wobbly legs as she spoke.

He started upright. 'Married, course I am. Didn't think I'd be moping after you my whole life, did you?'

She matched his flash of spirit. 'Hardly. You didn't mope after me for five minutes, always off with one girl after another.'

'Would you rather it was two at a time?'

'Two-timing, don't even get me started on that. Sharing the grief around. I can't believe I'm letting you drag me back to those times. For years you gave every appearance of hating me, but I wasn't going to let you see how it hurt. And now you're trying to tell me I was your great lost love. Fair enough in your crazy little bubble of batshit nostalgia, but that's not where I live. I'm not having it. I won't have it.'

He noticed her clenched fists as she gathered her breath. 'All right, don't get excited. I know you must be upset about your mum, I lost my dad remember, but I didn't mean to make you cry. Can I ask you one more thing?'

'Go on, let's have it, get all the poison out.' It was her turn to sit back in her chair, arms folded across chest.

'Did you keep your promise to your father?'

She looked at him blankly. 'Promise to my father?'

'You know, about staying a virgin till you were married or something.'

Her reaction surprised him. 'I'm sorry, if I didn't laugh I'd have to start crying again. Are you for real? I grew up Ray, I grew up. Did you not?'

'If you're in Florida, we're almost neighbours you know.' He tried another tack, dimly realising things were not going well. 'I'm in San Juan, Puerto Rico, *La Isla del Encanto*, do you speak Spanish, Island of Enchantment? You should give me your number at least.'

'Tina, is he bothering you?' Angie put a hand on her friend's shoulder as she and Omie came to the table from the dance floor.

'Here come the cavalry. Omie, you'll stay away if you know what's good for you, from me and from her too. Go and fetch Mick if you think you can mess with me.'

'He was the one sent me over, said he wants to see you outside. And he'd better not have to come and fetch you, he said.'

'You're shitting me. Mick wouldn't use you as his errand boy. I expect you and Roarer cooked that idea up to get me out of here. Well fuck you both and the horses you rode in on. And fuck Mick too. If he is waiting, let him wait a bit longer. Tina, can I have your number? Write it down for me, in a little note and ping it to me like you used to, I'm not even asking you to put it on my phone.'

'Why, does your missus check that? I bet that's it, Tina.'

'Don't make me tell you again, Angie. Mind your own.'

Omie now stepped between the two women and Ray. 'Leave her alone. You seem to have this strange idea we're all scared of you. Wind your neck in, you can hardly stand up to be knocked down.'

'Take more than you mate.' In standing Ray did not entirely disprove Omie's point.

'Here.' Tina jogged Ray's elbow and handed him a piece of paper.

'You sure that's the right number? Don't look like that, I trust you, but it's happened to me before. You won't need mine, I'll call you I honestly will. I do want to give you something though, wait a minute.' He fumbled at his throat before losing patience and tearing open his shirt, sending the second button flying. He lowered his head. 'Here if you can undo it at the back, it's not the one you gave me, lost that in a fight up London years ago, but it is a St Christopher.'

'What are you up to now? No, please, I don't want that, why would I?'

263

'I want you to have it. It's for travellers.' He ripped the touch-piece from his neck and put it on the table in front of Tina as she withdrew her hand, the fine gold chain pooling around the picture of the old man and the child. 'If you don't want it, give it to your mum from me, for… or whatever. I won't take it back. See Omie, I can stand up, still standing, don't get nervous mate. Tina, you know I'm serious, unless Mick kills me I'll be in touch.' And he set off to the bar.

'Is Mick really waiting for him, Stephen?'

'No Tina, Ray called that one right. Mind you, he's not far off getting a hiding from Mick or any number of people if he carries on like he is. Probably wouldn't even feel it, state he's in.'

6

I opened my eyes. I did not move, not sure I could. I didn't want to risk finding out for the minute.

'You're alive then.'

Only as Jan stated it did I realise I had been no more sure of that. Yet I doubted either celestial or infernal set designers would bother to reproduce so faithfully the bedroom my parents had shared when I was a boy.

'I was wondering.' She came and sat on the side of the bed, to my right. I was flat on my back, not a natural sleeping position I would have thought. I was wearing pyjamas I did not own.

'Are you all right?' While it could not be called concern, there was a tad more human interest in her tone.

'I'm fine. What time did I get home?'

'Home again, that's right. I'll spare you your whole Twenty Questions routine. Not that I can help you too much this time, I'm glad to say. You turned up about three. In an ambulance.'

'Yeah? Did I get mugged or something?' Was I paralysed? Why didn't I hurt?

'The paramedics said you were mouthing off when they brought you round, and back here you were talking about "smacking that cunt". They apologised to your mum for your usual charming chat as if it was their fault, but no, they didn't think you'd been attacked.'

'So why did they bring me home if I was all right?'

264

'You were drunk and incapable, a potential danger to yourself and others. I think that's the way they put it. You were lucky it was them. The couple that found you could have called the police, and they might not have been so sympathetic.'

'Found me where?'

'Far as I can judge you were paying a visit to an old flame.' Despite her lightness of tone, I felt the temperature had suddenly dropped a few degrees. 'Your mum recognised the address, Bateman Drive or something. A couple of pensioners, their Peke had been playing up, yapping, eventually the old man let it outside with a torch, found you flat out in his bushes. Even with the dog going mad they couldn't wake you, so he called an ambulance, a proper Good Samaritan.'

'It obviously wasn't an old girlfriend if it was an old married couple, don't start thinking that Jan.'

'I couldn't care less if it was or it wasn't. Good luck to you is what I say, if you think that's a good way of rekindling a romance, laying about snoring in the undergrowth, and as a special treat with your pants full of shit.'

That explained the pyjamas then. I suppose they must have been Dad's, kept by Mum for sentimental reasons rather than an eventuality like this.

'I told Agnes to ball up pants and trousers and all and chuck 'em in the bin, but she would insist on washing them, putting the machine on in the middle of the night, while I tried to get you in the bath. That's a picture you can explain to your daughter, she woke up and *was* worried for you. Denis slept through it all. Like you did yourself, pretty much. I've been telling your mum for years to get a shower fitted to the bath. If she'd had a hosepipe in the garden that's what you would have got, believe me.'

'I'm sorry, Jan.'

'It's them you need to say sorry to. Your mum was in here all through the night she told me, checking you were still breathing. She seemed to think I should have been with you, but I preferred the settee ta very much. She's the one who replaced the half bottle of brandy you insisted on taking to bed with that glass of water.'

'I could do with a sip of it.'

'Go on then. You don't expect me to pass it to you, do you?'

'I don't think I've got any feeling in my hand.'

'Probably only temporary paralysis.' Her tone now was brisk, cheery nurse. 'Here you go.'

'Cheers.' After taking a drink, I reached out my hand, which was indeed numb. To my surprise, she took it.

'I want you to listen carefully now, while you *are* sorry, and while you're halfway sober. Because we both know neither state will last long. This is permanent though; it's over between us. I'm leaving you. And before you start with your bullshit justifications, it's not because of last night.'

'The kids…'

'… will come with me, of course. You can be the Uncle Dad you've always dreamed of.'

'I was only joking. I never meant it. Jan, I—'

'I don't want to hear it. No more than I will when you feel better. I gave it a good go but I'm done now. I've had enough. I won't say anything to Agnes yet, nor the kids till we get things sorted out, but don't kid yourself that makes it any less final. You can turn your head away, you can go back to sleep, as long as when you wake up you're clear this is not a dream. It's for real.'

I would not give her the satisfaction of begging. I could have played the sympathy card of having been shitcanned, but my career was nothing compared to my marriage. And if my marriage was nothing…? She left me. I was asleep again before I had time to think I didn't want to wake up.

CODA

'Have you even been home?'

'Merry Christmas to you an' all, Jacky. What time was it last night you chucked us out?'

'Bout half two. You were sleeping so sound I was tempted to leave you sitting there in the corner, except I wouldn't have wanted you to miss out on Santa's call.'

'Cheers, and thanks for the Christmas pint. Only reason I came in here again.'

'That's what they all say, take advantage of my generosity. Remember, doors close at two this aft, with you on the other side of them.'

'You know we've only got a couple of hours till Jacky shuts up to stuff his face, and still you're late,' Ray complained peevishly to Jake after his mate was served his season's compliments drink from the guvnor.

'I didn't realise it was that serious a date. You on the rag or what?'

'I'm sorry mate. This is the first Christmas I've not been with the kids.'

'Try not to get used to it. I've been driving round all morning saying hello and dropping off Christmas boxes to mine, the ones still speaking to me anyway. Probably already over the drink-drive limit with the tots I've had. Nobody invited me to sit down, mind.'

'At least I'll be going to Jan's sister's to see 'em tomorrow.'

'Keep 'em on your side, you've always got a way back in then.'

'I don't know. They're not coming back to me in the new year.'

'I thought you'd got away with it that night you got totalled. Calling me to come help you do some cunt, saying you were on your way to the Bear but never showing. I've seen you in some states, but you sounded like you were *crying*, mate.'

'I thought I might ride it out as well. Turns out they only came back to San Juan to finish the school term and pack up their things. Sneaky bitch had already been planning to get 'em both in a school in Chelmsford, even before

that night. Must have worked it all out with her sister Lucy, I thought I got on all right with her, should have listened when I was told all them Roper girls are trouble.'

'I warned you myself sisters-in-law can be dangerous.'

'Yeah, but you were banging yours.'

Jake acknowledged the observation with a wistful shake of the head. 'Who was it you were banging, or trying to, that night of your old school reunion? You was yakking on about how much you loved her, all that malarkey.'

'Might have had a shot there, then the Old Dear only goes and washes me kecks with her number still in them, a soggy wad of paper when it comes out, couldn't read a thing.'

'Fuck me Ray, you do know what century we're living in? You shouldn't have no problem tracking her down.'

'I don't know. Maybe I need a bit of a break from women.'

'Don't go getting gun-shy. You fall off you gotta get right back in the saddle. I thought you had a bit on the side in Puerto Rico anyway?'

'That's all up in the air. I mean not the bird – she takes it up the council and everything – I mean I may not be out there much longer. Contract coming to an end and all that. Christ, I may be back in Feltwell for good, sitting down to Christmas dinner every year, on me tod with the Old Dear.'

'Just when you think you're out, they pull you back in, hey? You can do me a favour and invite mine round as well cos I'm not as fucking miserable as you. I'll defo be with someone else by this time next year. If not I'll be topping myself.'

'There's always that.' It was not the first time Ray had thought so.

'Cheer up mate, there's always the bevvy an' all. Before we go off to dinner with the Golden Girls, how about one last pint and a couple of chasers?'

'Never say it's the last one. And I might still get back with Jan, you know.'

'If that's what you want, good luck to you. Don't go getting all wobbly-gobbed, Ray. Not on Christmas Day.'

'Sorry, mate. Must be Jacky's prices making me eyes water. You buying?'

'Am I fuck. I've got more exes *and* more kids than you. Get 'em in.'

'You're right.' Ray tried to laugh. 'What the fuck. Jacky, if you want us out of here on time give us another couple of pints soon as you like. And two Jameson's, please. Big ones.'

THE END